The Glass Dancer

Laurie Sanford

RIVER LEAF PRESS

To my grandparents, Samuel and Doris Tooley. You have both inspired me in so many ways.

Note to Readers

Please be advised that this book contains some difficult issues, including attempted sexual assault and alcoholism. It may not be suitable for some readers.

One

Elsie resettled herself on the rocky shoreline and tucked a brown strand of hair behind her ear. Her pencil moved along the page in her lap, crafting the scene about her in words she never had use for at home. Now and then she paused, a thought lodged in her mind and refusing to budge. Then, in a surge of creativity, the pencil would magically whirl out another line and satisfaction would engulf her.

Breathing in the dusky air, she let her hazel eyes ramble over the cliffs and canyons rising like sentries before her. Far ahead, two massive waterfalls plunged into the depths of the green river running past her. They roared in mighty splendor as they hurtled into the water, crashing against the rocks and flinging their spray into the misty air. Even with her rampant imagination, Elsie could never have dreamed up a place this beautiful, let alone pictured herself living here.

Shadows crawled over the craggy bluffs, inciting a sharp gasp from Elsie's mouth. She glanced behind her to find the orange sun half melted into the horizon beyond. *Oh no, Mother will be cross.* She'd sent her off to the general store hours ago, chiding her to come straight home. Mother hated when Elsie squandered her time writing poetry or scribbling away at her drawings. A waste of precious hours, she called it. Time gave the opportunity for work, and work put food on their table.

Elsie shoved her latest poem into her scrapbook and wedged it beneath her arm. Gathering the paper sack from Turner's General, she carefully made her way over the rocks and back to the main road. The sun had nearly receded behind the mountainous Idaho countryside now, leaving the dirt road just a crooked line in the fading light. A sprinkling of Hoover wagons and Model As puttered down the thoroughfare, lending enough light to lead her back to the farmhouse nestled among the grasslands.

The kitchen smelled of garlic and sage, mingled with roasted vegetables. Mother was standing over a pot of soup steaming on the cast iron stove when Elsie slipped through the front door. She plunked two balled fists on her slim hips, her dark eyes shimmering and thin mouth crinkled. "Where have you been?" she demanded, coming forward to swipe the paper bag out of Elsie's hand. "I thought I told you to come straight home."

"I—I lost track of time." Silently she slid her scrapbook behind her, praying Mother's hawk-like eyes would overlook it. "I'm awfully sorry, Mother."

Sighing, her mother dropped the grocery bag onto the counter with a thud and reached inside. "You should be sorry." She wagged her head while pulling out a glass bottle of yeast. "I needed this to bake the bread that was supposed to go with dinner. Now your sisters will have to do with plain old vegetable soup. You know how Dorothy fusses."

Elsie bit her lip. She knew how hard her mother worked—the share of twenty women, it sometimes seemed. The Depression had hit her cruelly, just as she had four children to raise without the man who had sired them. Bread with dinner was just an expression of added care.

"I'll try to do better, Momma." Elsie felt behind her to a stack of magazines positioned on a table and shoved her notebook between them.

Mother placed the yeast inside a cupboard and mopped her hands on her apron. "Well, you can start by setting the table before you wash up for supper." Her firm hand stirred the boiling soup, then set the ladle on the spoon rest. "Your sisters will be home from school any minute now."

School. Something inside Elsie ached as she turned toward the china cabinet and lifted out a set of plates. Dorothy and Shirley still attended school in town, but Mother had seen fit to withdraw her at sixteen. A woman didn't need that sort of training, she said. Elsie knew how to read and to write, the basics of math and science and geography. She had much more value helping around the house and finding a respectable job, especially during these trying times. That's what Mother said, anyway.

Elsie's thumb slid over the thin glass of the mismatched plates they'd acquired from various places around town—the dime store, the grocery with purchase of food, even the cinema, where an entire family's admission tickets would return one piece of dinnerware. She set out a green one for Mother, blue for herself, pink for her little sisters. The yellow plate dove into place with a thump—Ralf. Elsie always saved her least favorite for him.

When the bulky Swedish salesman had first graced their doorstep, Elsie grouped him among the others—he'd bring them toys and candy, tell them fantastic stories of his adventurous life, pretend to be the father whom Elsie could hardly remember. Eventually he'd grow tired of Momma or move his business to a larger economy. But not Ralf. He'd courted their mother for months, moved in his clothes and wares, placed a plain silver ring on her finger. And so she'd have to grow accustomed to calling another man "father".

The front door clattered open, emitting the chill of the encroaching evening. Dorothy's twelve-year-old face, beet red from her run up the steps, beamed like a ray of sunshine inside the dreary kitchen. Shirley ambled up behind her, much calmer and demure at fifteen. The older of the two had blossomed in the last year, her blonde hair growing thick and curly, her form taking on a womanly pose. Dorothy still retained the wild streak that Elsie adored, her hair a raven color like their mother's, her smile always glowing with excitement.

"Something smells delicious!" Dorothy announced, trotting up to Mother's side and peering into her stewing creation. "I'm so hungry. I dropped half my lunch in the dirt at school today and I had to watch the birds eat it."

Momma gave her a weary look, but simply answered with a one-arm squeeze. "You must be more careful. We're lucky to have Ralf providing for us and we mustn't look a gift horse in the mouth."

"Oh no, Momma. I would never." Dorothy flattened her hand on her chest dramatically before her gaze darted around the small kitchen. "Are we only having soup?" Her little nose sniffed like a bloodhound on the hunt for prey.

Elsie's cheeks burned at the look fired back from her mother. "We're having crackers," Mother said flatly. Dorothy scrunched her face but said nothing, opting instead to skip off to their bedroom to remove her jacket and stow her books.

Dinner commenced when Ralf returned home from work. He often traveled great distances in a day, moving from house to house and peddling domestic items. He would stretch out his long legs under the dinner table, wrenching his shoulders behind him and exhaling as his back let out a loud popping sound. Mother abhorred rudeness at the dinner table perhaps above all else, but for Ralf she made an exception.

"What did you two girls do at school today?" he asked, lifting his napkin to swipe the soup from his blonde handlebar mustache.

Shirley stirred in her seat uncomfortably while Dorothy perked up. "We talked about our new president and how he's going to

4

fix everything bad that the last one did. He's going to give everyone jobs and money, then the whole country will be happy." The spoon she wistfully twirled in her soup halted. "Do you think he can do that, Momma?"

Mother's mouth crinkled. "I believe he will certainly try, my dear. That's the best we can hope for, isn't it?"

"He can and he will." Ralf aimed his spoon at the girl, his eyebrows an inch higher on his forehead. "Hoover was content to ignore us and leave us destitute, but Roosevelt has a plan. The economy will be as good as new by the time he leaves office, mark my words." He chuckled—a smarmy, snorting sound. "I've got to trust any man who takes the name of Commander in Chief and immediately sets to repealing prohibition. God bless him."

A shadow passed over Momma's face, but she went back to sipping her soup while Dorothy resumed her report. "We have nothing to fear but fear itself," she quoted, her voice leaping an octave lower to impersonate their new leader. "Teacher said he's right, but then Donald Watts said even if the president does fix all the jobs and make everyone happy, there will still be murderers in the world, and you should always be afraid of them."

Mother's mouth hinged open. "Dorothy, don't talk about such things. And don't put your elbows on the table." One hand jetted out to tap the rebellious elbows until they retreated. "Shirley, tell us about your day, will you? I've had enough talk of the economy."

Shirley raised her pretty blue eyes to look into the faces around the table. "It was all equations and American history, nothing of real interest."

Ralf laughed again, inciting a wince from Elsie. "All that time in school and you learned nothing significant? What a terrible bore that Miss Curtis must be."

"Well, she did give us an assignment to choose a poet, study their work, and then write an essay on what we learned." Shirley swiveled toward Elsie, seizing her wrist. "I thought perhaps you'd help me. You're so good with poetry, Elsie."

A feeling like jumping into a cold pond in summer washed over her. "Of course I'll help you. There are so many great ones you could write about." The family didn't own many books themselves, but Elsie had found ways around the problem. She had a friend in every bookshop in every town they'd ever lived.

Mother's dark eyebrows cinched. "I'm fine with you helping your sister, but you must finish your chores around here first. I need plenty of help with the house and garden."

"Of course, Momma."

"I have a basket of goods I'll need you to take to your brother tomorrow, then I want you down at the employment agency looking at job advertisements."

Ralf shook his head, his oiled hair staying perfectly intact. "It isn't as serious as all that, Lillian. I'm here to provide for your needs. Let her deliver Bus his necessities, then she can come home and tend to the garden while you're helping Mrs. Williams." He tried to throw her a reassuring smile, but Elsie's gut only coiled in response.

"Oh, I had forgotten about Mrs. Williams." Mother's slender hand rose to her hairline. "She'll certainly need my help at the farm now that her husband sprained that ankle. I suppose you can look for a job another day, Elsie."

Sinking back in her chair, Elsie attempted to conceal the relief surging through her. Before Ralf had entered their lives, money had been scarce and sometimes nonexistent. Elsie hated the days she'd spent lined up outside the employment agency seeking any type of work the day would proffer. For weeks, she'd sewn burlaps sacks together for the storage of barley and grains. She'd washed and ironed bed sheets for a local hotel. One day, the local mine had grown desperate enough for extra hands that they'd allowed women to haul chunks of ore into wagons.

Crueler than the work itself were the people she'd encountered on those dreary days—anxious, tattered, browbeaten people. Men once strong and robust, gaunt from going hungry to feed their families. Women grasping at any job they could acquire, leaving behind a house full of babies to fend for themselves. Vacant eyes, lonely souls, hearts and bodies crushed by the weight of poverty. One man had pushed her out of line, accusing her of thieving able-bodied men from their God-given right to work. Women had no place among them, he had shouted.

Despite her misgivings, perhaps Ralf was the absent piece that would knit her family together again. She certainly didn't love him the way she'd adored Mother's last husband—no one would replace Daddy Harry. But for all his quirks, his poor manners and ill-timed jests, Ralf worked extremely hard. He arrived home each night fatigued from putting his all into their livelihood. Gazing on the betrothed couple now, Elsie decided to hope. Momma had met a good man, and he would bring her the happiness she deserved.

After supper, the family gathered around the radio to indulge in their weekly entertainment. Normally Ralf reserved the radio for the newswire and sports, but ever since *The Lone Ranger* had volleyed itself over the waves and into houses across the country, the Dawsons couldn't wait to hear the cowboy's newest escapades with his horse Silver and Tonto the Indian. Elsie and her sisters had never even heard of a radio before Ralf carted one in from among his inventory.

Elsie helped her mother clear the dishes and wash them with water carted from the well out back. Grinning, she watched as Dorothy propped herself up on two elbows on the carpeted floor, her mammoth eyes fixed on the booming radio. Shirley sat beside her, legs tucked neatly beneath her. Behind them, Ralf smoked a pipe in his chair, the sweet-scented tobacco curling in hazy wisps to the ceiling.

The Lone Ranger had another hair-raising adventure, chasing bandits across the desert planes and winning every shoot-out with his swift pistol hand. As the last triumphant notes of the orchestra faded into static, Elsie felt her eyelids slipping shut. Her hand tumbled from beneath her chin, but she woke and caught herself before her face hit the kitchen table. Through bleary eyes, she saw Mother stooping to fold a slumbering Dorothy into her arms. Ralf and Shirley must have both gone to bed, as emptiness and quiet enveloped the kitchen and living space beyond.

Pushing up from the table, Elsie stretched her arms over her head and yawned, a most unladylike pose if Mother were to have spied her. Mother passed her on the way into her bedroom, planting a kiss on her cheek and disappearing into the bedroom that she and Ralf shared. Elsie always felt a cold ache in her stomach at night when she considered the two of them alone. She didn't wish for her father back—not the man who'd vanished from their lives before she could form a decent memory of him. But she vividly remembered the first day Daddy Harry had come to call. She'd felt the genuine love between the two of them, love that blossomed into her beautiful sister Dorothy. Ralf, for all his assets, could never hope to kindle such a bond with Lillian Potter.

A mild, late-spring breeze wafted in through the open window as Elsie stole into the bedroom and clicked the door shut. After tiptoeing to her clothing trunk, she used the moonlight to find her flannel nightgown. Noiselessly, she unbuttoned her dress and slid it from her shoulders, donning her nightclothes before stowing her dress in the trunk with the only other two she owned—another drab outfit meant for everyday work, and a pretty blue one designated for special occasions.

From across the room, Dorothy had already launched into her nightly unconscious whispers and giggles. Elsie's feet padded the cold plank floor. She bent to pull back her quilts, then snuggled in beside Shirley. The bobby pins holding up her hair slid easily out of place, the strands plummeting into a wavy veil around her face. Her fingers wove them with expert speed, braiding until she had nothing left but a tiny sprig of curls at the end.

Shirley rolled onto her side, watching Elsie fasten her braid with a ribbon. A smile lit her shadowed face, startling Elsie. She looked like a woman, and yet when could it have happened? She still saw the baby with bright eyes and ruddy cheeks crawling around on the kitchen floor, the baby whose yearning for adventure had led her out of the house and under a horse before she could even walk.

Settling her head on her pillow, Elsie swept a hand through her sister's hair. The German descent of their father emanated from every plane of her maturing face—in her soft pink skin, in the blue pools of her gentle eyes. Andrew Dawson had stuffed his belongings in a suitcase and marched out the door as Shirley still matured in her mother's womb. If only he could see her now, a stunning picture of the heritage he'd given her and then chosen to leave behind.

"I want to write about Elizabeth Barrett Browning," Shirley whispered. "What do you think? I know I've heard you quote her."

Elsie's mouth curled. "How do I love thee? Let me count the ways." A teacher long ago had implanted an adoration in her heart for the eloquent poet. "I think you will love her as I do. I'll write out the poems I know tomorrow."

Shirley's eyebrows tapered. "Mother will have a fit if you help me before all the chores are done. Even then she'll find fault with the idea."

"You let me deal with Mother." Elsie clutched her pillow, an idea blooming in her mind. "I'll take Bus his supplies in the morning, then I'll write the poems down before she comes home from helping Mrs. Williams. I'll still get all the chores finished in time."

"Let's hope she doesn't catch you this time. I'd rather not spend the next week nursing your welts."

Elsie grimaced, recalling in lurid clarity the day she'd defied Momma when commanded to finish the laundry and felt the willow switch's sting on her legs. "I'm seventeen. Momma hasn't hit me like that since—" *Since Daddy Harry broke her heart.* "Besides, she didn't catch me today, did she?"

Shirley's eyes broadened. "What did you do? Did you go out with a boy?"

"Shhh." Elsie stuck a finger to her sister's lips, glancing back to be sure Dorothy hadn't woken. "No, I didn't go out with a boy," she hissed, holding in a giggle. "I *wrote.* And I will keep writing no matter what stands in the way."

Mirth still danced in Shirley's gaze, even as her mouth drooped. "Well, I hope one of these days you will be writing about a *boy!*" Every youngster in town wanted a date with Shirley, but Elsie had yet to attract anyone other than their freckled neighbor who always smelled like an onion.

Elsie bolted upright in bed. "I almost forgot!" She flung back the sheets, her feet landing with a thud on the floor. Dorothy merely squirmed and snickered as she trotted past her, grappling for the bedroom door in the dark and yanking it open. The clock in the kitchen ticked to the rhythm of her feet as Elsie dug in the stack of magazines beside the door and located the prize within. She inhaled a breath to her toes, clutching her notebook to her chest.

Mother might not appreciate the call of the empty page, but Elsie had heard its melodic song since she'd learned to read from riddles on the sides of cereal boxes. The longer she ignored it, the stronger it pulled her to its breast. She went to sleep with her scrapbook secure in her pillowcase, her dreams housed safely inside. She would keep on writing, she would keep on dreaming, until reality caught up with the world inside her.

Two

E lsie woke before dawn, eager to visit her brother and hear news of his latest venture. Buster lived wherever the wind would blow him toward his next good meal and a steady paycheck. In the summer of 1930, he'd voluntarily quit school at the age of fifteen and lent himself as a farmhand to any rancher willing to hire him. He'd driven cattle in the stockyards; he'd mined for phosphate in Soda Springs. When the Union Pacific Railroad had publicized their intentions to employ sturdy men to refurbish and repair their southern track to Montana, Buster had waited outside all night to report first.

Elsie selected the lighter of the two work dresses she owned, anticipating the effect of the morning sun on her 45-minute walk to her brother's work site. She fastened the buttons on the collar of her gray cotton smock, then sat on the chest to tie her brown leather boots. Shirley and Dorothy both still snoozed from their respective beds as she stepped into the kitchen and eased the bedroom door shut.

The spicy aroma of brewing coffee satiated the little space. Elsie let it rush into her nose a moment before stepping forward, finding a fresh pot of porridge cooking on the stove. One quick glance out the front window told her Ralf had already departed for work. The dawning sun spilled over the mountainous horizon in oranges and sparkling yellows, exposing the vacant spot where her mother's fiancé usually parked his Model A. Relief spread from her tense shoulders to her fingertips, though she couldn't explain its presence.

Her fingers brushed the basket Momma had left for Buster on the table, the bristly woven wicker and glossy bow of ribbon knotted at the handle. Her mother had packed it full of blackberry and peach preserves, handmade shirts and work gloves, a letter she'd sealed with candle wax. Nothing he couldn't do without, surely, except a tender reminder that his mother's love would follow him even into manhood.

The mellow hum of a soprano voice propelled Elsie toward her mother's open door. Halting steps from the threshold, she caught the woman's reflection in her vanity mirror, standing before the open window. Her ebony locks, pinned loosely to the back of her head, glittered in the light of sunrise like obsidian gleaming off the hills. Her knee-length floral robe elegantly hugged every curve of her slender body.

Elsie clutched the doorframe, mesmerized. Even after forty-one years and the birth of six children, Lillian Potter still looked like a seraph born for the stage. Two wells of black ink looked out on the world from behind a curtain of feathery lashes, eyes that could stare through a person. Her cheekbones sat high and pronounced on her face over a strong nose and lips like pink rose petals. Rumors swirled in her family that far back in her line, a French fur trapper had wed an Indian woman of the Iroquois, lending her such bold features and copper-hued skin. She'd never admit it, of course. Not with the stigma attached to such heritage.

Drawing in a quivering breath, Lillian stared at the bursting sky clashing into the purple Idaho landscape, pressing her palm to the glass. A stray tear trickled down her cheek and fell from her chin, but she didn't bother to wipe it away. Pained yearning enfolded her wilted frame, a vulnerability she didn't display for her children. Elsie had rarely seen her mother cry.

Suddenly aware of her intrusion, she hurried to the table and snatched up her brother's basket. She hadn't meant to pry, and Mother would have her head if she knew. Just as she reached for the door handle, Lillian's voice touched her ears. "You're going so soon?"

Elsie pivoted back, expecting to find her mother's eyes swollen and shaded with red. Instead, Lillian's usual stoic beauty greeted her. "I—I wanted to get to Buster and home again in time to finish all the work that needs to be done around here." Her gaze shifted to the kitchen window, where leafy rows of plants peeked up from the garden. "There will be plenty of lettuce and broccoli ready to pull up when I get back, and I'd like to launder the bed sheets."

Mother's eyes narrowed warily, but whatever suspicions she had remained unspoken. "At least take some breakfast with you." She plucked an apple from the fruit bowl and handed it to her. After whirling toward the bread box, she returned with a miniature loaf of freshly baked rye.

Elsie accepted it with a nod and an appreciative grin. Leave it to Momma to complain about waiting for yeast, then stay up baking all night.

The fields stretching from the highway to the base of the foothills had ripened into a sea of rolling greenery. Here and there, a yellow dandelion or patch of purple lilacs peeped out. Elsie inhaled the mountain air, watching the ravens soar across the cloud-dusted sky of blue, diving and spinning in alternate waves. Somewhere beyond the ranges rising against the wind, a world of cities and exotic places waited to be explored. Yet still, she thought with a little smile, she'd be content to choose her country home over it all.

Elsie bit into her apple, the crisp skin rupturing loudly and covering her tongue in a spurt of sweet juice. She hiked down the road for several miles, the sun climbing high above her and showering her skin in warmth. Off to the side, she noticed a small shanty town constructed in a vacant field. Makeshift houses of cardboard and shipping crates crowded together, a crude display of desperation among the wilds of creation. Elsie couldn't silence her conscience until she'd deviated from her journey and left them with Mother's bread.

Bus's work crew had camped on the south side of the winding river, sandwiched between the gorge and the eastern-bound railroad track. Dozens of tents littered the tall grasses, and the occasional bedroll told Elsie some just slept in the open when the work day concluded. Her cheeks flushed hot as she wandered among the pairs of inquisitive eyes, finding her brother pounding spikes into newly fashioned wooden ties.

At eighteen years of age, Bus stood tall and strong among his comrades. He had sandy hair like Shirley and the regal features of his mother. When he'd left for Soda Springs three years before, he'd possessed the scrawny frame of a country schoolboy. Now, as he swung his anvil through the air and beat the iron spike into the ground, Elsie felt pride at the man he'd become.

Her brother paused to swipe an arm over his brow, the hair beneath his straw hat dripping with moisture. A clever smile wrinkled his mouth when he noticed her waiting there with her basket full of goods. "No finer sight can a man behold than his beautiful sister bringing him food," he said, letting his anvil plop into the dust.

"Oh, Bus." Elsie's cheeks flamed. "You shouldn't say things like that. What would your workmates think?" Her gaze darted around to the horde of railroad laborers, most of whom had gone back to their respective jobs.

"They would think I'm stating the obvious." Bus ambled toward her, drying his clammy hands on his cotton trousers. "I have three beautiful sisters, the oldest of whom should remember she is." He stopped before her, his shoulders shrugging. "I would hug you, but I don't want to ruin your pretty dress."

"Oh, bother." Elsie rolled her eyes, catching him in a tight squeeze. He always made a fuss of his sisters, turning whatever tired frock they wore into a ball gown straight out of French court. "You have *four* sisters, remember?" She pulled away, noting the disquiet rippling his brow.

The family didn't speak often of the two eldest siblings sent to live with their father when their parents divorced. They'd visited on occasion as children, but as the years sprinted onward, the distance between them only expanded. Dorothy had never even met John and Emma, and Elsie's recollection of the two young faces grew foggier with each passing day.

"Have you heard from them?" Bus asked, a spark of hope glinting in his light eyes. He, among the siblings, remembered them best of all.

Elsie's shoulders slumped. "No. Momma still writes letters, but—" The sentence dangled unfinished in the sunlit air. They both knew the conclusion—either they never reached Papa, or he chose not to reply.

Bus removed his hat, revealing the slick shock of blond hair beneath. "How is Momma?"

What a laden question. The vision of her crying at the window still haunted Elsie. "She's faring well." Momma would be furious if Elsie disclosed what she'd seen. "She's helping at the Williams' farm today. Dorothy and Shirley are splendid as always, of course."

A dimple lit his cheek. "Of course." Darkness shaded his eyes as he turned his hat over in his hands. "And Ralf? I assume he's still living with you all." A muscle in his jaw clenched.

"Yes, he's still with us." Elsie long knew the disdain her brother carried for the man. "He's a good presence. Really, Bus. He provides for our needs and Mother isn't so lonely with him there." The words felt dry on her tongue, uttered more for her own relief than his.

A grunt issued from somewhere in his stalwart chest. "I should be the one providing for you." His eyes roved over the camp, the

15

host of workers hammering and sawing. "We'll be finished with this job in the fall, and then who knows where I might go."

Elsie gave his arm a gentle squeeze. "You've done well, Buster. You've helped us through our roughest moments, and now you can start earning for your own future." Momma never spoke of it, but Elsie had glimpsed the money peeking from the envelopes that Bus sent home with her.

His fingers clenched around the straw hat. "Leave you behind with a man who's a stranger to me?" He chuckled without humor. "I've seen all types on the road, Elsie, and I'd venture that a Swedish salesman is no different from the rest."

"You've hardly even met the man." Elsie let her hand fall away from him. "You gave the last one a chance, didn't you?" The absurdity of her own argument rang in her ears. The last one had left Momma heartbroken and their family in shambles.

Buster's eyes shone with fire. "Ralf isn't Harry, and we are no longer children." Fear and rage battled in his gaze. He cared so much, and yet he was powerless to stop a headstrong mother who insisted she knew best. Elsie's gaze latched with his for several agonizing seconds, the truth echoing between them. They both harbored a premonition against the man Mother had sworn her life and trust to.

"Well, lookie here!" someone said. Elsie turned to find a man of about twenty ambling toward them with his thumbs hooked in his suspenders. "Bus, you weren't about to bring a fine lady into camp and not introduce her, were you?" His wide grin beamed back, the brown hair beneath his hat tumbling rebelliously over his brow.

The tension visibly drained from Buster's shoulders as he clamped a hand on his friend's back. "Of course not." He swept one arm toward her. "This is my sister Elsie. Elsie, Walt Tully."

The young man tipped his hat to her. "Nice to meet ya, sister Elsie. Don't let him scare you from coming back now, ya hear? We need more of you around this place." With that, he kept on with his stroll, pivoting back to throw a playful wink at her.

Buster chuckled at her look of disbelief. "What did I tell you? Pretty, pretty girl." He cocked his head, his gaze plunging to the basket in her hand. "Now, were you planning to give me that ribbon-covered thing, or was I supposed to arm wrestle you for it?"

～～～～～ ～～～～～

The sun had nearly climbed to the heavens' summit when Elsie saw her farmhouse in the distance. Her legs were weary from the long walk, and her stomach grumbled. The whitewashed boards and green trim shone bright in the gleaming light, concealing the cracks and peels in the worn woodwork. Her steps quickened, her body eager to devour some of Momma's newly baked bread and leftover soup.

Elsie stumbled to a halt in the roadway, the dirt clustering around her in a descending cloud. She squinted as a hay wagon rambled past her, sure her eyes forsook her. There, in the crushed section of grass beside their wobbly fence, sat the old Model A Ralf used for work. She thought briefly of walking into town until he left, but the groans in her stomach drove her onward. She'd just have to go about her work and ignore him as best she could.

The house sat in eerie quiet as Elsie creaked the front door open. Ralf had left his jacket draped over a chair in the kitchen, his keys discarded on the table beside it. When she surveyed the room and didn't spy a soul, she wondered if perhaps he'd walked over to the Williams' to help Momma with their farm. Then a rustling from their bedroom sank her hopes into despair.

Ralf appeared at the door seconds later, one sleeve rolled to his elbow and his vest unbuttoned. "Ah, Elsie. I'm so glad you've returned." He moved into the kitchen, still folding up the other sleeve. "Your mother forgot to pack my lunch this morning in her haste to get out to the Williams'. Luckily, my calls were all nearby today. I thought perhaps you'd fix me a sandwich." His aging face crinkled warmly.

A foreboding pang bit at Elsie's already famished stomach. Mother didn't often neglect her duties, and she'd spent plenty of time in the kitchen that morning. "Of course. I was just about to make myself something."

Ralf dropped into a chair facing the counter and set his elbows on the table. Elsie pretended she couldn't feel him watching her pull meat slices and vegetables from the icebox, chop the lettuce, and slice the bread Momma had wrapped in butcher paper. The aroma of roasted beef drafted to her nose, and instead of enticing her hungry middle, it sickened her. Every movement she made, she felt as if on display for an audience at a packed theater.

Lunch passed in dreary silence. Ralf asked the occasional question—her interests outside her daily household chores, what she planned to do in her adult life. Elsie kept her answers polite but curt, choosing to fill as many moments as possible munching on her sandwich. When the last morsel had disappeared from their plates, she sprang up from the table and collected the dishes, hoping he'd grasp her hints and leave.

Grabbing a wash bin from under the counter, Elsie plunked the dishes inside and reached for the water bucket she'd fill in the well by the garden. A sensation like icy fingers crept up her spine when she heard Ralf's footsteps pulse toward her and stop. Rising to her feet, she clutched the bucket to her chest in trembling hands. *Don't turn around.* She could feel his presence, so near her skin crawled with a million invisible insects. *Just don't turn around and he'll go away. He'll go away.*

Her quivering breath froze as his fingertips grazed her arm, traveling the path from her elbow to her wrist. Elsie stiffened, her limbs going numb. Both of his roughened hands slid up her forearms, gliding over her dress to her shoulders. His fingers kneaded the taut plains of her shoulder blades, working at the muscles.

"Relax," his Swedish-tinged voice murmured against the wisps of hair cascading over her earlobe. "Don't be afraid, my little *älskling*." His thumbs pressed her back, sluggishly yet purposefully descending.

Elsie dug her nails into the wooden bucket until she thought they'd bleed. "I—" The words refused to dislodge from her arid throat. "I must be about my work."

"Shhhh." Ralf gently removed the bucket from her arms and let it jangle to a standstill on the countertop. "Work can wait." His hand compressed her hip, bunching the light material of her dress.

Cold sweat dribbled from her hairline to the flushed skin of her face. Over her thrashing heartbeat, her chest heaved in agonizing waves. Ralf swept aside the stray tendrils of hair on her throat and pressed his clammy lips to the nape of her neck. Elsie's mind sprinted outside her body, trying to conjure a means of escape, and yet her legs felt cemented to the floor.

"Ralf, stop it." Tears squeezed from her eyes. "Please, stop it."

Instead, his body crushed hers from behind. One hand held her ribcage firmly while the other reached around to her torso, working to undo her buttons. Panic rammed through her, starting at her churning stomach and spiraling out to her static extremities. Without thought, her fingers closed around his.

"Ralf, please." She forced tenderness into her voice, kindness into the fingertips brushing his knuckles. He allowed her enough space to rotate in his arms, to come face-to-face with the man meant to call her "daughter". Elsie searched his face for a long moment, trying to pinpoint where and how a man evolved into a beast. The blue eyes in his creased skin must have once looked on the world in hope, but now they only preyed, only sought to gain what they could from feeding on the weak. Elsie swallowed, vowing never to be that victim.

"Slowly, please." She coerced her lips to curl in a shy smile. "I'm not used to this quite yet." In truth, she'd never before felt a male's touch, never shared a kiss. She did not have to act afraid.

Compassion smoothed over his salt-and-pepper brows. Ralf relaxed his hold on her, letting the back of his hand sweep from her forehead over the curve of her cheek. Her heartbeat battered her eardrums. His fingers moved nearer to her mouth. She waited, the seconds expanding into enormous chasms of time. Then his fingertips skimmed her lower lip and her gut constricted, as if shoving her into action.

Elsie opened her lips and bit down as hard as she could, her teeth sinking into his salty flesh. A pain-laden yelp buzzed in her ears as he tore his hand away. She tasted blood, saw Ralf through a blurry haze holding his injured fingers close to his chest. He swore and reached for her, but Elsie darted below his arm and dashed toward the front door. His boots pounded the floorboards behind her. Elsie dove for the handle, twisting in one motion and leaping over the steps. Her body landed with a hard thud on the bristly ground, her face scraped and stinging.

Twisting her head around, Elsie made out Ralf's bulky form marching down the porch steps. That sickening ache in her middle mounted her throat, threatening to choke her. Battling her weak limbs, she pushed off the ground and raced across the field ahead. Ralf could follow her down the roadway in his Model A, but he could never outrun her. And so she sprinted onward toward the mountains until her legs refused to carry her.

Three

The blanket of night settled over the valley like a mother tucking her children into bed. The mountainous terrain faded beneath a purple sunset, transforming to a murky outline in the dusk before ducking behind a black canvas. A million stars emerged, shedding bits of fire over the heavens. As the moon mounted the treetops, crickets struck up their nocturnal song, celebrating the day's finale.

Sam shared dinner with the rest of the railroad crew, a can of beans cut open with a Swiss Army knife and warmed over the campfire. His muscles ached from hours of swinging an anvil under the blistering sun, but the pain seemed to lessen every day. Nigh a month had passed since his brother trotted in merrily with a notice from the Union Pacific advertising jobs on their decaying track. Nigh a month of canned beans and grueling labor, but he didn't mind. Eleven growling stomachs at home had a way of impelling a man to try his hardest.

The work camp had come alive with the setting sun, trading in their grinding toil for gaiety. All around their many fire pits, men shoved food between their bearded lips and guzzled from their canteens amidst conversation. Laughter echoed across the canyons, booming back with equal force. Here and there, men took to card or dice games in the dirt. One even plucked at a fiddle, its blissful notes carrying on the wind. Sam looked over the twinkling array of lanterns and smiled. Despite the sacrifices it required, nothing compared with life in the wild.

"You should have seen it!" his brother Walt declared to another man across the fire, his hands dancing in excitement. "His big hairy knuckles snatching girls out of windows, whirling people around. He even climbs the Empire State Building!" Both hands arched over his head, indicating the mammoth structure.

"I don't know." His friend wagged his head, unconvinced. "If I'm going to spend my hard-earned money, I'd rather plunk down a quarter to see the Marx Brothers. At least I know I'll have a laugh."

"I like the Marx Brothers as well as the next guy, but you're missing the point," Walt said. "Comedy can happen anywhere at any time. But this—this was larger than life!" He whirled toward Sam, his eyebrows shooting straight up. "Tell him, Sam!"

Sam slurped up another spoonful of beans. "You've never seen anything like it."

Ever since a group had ridden into town together and decided to take in a film at the picture house, Walt had spoken of nothing else. They'd enjoyed a scattering of movies through the years, but nothing like *King Kong*. The film had sparked a seemingly endless debate about how the makers had depicted the beast scaling buildings, how he looked so lifelike, and if something so dreadful could actually take place in their world. Sam hadn't been as fascinated as Walt, but he did revel in watching his brother pester whatever fool dared to mention the cinema.

"Well, maybe I'll go see it when the next paycheck comes in," said the reluctant man across the fire.

"It will be worth it just to see Fay Wray alone," Walt said between bites of dry biscuit. "Wow-ee, what a looker."

"She's got nothing on Delores Del Rio, if you ask me," countered their friend Donald from the shadows. "I saw her in *Bird of Paradise* last year and I couldn't think about anything else for weeks."

"Delores Del Rio," scoffed another. "Carole Lombard—there's a lady with class and beauty."

"If we're on the subject of blondes, Mae West is your girl!"

"There's only one reason you like Mae West," Donald said. The group of men howled, well aware of the movie star's charms. Even inflatable life vests bore her name.

"Hey, she's a serious actress!" The man's rebuttal only incited more laughter before he recoiled behind the fire and solemnly returned to his dinner.

"What about you, Sam?" Walt asked. "You've been awful quiet during this whole debate. Which girl do you find the prettiest?"

The right side of Sam's mouth lifted in a half-smile. He hadn't thought much about girls since he and his eldest brothers had stepped into the working world. There'd been one or two who'd caught his eye in high school; he'd even worked up the courage to ask a classmate to spring formal several years back. But out here, where the earth met the sky in a dazzling array of rocky crags and unkempt grass, he'd seen little beauty save for Mother Nature herself.

"I like Kate Hepburn," he said with a shy grin. His sister Sally had practically dragged him to the picture show to see *A Bill of Divorcement* last year. His shoes had skidded the cinema carpet walking in, sure he'd abhor two hours of watching John Barrymore woo yet another swooning lover. When the film reel had clicked into motion and cast her comely face over the screen, his reluctance dissolved as if ice melting off his limbs. He'd returned to the show alone twice more just to hear that deep, haunting voice again.

Several men nodded, but most wore dumbfounded expressions. "Who?" Donald asked, eyebrows askew.

"You'll know soon enough." Sam dipped his spoon into his can of beans and enjoyed another savory bite. A woman like that would take over the silver screen. He'd bet his last cent on it.

"Speaking of pretty girls," Walt said, "did you fellows see that dame who walked into camp today?" A high-pitched whistle squealed through his teeth. "What a sight for a poor man's eyes."

"Don't let Bus hear you talk like that," Donald warned. "He's awful protective of them sisters."

Sam glanced over his shoulder to find Buster Dawson playing five-card draw by another fire. The man had spoken often of his three sisters at home, but Sam had never met one. Rumor had it the middle one was fair and beautiful, but he'd never dare to ask. Before he and Walt had joined the railroad crew, she'd visited the camp and drawn considerable interest. Bus had run one man clear out of camp for propositioning her, or so the story went.

"Aw, I don't mean any harm." Walt waved a hand through the smoky air. "Just a bit of good fun. We need it once in a while, you know."

Silence draped itself over the men sitting around the campfire. Only the snapping of logs and spitting flames filled the void. Sam scraped the last bit of food from his tin can and let the spoon jangle against the empty bottom. Their family lived only miles away, close enough to visit on long weekends. Many men had traveled great distances, left behind wives and children, in order to secure their livelihood. No wonder the sight of a female excited them.

"I'm going to bed," he said, the words sounding dull from his dry throat. His knees protested as he stood and picked up the discarded can. Sam lobbed it into the refuse pile and rinsed his spoon at the water pump before sauntering off to untie his bedroll and lay it over the earth.

The hard ground rose up against his muscles as he sprawled out in his sleeping bag. Here and there, a rock gouged from the dirt, jabbing into his shoulder or leg. Sam pulled off his jacket, bundling it beneath his neck and relaxing into it. The booming voices and shared mirth still drifted in from camp, but here, beneath a canopy of glittering stars, he felt peace.

Sam gazed up at the night sky, seeing crystals peeping from a bed of coal. The warm spring weather had sprouted a host of wildflowers over the hills, their scents mingling sweetly on the breeze. His thoughts ventured past the boisterous railroad crew, over the endless fields and rugged countryside, to a little house on the river. He saw Mother, standing at the threshold with a wide grin on her rounded face and a child in each arm. He saw his father, seated at a rocking chair by the window, a Bible open upon his withering lap.

"Oh, God," the words hardly escaped his trembling lips. The stars flickered amid his tears. "I'm a man now. Twenty-two years old and expected to face the world with bravery, a world that has only trampled men like me."

Six brothers, two sisters—each face paraded across his mind's eye. If he didn't care for them, who would? He'd seen Pop's condition on his last visit. The family's aging patriarch tried to conceal it, but his rheumatism had only worsened. How many years until it crippled him altogether?

"Give me faith, Lord. Give me faith when I cannot see the way out." The moon emerged from behind a curtain of clouds, projecting its white rays over the gleaming mountains. He felt the promise deep from within. Even in the darkest of nights, the light would appear. He would never let them stumble.

Pulling in a shaky breath, Sam closed his eyes and thanked the God he had known from childhood. "Help me become a man of success and integrity. Give me the strength I need to face tomorrow."

⁂

Elsie's lips still quivered as the words to "Nobody Knows You When You're Down and Out" poured through them and into the chasm of night. The air had chilled, seeping through her light cotton dress and prickling her skin with a thousand tiny goosebumps. The jazzy tune, dreary as it was, still sweetened the lonely night and did its best to lift her sunken spirits.

Elsie had heard it many times while visiting their old neighbor in Montana. The family had owned a phonograph, a magical contraption to her adolescent ears. When her friend had rushed over with the new Bessie Smith album, the girls must have listened to it a dozen times. Now the words echoed in her mind and escaped her mouth in a cheerless sonata. Nobody could know her pain.

Her boots softly scuffed the porch steps as she ascended them to the front door. Since her escapade with Ralf, she'd wandered the bluffs with aimless abandon, staring into the snaking canyon and half expecting it to consume her. She'd kicked a smattering of pebbles into the craggy precipice and pictured herself as one of them, careening through the open air and tumbling to certain doom at the bottom. Wasn't she just like them, hurling to an uncertain future without control of her direction?

When her legs had tired and her eyes grown sore from crying, she'd found a hidden spot among the tall grasses of a field and gone to sleep. Even there, she could not shut him out of her dreams, could not stop feeling his course hands grabbing at her clothes. The sound of his cruel laugh jolted her awake in a cold sweat, and Elsie leaped up, expecting him to have found her. Yet only the setting sun had greeted her, melting into the landscape in a glorious array, even in the face of her broken heart.

Through the muntin bars in the window, she spied Momma and Ralf seated at the kitchen table with her two little sisters. Dorothy chattered away in her usual fashion, while Shirley listened with a polite smile. They looked happy, like a family should—free to laugh and tell stories and enjoy a pleasant evening after a hard day's work. Then she saw Ralf's hand brush back Momma's thick wave of hair, and a cold sensation stabbed her gut. She could never be safe with him here. *Her sisters* could never be safe with him here.

Elsie sucked in a piercing breath as she turned the knob and forced her arm to drive the door open. Her gaze swept the two girls,

THE GLASS DANCER COPY

now hushed upon her arrival, then Momma's mystified frown, before finally locking on the cruel eyes that had seared into her memory all day. Ralf's gleaming scowl, his curled lip and crinkled brows, shot a clear message like a poison arrow in her direction—tell anyone and he would do far worse.

"Elsie, where on earth have you been?" Mother demanded. "We waited over an hour to start dinner, and now we're eating it cold because of you."

Elsie walked into the room as if in a daze, her gaze meandering over the half-eaten mashed potatoes, meatloaf, and steamed garden vegetables. Mother had prepared a special meal and she'd missed it. "I'm sorry, Momma," she whispered, plunking into the vacant seat beside Shirley.

"As well you should be." Mother sat straighter and rearranged the napkin on her lap. "I planned all this for you in honor of the hard work you've been doing around here. Then I come home to find none of the chores finished and a basin full of dirty dishes."

Elsie glanced at the counter to find it spotless, the basin she'd left there cleaned and stowed back in its place on the floor. She'd forgotten about the dishes from lunch—forgotten evidence existed of Ralf's betrayal. The man couldn't have washed two plates in order to hide his indiscretions?

"Did you bring a man home and feed him lunch, then let him drag you around the rest of the day?" Lillian threw up her hands at Elsie's sharp look and flushed cheeks. "Well, how am I to know? You use enough meat for three men, then disappear for the rest of the day. Suddenly you're eating like your brother and acting like him too?" Even in her rage, the concern behind her anger could not stay buried in her ebony eyes.

Elsie's lips parted, but the words wouldn't come. Her skin tingled at the warning in Ralf's fierce gaze, in the way his body angled toward her in threat. Shirley laid a cool hand over her forearm, but it only made her jump.

"Don't press her, Lillian," Ralf grumbled. "She's here now." He dug into his mashed potatoes, motioning for the girls to follow suit.

Momma gasped in alarm. "Land sakes, Elsie." She thrust out a hand and pushed back Elsie's drooping hair. "What are these scratches on your forehead—and on your cheek?" Her fingers traveled from Elsie's temple to her cheekbone, prodding at her throbbing flesh.

Jerking away, Elsie glanced over at Ralf's bandaged fingers. "What happened to Ralf's hand?" she asked, her sarcasm manifest despite the fear expanding within her.

Momma shook her head. "He was bitten by a dog on one of his sales calls, but I don't see what that has to do with—" Her words dangled about the strained room as she looked from Elsie to Ralf, comprehension dawning. A horrified grief crept over Lillian's smooth brow, the suspicion a mother feared above all else.

"It doesn't," Elsie said quickly, squelching the fright in her mother's eyes. She couldn't stand it, not even when born of truth. "I went to the employment agency to find work, but I was pushed down in the crowd." She scrunched her dress in one balled fist beneath the table. Somehow, the lie felt necessary.

Relief visibly flooded her mother's body. She relaxed into her wooden chair, retrieving her fork from the table. "It is war there, I'm afraid." Slicing off a bite of meatloaf, she smiled at Elsie. "I'm proud that you went. I can forget the dishes today if you promise not to do it again."

Nodding, Elsie speared a carrot and brought it to her lips. The bittersweet vegetable crunched between her teeth, barely gliding down her burning gullet. Her stomach lurched, repulsed by the food. Elsie loaded her fork and kept on eating for Momma's sake.

"Can we talk about the wedding now?" Dorothy asked, rupturing the tension. All eyes reeled toward the animated little girl with rosy cheeks and pink bows tethered to her braided hair. "We read about a grand wedding in school today. I want you to have one just like it, Momma, with flowers and lace dresses and a symphony to play when you walk down the aisle."

Lillian let out a deep chuckle. "I don't know about all that, but you can certainly help us plan it." She turned an excited smile on Ralf. "What do you say about setting a date in the fall, Ralf? It will be beautiful that time of year with the trees changing color. I don't think the Williams would mind us using their farm."

Grunting, he didn't bother to lift his distracted gaze from his dinner. "We'll discuss it later. I may have to take a business trip that time of year."

"Oh well, no matter." Mother's lips curled despite his dismissal. "You and I will just have to arrange the whole thing, my girl." She cupped Dorothy's cheek and winked.

Elsie did the dishes without help that night, penance for abandoning her task earlier in the day. While the family chatted about the day's events and Dorothy read from her speller, Shirley sidled up to Elsie and tried to ask what troubled her in a whisper. Elsie only shook her head, daring to peer back at Ralf, who read the newspaper in his recliner. He would hurt her if she revealed his misdeeds. She would not let him hurt Shirley.

Her fingers were rough and wrinkly by the time she drained the last of the dish water on the ground outside and dried the basin with a towel. When she entered the kitchen through the back door, Mother stood by the icebox, one hand stroking the curling wallpaper above it. Elsie moved past her without a word, bending to stash the washbowl in the corner.

Mother's fingertips swept her hair as she rose. "I wanted to wish you goodnight." Her dark eyes hunted Elsie's face. She didn't voice it, but Elsie could see the questions written in the gentle pucker of her full lips. She didn't want to know the truth. She wanted assurance.

"Goodnight, Momma." The curtains in the window ruffled as the breeze drafted through it and unsettled the hair already falling from her pins. The air stung the scabbing wounds on her face. She caught her mother studying them once again. "They've already begun to heal." Elsie pressed her palm over the tender cuts, obscuring them from her mother's hawk-like stare.

"Just to be safe, we'll cover them in ointment tomorrow." Lillian's perplexed gaze flickered once more over her daughter before she pivoted on her heel and started toward her bedroom door.

Tell her! a voice screamed from Elsie's core. *Save her from certain misery!* Elsie clutched the back of a chair in a tense grip, her knuckles blanching white. If her mother wed the monster living within their walls, she could be mired in his presence forever. She could bear his children and never escape him. "Momma, wait!"

Lillian paused a long moment at her door, head bent low. When she turned back to Elsie, the sputtering kitchen lamp light unveiled the truth in the robust plains of her face. Deep down, she knew already. She could sense what manner of man slept beside her at night, and to destroy the fantasy she'd crafted would only rend mother from daughter. She wouldn't believe her, at least not anywhere but her heart.

"Sweet dreams, Momma," Elsie said.

Long after Mother had retreated to her corner of the world and Elsie had wrestled back the forces urging her to escape this place, she summoned the strength to move. Lifting the chair already in her grasp, Elsie dragged it over the cracked wooden floor and hauled it into her bedroom. Gentle snores drifted from both the beds inside as she snapped the door shut and wedged the chair beneath the handle.

When at last the cozy blankets enveloped her, Elsie's heart still galloped. She wrapped an arm around Shirley's sleeping form and hugged her close, her warmth both comforting and petrifying. Perhaps she could protect herself, but what happened when Ralf laid his sights on this blue-eyed angel? Elsie kept her wide eyes pinned on the bedroom door, her breath quick and high in her throat, until fatigue at last overcame her.

Four

Saturday meant freedom in so many ways. Dorothy and Shirley went begrudgingly off to school on the weekdays, but when the classroom bell rang on Friday afternoons, life became leisure and play time. Elsie performed her normal duties around the house, a skip in her step absent on the other days. For on Saturdays, Daddy Harry came to visit—and Ralf vacated the house until sunset.

Elsie whistled a jaunty tune as the midmorning sun beat down on her curling tendrils of brown hair. Swiping away the moisture on her brow with one sleeve, she crouched down in the earth once again and tugged at the weeds plaguing her garden. The cabbages sat in line on her right side, parading their beauty in green flowerets tinted with purple. On her left, the pea plants sprouted tall and proud, winding up the trellises like grape vines cleaving to their trunks. Patches of onion and garlic shot up from the earth in hearty stalks and scented the garden in a bright aroma.

"Still hard at work, I see."

The familiar man's voice volleyed a stream of good spirits through Elsie. She tossed a grin over her shoulder and yanked at the stubborn weed in her gloved hand. The toxic stem slid through the dirt, dragging with it a tangle of roots. "If I don't pull out the bad, the good cannot grow." The statement troubled her. How could healthy plants stay that way with something foreign choking out their life?

Pushing off the ground, Elsie stood and brushed the dirt from her soiled skirts. Harry held out his arms in spite of her mess, and she went into them gladly. His musky aftershave shrouded her as his tweed coat scuffed the cheek she pressed to his shoulder. Somehow when Harry came calling, the world felt manageable after all.

"Come to see your daughter?" she asked as she released him and stooped to pick up her basket filled with gardening tools.

"I found her," he said with a clever smirk.

Elsie merely chuckled while she pulled off her work gloves and laid them in her basket. Harry looked smart as always, clad in a charcoal gray overcoat with pointed lapels and double-breasted buttons. He wore a triangle-folded handkerchief in his breast pocket and a flat cap with matching ribbon over his reddish-blond hair.

"Dorothy's inside." She motioned for him to follow. Of course they were all his children, and knew it too, but Dorothy alone granted him the proper excuse to still visit them every week.

When the pair scooted through the back door, Dorothy lit with delight and charged at her father like a bull chasing red. "Papa!" she screeched, leaping into his already open arms. Harry lifted her up and cradled her against his solid chest, kissing the hair that so resembled their mother's.

Setting her basket on the kitchen table, Elsie stood back to watch the precious scene. Time could not erode her first memories of the Scotch-Irish fireman calling on her momma. She must have been only three or four years of age, Shirley just a baby. Elsie remembered his large, square shoulders and how they hardly seemed to fit through the door. She could still taste the black licorice he carried around in his pocket. Harry O'Donnell had altered all of their lives forever.

"Oh, my girl." Harry sighed, pulling away enough to look at her. "What is a healthy, twelve-year-old girl doing cooped up in the kitchen on such a sunny day? You ought to be outside enjoying your youth!"

Dorothy's feet hit the floor as he set her slight frame back down. "Momma says I have to finish my schoolwork before I play." She speared one finger toward the offensive papers waiting on the kitchen table. "I have just one more page before I'm finished."

Harry took the time to embrace Shirley, who'd put down her copy of *The American Magazine* to rise and greet him. "Well, then you'd best hurry. I've made plans for us today—all of us."

Dorothy's dark eyes twinkled. "Are we going to the hot springs?" She bounced from foot to foot. "Or to the river? I love it when we swim!" Her whole body wiggled, her civics paper forgotten.

"I will tell you when you've finished your work like your mother instructed." Harry pulled off his hat, the wave of hair beneath fixed in place. "Tell me about this assignment of yours so we can get it done as quickly as we can." He dragged a chair out from beneath the table, seating himself with his hat on his knee.

Face contorting, Dorothy trailed behind him and plopped into her abandoned spot. "I'm supposed to write about a foreign country and how we can learn from them. I wanted England, but Teacher assigned me Germany." She stuck out her tongue, arms crossed over her little chest.

Shirley chuckled from her spot in Ralf's lounge chair. "Why did you want England?"

"Because they have a king, and they ride horses, and they drink tea every day." Dorothy picked up her pencil and whirled it with a fanciful flourish. "I could have finished my five paragraphs in ten minutes."

"Germany has plenty of culture too," Elsie said as she threw her garden trimmings in the compost bucket and set fresh peppers on the counter to be washed.

"All I know is that they like to yodel and the men wear skirts," Dorothy said with a pout.

"Swiss people yodel, not Germans." Shirley shook her head, a good-natured smile capturing her face. "And you're thinking of Scotsmen. They're called kilts, not skirts."

Releasing a frustrated grunt, Dorothy slammed herself into her chair back and rolled her eyes. "See? I know nothing about Germany. It might as well be Neverland, for all I know."

"I hear they have a new chancellor." Harry tapped his finger on her empty page. "Adolf—?"

"Hitler!" Dorothy said, recollection dawning. She posed her pencil into ready position. "He makes all his soldiers march without bending their knees and he has a funny little mustache. Teacher thinks he's handsome, but I think it looks like he has a creature growing straight out of his nose."

"Dorothy," Shirley chided. "It's not nice to say things like that."

"He isn't *my* president." Dorothy's chin elevated, as if to defend her choice of insults. "Maybe he just likes it that way. He wears other silly things, too. Like the armband with the spider on it."

"Swastika," Elsie corrected as she moved to collect her gardening tools and replace them in the shed out back. "It's the symbol of the Nazi party."

"Nazis!" Dorothy bit her lip, jotting down notes in the margin of her page as the strange words and facts flew at her. Pausing, she cocked her head to the side and looked at her father through narrowed eyes. "It's an awful lot of show, isn't it, Papa? Do you think he needs it to be a good leader?"

Harry O'Donnell scratched his chin, the idea working his wrinkled brow. "That I don't know, my darling. I guess time will tell, won't it?"

Dorothy agreed with a nod and went back to eagerly scrawling her assignment over the bare page. Elsie toted her gardening basket to the water pump and cleaned the shovels out before drying them and storing them in the work shed among shelves of canned goods and supplies. Once she'd rinsed the dirt from her arms and towel dried them, she returned to the house to find Dorothy's pencil flying over the paper, scribbling out the last sentences on her diatribe against Hitler's army and overall fashion sense.

After quietly pushing up from his chair and ambling toward her, Harry leaned on the wall beside Elsie. "Do you expect your mother back any time soon?"

Elsie shook her head. "She's helping at the Williams' again today. They have so many animals to feed and maintain. Mrs. Williams is hard pressed enough with seven children to care for."

His lips pressed thin, but he simply nodded. The disappointment in his cornflower blue eyes spoke for him. A sensation choked Elsie's throat, the driving instinct to blurt out everything—that Ralf was wrong for Momma, that she would only ever love *him*, that Ralf would hurt them all if he stayed. Then she remembered Momma's face the day she'd packed up her four children and left Harry behind, the endless string of nights she'd spent crying on her pillow over their divorce. Life with him had never been as easy as she liked to imagine.

"We struck a hotbed of ore at the quarry. Earned us all hefty bonus checks. Thought I'd treat you girls to lunch and a soda pop in town to celebrate." He squeezed her shoulder, so different from Ralf's touch when he'd done the same.

Elsie's hands shot to her sweat-ridden, frazzled head. "Just give me a moment to redo my hair." She couldn't remember the last time she had the privilege to dine in town, and she refused to be seen with a crow's nest sitting atop her head.

Upon stepping into the bedroom and finding the table between their beds empty, Elsie recalled washing her hairbrush and setting it out to dry early that morning. A wood thrush flapped madly away when she opened the front door and trod across the rickety porch. Ralf had promised to fix it a month ago, but still the boards swayed and creaked as she crossed to retrieve the brush she'd left atop the railing.

The mountains sparkled in the sunshine as Elsie pulled the pins from her hair and set them in a neat row next to her brush. The snow caps had nearly melted, but still a patch of glistening white peered out among the dents and curves of the sprawling ranges. Elsie tempted herself to stop and write a poem about the mountains and the fields below them, but knew time wouldn't permit. She could already hear Dorothy inside celebrating the demise of her time with Germany's unconventional leader.

A tractor trundled by, spitting out diesel fuel and clouding the air with dust. Elsie dragged her hairbrush through her snarled mane, gently tugging at the knots and freeing tangles. Just as the tractor had faded away and the dirt had settled, she saw a 1920's Chevy truck sputtering down the lane. Elsie held her breath and slid the brush through her hair again, sure the old vehicle would stir another unpleasant haze of filth.

The breeze filtered through her free wisps of hair as the truck rolled past her front porch, engine roaring. The once red paint had worn to a burgundy with sun damage, evidence of its former beauty still seeping through the cracked and rusty frame. Two people sat inside—the passenger too far to make out, the driver a young man in his early twenties, one arm slung over the wheel and a fedora across his thick brows.

Elsie gripped her hairbrush, halting in mid-action. The man had pinned his gaze on her, a firm yet quiet look that sent a thrill up her spine. The cool wind blew over her face, fanning the flaming skin beneath. She tried to look away but couldn't. He studied her for several agonizing seconds before his mouth tilted in a lopsided grin and the truck rumbled off toward town.

Stepping to the rail, Elsie set down her hairbrush and stared after the parting truck until it rounded a corner and vanished behind the neighboring farms. She clutched the post beside her, feeling as if in a trance until Dorothy's running footsteps announced the time. Elsie made quick work of refashioning her hair with her bobby pins and joining the others, attempting to put the man and the truck behind her. Yet as they all piled into Harry's old Model T and took off for lunch, she doubted she would easily forget.

⚜ ⚜

M other and Pop lived in a farmhouse at the edge of the Snake River. Sam's brother-in-law had purchased it years before and moved the family in when times turned rough in the minefields of Nevada. Now the little abode practically burst at the corners with Tullys, old and young, running about like a wild pack of monkeys.

The family's corroded Chevrolet pickup cranked angrily as it climbed the last hill to their temporary home. Sam shifted gears, compelling the tired truck up the slope and over the rocky terrain. Beside him, Walt whistled a jolly tune, some anthem to good spirits he'd picked up in the railroad camp. The spinning tires jostled them to and fro, one minute into the air, the next back down with a painful thump.

"Do you think we'll go back to the mines in Delano?" Walt asked, his gaze fixed on the white bark pines parading along the roadway.

"Can't say." Sam shifted the idea around in his mind. "If Pop gets another contract, we will." As much as he hated them, the mines had provided well for his family. Sam had worked as a driver, hauling ore in the bed of his truck in Delano, one of the barest, most desolate places he'd ever hoped to see.

"I'm partial to the railroad," Walt said with a sigh.

Sam let the rumble of the Chevy's engine answer his brother's thought. He liked the railroad better than the mines, but still he couldn't quench the desire for more. Their father had taught them the value and respectability of manual labor, but Sam wanted to use his mind. He couldn't help dreaming of running something that he had created himself, rather than taking orders from whatever boss would hand them a day's work.

The juddering truck crested the hill and dipped low again. Sam rolled down his window and thrust his hand into the hissing wind, letting it rush over his skin and lift the hair of his arm. The spicy scent of pine needles filled his senses as the remote farmhouse rose into view, a charming display of yellow and white trim against the sparse forest beyond. He could already spot several children running around in the yard, the tail end of the Tully clan.

The tires crunched over the gravel drive, the motor clanging as they slowed. Sam shifted gears and broke the truck near the white columned front porch, delighted at the squeals and giggles bounding around the yard. Three pairs of legs dashed toward the rickety Chevy, undeterred by the cloud of exhaust congesting the air.

"You're home!" their youngest sister Lizzy shrieked, an eager smile stretched across her seven-year-old face.

"Want to play three flies up?" ten-year-old Ollie asked, a ball ready in his hands.

Sam swung the truck door open and climbed down, ruffling his adolescent brother's head. "Maybe in a few minutes, sport. I'd like to see Mother and Pop first."

"I'll play with you." Walt surged forward, snatching the ball out of Ollie's hand. "You'll have to catch me first, though!" He tore across the front yard, three screaming children at his heels.

Sam's boots clattered up the porch steps, where pots of geraniums dangled from the eaves. Pulling back the screen door, he thrust open the wooden one beyond and let both clang shut behind him. His sister's empty sitting room was neat despite the horde residing within her walls, adorned with fringed lamps and quilted throws. The pleasant hum of laughter and conversation trickled in from the kitchen.

Following the trail of female voices, Sam tread into the kitchen to find Sally busily scrubbing the countertops while his mother cooked the evening meal. A rather hefty woman, Olive Tully had her first grandson hoisted on her hip and one arm curled around him. With the other, she stirred a pot of boiling stew, a cloud of steam lifting and moistening the air. A smile touched his lips. Mother always had a child in her arms, no matter the task at hand.

"Room for two more?" Sam asked, leaning against the door-jamb.

Sally threw down her scrub brush and hurried over, cupping his face in her hands before rising on her tiptoes and kissing his cheek. "It's good to see you, brother." Her dark eyes soaked him in a long moment before she fell back on her heels and scowled. "Now, where is Walt? Apparently, he taught my son how to make spit wads on his last visit."

"He's in the front yard with Lizzy and the boys." Sam chuckled as his sister marched off with shoulders squared. Though Sally had never been considered a particularly beautiful woman, her dogged personality sufficed.

"And how are you, Momma?" Sam laid his palm over her soft back.

Olive's rotund face lit with joy as she kept on tending the food on her porcelain stove. "Faring well, my dear. All are healthy and content, and that's all we can ask for." She pitched him a questioning look, her eyes making a quick scan of his physique. "How are you boys? Eating well, I hope. You look rather thin."

Sam pressed a hand over his lean midsection. "We're amid a depression. Aren't we all a little thin?"

His mother's ample chest shook as she laughed. "Not all of us, I'm afraid. Not after welcoming nine children into the world."

Drawing near, Sam dropped a peck on her forehead. "You're beautiful, Momma. Always have been and always will be."

Olive narrowed her eyes but smirked, tossing a graying strand of hair off her brow. "You go on and say hello to your father. We'll sit down to eat as soon as Bert and Bill are home from work. Shouldn't be more than a half hour."

Sam found his father in a familiar place—hunched over an atlas in the study with his teenage brother Jim. Though he'd never see most of it, the world fascinated their father. Distant lands and exotic cultures came alive as he wove tales of their peoples and practices. A poor man's purse would never get him far, but still his finger could travel the roads of his map, his imagination filling the void between.

Jim turned and noticed Sam standing in the doorway. "Sam!" He strode forward and clapped Sam's back. "Are you home for good now?" He flung his head back, shifting the mop of flaxen hair out of his eyes.

"No, not for good." Sam dug his hands into his pockets. "The railroad repairs won't be finished for another few months."

"Dad and I were just talking about taking a trip to California," Jim said. "I thought maybe we could all pile into the pickup." His youthful chuckle filled the little space, bounding off the row of bookshelves. The family had made many journeys together from house to house, weighing two vehicles nearly to the earth and breaking down whenever they bottomed out on a hill.

Sam's gaze drifted back to the aging man standing over the desk, one withered finger still pinned on his map. His shoulders drooped a little more than Sam remembered. His hands looked more crooked. The head over his bushy eyebrows was exposed nearly to the back, a patch of chestnut hair on either side above his ears. The kind blue eyes he cherished still remained, laced with sorrow, worry, and hope in kind.

"Jim, why don't you give us a moment to catch up?" Herman asked, voice gravelly.

Once the boy had obeyed and shuffled into the hallway, his father opened both arms and silently welcomed Sam into them.

His linen shirt smelled of lemon verbena, his leathered skin of hay and alfalfa. Sam's strong arms enveloped his father's fragile form in a reverent embrace, nearly afraid his bones might crush with the slightest pressure.

"It's been too long, my boy." Herman stood back to look at him, pride swelling in his features. "Too long."

Sam squeezed his hand over his father's shoulder blade. "Won't be long until the repairs are made and we'll be back home with you and Mother."

Herman swiped a hand through the air. "Don't go worrying about that." He shook his head. "A man with grown sons expects them to fly the coop after so many years. I left my father in Oregon. He left his in Indiana. It's been the way of things since the children of Adam." He leaned on the desk, gazing down at the hands in his lap. "Doesn't mean I won't miss my firstborn boys."

Out the six-paned window, Sam watched Bert and Bill trekking up the hill behind the chicken coop. "It's a lucky thing you have so many," he said thoughtfully. "Your home won't be quiet for a good while."

His father's shaggy eyebrows rose as he inhaled a long breath. "Yes, the Lord has blessed me. Sometimes I feel like Israel, raising up a pack." He glanced up with a spark in his eye, his mouth crinkling wryly.

A sudden chuckle burst from Sam's lungs as he thought of them all together—the overwhelming number, the sheer noise. Sometimes he wondered if he ever did meet a girl he fancied, would she run away as soon as she beheld the circus he'd rope her into? Surely a woman with sensibilities would think twice before entangling herself with such a brood.

"There are certainly many of us," Herman said, compelling Sam to look at him. His face had grown solemn, his brows pinched and his jaw fixed. "There's something I've been meaning to talk with you about, son. Go on and close the door."

Five

Though the temperatures had warmed and the sun begun to descend over the landscape later every night, Sally still found it pertinent to keep a fire in her hearth. She said it brought her comfort, the sense that even after a grueling day, she could retreat into a world free of worry. A pile of wood was stacked proudly next to their brick fireplace, replenished weekly by her husband. Sam knew she would keep on kindling a new fire in the evenings until the heat of summer forced her to stop.

Reclining on her brown chenille sofa, Sam watched the flames flicker and dance behind the glass grate. Sally sat at the sofa's opposite end with a lapful of knitting, her young son Jackie asleep and nestled between them. Their parents had long retreated to bed, along with a houseful of rambunctious siblings. Only Walt and Jim still convened on the porch, bits of their conversation floating through the window.

Sam had always been able to sit in the stillness of his sister's company, neither expecting the other to entertain them. What a welcome relief after a dinner table crammed with twelve people, each straining to get a word in. And yet, as he mulled over the ideas presented by his father that afternoon, talking felt like the only way to settle the questions haunting his troubled mind.

"What is it?" Sally asked, cocking her head to the side. "I haven't seen your forehead scrunched like that since the Yankees beat the Cubs at the World Series."

Sam's frown converted to a grin, remembering his annual favorite day of the year. "What can I say? I like to root for the underdog." At her serious gaze, he relented. "Pop told me about the house. I had no idea things were so rough around here."

Sally heaved a prolonged sigh. "Cap doesn't like to admit it." She lowered the project in her hands. "He told everyone he's away on a business trip, but really he's scouring the countryside looking for something we can afford. Pop's scraping together what he can to pay the mortgage, but we're still months behind our agreed schedule."

The very words twisted Sam's gut. "I wish I had known. Maybe I can get some extra hours doing labor on the weekends. There are plenty of farms around the railroad camp."

"Don't you dare." Her dark eyes snapped. "I know how hard you and Walt work out there already. I won't have you killing yourselves just to keep this large of a roof over our heads. We'll make do, one way or another."

"With eight extra mouths to feed?" The foul-tasting cynicism on his tongue blared.

His sister's gaze pinned him squarely. "We're family, Sam. We're a team." She brushed a gentle hand over the hair falling into Jackie's closed eyes. "When times are the hardest, at least we know we can stand together."

Sam squashed his back against her spongy couch, his wrist laid over his forehead. "I just wish I could keep us all in one place. Pop is talking about going back to Nevada." Somehow, the prospect brought a strange foreboding he just couldn't shake.

"Maybe it will be the best thing." Sally resumed her knitting, the click of her needles ticking to the rhythm of her moving hands.

"Mr. Hargrove owes him a lot of money, and he has a cabin he'll let Pop use for free. It's only a temporary solution, but it might work."

"Do you want to see Mother working in the mines again?" Sam couldn't dislodge memories of toiling by her side, watching the sweat and soot accumulate on her face. Olive Tully would work as hard as any man and never complain, then return home at night to cook dinner for a crowd.

"Of course not." Sally's deep brown curls shook. "But the younger boys are coming of age now, and there are plenty of hands to work. She might not need to."

Sam retreated into his thoughts, hoping his sister's words proved true. A heady pine scent filled the room as the wind moved through the trees outside. Walt and Jim's footsteps plunked over the porch outside until the front door creaked open and they waved goodnight as they passed in the hallway. Even amid the turmoil, so much peace existed. It had to in a place this crowded with love.

"The future is yet to be built, Sam," he heard Sally say through the dimly lit room. "Have faith that it will take you beautiful places."

Beautiful places. Despite his fear, Sam longed for the unfolding days ahead, for the adventure hiding behind each new bend. An endless field of possibilities awaited—he could be sure of it. His face crinkled into a smile. When he imagined the future, he couldn't help thinking of the girl on the porch brushing her hair, and how her angelic face had stolen his breath away.

Ralf's newly polished Model A grumbled its way down the country drive, whizzing past expansive fields and thickets of trees. Momma was perched beside him in the front seat, pointing out natural wonders among the spring scenery, while all three girls had piled in the back. Elsie held tight to Dorothy's hand, as if she might protect her whenever the tiny town car hit a divot or bump in the road.

Squished beside her little sister and directly behind Momma's head, Elsie alternately concentrated on her mother's chatter and the landscape rolling by. Alder and birch trees ripe with green leaves dotted the sparse grasslands. The mountains and canyons adorning their home had vanished, replaced by boundless flat plains extending as far as she could see in every direction. The drive felt like half a day's time had elapsed, yet she doubted they'd ridden for more than a half hour.

Elsie readjusted her confined body, her head hitting the vehicle's canvas top as she did. Her eyes met Ralf's wicked stare in the rear-view mirror an instant before she snatched them away, determined to ignore whatever communication he attempted with her. Weeks had lumbered by without a second occurrence, yet still her skin crawled whenever he stood within a foot of her. The resentment in his gaze said his wounded pride would be avenged. She had only to wonder when to expect it.

"Must we go all this way just for a picnic?" Dorothy chirped above the growling motor. "I want to go swimming!"

Mother reached back to pat her little knee. "You can swim where we're going, dear. It's much safer than the river, anyway. Besides"—her striking eyes gleamed with mischief—"Bus said he would come. You want to see your big brother, don't you?"

"I guess so." Dorothy wiggled back in the seat, impatience glowing in every curve of her freckled face. She glanced at Elsie then out the window behind them, but the Model A had abandoned their friends long ago. Most people had rigged their cars with horses, unable to afford the gasoline needed to power them.

"Good things come to those who wait," Momma said, sighing as she peered across the automobile at her fiancé. "We'll have this beautiful picnic today, then us girls will go to the carnival before your school lets out for the summer."

"Oh boy, the carnival!" Dorothy popped up again, her fists lifted in excitement. "I'd nearly forgotten."

Elsie swapped a grin with Shirley behind their bouncing sister's head. She still cherished her own memories of her first experience under the big top—the parading elephants, the fireworks and acrobats, the wonderment in each new illusory display. Bus had convinced her to spend her last penny to see the littlest lady in the world, a beautiful dwarf who lived in a miniature house with equally tiny furniture. Elsie's childish dreams had soared as the little lady looked at her and sang a Great War song about a winding road beneath the moon.

"Are you sure you can't take the time off work?" Momma asked Ralf. "It would be such a treat for the girls to go as a family."

The sour ache in Elsie's stomach lessened when Ralf shook his head. "I've told you once already, Lillian. I'm too busy to take two whole days and nights away from my job." His tone hardened. "Take the car to Mountain Home if you'd like, but I have to work."

Lillian retreated, but Elsie didn't miss the sag in her normally elegant shoulders. Since that day in the kitchen, he'd become increasingly short with their mother.

"Well, I don't think I'll go either," Shirley said. "That's just before graduation, and I'm beholden to help out. I *am* the chair of the social committee."

"What a pity." Momma swiped a gloved hand over her perfect brow. "I guess it will just be the three of us, then."

Panic stiffened Elsie's arms and wound up her throat, suffocating her. She couldn't leave Shirley home alone, not with the fiend who'd be there with her. "If Shirley's not going, then I'm not going either," she said, crossing her arms over her chest.

"You must be kidding." Lillian pivoted all the way around in her seat, holding onto the flowered hat sheltering her hair. "Elsie, the carnival is one of your favorite things. You haven't missed it ever since that first carnival came to town."

"You have to go!" Dorothy tugged at her elbow. "You said you would ride the ponies with me this year and help me win the high striker."

Even in the face of her darling sister's petitions and her mother's searching gaze, Elsie refused to budge. "I *said*, I'm not going." Ralf's icy gaze latched with hers again in the mirror, and this time she held firm, silently promising him hell if he touched a hair of Shirley's head.

Momma turned back around and sank into her chair, smoothing out her rayon skirts. "I feel like I don't know my own children anymore."

Ralf flipped on the radio for the rest of the journey, listening to a news broadcast highlighting Roosevelt's plan for national security, along with the Senate trials of millionaire J.P. Morgan and Judge Harold Louderbeck. No one spoke, not even when their destination rose into view, a sparkling lake framed in rolling hills. Ralf simply parked the car, and they all tumbled out in various directions.

Within the hour, their neighbors had caught up and the picnic commenced. Elsie helped her mother spread out blankets over the verdant earth, selecting shady spaces under the sprawling oak trees. Baskets soon peppered the ground, bringing forth meats and cheeses, baked goods, and a delicious array of fruits. Families gathered in clusters on the blankets, passing around the assortment and loading their plates. Within the jovial assembly of laughter and community, Elsie felt so much more at home than the cramped space in which she lived.

The flavors erupted on her tongue one after the other—roast pork, potato salad, marshmallows and yams. Elsie bit into a fresh slice of watermelon, certain she'd never tasted a food so sweet and succulent in all her life. Momma warned she'd get sick, but still Elsie couldn't resist the piece of boysenberry pie that topped off her meal. The rarity of such feasts called for a little indulgence, she told herself.

Bus wandered into the party not long after Elsie had finished eating and Shirley taken Dorothy to swim in the lake with a group of giggling children. He had his jacket slung over his shoulder, his boots covered in dirt and a crooked smile on his face. Momma leaped up and made quick work of introducing her handsome son to all her neighbors, though Ralf gave him no more than a cursory nod. Bus saved his last greeting for Elsie, the sister of his youth, the one who knew him best.

"He's looking more sullen than usual," her brother whispered as he pulled her into a hug. "Did he and Momma have a fight?"

Elsie followed Bus's gaze to the Swedish man now inclined against a tree, hands buried in his pockets and face drooping. "That's how he looks all the time now, I'm afraid." She bit her lip, resisting the urge to tell him why. "Let's not talk about him, Bus. It's a beautiful day and I don't want to spoil it."

Her brother's eyebrows lifted. "My, you've changed your tune." He chuckled. "What happened to, 'Give him a chance, Bus? He's better than you think, Bus?'"

"Perhaps I just got some good sense." Elsie exhaled sharply, snatching her older brother's hand. "Let's walk down to the lake and not talk about this again. I want to hear about your life."

A mild wind swept through the unkempt grass at the water's edge as Bus flung the jacket from his shoulder and laid it out for Elsie to sit on. Selecting a spot in the dirt, he plunked down beside her and nested his elbows on his bent knees. Dorothy's chortles and playful screams sailed through the sun-drenched air, rushing over the bare earth. She and several playmates frolicked in the rippling water, splashing and chasing one another, while Shirley floated on her back farther out, looking like a film star in her sunglasses and pink cotton suit.

"Have you thought more about where you're going in the fall?" Elsie dared to ask. She saw the indecision in Bus's eyes, still watchfully pinned on their sisters. He had hopes and dreams, but the four women at home would always overshadow them.

Bus plucked a long blade of grass from the turf and stuck it between his teeth. "Some men have talked about the mining in Nevada, others about the lumber opportunities in Washington." The hands between his knees worked as he spoke. "I've thought about both—and neither. There are oil fields in California, farming, pastures as far as the eye can see."

Elsie stared at the floral print of her dress stretched over her crossed legs. Her heart ached when she imagined him moving. "You could always take a train to Hollywood and have a go of it. You could be the next Clark Gable."

His baritone laugh made her smile. "Wouldn't that be a sight." Bus squinted through the sun's rays, rolling the blade of grass around with his tongue. "Mr. Perrine has made such a success of himself here, I can't imagine why I couldn't do the same." The local agriculture tycoon and rancher had certainly crafted a prominent name for himself, but hordes of others had attempted the same feat and failed.

"You can't stay here, Bus." Her throat closed in on itself. "The good land is already claimed, and hundreds of men are still out of work." Her palm gently pressed his forearm. "Go someplace that needs you, someplace where you can make a real name for yourself." They both knew Idaho would never fulfill his vast vision of the future.

Bus's gaze rolled up to hers, eyes flashing. "I *am* in a place that needs me. Why are you always telling me to go? Are you trying to say that Mother doesn't want me around now with Ralf to take care of her?"

"Of course not. She will always want you near."

"What then, Ralf? Has he told you to chase me away?" His eyes narrowed, more from hurt than distrust.

"*I* want you to go, Bus!" she burst, instantly regretting her words when she saw the wounded confusion on his face. Elsie's fingers tightened on his wrist. "I want you to go, and I want to come with you." Her voice softened, head shaking. "Momma is happy now with Ralf. I'm unmarried and will only be a drain on their resources."

Bus's eyebrows cinched. "You're speaking like you're an old maid, Elsie. You're seventeen years old." His head cocked, sandy strands of hair tumbling into his eyes. A muscle in his jaw tensed. "What's happened to make you feel this way?"

A surge of pain welled in Elsie's chest. Bus's eyes seared into her, begging for a reason to act on the instincts plaguing him. He had detected Ralf's character from the first lines Momma had written about him. Bus would beat him, *kill* him if necessary, to protect the family he treasured. He would destroy himself for their sake.

"Nothing," she said, squelching the tears trying to crowd her eyes. "It's just time, is all. I can't live the rest of my life in Idaho, and Momma doesn't need me anymore. I'll work extra hard and save up the money." Swallowing back her emotion, she folded her hands and peered at the lake, sparkling beneath the flaming sun.

"What about Dorothy and Shirley? You'll miss them far too much to simply leave them behind."

Elsie endeavored to keep her head level and her eyes on the children at play, though she wanted nothing but to cry until all the tears inside dried up. "We'll figure out a way to bring them with us. Momma has Ralf, and we'll have each other." *Just please—rescue us before he slashes us apart.*

The prattle of their neighbors melded with the baying wind as Bus left the space between them silent. Shirley had swum to shore and reclined on a towel near the shallows, attracting two teenage boys to join her. The children had tired of their game and commenced races across the narrow lake, hurtling through the water like little fish fighting their way up stream. Her plan invited no further discussion, though Elsie could feel it looming close by, a heavy tension she had no desire to breach.

"Maybe we'll go to Oregon," Bus finally said. "I hear there's no place greener and more beautiful on Earth." Elsie glanced back to find a placid look on his face, the promise that he would propel her dreams forward as she always did with his. Both knew they would never abandon the mother who had loved and reared them.

"Oregon sounds nice." Her mind traveled over the stories Daddy Harry had told of the place. "I hear they have nothing but miles of forests and waterfalls that reach to the sky."

"You believe too much." Bus poked her in the side with his elbow.

Elsie lifted an eyebrow. "And you never believed Harry's stories about Indian attacks and rain dances?" She laughed at his beet-red grin. "Please, I'll never forget you wiggling around in the backyard trying to make it rain."

Bus tossed his head back, his chuckle broad and robust. When his laughter faded, the air seemed to warm and the sun shone brighter. "The boys are having a good old-fashioned barn dance on Saturday. I would like you and Shirley to come. You deserve a little fun, sister."

A crowd of strange men all waiting to swing her around sounded more like work than fun. "Dorothy will have a fit. She hates being left behind."

"Well, she can come too if Momma lets her."

"You must be joking." They both watched as their mother marched down to the water and separated the neighbor boys from their sun tanning sister. "Shirley will be lucky if she makes it there alive. Dorothy has no chance."

Buster threw his blade of grass into the lake and rose to his feet, extending his arms high above his head in a stretch, then resting his hands on his trim hips. "If all the things in this world we lack, at least we have a mother who cares."

Six

S am stood at the trail to the railroad camp, mesmerized by what he saw. It had taken mere hours to convert the dusty, disheveled train of tattered tents and bedrolls into a place fit to invite women. The piles of trash and compost scattered about the camp had disappeared, the firepits cleaned, and any evidence that the men lived outdoors stashed in their tents. The old barn where many workers chose to sleep had been cleared and sprinkled with fresh hay, lanterns suspended from the rafters. Without a doubt, a woman could motivate a man like nothing else.

The whole harebrained scheme had begun when Walt announced he was bringing several ladies he had met in town to visit camp. Women did appear from time to time, usually someone's wife providing their husband fresh clothes or a homemade meal, but rarely a group of them. Walt's new acquaintances had tittered about it with their friends, and suddenly an intimate tour around camp had blossomed into two dozen girls from Twin Falls coming for a hoedown. Walt had overseen the camp's overhaul, insisting that proper ladies needed a clean environment. Sam guessed he'd taken a shine to one of them and felt the need to impress her. Good thing he commanded the clout to do it.

The first notes of Gillingham's fiddle had already breached the evening air when Sam stepped up to the doors of the old barn. The purples and hazy pinks of dusk were melting into the horizon, crickets chirping between the violin's strains. Men lit the scattered firepits, the hissing flames igniting the camp in swirling light. Walt had positioned himself at the barn's corner, where a table held a punchbowl he'd gotten goodness-knows-where. Several women crowded around him in slim dresses, one wearing a jeweled veil in her hair, another a hat that covered half her head.

"Never thought I'd see the day we'd be entertaining ladies in the middle of nowhere," Donald said as he sauntered up behind Sam. He fixed his stare on the camp's trailhead, where another truck overflowing with ecstatic women ground to a stop.

Sam watched them hop down from the truck bed with the men's assistance, amused by the way they daintily tried to carry themselves despite the rugged terrain. "Must not be much entertainment in town."

"No men, either. The Depression has hit hard in these parts, I hear. Most men have been forced to find work elsewhere, leaving a pack of lonely women behind." He chuckled as they observed a redhead strutting elegantly over the field sink her heeled shoe right in a thick patch of mud. Donald clicked his tongue. "Their loss is my gain," he said with a wink. "Excuse me, I think someone needs rescuing."

The barn and the expanse of dirt around it hummed with chatter and giggles before half an hour had passed. Sam preferred to stay leaning against the barn wall, simply surveying the bizarre spectacle. Now and again, a woman would pass with inquisitive eyes, a silent petition for him to dance or at least converse with her. Sam would cross his ankles and look down at the toes of his boots, sure she'd rather dance with a partner not liable to stomp on her feet.

Walt had wasted no time in absorbing attention from all the girls who would give it. Beside an orange raging campfire, he whirled one around while a semi-circle of others clapped along. His rapid feet hammered out the Dixie Stomp, his whole body leaping and jiving to the fiddle's quick chirps. The girl in his arms, red-faced and laughing, could barely keep up with the steps but didn't seem to mind in the least.

"Would you look at that," said Miles, a man who'd joined their crew not a month past. Sam followed his astounded gaze to the rim of camp behind the fires, where Buster Dawson had arrived with a young blonde no more than sixteen years of age. "I've never seen anything like that in all my life."

Indeed, the girl had swiftly drawn the gawking stares of most every man in camp as she gracefully sashayed between the fires. Her long golden hair draped freely over her shoulders, parted on the side and cascading in bold waves down the right side of her face. Shimmering white satin hugged her willowy frame, accentuating a body too mature for her age. Even at a distance, her blue eyes sparkled in the rolling flames, dazzling above her high cheek bones and pouty pink lips.

"That must be Buster's sister I've heard so much about," Sam said. He turned to say something else to Miles, but found the spot beside him vacant and the man wandering toward her like a moth drawn to a lantern's glow. A whole swarm of men were tripping over themselves to reach her, all far too old for a girl her age, Sam inwardly worried.

Suddenly Sam's throat went dry. For all the interest the first girl had sparked, he hadn't seen the one emerging from the shadows behind her. Clad in a simple blue floral-printed dress, she trailed the other with modesty in her stride. Her chestnut brown hair was pinned, the curls not extending below her chin. She bore a resemblance to Kate Hepburn, the film star he admired, yet her nose turned up sweetly and her mouth had a gentler curve. Sam felt his shoulder muscles launch him away from the barn wall and stiffen. He'd seen her before, noticed her as she brushed her hair on the porch that dusty day as they drove to Sally's house.

Fire shot down his muscled arms and into his hands as Sam watched the flock of admirers descend on the pair like birds hunting for scraps of food. They had come for her companion, but easily swept the second girl into their plot. The pair had obtained partners and joined the whirling ruckus before he could even form suitable words with which he might greet her. Sam counted every man who danced with her—Jake, the wanderer from San Antonio. Timmy, the one who'd journeyed here from Canada. Dave, the construction worker who could pound two stakes to every other man's one.

"Care for a drink, brother?" Walt's casual inquiry ruptured his concentration. Sam glanced over to find his brother, chest heaving, extending a flask in his giant hand.

"No thanks." He swung his gaze back to the festivities, where the girl had just been deposited near the water pump. The blonde still had dancers galore lined up for their chance to woo her, but her friend now stood shyly in the flickering shadows, hands clasped behind her back.

Sam looked back in time to catch his brother tilting his flask over the punchbowl. "Don't you dare!" He halted Walt's wrist in mid-action. "Do you want to have the coppers out here? Put that thing back in your jacket." They couldn't afford to lose employment over such a useless defiance of the law, and more than one Tully had suffered a cruel end due to overindulgence.

"Fine." Walt huffed, thrusting the gleaming steel flask into his brother's hands. "But live a little, would you? Have some fun." His hand swept over the animated gathering. "There are girls of every variety here. You can't tell me one doesn't strike your fancy."

Sam swallowed, Walt's flask clenched in his curled fingers. He could still see her, silently viewing the party from the darkened edges of the gathering. Her nodding head and tapping foot bespoke her desire to rejoin the fun, yet every time a man ventured near her, she swept her eyes aside and angled her body away.

Walt anchored his hand on Sam's shoulder. "That's the one!" He speared a finger toward the brunette girl who'd captured Sam's entire awareness. "You're staring at her harder than you do the sports section when the Sunday morning paper comes."

A scowl dragged the corners of Sam's mouth. "You're insane."

Walt clapped his hand against Sam's broad back. "She's the one I told you about before, remember? Buster's sister, the older one. Elsie, I think her name is. She came to see him that day you were out picking up supplies." A low, protracted whistle hissed through his teeth. "She's an eyeful, no doubt about it."

He leaned in close to Sam's ear. "Well, go on, little brother. Go on and ask her to dance. She ain't liable to jump up and bite ya."

A similar prodding jabbed at Sam's insides, even as another voice warned him to stay put. What if she rejected him? What if she laughed in his face? Worse still, what if she liked him and he had to invent all sorts of fancy things to say in order to keep her liking him? He leaned his elbow on a hay bale, feigning a shrug at his brother. "I don't know what you're talking about. She just looks like any other girl to me."

"Oh, really?" Walt hooked one eyebrow, mischief skittering over his newly shaven face. "I think I'll just scoot on over and claim her, then." As if a match had lit beneath his feet, he vaulted headlong toward the unsuspecting girl.

Sam watched in annoyance as Walt seized one of her hands and pulled her toward the capering mass. Her cheeks pinkened from joy or embarrassment, he couldn't tell which. Gillingham's violin had just commenced a spunky round of "Camptown Races", and Walt couldn't resist hopping around her and clomping his heels, his fine baritone voice yelping the words to the old folk song.

"Camptown ladies sing this song, doo-dah, doo-dah!" he crooned, thwacking his palms to the rhythm of the fiddle. "Camptown race-track five miles long, oh, doo-dah day!" He grabbed her hands again, winding her in a circle before pulling her in and pumping her right arm dramatically up and down, his left arm coiled around her waist. The woman's laugh kindled the smoky air, a rich and beautiful tone that sent waves of warmth over Sam's head and chest. He caught his big brother volleying a playful wink back at him, the same challenge he'd presented when they'd ridden their first bike, played their first game of football, tried their hands at their first job. But this time—this time, the prize felt so much grander.

Clutching Walt's flask, Sam unscrewed the top and threw back the remaining liquor inside. The sweet whiskey burned as it slid down his gullet, warming his stomach and prickling his tongue. Sam chucked the flask into the hay and trekked forward. He could stand in the shadows, or he could take a chance on what he already knew he wanted.

Walt had the girl spinning about in a three-step jig as Sam neared, still giggling as he serenaded her with mostly wrong words to Camptown Races. He halted at Sam's approach, approval capturing his face. "What can I do for you, brother?" he asked, a rascally glint in his gaze.

Sam took one look at those doe-like hazel eyes staring timidly up at him and knew his answer. Flattening his hand over Walt's surging chest, he propelled him backward. "Get out of my way."

❧❧❧❧❧ ❦❦❦❦❧

"**M**ay I have this dance, ma'am?" he asked in a fathomless tenor, and she felt herself nodding.

Elsie's skin tingled when his large hand covered hers. His other hand reached around, softly pressing the valley of her lower back. Despite the hurried pace of the folk tune singing from the fiddle, he led her slowly, in a purposeful circle amid the bustle of springing dancers. He moved as if the world might go on without them, as if he'd created some magical sphere safe from outside worry.

"I'm Sam," he said, the words simple yet full.

"Elsie." It sounded so little next to this tall, hearty man. His muscled arms felt as if they could crush her in their superior strength, and yet he held her with the tender care one might handle an injured bird.

Elsie blinked, hazarding a peek at where her previous partner might have gone, and found him already swinging another girl around inside the barn. One moment, she'd been watching one lad after another attempt to steal Shirley's heart with his dancing skills. The next, Walt Tully, the flirtatious fellow she'd met on her last trip here, had practically yanked her onto the dance floor and worn her out with his eccentric steps. Then this man had shoved him away. Elsie wondered if she might not be walking through a strange dream.

With a breath of courage, she dared to look back at the face angled downward toward hers. Sam wore a lopsided smile below a long nose, thick eyebrows, and the kindest eyes she could ever remember seeing. Handsome despite his prominent nose and large ears, he had a placidity and charm to his features that made her own cheeks grow rosy.

"I hope my brother hasn't scared you with his foolishness," he said with a clever purse to his thin lips. "He terrifies many a woman."

"Yes." Elsie's body jerked, her skin aflame. "I mean no. He wasn't so bad." Of course she would insult his family with the very first words from her mouth.

Sam peered back at the man now jumping from one bale of hay to the next. "That's all right, we all know he's crazy. Isn't much we can do about it."

Elsie laughed, her eyes pinning to his white cotton shirt and brown suspenders. "My brother Bus works here in camp. And my sister"—she gazed across at the lamplit barn, where Shirley sipped punch with half a dozen enamored males crowded around her—"my sister Shirley is here also."

"Yes, I saw her when you came in." Sam stared over Elsie's head at the spellbinding girl daintily drinking punch and chatting with a man who looked twice her age. How silly of her to mention Shirley. She hadn't met a fellow yet who didn't overlook her as soon as her little sister swanned into a room.

She sighed in the predictability of it all. "She looks like a model in that new dress." Better to declare the truth right out than ignore it.

"She looks like a very young girl," Sam said, surprising her. His gleaming eyes bore into hers again, his admiration gentle but clear.

Elsie clutched his strong shoulder, wanting to tear her gaze from his but finding it anchored there. The music had switched to the Lindy Hop, and still his frame directed her in a leisurely tempo, the arm encircling her firm at her back. The warm fingers grasping hers constricted. The muscles beneath his rough cotton shirt shifted with each step beneath her palm. He smelled of aftershave mingled with a hint of earth, as if he'd toiled all day and washed up before the revelry began.

"I'm new to these parts." His half-smile angled higher, propelling electric tingles down her limbs. "Got anything fun to do around here?"

Fun in a tiny wilderness town? Elsie imagined her days and could pinpoint little enjoyment she derived from them. Maybe if they lived in some grand place like New York City or New Orleans, she might have a storybook of tales to reveal. One could only frequent the picture house so many times, and Momma would have a fit if she discovered Elsie even knew an underground dance hall existed.

"A carnival comes to Mountain Home every June." She winced, thinking better of it. "I promised I wouldn't go this year, though." Shirley had clearly budded into womanhood, and no doubt Ralf had noticed her.

Sam's brows skewed. "You promised someone you'd avoid a carnival?" He chuckled, his teeth catching the lamplight. "Bring too much trouble to the place, do you?"

Elsie's face heated. "It's a complicated story." She tried to look as serious as the hidden tale behind her statement, but somehow mirth crept over her lips and she wound up laughing. How silly her words must have seemed.

"Sounds like it." Sam joined with her irrepressible laughter, their chortles rising and fusing with the warbling fiddle. "Are you concealing your identity? Running from the law?"

Nodding, she captured her hurried breath. "Something like that."

"What a shame, then." His masculine face took on a solemn look. "I have at least four brothers and a little sister who would give up a lifetime's supply of candy just for one night at a carnival."

Elsie shook her head. "Well, just because I can't go doesn't mean they can't."

Sam halted their metrical dance, the hay beneath his feet crunching. "You think I would be safe chaperoning that many children alone?"

"Well, Walt—" Her open hand indicated Sam's spirited brother, who now had Shirley by a fire, attempting to teach her the Charleston. Shirley wore a mortified expression as Walt pranced around her, his calves twirling from his knees as if made of string. "Walt is another child to watch," she said, garnering agreement from Sam.

Her gaze slid to the ground, where her Mary Janes met with his dirty boots. "Well, I'd like very much to go, but I can't."

Sam had dropped his arm from her waist but his fingers hadn't forfeited their grip on her hand. The couple stood there a moment, his thumb compressing the veins of her palm, the warm breeze bearing traces of lavender and sweet peas. The yellow glow of lamplight glistened against the black night, steady above the dying fires. The swell of the violin and snapping logs had receded, and Elsie could hear only her pulsing heartbeat, mirrored in the gentle throb of his hand.

He took a deep, shivering breath before his voice lit the air. "Maybe I could—"

"Elsie, there you are!" Bus said, materializing from the darkness. He snatched her free hand. "Come on, let's get going. It's after ten already, and Mother is going to be in a panic if I keep you girls out any longer."

Alarm seized Sam's face, his body bolting upright. His fingers squeezed tighter, then loosened as Bus hauled her away. "I can give you a ride in my truck if you like!" he called after the pair, Bus trooping on determinedly and Elsie tripping behind him.

"Thanks, Sam, but Miles has his Dodge all rigged up to go. Shirley's already inside." Bus waved his hand amiably, not even pausing in his duty to get his sisters home in a rush.

Elsie pivoted back to find Sam standing in the waning firelight, his hands planted in his trouser pockets. Disappointment crushed her as Bus shoved her into the pickup seat beside Shirley and squashed himself on her other side. Miles hit the gas pedal and the Dodge's engine thundered to life, driving them over the rocky trail. One glimpse out his sullied window was the last she had of Sam Tully.

Seven

"Hurry! Miss Curtis said we get a peppermint if we show up early for school today!" Dorothy shouted, already twenty steps ahead of her sisters. She had on a red checkered jumper that Momma had made long ago and new patent leather shoes. Her eager feet skipped in a zigzag pattern, a haze of dust lifting behind her.

Shirley sighed, her school books tucked neatly over her chest in one arm. "Do you think she'll ever grow up?" she asked, watching their younger sibling hoot and holler.

"She's only twelve. Give her a couple of years." Elsie sent her a knowing look. "You weren't much different yourself at that age."

Giggling, Shirley shook out her blonde curls. "I suppose you're right. It seems so long ago now, but I could fit into that jumper only two years ago."

Time had always hurtled on too quickly for Elsie's taste. Sometimes she closed her eyes and wished she could bask in the moment, bottle up the feeling of the wind on her face, or capture a perfect memory of the colors at sunset. She could still hear the happy coos gurgling in her baby sister's throat, and now, seemingly only days later, that same voice belonged to a plucky juvenile.

"I saw you with a fellow at the barn dance." Shirley's beautiful mouth wrinkled slyly. "Walt said he had taken a shine to you."

Elsie kept on walking, sure her face betrayed her. In the grove of birches sprouting from the side of the road, a squirrel scurried down a tree trunk with an acorn lodged in its paws. The little town's uneven silhouette rose out of the morning fog, a muddled gray against the brimming sun. She had meant to distract herself from thoughts of him, and yet everything reminded her of that night.

Folding her arms against the chilly gusts of dawn, Elsie closed her eyes and let the smell of dewy grass steep her senses. "Walt says a host of crazy things. I danced with several young men that night."

"Not like you danced with that one." The crunch of their boots on the gravel-paved road disguised Shirley's certain snickering. "You two were so cute out there dancing like there wasn't anyone else around. I told Bus not to bother you, but he insisted on rushing home right away. I don't think he liked the thought of another man stealing your heart."

Elsie peered at her sister curiously. "What about you, Miss Cosmopolitan? I don't think a person there missed your charms." She said it sweetly, but still a hint of envy managed to leak into her tone.

"Clever way to change the subject." Shirley brushed back a single curl, returning it to the dense cascade tumbling down her back. "I would tell you about who *I* met there, but clearly you won't reciprocate." She grinned mysteriously, her peach skin glowing in the light of daybreak.

Curiosity tugged at Elsie's indifferent façade. Who among all those sweaty railroad workers could have ensnared her sister's fancy? The quarterback of the football team hadn't yet, much to their mother's vexation. He'd shown up at their house decked in a houndstooth suit and tie with his hair slicked back, a bouquet of fresh pink roses in one hand. Mother had ushered the boy hastily through the front door, offering him cookies from her newly baked batch and a glass of lemonade. Few in town didn't recognize him, son of the wealthiest rancher in the region, valedictorian and star of the local high school. He'd taken Shirley out one time before she turned up her nose, citing that he was three years her senior. Elsie had discerned the true reasons behind her glazed eyes and covered yawns—the poor predictable boy bored her sister to tears.

"Who is it?" Elsie attempted to discern a clue from Shirley's laughing eyes. "Is it Walt?" The boisterous man certainly wouldn't fear the challenge of pursuing her.

"Of course it's not Walt!" Shirley clapped a hand over her full mouth. "Walt is twenty-four years old."

"Well, he behaves like he's seven. How should I know?" Elsie scratched her chin, her gaze wandering to the purpling sky. "What about that Miles fellow who brought us home? He seemed rather keen on you."

Shirley scrunched her face, her pink tongue jetting out from between two rows of pearly teeth. "Miles is a twit. I asked him about his favorite book and he started quoting Bing Crosby lyrics at me, trying to pass them off as poetry." She pressed the back of her hand to her brow in a melodramatic fashion. "It was all nightingales and the sandman bringing dreams of me."

Elsie burst into a fit of giggling while Shirley wagged her head and sighed. "You laugh now, but it's terrible." Her arms flailed outward, the pages of her school books flapping. "As if I'd believe Shakespeare wrote about the sandman! How dim do these men think I am?"

The ground had evolved into asphalt, the town and its quiet buildings looming around them. The schoolhouse lay on the outskirts of main street, a plain structure of brown brick and sash windows with a fenced yard in front. Unable to contain her enthusiasm, Dorothy threw open the gate and bashed it against the fence, tearing up the walkway like a wild bird escaping capture.

A short walk through town brought the other two girls to the high school. The city had just woken with the mounting sun, shopkeepers flipping over their "open" signs and sweeping their front stoops. The courthouse next to Shirley's school already had men in business suits running across the grass and up the front steps, clutching their briefcases as they rushed between the pillars. From inside the brick school, a screeching bell announced that fifteen minutes remained before first period.

Elsie took Shirley's hand before she could trail her swarm of classmates into the building. Sweeping the tips of her fingers through her sister's shimmering hair, Elsie smiled. "They don't think you're dim, my love. They just don't know how to handle themselves around intelligence and beauty and a good heart. All three rarely arrive in one package."

Shirley's eyes filled, her head tilting thoughtfully. "Oh, Elsie." Leaning over, she planted a kiss on her cheek. "You always have the most beautiful things to say, and I'm sure I'll never deserve them."

"You deserve every word." Elsie lovingly crushed her hand. "I'm sure this boy, whomever he is, must be very special to have sparked your interest. I can't wait to meet him."

A crinkle of worry dimpled Shirley's brow. "You won't tell Momma, will you? You know how she meddles, and I don't want her fretting before anything has really happened. I just met him, and I've only agreed to one dinner." Her lithe shoulders shrugged. "Who knows? I might not even like him so much after I get to know him."

"A *secret* affair." Elsie tipped one brow, her lips puckering. Leave it to her sister to live out a storybook romance at fifteen years of age. "Mum's the word, I promise."

Elsie watched Shirley trot off happily through the double glass doors, trying to thrust her own worry aside. Shirley had already reached womanhood, and the days fast approached when Elsie nor Momma would have any say in what the beautiful young girl chose to do in life. Better to be on her favorable side and keep guard from a distance.

The town had blossomed under the gilded sunlight and cerulean sky. Elsie moseyed through the streets, peeking in store windows at frilly dresses and high-heeled shoes she'd never have the money to purchase. The vibrant aroma of roasted coffee mingled on the wind with freshly sugared donuts, enticing Elsie to a storefront displaying three shelves of assorted pies and slices of cake. Beside the bakery, a newsstand held papers proudly broadcasting the Chicago World's Fair in bold black letters.

Farther down the street, a drugstore with a huge sign in the window proclaimed their newest elixir could cure anything from gout to the common cold. Wilson's Hardware had a sale on socket wrenches. She spun around and peered across the motor-lined street at the cinema, where beneath the unlit neon emblem, the marquee read *"Don Quixote"*. At home, money didn't seem like such a terrible thing to lack. In the city, every sight demanded one possess it or stand back and dream of doing so.

Elsie picked up the groceries as she'd promised her mother and started for home with a brown paper bag in her arms. Traversing the busy street, she angled her body between two Chevy sedans with tires on their rears and trudged up the sidewalk to the employment office. As much as she detested the idea, new job postings might mean funds she would desperately need if she ever wanted to leave this place.

The help-wanted ads proved sparse that day—an opening for a trained secretary at City Hall, another for a law professional. The dam needed several workers for a digging project that summer. Elsie had nearly given up hope when an announcement behind the others caught her notice. Folding back the papers around it, she scanned the bill with ferocious energy. "Wanted: kitchen help and hospitality workers for immediate hire at the Larkspur Hotel in Shelby, Montana." Ripping the page from the bulletin board, Elsie's trembling fingers curled around the edge. Her eyes fixed on the closing line, her lips barely forming the words. "To apply, please contact owner Andrew Dawson."

C onfusion swirled about Elsie's mind as she plopped down on her front porch and set the grocery bag beside her. Her father resided in Montana—she'd known that ever since she'd first spied a desperate letter scrawled in Mother's handwriting, begging to see her eldest children. Perhaps he'd moved, she'd surmised. Maybe he never received the string of letters Momma wrote in the deep hours of night after tucking her other children into bed.

Dragging the job publication from her pocket, Elsie unfolded it and stared at the creased letters. Her father was successful, a proprietor. He owned a flourishing business seeking to appoint new employees. Momma had mentioned once that his family owned horses and he worked as a liveryman, but she always imagined a poor laborer under the thumb of a rich employer. Never would she have envisioned a businessman thriving amidst a pitiful economy.

Elsie let the paper plummet to her lap and gazed out at the jagged mountains, still misted with morning dew. The truth conveyed questions—problems she couldn't discount with the usual excuses. Only the hazy contours of a face her three-year-old memory had stored remained of the man whose name she bore. Why, if he possessed the means to do so, hadn't he chosen to know her? What could have kept a group of siblings so fractured, they hardly remembered each other's names?

The only conclusion she could draw was Momma. Rising on unsteady feet, Elsie sucked a long breath through her nose and hoisted the shopping bag into her arms. Her mother's unreasonable temper could drive a litter of adorable puppies away. Daddy Harry had only condoned it so long. Ralf, if she ever really let him in, would respond far worse. Perhaps Andrew Dawson had deemed it best that John and Emma start anew without maternal influence despite the woeful pleas of his former wife. But that still didn't account for his absence in his three other children's lives.

Tears pricked her eyes, but Elsie shoved them back as the screen door creaked open and she reached for the knob beneath. Ralf was at work and Momma had offered her day to a widow working a small farm a mile down the way. At least she'd have a handful of hours to reflect and cry in seclusion if need be.

Arms full of groceries, Elsie entered the kitchen and closed the front door with her foot. Oddly, the radio still blared through the empty house, broadcasting a baseball game from Yankee Stadium. Elsie listened to the anchor's gregarious chatter a few moments while she stashed the foodstuffs in the cupboards and the icebox, folded the paper bag, and piled it with the others between the cabinets and the stove. The broadcaster yelped, hailing a homerun by star player Joe Sewell to the rumble of a screaming crowd of feverish fans.

Temporarily distracted from her worries by the joyful sounds booming from the speakers, Elsie thought perhaps she might take a minute to sketch out a drawing before Momma came home. Bending over the wireless, she flicked the knob and drowned the room in silence. An odd sensation inched down her spine an instant before a flash of movement caught the edge of her sight. Whirling, Elsie felt her heartbeat leap to her throat at the face staring back.

"Ralf! How did you—" The man must have been skulking in the shadows of her bedroom. Now he stood breathless before the open front door, his hand twisting a key in the outer lock. Panic blasted through Elsie's veins. She sprinted toward the back door, but found he'd bolted it from the outside already. He'd barred her in, knowing she could outrun him.

"How did I trick you?" he asked in a sarcastic lilt, slamming the front door shut. "I parked my car at the service station and walked here."

Her quaking hand still grasped the doorknob, her mind conjuring escape tactics. She could throw something solid through a window and break the panes, but the idea of Ralf with shattered glass at his disposal sprung the taste of bile in her mouth. When she finally found the courage to turn and face him, she watched him slip the key into his bookshelf safe and rotate the lock to a random number.

Ralf removed his jacket and slung it over the assorted sweaters on the coat rack, rolling up his sleeves like a man about to embark on a serious assignment. "I found your mother another charity case and I made sure she put items on your grocery list that would require you to return home right away and put them in the icebox." His mouth sloped wryly as he strode ominously toward her, his polished shoes clicking on the wooden floorboards. "I waited in your bedroom for hours, looking through your notebook, reading your thoughts."

Elsie pressed her body against the door as if it would cave in and release her from the approaching madman. "I should have told her." Tears burned her eyes and plunged down her reddened face. At least Momma might have listened, might have saved her from this fate. Elsie had trusted in her so little, she'd sealed her own doom.

"Yes, you should have." His deep Swedish drawl lodged a scorching ache in her gullet. His breath quickened with every step he moved toward her, his eyes hunting the hills and planes of her figure. "But we both knew you wouldn't. You wanted this, my little älskling." His lips snarled, his tongue spurting out to wet them. "You wanted me to make you a woman."

Elsie cringed at his growling words, her hands grabbing at the air behind and around her, vainly searching for anything to defend herself with. "You stay away from me," she warned, her fear all too evident in her quivering voice. She thrust out a hand in desperation, trying to block his approach.

Laughing, Ralf seized her wrist and angrily wrenched it downward, fastening it to the small of her back. Arrows of pain surged through her arm while his other hand captured her waist. His rum-laced breath flooded her cheek, his wrinkled face so close she could see the flecks of gray in his yellow brows. His mouth moved to cover hers, but she swung her head to the side before it could. Grunting, he thrust his heaving torso against hers and angled her head straight again with one clenched hand to her chin. Elsie took one look into those seething, devilish eyes and spat in the face staring back.

Undeterred, he yanked a handkerchief from his waistcoat pocket and dabbed at her saliva before pitching the cloth to the floor. His creased blue eyes studied her a long moment, journeying over her young face. "I didn't expect you to make this easy," he said, so close his spittle showered her skin. "I would be disappointed if you did." Clamping a hand firmly around her ribcage, he spun her and shoved her toward her mother's open bedroom door.

Elsie seized the doorjamb in throbbing hands, the vision of Momma's pristine lacy pink bedspread blurring through her tears. One shove to her spine catapulted her into the room, her outstretched hands colliding with the pliant mattress. His footsteps sounded like giant weights crashing against the floorboards. Gasping for breath, Elsie scrambled over the bed and snatched the two pillows beneath the headboard. One after the other, she hurled them at him, frantic to escape the hazy form trundling toward her.

Just as she reached for the ivory hairbrush laying atop her mother's vanity, one strong hand yanked her backward by the hair. Screaming in agony, she heard only the plink of her hairpins on the floor before Ralf pinned her against the wall between the dressing table and the bedframe. Elsie had heard once that a swift kick to the trousers would buckle a man. Her feet kicked madly, flailing without direction, one bashing into Momma's vanity and splintering the mirror into a thousand tiny shards.

Ralf thrust her higher, forcing her legs to straighten until her feet barely touched the floor. Wedging her elbows against the wall, she planted her palms on his shoulders and tried to drive him off her, but his superior strength effortlessly resisted. Salty sweat leached from his pores, his heartbeat booming as he unfastened his belt buckle. His hand slithered up her thigh, her skirt inching up with his intrusive fingers.

Elsie's fingers went numb, her mind giving into the darkness. He'd won; she'd let him win. Momma had asked the night of his first attack—not with her words, but with haunted black eyes now singeing Elsie's memory. She could have run, taken her sisters, freed them of this inevitable fate. Fear had utterly crippled her. Her mind conjured images of Sam holding her gently under the moon, swaying her to the singing violin. A hard lump stuck in her throat. She'd never be able to give a man all of herself—not really, not after this monster ripped it away.

Panting for air beneath his heavy frame, Elsie rolled her head to the side and let her loose hair spill over her face. Through the wavy tendrils, she glimpsed an odd shape jutting out behind the bed—a box-like shelf built into the headboard. Her brows furrowed, her memory racing back to the day she'd found Daddy Harry bent over it, his hammer thrashing the wood. "Don't ever look back here," he'd said. "And don't tell your sisters. But if you're ever in real trouble, remember it's here."

Extending her quaking hand, Elsie eased her forearm behind the bed frame until her fingertips brushed the hiding place Harry had fashioned. Splintered, unfinished wood punctured her skin. Warm blood trickled from the open cuts stinging her hand. Elsie kept prodding until she felt icy steel beneath her fingertips.

"Let me go," she strained, her voice a painful rasp from her arid throat. "Let me go *now*." When Ralf only chuckled and slid his hand higher, Elsie gripped the weapon and soundlessly guided it between the headboard and the wall. Summoning every last ounce of courage she possessed, she wrapped her fingers around the hilt and shoved it beneath his chin. "I told you to let me go."

His grip on her body slackened but didn't retreat. His eyes rolled downward, assessing the gleaming revolver in her white fist. "You won't shoot me," he said, never daring to glance away from it. Elsie could see in his careful gaze the plans emerging within. He would wrestle the gun away if she hesitated another instant.

Elsie tipped her thumb over the hammer and pressed it toward her, the revolver's click deafening in the quiet bedroom. "I *will* shoot you, Ralf." Her eyes filled, the lips over her clenched teeth trembling. "I will shoot you," she said again, reminding herself.

His light eyes searched hers a prolonged moment, challenge and defeat sparking around his hollow pupils. His giant hands constricted and then released her, alerting her muscles to relax from their stone-like trance. Ralf took two steps backward, his hands raised on either side. "You win." His teeth gritted. "You win this round, but it will not be the last. Your mother will never believe you—not while I pay her bills."

Flames of heat scorched her arms as she stepped forward with the firearm extended, forcing him out of the bedroom and into the living area. "She can believe you or me; it doesn't matter. If she refuses to listen, I'll run."

Ralf's whiskered mouth tipped. "Then I'll enjoy every last bit of your little sister." Malicious hatred swarmed his eyes. "She really is a lovely girl."

Her hand clenched around the revolver's silver hilt, her finger pulsing on the trigger. "What is it in you that compels you to hurt people? Does it make you feel stronger?"

Ralf swallowed, his fists scrunching and loosening. "I am a man. Some may pretend to play a loftier part, but we're all the same and we all live for similar ends—power, money, *sex*." His lips crushed into a sinister scowl, all traces of the generous beau Momma had brought home that first night erased. "If it isn't me, some other man will find you and gladly finish the job."

True or not, his words slashed her open like a lamb butchered for Easter dinner. Her stomach turned sour, her throat refusing to gulp back the enormous lump lodged there. Elsie saw her father, cramming his clothes into a valise and storming out the door without even throwing her a glance. She saw Daddy Harry, tie half undone and suit disheveled, clutching an empty bottle of bourbon on the kitchen floor. They were all the same, Ralf had said—cowards, liars, thieves, and philanderers. A faint voice inside urged her to squeeze the trigger and send at least one of them to death. Then the front door swung open, and reality silenced her musings.

"Why was the door locked?" her mother asked, head still bent as she jerked the key from the lock. "We finished our work early, and I thought I'd surprise Dorothy with a—" She froze at the threshold, the key slipping through her lax fingers and clanging on the floor. "What's going on? Elsie, where did you get that?" Her rounded eyes glanced from one person to the other, horror masking her face in white.

Elsie threw Ralf one last glare before she let the gun drop to her side and crossed the room. "Here, Momma." She deposited the revolver in her mother's open hand. "If you marry this man, you're going to need it."

Eight

E lsie stood like a bronze statue in the garden she'd sown with her own hands, the flourishing rows of plant life comforting her as much as any human arms could hope to. The minute corn seeds she'd stuffed into the earth and covered with soil now brushed their tender shoots around her ankles. Yellow bulbs of squash peeped out from beneath massive leaves, reminding her that she'd fostered their entire lives, affirming some sort of value in this world.

Shading her eyes with a flattened hand, Elsie gazed back at the house, past the white-washed boards cracking in the sun to the back door that Ralf had deadbolted. Momma had requested she speak with her fiancé alone, and it felt like they'd penned themselves in that ravaged bedroom for hours. One glance at the glowing sun overhead and Elsie realized it couldn't have been more than ten or twenty minutes.

When at last she heard the front door screech open and saw Ralf tramp down the roadway, anxiety lurched within her. She supposed he would point himself toward his Model A at the Texaco station and speed off to whatever destination helped to bolster his ego and quiet any conscience he had left. The corner bar had converted to a malt shop with the instigation of prohibition, but everyone knew what lay beyond the double doors and down a flight of stairs.

Inner voices battered her as she stepped neatly around her precious herbs and vegetables, winding a path to the house. What would she tell Momma after all this time? *Tell her you're sorry, that you should have revealed the truth sooner. Tell her nothing—she won't believe you anyway. She needs Ralf to survive and to feed her children.* Elsie's anger rose, yet she couldn't comprehend who had inspired it—Ralf, for his depravity, for wanting to hurt her and steal her innocence. Momma, for bringing him into their lives and overlooking the suspicions she obviously harbored. Herself, most of all. Something about her—something in the way she moved or spoke or dressed, must have permitted Ralf to treat her that way.

Elsie swung the back door on its hinges and moved cautiously inside. Even the air in the tiny house buzzed with tension, so silent and yet so heavy. Heartbreak overwhelmed her to look at Momma in her bedroom, staring listlessly down at the pieces of her shattered vanity mirror, peppering the floor like a million glimmering stars across the heavens. Her regal shoulders had wilted, her normally radiant face sagging with the age it seldom divulged. She sank onto her bed and gathered a misplaced pillow on her lap, hugging it close to her slender body.

"It won't be easy cleaning this mess up," she said without glancing away from it. Her voice sounded like a droning guitar continually playing one string. "I'll have to finish before the girls get home from school."

"I'll help you." Elsie clutched the doorframe, her heart pitching against her ribcage. Momma looked just like the bird with the injured wing she'd found last spring among the geraniums and nursed until it flew again. "Momma, I'm sorry. I'm so sorry."

Lillian turned expressionless eyes to her, as if staring into a hollow abyss. Her lips compressed as if she might cry, but no tears came. "Why should you be sorry? Accidents happen."

A cold premonition punched Elsie's gut. She couldn't lie, not again, not with the damp feel of Ralf's touch still sticking to her skin. "It wasn't an accident, Momma. None of this was an accident."

Her mother's elegant fingers worked at the fringed pillow in her grip. "Ralf said it was. He said you came in here to clean and you struck it with the broom handle when you bent over for the dustpan." Her words tumbled out like a script, both rote and unconvincing. "He said you worked yourself into a frenzy over it, terrified of what I'd say."

Elsie crossed her arms over her chest. "Did he tell you what he was doing home in the middle of the day?"

"He came home to catch the Yankee game on the wireless. He missed it Sunday night because of Dorothy's recital."

"And you coming home to find me holding a gun to him? I suppose he had an answer for that, too." Elsie's head cocked in sympathy. He had an arsenal of falsehoods stored up for his every indiscretion.

Lillian blinked, her ebony eyes glistening. "He said you went crazy when he tried to help you. He said you accused him of attacking you." She paused, an array of hurt and confusion coloring her face. "He told me you threatened to kill him if he didn't leave our family immediately, that jealousy drove you to madness." She choked on the final, vile words.

Stepping into the bedroom, Elsie leaned her back to the wall and drank in a long breath. "And do you believe him, Momma? Can you suspend all logic and trust in a story that smears me and absolves him?"

Momma threw one hand in the air, the other still blanching on her pillow. "What else am I supposed to believe, Elsie? You haven't told me any different."

An agonizing moment trundled by, the birds chirping gaily in the tree outside her mother's window, several motors grumbling up the road on their way to town. Elsie searched her mother's forlorn gaze, following the emerging wrinkles she hadn't noticed before. She had so much to lose no matter what she decided—comfort and money, the ability to easily feed and clothe them if she pitched Ralf out the door. Her dignity if she didn't.

"Will you listen if I tell you?"

"Oh, Elsie." Lillian tossed the pillow on its matching bedspread, rising to stand before her. "I just want the truth." Gentle fingers pushed back the twisted tendrils of Elsie's hair. "I am supposed to marry this man. How can I do that if I don't have a complete picture of who he is? No matter what you say, I want to hear it." Her beautiful brows lifted on her alabaster forehead, her eyes pleading in earnest. "Tell me what happened here today."

Elsie felt drawn in like a magnet straining for its mate. She could say anything to *this* mother—the woman whose fingertips smoothed her heated skin, the person whose very heart shone from her frightened eyes. How many times had she longed for the authentic, vulnerable soul obscured within her mother's spotless shell? Yet even now, with the truth driving to the surface, begging for freedom, she still found it lodged behind a swollen tongue.

"I—" How could she speak the ugly words? How could she relive them? Stinging tears brimmed in her eyes just to picture the dreadful ordeal again. Lillian's thumb swept her cheekbone, compelling her onward. "I came home and found the radio on. He was hiding in our bedroom." Her body quaked, rising up in waves until her shoulders tremored. "He tried to touch me, Momma. He tried to *rape* me."

Lillian's hand fell limp at her side. She shut her eyes, anguish moving across her lofty cheekbones, over the supple lips and straight nose Elsie had always admired. Her body shuddered once, a gentle moan escaping from between her teeth. Her fingers wound around each other, squeezing until the blood ran out. When her abundant lashes finally fluttered open, the hardness had returned, so much mightier than before.

Elsie inhaled tightly at the stern glare issuing from her mother's eyes. Lillian's palm jetted out to thwack her cheek, the startling action immobilizing her. She held her throbbing face, mingling emotions battling one another as she stared back at her mother. The woman had armed herself in ice.

"Don't ever lie to me again!" Lillian demanded, and within the space of only seconds, she'd transformed into an enemy in her daughter's eyes.

E lsie stared into the wooden grains of the porch posts, tracking their curving path from the floorboards to the unstable railings above. The still night showered a sense of trepidation over her—the unseen mountains and blackened fields an eerie void beneath the moonless sky. Summer warned of her approach, washing a balmy warmth over Elsie's skin. She held onto Dorothy tighter, wondering if her sister had fallen asleep while waiting for Momma and Ralf to finish their spat.

Across from them and near the steps, Shirley leaned her head against the posts and heaved a sigh. "How long do you think they've been at it?" she asked, the fatigue on her face reflecting worry more than sleepiness.

Elsie glanced at the cloudy sky, but she could tell nothing from the hidden moon. "Too long." From inside the house, the shouts and screams between her mother and Ralf chilled her to the core, and she felt powerless to end it.

A worse day in her life, she couldn't recall. After Momma had accused her of lying, she'd demanded Elsie leave until she could look at her again. Had she obeyed her first instinct, she'd have run the entire way to Bus's railroad camp and cried in his arms. But Bus would kill Ralf if he knew, so Elsie had languidly walked the streets of town all day until her feet ached and her shoes felt worn through. Momma had served them a cold dinner of sandwiches and carrots, the atmosphere as chilly as the food. When Ralf stumbled in around seven o'clock with a bouquet of flowers, Momma had ordered the three of them outside so the couple could have a "talk".

Elsie's shoulders jerked as something solid smashed against the wall near her head. He had better not hurt her. Her blood simmered just to imagine it. Momma had pulled down the window shade, thwarting any attempt Elsie could make at spying. Going inside to check would only heighten the already volatile situation.

"Elsie?" Dorothy asked from inside her warm hold.

Elsie ironed a hand over Dorothy's braided hair. "Yes darling, what is it?"

"Is Ralf going to leave Momma like Momma left my papa?" Dorothy was twelve, and yet the voice belonged to a scared little girl, lost in a world of confusion.

If God is merciful, a cynical voice echoed inside of Elsie. "I don't know." She tucked a loose strand of raven hair behind Dorothy's ear. "Sometimes relationships last a lifetime, and sometimes they fizzle out quickly." She had yet to behold the former, but she'd heard of marriages that survived until death.

Dorothy exhaled, her tepid breath blasting over Elsie's arm. "I don't want him to go."

Shirley lifted her head, her perfect brows scrunching. "Do you like Ralf, sweetie? Is that why you want him to stay?" Or perhaps she had just grown weary of Momma's every romance concluding in heartbreak.

"He's all right." Dorothy mulled the thought over a moment before a tear slid down Elsie's hand. "But if he goes, who is going to take us to Mountain Home for the carnival next week? We don't have a car."

Eyes reeling, Shirley collapsed against the porch. "What about Daddy Harry? I'm sure he'd be happy to take you."

Dorothy sat up, rubbing her eye with one fist. "Papa says his car is broken, and he doesn't have enough money to fix it until he gets paid next."

"Well, I'm sure some of the neighbors will be taking their children to the carnival. You can ask one of them if need be." Shirley's head shook. "You needn't be so selfish, Dorothy. There are much bigger problems going on right now than you getting to see the ponies in Mountain Home."

"I'm not selfish," Dorothy whined, her tapered eyes and puffed out rosy cheeks glowering at Shirley. "We go to the carnival every year, and Momma said I'm finally old enough to ride the big Ferris wheel. I've been waiting to go my whole life!"

Elsie swapped an amused look with Shirley. "I'll make sure you get to ride the big Ferris wheel, Dorothy." Her skin warmed at the thought of the man who'd twirled her about that lamplit night and offered his truck to take her home. "I have a friend at Bus's camp with a car that can take us. That's if Shirley will help me ask him."

Shirley thrust a hand on her reedy hip. "How am I supposed to help with that?"

Giggling, Elsie almost forgot the dire battle raging inside her house. "As if I haven't seen you trotting off down the road to go visit that beau of yours."

At Shirley's exploding eyes, Dorothy joined in the tittering. "Even *I* know that, Shirley. I've never seen you tie so many bows in your hair before."

Shirley bolted upright in the face of their mockery. "Maybe you two know, but Momma doesn't and I'd like to keep it that way, please." She shook one finger at Dorothy's freckled grin. "You'd do best to watch yourself, missy. I will deliver your message, but only if you promise not to breathe a word. If Momma has so much as an inkling because of you, no carnival and *no Ferris wheel.*"

Shirley's threats washed the smile clean off Dorothy's face. "I promise!" She clamped her lips tightly. The little legs beneath her plaid print wiggled, and Elsie surmised she was already imagining the wind on her face and the thud of her heart as the ground moved away and the Ferris wheel climbed toward the sky.

Shirley's bright eyes locked on the door again, through which rose the wail of their mother's cries and Ralf's rebuking barks. "How did this even begin?" She frowned, glancing at Elsie, seated against the wall with her knees high. "Elsie, you were home today. Did something happen out of the ordinary?"

Just the thought of it made Elsie's tongue dry. She swallowed, her parched throat collapsing on itself. "Nothing." Shame threatened to crush her. How could she tell them that Ralf had thought her so weak, he could prey on her like a hawk hunting an innocent mouse? How could she explain how she'd unconsciously permitted him to look at her, to think of her like that?

Unaware, Shirley leisurely wound her curled hair around her hand. "I've never seen him so much as raise his voice to her before. Sometimes he was brusque but *never* so unkind." Her deduction propelled the guilt further into Elsie's gut. Before her mistake, Momma and Ralf had enjoyed a happy engagement. Whatever she'd done, it had ruined Momma's chances at living a contented existence.

Elsie breathed the mountain air, the blame of it suffocating her. A flock of geese flew low and skittered over a tiny pond among the weeds, the outline of their flapping wings all she could see in the darkness. Above the honks and splashing water, an ominous foreboding fed her fears. Something hateful existed inside her, something she could not see but others well understood. Father had left. Daddy Harry had given up. Now Ralf struggled with Mother over this invisible force inside her. Every man would see it, and every man would run.

The little house's walls reverberated with the shatter of glass in the kitchen. All three girls spurted to their feet, Dorothy clinging to Elsie around the waist and Shirley gripping tight to the porch column. Ralf screamed a curse word at Momma before his heavy shoes battered the wooden floor and the front door punched open.

Elsie secured Dorothy to her as Ralf's sunburnt face appeared behind it, twisted and red with ire. His beady eyes secured on Elsie, his loathing manifest. "I hope you're happy," he snarled, spitting into the grass beyond the porch railing.

Elsie held her breath as Ralf's boots pounded the steps and he staggered to the Model A crookedly parked beside the road. After heaving himself inside, he smashed the car door shut and jetted off the moment its engine rumbled to life. The Ford flew down the highway faster than she knew it could go, careening this way and that, until its brake lights disappeared beyond a bend.

Frantically reaching for the door handle and hauling it back, Elsie led her sisters into the kitchen, where glass littered the floor and Ralf's bouquet of daises was strewn over the mess. "Be careful where you step," her mother said, sniffling. "He broke the vase I used for the flowers he brought home."

Elsie's heart plunged to her stomach when she saw her mother seated at the kitchen table, tending an eye wound with a wet cloth. "Oh Momma, what did he do to you?" She rushed forward and crouched near Lillian's chair, horrified at the inflamed skin of her cheekbone already beginning to purple.

Mother held out a halting hand, pushing back her chair to stand. "It's just a little bruising. Nothing to panic about." She directed her gaze toward her other two daughters, who stood gaping in the doorway. "Girls, go on off to bed. It's far past that time already."

Despite their mystified expressions, Dorothy and Shirley heeded their mother, shuffling off to the bedroom and clicking the door shut. Elsie stepped back, the silent kitchen unnerving her after their earlier meeting. Still, the suffering in her mother's crumpled form extinguished the resolve she'd summoned to remain callous against her. "Momma, I—"

Lillian gusted forward, her arms enclosing Elsie before she could articulate another word. At first stiff within her mother's embrace, Elsie's muscles eased as she felt Momma's frame shuddering with tears. Desperate hands clung to the back of her dress. Arms held her as if she'd dissolve without their touch. The floral scent of Momma's perfume satiated her nostrils, the subtle sweetness of rose hips transporting her back to days gone by when the strict yet loving hands about her had nurtured her as she grew.

"I'm sorry," Momma whispered, her breath tickling Elsie's ear. "My little girl, I'm so sorry." And at long last, Elsie knew she meant it.

Nine

Morning greeted Elsie with a tender caress, the sun peeking in to kiss her neck and shoulders. Tossing back the thin quilt she shared with her sister, she glanced around to find herself alone, the room much brighter than she normally woke to. Movement stirred in the kitchen beyond, brewing coffee and frying sausages fanning their enticing flavors through the space under her door.

Curious, Elsie slipped on her newly laundered brown dress and combed out her hair before pinning it up in her usual style. Peering sidelong through the window, she noticed automobiles driving up the roadway, the air a haze of dust and fumes. Farmers worked the fields beyond the meadow, John Deere plows churning the dirt in precise rows.

Elsie entered the kitchen to find Mother standing over the stovetop with spatula in hand, an array of breakfast meats sizzling and snapping in the frying pan's hot oil. A platter of melons and strawberries graced the table, around which sat three empty plates and another with a fried egg and a thick slab of French toast atop it. She even had a glass pitcher of maple syrup next to her delicious display, its amber liquid glowing in the morning sunlight.

"I see I missed breakfast with the family." Elsie noted the crumbs and remnants of strawberry stems sprinkled over the other plates.

Momma turned from her cooking, her complexion pink and a delighted smile on her lips. "The girls left for school about thirty minutes ago. I came in, but you were sleeping so peacefully I didn't want to disturb you." Even her posture, so wilted the night before, had sprung back to its usual queen-like pose.

The small clock above the bookshelf said 8:32, but Elsie could hardly believe it. Her body normally roused her with the dawning sun or before, eager to get about the day's errands. "I suppose I haven't slept much since..." Her words trailed off at the long-buried glow in Momma's eyes. How could she demolish it by mentioning Ralf's betrayal again?

Lillian's solemn nod said she understood, but she whisked past it. "Why don't you sit down and eat your breakfast before it gets cold?" Lifting the pan from the scorching burner, she carted it to the table and slid her metal spatula under the hissing meat. Three plump sausages plopped onto Elsie's plate, the picturesque completion to an already beautiful meal.

"Momma, where did all this food come from?" Elsie asked, sinking into her usual chair. "Yesterday we had nothing but lunch meat and a bit of milk in the icebox."

"Hanson's General has a delivery boy who makes his rounds early," Mother said proudly, setting her frying pan atop a cold portion of the stove.

Elsie palmed the linen napkin beside her plate and unfurled it over her lap. "But can we afford all this? I haven't seen a meal this fine since Dorothy came home with good marks on her report card." Not to mention their means of support had stormed out of the house last night, hopefully never to return.

"You let me worry about that. I have a little saved." Momma lifted the coffee pot and poured a generous helping of the steaming liquid into two mugs on the counter. Seizing them both carefully by the handle, she set them on the kitchen table—one in her place and one in front of Elsie. "Do you want cream and sugar?"

Elsie barely managed a nod. "You've never let me drink it before. You always said it would impede my development."

With a little laugh, Momma poured a dollop of cream into Elsie's cup from the decanter and followed it with a spoonful of sugar. "You're a woman now. You have no more development left, at least in the physical sense."

Elsie swallowed, tentatively cupping her hands around the blistering mug. Momma had never said it before—never called her a woman, never trusted her with true adult responsibilities. After several cautious glances assuring Lillian's approval, Elsie wrapped her fingers around the mug's handle and pressed it to her lips. The beverage scorched her sensitive skin and flushed a river of fire down her throat.

"Well, wait for it to cool first." Mother chuckled at the grimace on Elsie's pinched face. "Here, you haven't even stirred it yet." She reached over and twirled her spoon around in Elsie's coffee a few times before clinking it on the edge and setting it back on her placemat.

"Thank you, Momma." Elsie blushed, chagrined by her lack of practice. Her gaze wandered over the living space, where she spied an empty spot of clean carpet indented in a perfect rectangular shape. Ralf must have returned late at night and collected his belongings, wireless included. The thought prompted a flood of relief through her, though she knew Dorothy would miss her weekly adventures with the Lone Ranger.

"He's gone," Momma said. "He's gone for good."

Peering back at her mother's stalwart face, Elsie's pride swelled. Momma had selected the difficult path, an uphill struggle that would require cuts and scrapes, bruises and bumps along the way. She would ascend it for her children. "I'm sorry, Momma."

"I'm not." Lillian plucked a ripe strawberry from among the assortment and whirled it between her fingers. "He had a girl at the laundry and two more down at that restaurant he always went to for lunch. I found that out long ago, but I never supposed he would endanger my girls." Her voice choked, regret shining clear in her dark eyes.

Elsie reached out to clutch her mother's supple wrist. "It's not your fault."

"It *is* my fault for letting him stay, but I don't want to dwell on it forever." Lillian gripped her wrist so their hands entwined around one another. "You showed strength yesterday, Elsie. You possessed clarity of mind and moral courage. Life will always throw obstacles in your way, but you will overcome if you maintain those qualities."

Touched, Elsie forgot about her breakfast until her mother motioned toward it with her head. Letting go of Lillian's arm, she picked up her fork and sliced off a piece of sausage, the spicy taste of sage satisfying her tongue. She slathered warm maple syrup over her French toast and delighted at the rich flavor mingled in butter. She couldn't recall a better breakfast, not even on Christmas morning.

"You come from a line of strong women, Elsie," Lillian said as Elsie cut into her fried egg. "My mother died very young. I was only a child at the time, and my little sister Kate just a baby. My sister Mabel helped my father in every way she could, raising us up to be proper young women despite our mother's absence."

Lillian took a bite of her strawberry and smiled, the memories alive on her radiant face. "Her face is foggy now, but I do remember my poor Irish grandmother slaving away on her farm in Wisconsin. She raised eight children with a husband off fighting the Confederates, and managed without him when he died from his wounds not long after the war ended." Her eyes shimmered, so far away and yet happy. "I've always wanted to be like her—the little old woman born across the sea who raised a herd alone, kept a farm on a lake, and never even learned to read."

When Elsie tried to picture her, she saw a gray-haired woman in a 19th century calico dress chopping down trees with her lumberjack sons. "And she raised upstanding children to be proud of."

"Oh, goodness no!" Lillian laughed, displaying her lovely white teeth. "They were a gang of hooligans—one a horse thief, another probably a murderer. You'd be hard pressed to find a worse lot in all of Wisconsin."

Elsie's face fell. "Well, Grandpa at least turned out good, didn't he?" One crisp memory from the age of three still shone in her mind of a thin man with a large mustache driving them into town on a wagon, peppermints stashed in his shirt pocket. Elsie could still remember holding her arms in the air with Bus, the pair attempting to mimic their grandfather's grip on the horses' reins.

Lillian took a sip from her mug and held it in front of her. "Yes, my father was a good man. A bit rough around the edges sometimes, but he cared for us. It couldn't have been easy losing my mother so early."

Hesitant to voice her next thought, Elsie jabbed her fork in her melon. "Ralf told me men wanted nothing but power. *All* men."

The steam rose in curls from Momma's coffee cup several moments before she took another swig and set it on the table. "For the most part, he's right. I've encountered many men in my lifetime, and only a handful didn't fit that description. They run this world and they know it."

Elsie's eyebrows pinched together. "What about Harry? He isn't like that."

"Harry has problems too." Momma sighed. "Perhaps you don't remember the nights he stumbled in here drunk, but I do. So many hours waiting up, worrying that he'd get himself killed. It was no way to live."

And yet, Elsie sensed the regret peeping out from behind her words. She let her fork drop to her plate with a tinkling sound. "But you loved him."

With an uncomfortable jerk, Momma began collecting Dorothy and Shirley's dishes and stacking them on her own. "Love doesn't mean everything, Elsie. It can't fix a broken home. It can't put food on the table." Her fingers shook as the silverware clattered over the dishes. She looked across at Elsie's puzzled expression and her face softened. "I hope you do find love in your life, but please don't make it your goal. *Survival*—that's what matters in this world."

Elsie stared into her half-eaten breakfast while her mother rose and deposited the dishes on the kitchen counter. The world Momma depicted appeared so bleak, a maze of tangles and snares designed to kill anyone who ventured into it. As a woman, her existence largely depended on the male race that Momma so effortlessly reduced to an assembly of rogues.

Her eyes lifted to Momma, who stood sorting dishes in the window's streaming light. "Momma?" The voice in her throat belonged to the frightened child she felt lurking within. "How do I survive it?"

Reeling around, Momma gave Elsie a square look and gripped the countertop behind her in clenched hands. "You have courage. You rely on your own strength and not your husband's. And whatever you do, don't give too much of your heart away." Her eyelids fluttered, pain glossing her lustrous eyes. "The minute you do, they keep it for themselves, long after they've left you."

The clank of anvils beating spikes into the railroad track reverberated throughout camp, creating a buzz in the afternoon air. All across the long bend in the Idaho route, men littered the rails, replacing wooden ties or repairing trestle beams over the river's yawning gorge. A stray breath of wind rustled the tree leaves here and there, but the high sun dictated the climate, slathering heat over the laboring men.

Sam broke from his work to sit in the shade of an elm and mop the sweat off his blistering brow. The blue sky looked like a painter's canvas stretched over the mountains and fields, splotched with clouds bursting in gold-rimmed glory. Sliding his canteen from his pack, Sam lifted it to his cracked lips and rejoiced at the renewing torrent of cold water rushing down his dry throat. Dirt caked his neck and face. Blisters throbbed on his fingers. Still, he couldn't complain about an honest day's work. Nothing made him feel more alive.

Beyond the tent canvasses whipping in the breeze, Sam couldn't help but notice Johnny Mills sneaking off to a grove of swaying birch trees. A boy of eighteen, Johnny still carried himself like an arrogant high school track star, swaggering around campus like he owned every student. For all the good looks and charm he possessed, his parents hadn't managed to afford him. The moment he'd come of age, they'd shown him the door and his days of reigning as teenage heartthrob had ended—until Shirley Dawson had appeared at camp with her long legs and glittering blonde hair.

Buster Dawson hadn't missed the youth's disappearance either. Hopping down from a low point on the trestle bridge, he screwed on his hat and marched toward Sam's hideout in the shade. "Have you seen Johnny Mills lately?" he asked as he approached. "He was working on the ties just a few yards from me and when I looked up next, he was gone." His bronzed face scanned the fields with eyes squinted. "Thought he might have left to relieve himself, but he hasn't shown back up in twenty minutes."

Sam well knew Buster's cause for concern. Since the night of Walt's impromptu hoedown, he'd spotted Shirley a handful of times chatting with Johnny under the trees, or walking off with him alone. Rumors circulated that Bus had warned the little twerp to dump his sister or else, but Johnny had laughed in his face. Sam doubted the whispers contained much truth. Buster would clock anyone who talked to him like that, especially over one of his sisters. Not to mention his superior size and strength to the stringy kid.

"He went that way." Sam pointed toward the birch trees now concealing Johnny's swaggering form. "Saw him go in there just a few minutes ago. Didn't look like he was relieving himself from the way he was glancing around."

Bus dislodged a rock from the dirt with his foot, sending it careening over the grass. "I'm going to string that kid up by his feet." His hands constricted into fists. "No doubt my sister's out there waiting for him."

"You told her not to come out here, didn't you?" Or so the story went from around the campfire.

"Shirley doesn't listen to a word I say." Buster pulled off his straw hat and brushed a hand through his blond hair before replacing it. "Why don't you come with me? I need someone to stop me from killing him."

Scrambling up from the dirt, Sam threw his canteen into his pack and grabbed it before trailing Buster down the mild incline. Fueled by wrath, Buster's long legs conveyed him over the meadow so fast, Sam almost had to jog to keep up. When they reached the grove of trees Sam had indicated, a woman's laugh laced the air.

Buster glanced back before he ducked under a tree branch, his brows cinched and mouth twisted. The outline of two forms standing close together emerged from within the white trunks. A few more steps around the creaking trees and Sam could see the overconfident young man with one arm draped around Buster's sister, his lips pressed to hers. Shirley looked like a woodland fairy with the sunlight filtering through her golden hair, an enraptured glow to her fair skin.

"Take your hands off my sister this second!" Bus commanded, thundering in and snatching Shirley's free arm. Before she could protest, he yanked her away from her wooing companion and placed her safely behind his back.

"Bus!" Shirley cried, attempting to claw her way around him. "Bus, what are you even doing here?"

Buster tossed her a disapproving scowl. "I could ask the same of you." He whirled back on the cocky boy with his arms crossed over his broad chest, one foot already tapping. "And you. I thought I advised you to stay away from her."

Johnny pitched his dark hair back defiantly, his chiseled jaw setting in a smug expression. "I'm a grown man. I don't take orders from you."

"Well, she isn't!" Buster's brows rose to mid-forehead as he signaled toward his sister. "She's *fifteen* years old. If you don't listen to me, maybe you'll listen to the coppers when they drag you off to the county jail!"

"We haven't done anything wrong!" Shirley lurched forward, seizing Buster's arm. "We were just talking, Bus, I promise."

He met her terrified gaze. "Do you think he plans to stop there, Shirley? Do you think a boy like this just wants to *talk* to you?"

"Don't listen to him, Shirley," Johnny said, directing a cool smirk on Buster. "They'll sooner arrest you for threatening me. I haven't made a formal complaint yet because you're my girl's brother, but now I think you may be stalking me."

"I'm going to ring your neck, you little jerk," Buster sputtered through gritted teeth. He lunged at Johnny with fingers curled in a strangling pose, a livid flush spouting color up his neck and into his already sunburnt face. Sam dove in the way just in time to catch Buster's fist, aimed squarely at the boy's nose.

"You don't want to do this, Bus." His muscles strained to confine the struggling man. "You don't want to get in trouble and lose your job just because some idiot doesn't have the sense to keep his mouth shut."

Buster grunted angrily, his frame quaking in fettered rage. "I won't let him hurt my sister!" His light eyes shot flames of fire at Johnny.

Sam clutched Buster's work shirt, catching his gaze and locking it there. "We won't let him. We'll watch him. We all will. We'll protect Shirley as if she's our own."

The muscles pushing against his hands slackened, Bus's glower melting into a wary expression. He looked between his sister, who stood helplessly in a ray of sunshine, and the man who'd inspired his fury, leaned up against a tree as if out for a summer picnic. "Fine." His square jaw flexed. "But from now on I *am* stalking you. Everywhere you go, I'll be there." He speared a finger at Johnny. "And if I see you within ten feet of my sister, you won't keep that tongue you're so fond of making smart remarks with."

Johnny's eyes narrowed. "I'd like to see you try."

"Johnny, please." Shirley sent him a pleading look, the sunlit shadows on her face revealing her puppy dog eyes and quivering mouth.

"Go on home, Shirley," Bus said without ripping his stare from Johnny. "Don't come back this time."

Shirley stepped forward with her arms extended, the breeze fluttering the skirts of her floral print dress. "I'm your sister, not your child. You can't mandate everyone I see forever."

Buster swung his gaze on her. "I doubt Mother knows about this little courtship." He swallowed as doom overtook her pretty features. "If I see you back here one more time, I'll run over there and tell her myself."

"Oh Buster, you wouldn't!" Tears sprang into her eyes, the fear there twisting Sam's gut.

"I *will*," Bus said. "She allows you too much freedom, but she won't once she finds out about the two of you."

Her porcelain hand reached up to wipe the moisture from her cheeks, but her mouth fixed into a dogged line. "Johnny isn't the only reason I came here today," she said with a snarl in her voice. Her gaze darted unexpectedly to Sam. "Elsie says she'd like you to bring your truck by the house after all so you two can take the children to the carnival Friday night."

Suddenly the focus of every eye in the group, Sam staggered backward. The distrustful glare Bus had reserved for Johnny revolved on him now, picking him apart for inspection. He tried to conceal the enjoyment her revelation brought him, yet still he felt it rushing over his face like an inescapable tidal wave.

"Well, Bus," Shirley said with a vain little simper, "it appears as if Johnny isn't the only man you have to worry about anymore."

Ten

E lsie hummed the notes to "Night and Day" as she groomed herself for the carnival, a band of violins and saxophones performing the song in her head. She'd heard it several times on the radio, before Ralf had confiscated the contraption and immersed their home in silence. Now, staring into the mirror at her wide, amber-flecked eyes and her turned-up nose, the words frolicked through her mind like a ballet dancer leaping and spinning in the air.

Reaching up, Elsie pulled out her pin curlers one at a time, removing the bobby pins and unwinding each spiral until she had a head full of curlicues. Elsie normally wore her hair fastened at the back of her head, but Shirley had convinced her to brush out her curls and wear waves about her face like Marlene Dietrich in *Shanghai Express*. The first time she'd attempted the feat, she'd wound up with a giant frizzing rat's nest. After hours of combing through her tangles and patient assistance from Shirley, Elsie had finally grasped the trick of it, at least enough to last one night.

Bursting into the room, Dorothy cocked her head impatiently. "Aren't you almost ready?" She hopped from one foot to the other. "You've been staring at yourself in the mirror for hours now."

Chuckling, Elsie gently drew her hairbrush through her ringlets and shaped them as Shirley had demonstrated. "Beauty takes time, my little one. Besides, Sam isn't expected until five o'clock. We have to wait for him anyway."

Dorothy released an anxious huff and galloped back to the kitchen, where Momma sat weaving a basket at the table. "I bet the carnival will be even bigger and brighter than last year!" Elsie heard her crooning. "I'm going to win the fluffiest bear at the ring toss. That scoundrel Mickey Donovan isn't going to knock me off balance this time—not when I'm taller than him now!"

Elsie took one last gander at herself in the bedroom mirror, unpredictably pleased with what she saw. Her walnut-toned hair framed her face in a flattering way. The skin she usually just washed and dried in the mornings she'd powdered with a shimmering bronzer, followed by a blush that pinkened her cheeks. Her lashes looked thicker with mascara, her eyes bolder with a hint of gray shadow. She'd always believed Shirley's perfect visage came from nature itself, but apparently, she'd had help all along.

Turning aside, Elsie snatched her black cardigan from the bedpost and flung it over her shoulders. Shirley had leant her a favorite outfit for the evening—a red dress that hugged her torso and flared out at her knees. She'd suggested Elsie wear matching stilettos to give a shapely appeal to her legs, but Elsie imagined tripping over her feet all night and opted for Mary Janes. The idea of drawing attention to her legs mortified her anyway.

After tucking a lipstick, a handful of coins, and a wad of tissue into her clutch, Elsie snapped it closed and strode into the kitchen. Initially, she hadn't understood the need for a purse, but Shirley had assured her that no outfit was complete without the holy accessory. She'd just have to endeavor not to leave it behind during carnival games and rides.

Momma's eyes flickered over her, pride and worry indenting lines around them. "You have money with you?"

"Two dollars," Elsie said. It had taken a year to collect the sum.

"What time will you be home?"

Elsie glanced at the wall clock, the hands indicating 4:56. "No later than ten o'clock. Sam has to drive his siblings home after he drops us off." At nearly an hour's drive, the trip to Mountain Home usually involved an overnight stay for the family. This year, Momma had chosen to remain at home.

Lillian continued lacing strands of wicker, her fingers nimbly weaving an intricate pattern. "And you're sure this Sam fellow is safe to go with? You've only known him a short time, haven't you?"

Gripping her clutch, Elsie attempted to suppress the color blooming up her neck. No need to reveal her feelings for the man and kindle Mother's concerns. "He is a friend of Bus's, and a very nice man. Talk to him when he gets here, if you like."

"I would still feel better if Bus came along." Momma shook her head. "He gave me some excuse about needing to stay at the railroad camp, but I can't imagine what would keep him there on a Friday night."

Elsie clamped her mouth shut. On his visit Sunday last, Bus had made his troubles clear in the privacy of the garden while Momma cooked dinner. He placed no trust in the young man courting Shirley, and he would watch him every waking second. Cautioning her to do the same with Shirley, Bus had a mile-long list of complaints against this Johnny Mills. He came from a family even poorer than them, he walked around giving everyone orders and making up facts to sound smarter than he was, he wore his pants too tight. Inwardly, Elsie wondered if his suspicions stemmed more from the man himself or the idea of their sister alone with him. He certainly hadn't welcomed the news that Sam was taking her out until she had told him how many children would accompany their little adventure.

The hum of a motor breached the kitchen's silence, prompting Dorothy to whoop and spring from her chair toward the door like a baby kangaroo. Tension clamped on Elsie's limbs, her stomach whirling and rising to her throat. Gripping her purse close to her fitted satin bodice, she drank in a long breath and trailed Dorothy, who already bounded down the front steps two at a time.

"Elsie?" Momma called after her just as her feet hit the threshold. Elsie's head reeled around to find her staring back, basketwork sitting atop the table beneath her folded hands. "Remember what I told you about men. Guard your heart like it's your greatest possession."

The brake lights of Sam's old 1920's Chevrolet truck cast a red glow over the grass beyond their porch. Elsie strode through the front yard, stepping around dips and pebbles toward the vehicle teeming with giggling children. She counted three boys and two girls, including Dorothy, squirming in the truck bed, all atwitter about their trip to the carnival. The pick up's engine purred, clouding the air in diesel fumes.

From beyond the excited ruckus, a tall male form emerged within the haze. Clad in a white cotton shirt and suspenders, he had on cuffed trousers that rose high on his waist and the same fedora hat sloped over his brow as the day she'd first laid eyes on him. Elsie tried again to squash the goofy smile edging her lips as his mouth tipped and he swept an arm toward the passenger door. Somehow, she had a feeling this year's carnival would turn out different than all the others.

❧❧❧❧❧❧ ❦❦❦❦❦❦

*E*lsie Dawson. The woman looked like a siren in her snug-fitting red dress, a matching rouge on her lips. At the camp, he'd lost his heart to a simple country girl blushing under his touch. Here stood a goddess with brunette hair grazing her smooth skin in curls. Heart pounding, Sam endeavored not to stare at her as he led her up to the Chevy and popped the door open. He held out his hand to help her into the cab, her thin fingers leaving his tingling. Catching his breath, he threw her door shut and paused a second to still his pumping blood.

"You settle down back there," he told the five children bouncing in the truck bed as he rounded the back. "It's a long drive to Mountain Home and I don't want one of you falling out on the way." He grinned at Elsie's little sister, who already had Lizzie by the hand, chattering to her about the midway games.

Sam dragged the door open and slid in beside Elsie, keenly aware of her rose-tinged scent filling the cab. "There certainly are a lot of them," she said as he twisted the key in the ignition and threw the truck's shifter into drive.

"I convinced Miles to let us borrow his truck so Walt could bring my sister and her son along with the rest of my brothers," he said with a laugh.

Her face went white. "How many siblings do you have?" She turned and began counting the ones in back.

"Six brothers, two sisters. There are nine of us in all." Sam gripped the steering wheel and pressed his right foot to the gas pedal, propelling the truck into motion. "Sally came first, and Mother says she loved raising her so much she had to keep trying for another girl. Seven boys later, Lizzy finally graced us with her presence."

Instead of the revulsion Sam feared, he glanced over to find delight swimming on Elsie's features. "That sounds like a party!" Mirth lit her eyes.

Sam nodded. "Sometimes it feels that way. Other times you have to take a walk just for a minute of peace." He gazed back at the road, where only the occasional automobile passed. "What about you? Is it just the four of you at home?"

A quiet moment lumbered over them before Elsie bobbed her head. "Yes, there are just four of us at home."

The road to Mountain Home curved through infinite potato and grain fields, row after leafy row stretching under the soft blue sky to the hills afar. Most of the journey they spent in silence, the engine's roar and the children's gleeful laughter filling the space when no words passed between them. Sam would let his gaze slip to the girl beside him, relishing the shy glances he received back before she held her handbag closer and looked out her window at the trees whizzing by.

The old truck ground to a stop in the parking lot outside an archway flashing the word "carnival" in white lights. After helping Elsie climb down, Sam opened the back gate to a troop of scream-ing youngsters, stomping their way out of the bed like so many crazed chimpanzees. They purchased their tickets at the booth, where Sam instructed the trio of boys to stay together. Lizzy and Dorothy, he decided, would be safest close to them.

"Oh boy, I've never seen so many rides before!" Dorothy said, her hands sheltering her freckled cheeks as she scanned the land-scape from carousel to spinning swings.

"I want to ride that one!" Lizzy stabbed her chubby finger to-ward a lurching dragon with flickering red eyes, heaving a group of screaming fair-goers through the air.

Sam spied Sally standing in line with little Jackie in her arms, waiting for admittance into a sideshow advertising a tattooed man, a girl with fourteen fingers, and a woman weighing in at 600 pounds. Not far away, Bert and Bill loafed around near a conces-sion stand, throwing popcorn into the air and trying to catch it in their open mouths. He wondered where Walt had run off to before a piercing whistle blasted through the air behind them.

The whole group revolved to see Walt sauntering up to them, thumb and forefinger leaving his mouth while the other hand moseyed up and down his suspender. "Wowzers, would you get a load of this?" His astounded gawp unabashedly appraised Elsie from the curves of her legs to her shoulders. "Looks like we have one sweet momma on our hands."

Elsie tugged on a wave of her hair, the blushing skin beneath heightening her beauty. Sam shoved his brother hard in the chest as he moved past him. "Have a little respect, would you?"

Thrusting his hands out on either side in a harmless stance, Walt didn't withdraw his stare. "What? I'm just observing."

"Well, observe somewhere else." Sam ticked his head toward the animal pens. "Come on, girls," he said to the young ones still drooling over the carousel horses plunging and leaping in a circular pattern. "Let's go take a look at the ponies."

Walt draped his arm over Elsie's shoulder while she followed Sam. "Don't forget to save me a seat next to you on the Tilt-tee-Whirl." He tossed her a playful wink as he rejoined his brothers at the concession stand.

The group wound through an assortment of farm animals residing behind wire fences, the girls finding it necessary to stop at each enclosure. Dorothy made friends with a pig named Wilbur. Lizzy giggled wildly as a sheep munched alfalfa from her hand. Despite the sour stink of manure, peace descended over Sam as he watched Elsie cradle a horse's snout to her cheek, her lithe hand smoothing the velvet hair between his mammoth eyes.

As the sun set and evening blanketed the fairgrounds, Sam bought them a hasty dinner of corndogs and caramel corn. The midway sparkled in strung lights as they meandered among merchandise booths, the girls chattering about jewelry and toys between enormous bites of corndog. Sam kept them distracted watching a traveling fortune teller and a man with a hand crank organ and a monkey while their little bellies digested their food. At around Dorothy's age, he'd learned the hard way that carnival food and rides didn't blend well.

"Step right up! Take your chance!" the booth workers bellowed, hands full of baseballs or darts, or whatever game they peddled to the passersby. Dorothy marched right up to the ring toss, tickets extended, and rubbed her hands together as the operator gave her a set of colored rings. Licking her lips, she posed one graceful foot behind the other and lobbed all five rings, four of which hit their mark and spiraled down the wooden pegs. Squealing with glee,

Dorothy bounced into the air, her finger jabbing toward a tan bear with a red bowtie hanging off the booth.

"What game would you like to play?" Sam looked at Elsie, whose hazel eyes glinted excitedly in the dazzling lights of the midway.

She crossed one arm over her body and held her elbow as she perused the array of flags and painted signs. "That one." She nodded toward a stand with milk bottles piled into a pyramid.

Sam found his brothers one station over, Bert and Bill locked in a heated contest over who could shoot the most wooden ducks speeding across the board. Both teenage boys had air rifles positioned at their ears, their faces a cherry red and eyes darting back and forth like wild rabbits. Planting a straight finger over his lips, Sam snuck up behind them, his boots soundlessly treading the dirt. Just a few inches from their backs, he reached both arms out and poked a finger into the exposed armpit of each brother.

"What in—?" Bill hollered, dropping his gun and whirling.

"Aw, Sam!" Bert said. "You made me miss my mark. I could have hurt someone, you know."

Sam chuckled, seizing the boy in a headlock and ruffling his hair with a fist. "Relax, you're firing blanks."

"Such a spoilsport." Bill retrieved his gun from the dirt and slammed it back on the counter. He tried his best to pout, but a grin still boosted the corners of his mouth. "I'll get you next time, Sam." Freeing Bert, Sam clapped Bill on the back. Of course he would. The relentless rivalry of brotherhood never really ended.

Sam presented his tickets to the man at the next booth over and received two handfuls of baseballs in return. "You first," Elsie said when he held them out to her. She still had that purse tucked up under her arm, like someone might snatch it away the moment she let go.

"Sam could have been a professional," Bert bragged to Elsie. "He was the best pitcher in school. Struck 'em out every time."

Setting the baseballs on the American flag-adorned counter, Sam lifted his fedora and laid it down beside them. He rubbed his palms over his trousers, suddenly wet and sticky with perspiration. Did they have to tell her all that *now*, just when he stared the public test of skill right in the nose? Grabbing one ball, he rolled it over and again in his hand before shifting it to the other and flinging it at the taunting pyramid of milk bottles ahead. *Whoosh!* The baseball hit the curtains behind the target, cackling at him as it slammed into the dirt and rolled out of sight.

An outbreak of groans and lamentations ruptured behind him. "I haven't seen you throw that bad since you pitched with the flu!" Bill said.

"Keep your eyes *open* this time, Sam," Bert said.

Sam spun around to shoot them a silent warning, but they hardly noticed in all their carousing. Between them, Elsie stood demurely with her hands folded in front of her.

Gripping the next ball in his clenched hand, Sam focused on the middle of the stack and visualized the whole thing toppling over. He *had* pitched hundreds of perfect games before a screaming crowd, many of whom were pretty girls. Why did this one get his goat? Balancing on one leg, he hinged his right arm back and chucked the ball past his ear, watching as it thwacked the very top bottle and knocked it from its spot.

"That one sure felt your wrath," the cheeky booth operator mocked him this time, twisting the end of his handlebar mustache.

Grunting, Sam seized the third ball in whitened knuckles. Not much got his hackles up, but the thought of failing at a talent so easy to him in front of the one person he wanted to impress sent his blood racing. The baseball's rough stitching scuffed his fingertips as he spun it around in his hands and glared at his target, time freezing solid. Either he would win, or it would. With one decided breath, Sam hurled the baseball into the stack of milk bottles. Triumph exploded in his chest as the ball crashed into the center and sent the pyramid tumbling.

To his brothers' cheers and exultations, Sam twisted around to grin at the girl still standing there shyly, a sweet smile on her glowing face. Grabbing up the remaining two baseballs, he lobbed them at the triangles of bottles on either side, easily demolishing them all.

"What a show-off!" Bert hooted through his cupped hands as Sam danced around in a circle, lifting his arms and knees the way Walt had frolicked about at the hoedown. Elsie's soft giggles lit the air of twilight, lending it a warmer feel.

A glorious sensation abducted him, as if he'd just won a thousand dollars. He whisked over to Elsie, chest pumping and sweat glistening his skin. "What would you like from the prizes?" His hand swept toward the booth. "You can pick anything they have if you knock down all three."

Elsie's eyes widened. "Me?" Her hand flattened on her chest. "But Sam, I didn't knock anything over. *You* did."

His mouth crinkled at her unassuming look of surprise. "I want you to have it. Come on, let's look at what they have."

Sam led Elsie over to the booth with a gentle hand on her shoulder. The operator had an array of rewards to choose from—candies, ribbons, stuffed animals of every size and color. An assortment of toys festooned the lower shelf, ranging from jacks and marbles to spinning tops and slingshots. Sam felt certain Elsie would stop in front of a glass case boasting fancy hair bows and lipsticks, but instead she moved to the very end and plunked her elbows down, focused on a darkened corner it appeared no one ever picked from.

"There." She speared her finger toward a long package beneath the glass. "I'd like that one, please."

Following her direction, the booth worker bent low and retrieved her selection from his cache. His hands brought forth a simple cardboard box with swirls and designs adorning the label and passed it to Elsie. Squinting, Sam made out words he hadn't expected—paintbrushes. Atop the label, a plastic window displayed thin wooden sticks with soft black brooms sprouting from the top.

"I didn't know you painted." He'd seen only a handful of paintings in real life when the family passed a gallery on their way from town to town. He'd never known someone who actually created them.

Elsie turned them over in her hands, admiring them. "Well, I don't."

A chuckle burst from Sam's lungs, his forehead scrunching. "Then why did you pick them?"

Her eyes shone lovingly down at her new possession before they turned up to Sam, stirring something inside of him. "Because I've wanted paintbrushes for a very long time." Her head cocked sideways. "I've always wanted to paint, but I've never had the means." Her lashes fluttered once. "Thank you, Sam. Today I'm one step closer."

✤✤✤✤✤ ✤✤✤✤✤

E ven with the cool evening breeze kissing her skin, Elsie couldn't seem to calm the rush of heat still steaming her cheeks. Strolling up the midway beside Sam with the girls prancing ahead of them, she passed one stall after another, each boasting bigger prizes and better chances at winning. With her new paintbrushes tucked safely into her purse, she didn't give the carnival workers a second look.

Sam had used his win to give her a gift grander than she'd ever received before. After his impressive feat, she imagined they'd wander over to the rides that Dorothy had blathered about since they first left the house. Sam, however, had paid the vendor more tickets and handed her the next set of baseballs. Emphatically wagging her head, Elsie had insisted she couldn't follow his victory up with her pitiful lack of skill, but Sam had coached her until she hit her mark and managed to topple most of one pyramid.

As they walked by the bumper cars, most filled with zealous children bent on crashing into their friends, Elsie stole a sidelong glance at Sam. She could still feel the brush of his fingertips against her elbow as he guided her arm in an arc toward her target. The smell of his bay rum lingered in her nose, transporting her back to the moment he'd stood so close and murmured how to aim in her ear. Now, the carnival lights danced in his light eyes as he stared up at the Ferris wheel in quiet awe.

"Can we ride it now?" Dorothy asked, tearing Elsie from her trance. She looked over to find Dorothy hopping in circles as if on springs. "Oh please, oh please, oh please? I've been dying to ride it for so long!"

The others trailed her to the massive revolving ride, where pairs ascended to the night sky and back again to the jaunty music of a calliope. Dorothy was first to the height sign, her shoes flat on the ground, but her back stretching as far as her spine would allow. Her head crossed the mark by an inch or so, prompting her holler of triumph and corresponding victory dance. At eight years of age, Sam's sister Lizzy barely hit the designated line.

"That's not fair!" Dorothy knit her arms over her chest, her lower lip protruding. "Last year I couldn't ride the Ferris wheel because I was too short, and I was eleven years old!"

Elsie smoothed a hand over her braided head. "You're little for your age, Dorothy. Lizzy is just taller."

Dorothy peered suspiciously from one face to the other, as if a fantastic conspiracy had been waged against her, until the ride operator lifted the gate and motioned her inside. All jealousy forgotten, she climbed the steps and sat on the swaying bench like a queen taking her throne. Lizzy nestled in beside her regal partner, wiggling in anticipation as the operator clamped the handlebar across their laps and tugged it once.

Dorothy shrieked with joy as the Ferris wheel chugged into motion, propelling her into the air. The clanging ride made half a rotation before the engineer halted it to let two passengers off.

Trepidation bounced in Elsie as she snuggled into the seat and folded her hands in her lap. She hadn't anticipated the goosebumps that prickled her arms when Sam stepped in and plopped down beside her, rocking the swinging seat. Shivers burst over her skin at the thought of an entire ride alone with him.

The bar locked over their knees and the Ferris wheel lifted them off the ground, over the crowd of carnival goers. Elsie gripped the bar, her stomach churning as the earth moved farther away. The higher they climbed, the more anxiety squeezed her. She clenched her eyes shut, and still the swaying motion of the bench forced her muscles to tauten.

"Are you afraid of the height?" Sam gently asked, inciting Elsie to open her eyes and look at him. The gray-blue of his eyes sparkled in the flashing lights, concern emanating from them.

Managing a nod, Elsie gazed down over the buzzing fairground. The people looked like bugs from up here—crawling over the hay-sprinkled earth in wanton frenzy. The flying lights of the The Whip and the carousel sped on in continuous motion until they looked like unbroken streams of red and yellow and blue. "I ride it with Shirley every year, and still I haven't grown used to it." Elsie's stare wandered over the quiet parking lot, a blackened field of pickups and sedans under the moonless sky. The ride had jerked to a stop again, suspending them near the top with no safety but the thin wall at their backs.

"Look here," Sam directed, pointing toward a cluster of stars shaped like a broom. "That's Scorpius. Orion once bragged that he could kill all the animals on the planet, but the scorpion defeated him and that's why he's in the sky now."

Elsie's gaze traced the constellation from its spindly end to the tail forming a "j" shape before she looked back at him with a skeptical grin. "You're making that up."

"No, it's true. I read it in a comic strip." Sam's eyes smiled as a chuckle erupted from his lungs. He lurched his finger higher, his enthusiasm rocking the chair. "And that one's the Big Dipper. You can usually see it, no matter the time of year."

The familiar pattern of stars glimmered from their ebony canvas, forming a pot-like design. "It's part of Ursa Major," she said. Oh, how she missed school and the thrill that accompanied each new discovery.

Sam nodded, his face thoughtful. "That's right, the bear." At Elsie's questioning brow, he shrugged. "I read a lot of comic strips."

Elsie's lips pressed into a timid smile. How skillfully he'd distracted her, caused her to forget they sat fifty feet in the air with no escape until the ride proceeded. She looked down at her hands, still trembling a little on the cold steel bar across her lap, and noted how close his fingers lay to hers. Sam could spread them an inch to his right and touch her. A part of her wished he would, while the other panicked at the prospect.

Her eyes swept his arm until they reached his face, anchoring there. He'd removed his fedora and settled it on his legs, giving the breeze free reign to lift the short strands of his ash-colored hair and toss them at will. The scent of barbeque chicken roasting on the spits drifted high, the roar of the rides and the squawking children drowning into a distant whir as his eyes searched hers. Elsie achieved a quivering breath, her lungs aching to let it out again.

Fear and longing took hold as he shifted beside her, his arm extending behind her shoulders. His nearness brought warmth, excitement, terror. How desperately she wanted to stare back into the swirling scenery below, and yet as the wind stirred her loose curls against her cheeks, her gaze refused to tear itself away from him.

"I like you, Elsie," his deep baritone hummed in the chilly air. "You know I like you, don't you?"

She meant to say yes, but the words wedged in her throat. Elsie nodded, delighting in the joy crinkling the skin beneath his scruffy brows. "I like you too, Sam."

One side of his mouth lifted in a boyishly handsome grin. His hand fastened on her shoulder. Elsie held her breath as he moved nearer to her, the woodsy scent of bay and clove filling her senses. The mounting breeze knocked their chair in swift movements, but somehow she forgot to care with his body looming, his gaze clamped on her lips.

The Ferris wheel jolted, thrusting them into motion. A nervous giggle escaped Elsie's mouth as their chair descended and swung them through the bottom again, past a line of eager children. Sam set his elbow on the lap bar and simply grinned, releasing a lengthy breath. Their moment had ended long before it had wings to fly.

The couple revolved around the Ferris wheel's spokes seven more times before it ground to a halt and deposited them on the platform. The ground swayed beneath her feet as Elsie stepped off the ride and accepted Sam's support down the metal steps. Both sisters waited in the crowd beyond the gate, their faces ruddy and their mouths bursting with enlivened chatter.

"That was the greatest experience of my life!" Dorothy said, her whole body wagging like a puppy dog's tail. "Can we go again, Elsie? Please, can we go again?" She crushed Elsie's wrist and cuddled close to her chest, her enormous eyes imploring.

Elsie swapped a look with Sam, her cheeks pinkening but her eyes full of good humor. "How about we get some cotton candy first?" She noted the way Lizzy's shoulders popped up at the idea. "Do you think maybe Lizzy would like that?"

Bobbing her head, Lizzy seized Dorothy's other hand. "Let's get cotton candy, Dorothy. It's so much fun to watch them make it."

The carnival lights looked like fairy lanterns as they started off toward the cotton candy stand, Dorothy and Lizzy already halfway there. Strings of bulbs crisscrossed over the midway, buzzing and flickering as if fireflies dotted the black night. Sam's boots tramped the dirty pathway, his form closer than their walk to the Ferris wheel, his arm brushing hers on occasion. Elsie felt the back of his hand graze hers and knew he had meant to. She turned her palm, her heartbeat hammering as his skin met her hand, his fingers lacing the spaces between hers. Without even a glance at the other, the couple kept on walking, cutting a path under the magic lights of the midway.

Eleven

The lyrics to "I Found a Million Dollar Baby (in a Five and Ten Cent Store)" rang over the railroad camp. Walt's thick voice clouded the air, his cheerful tenor lightening the workload. He held out the final note as long as he could, theatrically crooning the romantic strains with his eyes shut and lips protruding.

"You better open those eyes before you cut one of us," Sam warned, yanking the crosscut saw they shared through a block of wood perched on a frame.

Walt dragged the saw his way again, its jagged teeth digging deeper into the lumber. "I am most excellent at both singing and sawing, brother. Together, they make an unstoppable combination."

Wagging his head, Sam kept on with his work. "When was the last time you met a girl in a five and dime anyway? If you did, you'd have her running with that song."

Letting go of the handle, Walt straightened and swiped his arm over his perspiring forehead. "Well, excuse me. We can't all have the prettiest girl at the carnival on our arm all the time."

Sam scratched his jawline, attempting to stifle the grin festering there. "She was pretty, wasn't she?" He shook his head, the memory still thriving as if shown beneath a spotlight in his mind. "I forgot how to talk when I first saw her like that."

"Are you kidding?" Walt lifted his metal canteen and tipped it toward Sam before guzzling a swig of water. "I saw you showing off at the milk bottle toss." He screwed the cap of his canteen on. "It's a shame to see a girl like that wasted on my goofy little brother—especially when *I* saw her first."

"Saw her, but didn't really look at what was there."

Waving Sam off, Walt leaned his hands against the brace and stretched his back. "I should have filched her out from under you at that barn dance. We had a connection, you know."

Sam hugged his arms around his torso and swung them out repeatedly, his muscles sore and stinging from hours bent over. "Well, you still have your chance." He squinted out the harsh rays of sun overhead. "She did let you take her on the tilt-a-whirl after all, didn't she?"

His brother looked like a soaring reed against the field of dry grass behind him. He stood taller, pride and amusement denting his bristled mouth. "That ship sailed off to Panama, my friend." He let out a hefty sigh. "I laid on all the charm I have in my reservoir. I complimented her clothes. I took every opportunity to scoot closer whenever the ride spun around." He bent nearer, as if sharing a secret. "I even pretended to be scared just so she'd try and comfort me. And you know what she did?"

"What?" Sam asked, savoring the break from Walt's usual good luck with women.

"She told me *you* knew how to help if the ride made me nervous. Apparently, you have some kind of gift." His brown hair shook at Sam's chuckling. "She spent the whole time staring at you like she was drowning in a river with me and you were the lifeboat to save her. I haven't felt that ineffective since I was thirteen and my voice broke just as I tried to ask Ginger Downs to the church social."

Crippled with laughter, Sam doubled over and slapped his knee. "Serves you right for trying to spoil my night. You've never met a girl who didn't fall for your antics."

Walt glared at him sideways through one scrunched eye. "Yeah, and I don't like meeting one now." The fabricated annoyance on his face dissolved into a serious look. "But truly, Sam, how did it go? You both looked very happy."

Standing to his full height, Sam let his laughter subside as he thought about the girl in the red dress with curls in her hair. "I *was* very happy. I am." Just remembering volleyed an unexpected thrill through him. "She's—" How could words describe the beauty he'd encountered that night? A shy grin tickled his lips. "She's very special."

Drawing close, Walt wrapped an arm around Sam and clapped him on the shoulder. "I'm glad to hear it, little brother." He turned to the work they'd left behind—a saw stuck in a piece of wood and a pile of lumber stacked beside it. "We'd better get back to work before the foreman has our tails."

With much effort, the brothers managed to saw through their batch of planks before the noon bell rang for lunch. Walt whooped and sprang toward the gathering group with fire beneath his feet, but Sam sauntered behind him, enjoying the warm summer breeze whisking the beads of sweat from his skin. Fields of rolling grass glistened beneath the sun, forming gentle waves clear to the foothills. Ravens circled and dove through the clear blue sky. The world somehow looked brighter; the air felt crisper. Life flourished.

The future looked full as Sam plodded toward camp, the dry grass crunching beneath his boots. He'd shared so few words with the girl at the carnival, and yet they'd said so much. Her eyes burned in his memory—the gold-dusted brown beneath her copious lashes disclosing her innocence. How strongly he'd wanted to kiss her atop that Ferris wheel, under a canopy of blinking stars, with only the night sky watching. Yet something had cautioned him to slow his ardor and get to know her, find out who she was.

Buster Dawson roosted on a log near the fire pits with one foot perched on his knee and a baloney sandwich in his hand. Ignoring Walt's impatient gesture to join their friends under the elm trees, Sam turned aside and approached the man seated by himself, demolishing his lunch. Sam wondered why he concentrated so hard until he followed Buster's gaze to the line of men at the tables waiting for their meal. Sure enough, Johnny Mills stood among them, chattering and snickering loudly.

"You still spending all your time on that kid?" Sam asked, advancing toward Bus with his thumbs in his belt loops.

Bus glanced at Sam before pinning his stare back on the cocky youth. "Have to. He's slippery. He pretended to be sleeping the other night, and when I went to check his tent, I found it empty. Looked for him for three hours before he came moseying back into camp, looking like he'd won the Kentucky Derby."

"Do you think he was with Shirley?" Sam stopped next to the fire pit and looked back at Johnny, who now balanced on one leg with the other extended atop a stump, apparently flaunting some trick to the other workers. "She didn't go with us to the carnival."

"Yeah, but she had some school event." Bus shook his head, the sunlight playing in his blond hair. "Can't see how much trouble they could have gotten in. I know my sister well enough. She takes all that social stuff too seriously to let him drag her off anywhere."

Sam crossed his arms over his chest. "Well, then maybe it isn't so bad that he sees her. Maybe Shirley is smart enough to keep him at a proper distance." Maybe Bus could relax his watch on his sisters enough to trust someone with their well-being.

"She's smart, but she's fifteen." Bus took a bite of his sandwich. "She's too young to know how to defend herself if something happens. My sisters don't have much exposure to men. Good ones, anyway."

With a sizable gulp, Sam looked at the dusty toes of his boots. He hoped he was a good one. Despite his imperfections, he wanted honor to win out. "Are you upset I took the girls to the carnival?"

Bus shot him a look like he'd lost his mind. "Of course not. Dorothy's been yapping about riding that Ferris wheel since she could talk."

Sighing, Sam sauntered forward and eased onto the log beside Bus. "But you know that wasn't my only reason." He looked Bus in the eye, determined to share the truth even in the face of his discomfort. "I asked Elsie out again for Saturday night. Alone this time."

Buster's gaze held his a long while before it flicked away and soared over the mountainous terrain. "Elsie's a grown woman. She can make her own choices."

"She's only two years older than Shirley."

That suspicious stare swung back. "Are you saying I need to worry about you too?" Humor dented the skin around Bus's mouth.

Sam laughed, shaking his head. "No, but I know you love her and you'll still want to protect her no matter her age." He reached out to clap Buster's shoulder. "I want you to know that I intend to respect her and care for her in the time that she lets me. I wouldn't feel right about taking her out without your approval."

Bus stared at Sam's hand a lingering moment, deliberation knitting his brow. Most of the camp had passed through line, only scraps of bread and sandwich meats remaining on the tables. From beneath his belt, Sam's stomach rumbled its displeasure at his delay. At last, Buster lifted his head and gave him a nod. "You're a good man, Sam Tully. Elsie is lucky you found her before one of these other fools."

S eated at the kitchen table with her hands in a bowl full of warm water, Elsie giggled as Shirley massaged her fingers from the tips to the rounds of her knuckles. A warm wind wafted in from the open window, blowing back their mother's lacy curtains and shedding a little air through the stifling house. Momma had left meatloaf baking in the oven, its savory smells swirling about the kitchen.

"I still don't see why I have to have a manicure," Elsie said as Shirley set her fingers out on a towel and dabbed them dry.

"Because you're going on a date, silly." Shirley beamed, the excitement as true for her as it was for Elsie. "It's not every day a man picks you up in his car and takes you out on the town. You want to look your best."

Sighing, Elsie wilted in her chair. "I already dolled myself up and curled my hair the last time. I even wore your favorite dress. How much more do you think he expects?"

Shirley laughed, flipping her long waves of tawny hair over one shoulder. "It doesn't matter what he expects. It's your job to always impress beyond the last time. That's what all the magazines say."

"Well, if the *magazines* say it." Elsie tried to curb her sarcasm as she watched her sister pluck dead skin and hangnails off her work-worn hands. "We're in the midst of a depression, for goodness sake. Who has time for manicures, anyway?" Seeing her hands so idle only drove the guilt deeper.

"Claudette Colbert." With expert quickness, Shirley buffed her emery board over the tips of Elsie's nails until they bore an oval shape.

Elsie scoffed. "Claudette Colbert is a movie star. What does she have to stress over?"

"Even if you aren't a movie star, it does no harm to look like one." Shirley's nail file jetted back and forth, the coarse edge hot against Elsie's fingertips. "Just because we're in a depression doesn't mean we have an excuse to look like hobos."

Lifting her feet, Elsie set them on the chair across from hers and crossed them at the ankle. "Momma spends ten minutes on her hair in the mornings and she hardly ever puts anything but blush on her face. She's twice as pretty as *Claudette Colbert.*"

Shirley smirked, her eyes still fixed on her meticulous task. "That's because Momma is secretly a goddess." Her thin eyebrows pinched inward. "Where is Momma, anyhow?"

"She's off trying to find a job, like I should be. If not that, there's so much to do around here." The quiet house screamed at Elsie with all the work left unfinished. A garden full of weeds sprouted in the dirt outside the window. The kitchen floor needed mopping, and Dorothy's trip to Harry's house presented the perfect time for Elsie to wash and wring out her extra clothes.

Shirley opened her clippers and squeezed them over an unruly section of Elsie's nail. "Oh, relax. The work will still be here when I'm finished. I'll help you."

A new worry budded as Elsie watched her nails taking a lovely shape. "I'm afraid I'll ruin all your hard work."

"Just be careful." Shirley reached for a bottle of dark rough polish she'd left beside the water bowl and shook it out before she unscrewed the top. "At graduation setup, I just tried to keep my fingers straight when I could and not dig my nails into anything."

The acrylic smell of Shirley's nail polish assaulted Elsie's nose. "How did that go?" she asked, averting her face away from the offensive odor.

Shirley shrugged. "As good as any, I'd guess." Carefully, she swept her brush over Elsie's fingernails, leaving an unpainted moon shape near her cuticles. "The seniors all told me they had a good time at the mixer." Her pretty mouth dimpled. "All except for Joseph Hatley, anyway."

"What was wrong with Joseph Hatley?" Of all the boys at Shirley's school, Elsie expected the football team's quarterback to have the best time.

"Oh, he didn't like that Johnny was there." Shirley blew on Elsie's wet fingernails, fanning the air with her hand. "He saw us dancing and he tried to come over and pick a fight. He said Johnny shouldn't be there since he doesn't go to school with us."

Cold fear blossomed in Elsie's middle. "Johnny didn't fight with him, did he?"

Shirley wagged her head. "Of course not." She chuckled. "Johnny is far too mature for that type of high school nonsense. He just laughed it off." She dipped her brush into the bottle, returning to Elsie's unpainted nails with fresh polish. "I told him if Johnny wasn't welcome, then I didn't want to be there either, and we left."

Elsie bolted upright in her chair, knocking Shirley's gentle grip off balance. "You two left by yourselves? Shirley, you're supposed to have a chaperone."

Her sister huffed, her glossy pink lips billowing. "Elsie! You made me flub up." Seizing Elsie's rebellious hand, she plunged her towel into the water bowl and scrubbed at the fingers now doused in crimson. "Calm down. You sound just like Buster. All we did was walk around town for a little while. He bought me a soda pop. It wasn't whatever disaster the two of you might imagine."

Attempting to coax herself into relaxing, Elsie leaned back in her chair and let Shirley finish the job she'd begun. "Bus would be very upset if he knew. He's only doing what he thinks is best, you know."

Shirley sighed as she slid the brush over Elsie's nails. "I wish what he 'thinks is best' was minding his own beeswax. Do you know he's been following Johnny around everywhere he goes? He even follows him to the outhouse."

A spontaneous giggle burbled in Elsie's throat. "Well, that can't be a pleasant experience for anyone."

Hooking one eyebrow, Shirley glanced up with a simper before aiming her attention on Elsie's other hand. "I'd imagine it's not, and it really only makes me want to see Johnny more. It's just like when Momma bought those popsicles and told Dorothy she had to wait until Sunday to eat them. She'd best have left them in the icebox without mentioning it than tempting the poor girl until she broke in and ate them all."

"Oh, Shirley." Elsie bit her tongue, another reprimand pleading to launch out. Shirley was right; added mandates from family members would only fuel her straight into Johnny's arms. "Maybe there's a way you can see Johnny and still put Bus's mind at ease. Bus wouldn't be so quick to distrust Johnny if he didn't always drag you off alone. Show him there's nothing to hide, that it's okay if other people come along too."

Shirley's eyes narrowed as she put the finishing touches on Elsie's pinky. "Do you think Bus would go for that?" Recapping her nail polish and fastening the lid tight, she plunked it on the table. "I certainly don't want *him* to chaperone us. He'd spoil the whole date."

"Of course not him, you silly goose. I mean *me*." Elsie spread her fingers out like a fan, impressed with the practiced way Shirley had painted around her nail beds, leaving only the moons and the tips exposed. "If Sam and I went with you sometimes, maybe Bus wouldn't be cross about the two of you seeing each other."

With squirrely delight on her sunny features, Shirley sent her an approving grin. "Listen to you, talking about going out with Sam again." She snatched up her polish and emery board and stuffed them into her beauty kit. "Elsie, I do believe you have an idea that just may work. You're going to like Johnny more than you know."

Twelve

From the moment he first saw Elsie, Sam had stored away what little excess money he earned after paying for gasoline and sending a portion to Mother and Pop with the idea of buying a suit. A proper girl should be taken out by a man in stylish attire, he thought, yet still he'd only raised the funds to purchase the tie alone. Most of the clothes he'd ever owned were lovingly hand-sewn by Olive Tully's deft hands, and usually fit for Walt's lanky form first. When he outgrew them, he'd watch the outfits he'd worked and played in pass along from one brother to the next. Poor Ollie had never owned a new shirt in his life.

Sam yanked on the new checkered silk tie, tightening the knot beneath his chin until it rested just under his Adam's apple. He swung the sport coat he'd retrieved from home over his shoulders, aware the sleeves didn't quite reach his wrists. At the water pump, he wet a comb and ran it through his hair until it sat neatly off his forehead. His tired red Chevy truck waited near the tracks to carry him off to Elsie's house, somehow graceful despite her chipping paint and a layer of filth caked on by driving through the camp's dusty fields.

The trusty pickup trundled over the rutted road between vast fields of golden grass, just turning in to sleep under the purple strands of sunset. He imagined her there, sitting next to him in the cab of his truck, and felt sweat slick his palms on the steering wheel. They'd never spent time alone together before, never shared the awkward silence as conversation lulled. He'd never had so much time to contemplate whether to touch her or not, whether to kiss her or not, with no audience of siblings close by to watch.

When he rolled up to the weather-beaten farmhouse with cheerful green trim, Sam noticed a black Model T parked by the mailbox. Dorothy had mentioned their mother's fiancé owned a car, but from what he understood, the man had recently left her. Sam grabbed the bouquet of wildflowers he'd spent the afternoon plucking from the pastures off the passenger seat and marched between the cars up to the sagging front porch.

Inhaling a breath of courage, he pounded out four steady knocks on the door, a queasy sensation sprouting as he heard footsteps from within. The door opened, revealing a woman who looked just like Elsie, save for a darker complexion, a harder face, and a strong nose jutting from beneath her eyes. She appeared too young to have grown children, and yet the wise quality in her gaze as she surveyed him said she'd sired a pack of them.

"I assume you're Sam Tully." Her unapologetic stare assessed him from the toes of his shoes to his necktie.

"Y-yes ma'am." His face reddened as he stumbled over his words. The woman possessed an intimidating air, so different from her unassuming daughter. "I've come to pick up Elsie," he said despite the thick tongue attempting to trip up his every word.

"Yes," Elsie's mother stretched out the word, her lovely face placid yet judgmental. "I hear you work with my son at the railroad camp." She crossed her arms over her slim figure. "You're not one of these hoodlums I hear stories about, I trust."

Sam stiffened. "No, ma'am, of course not." His muscles relaxed at the humorous glint looking back. "Buster is a friend—a good friend. He approves of me, as I hope you will." Gulping back his anxiety, Sam lifted his eyebrows in supplication.

The woman tilted her head, a small smile playing on her ample lips. "Very well." She stepped aside to admit him. "Why don't you come in then, Sam Tully?"

A tiny house lay beyond its guardian—only a kitchen with a connected living area and two doors Sam assumed led to bedrooms. The chatter of two female voices coasted through one of them, while Dorothy sat at the kitchen table playing checkers with an older blond man. His presence interrupted their game, revolving both heads up and igniting elation in the little girl's freckled face.

"Sam!" she burst, jetting up from the table and rushing over to embrace him. "I knew you'd come back. We had so much fun at the fair. Did you bring Lizzy with you?"

Sam patted her head as her arms wrapped tightly around his waist. "Not this time, Dorothy. This time is just for Elsie and I."

The child let him go and stepped back, her face slumping only a little. "Okay. But next time bring her, okay? I want to teach her cat's cradle with the new strings I braided."

"There's no promise there will be a next time," Elsie's mother said before Sam could answer. He turned to see her sashaying past him toward the kitchen counter, her features shrewd. "How old are you anyway, Sam?"

His fingers nervously clutched the bouquet of wildflowers at his chest. "Twenty-one, ma'am. I'll be twenty-two in September."

The man at the table leaned back in his squeaky chair. "Leave him alone, Lillian." He thrust out a hand to Sam. "I'm Harry O'Donnell. I'm Dorothy's father."

Lillian watched the two of them shake hands with venom in her gaze. "Yes, and you are not *Elsie's* father, so you don't have a say in it," she shot at her former husband before swinging back to Sam. "She's only seventeen. I hope you appreciate just how young of a girl she still is, Sam."

Despite his dry mouth, Sam bobbed his head. "I only have the best of intentions, Mrs.—" What did he call her? *Dawson? O'Donnell?* A cold sweat broke on his forehead as her scathing glare appraised him.

"You may call me *Miss* Potter. And you know as well as I that the best of intentions does not always lead to the most upright of actions, now does it?" Her brows rose.

"Momma!"

Sam's body jerked, his neck rotating to find Elsie at her open bedroom door, mouth agape. He sucked in a trembling breath. *Oh Lord, let my actions match my intentions. Let me do right by her.* She robbed him of breath, clad in a muted blue polka dot dress that padded her shoulders and supplied her a sleek silhouette. Her hair, shorter than he'd last seen it, curtained the sides of her face in soft waves beneath an angled hat with a wide brim. She looked like something out of a magazine, and yet as simple and modest as the moment she'd first stolen his heart.

"I'm sorry, Sam, I don't know what's gotten into the members of this family." She cast her mother a reproving glower. "I apologize for our rudeness."

"That's all right." Lillian's remarks forgotten, Sam's attention locked on the elegant woman standing before him, so dissimilar to the naïve little girl her mother had defined. He held out the bouquet to her, attempting to still his unsteady hands.

"Thank you, Sam. They're beautiful." Elsie held the flowers to her nose, inhaling the mingled scents of lilac and poppy in his collection, before handing them off to her eager sister. "Dorothy, do you mind putting these in some water while Sam and I are out so I can enjoy them when I get home?" Dorothy fervently nodded, dashing off to find a vase in the cupboard.

Without a word, Elsie reached for Sam's extended elbow and locked her arm with his. A shy smile dimpled her mouth as he led her toward the door. "We won't be out late, Momma. I promise."

"Not past *ten*," Miss Potter called after them. "You remember that, Sam Tully."

Sam tipped his head to Lillian as Elsie dragged him out the door. He didn't know whether to like her or fear her—a woman so filled with passion, yet clearly in love with her daughter. Once he'd settled his date into her seat and rounded the bed of his truck, he noticed that face at the window inspecting his every step. If she ever discovered Shirley's relationship with Johnny Mills, he doubted Johnny would live until sunset.

A short drive transported them into town, just a silhouette of buildings and a church spire under the hushed gray-blue of dusk. Lamplight cascaded onto Main Street from shop windows arrayed with daily deals and creative displays. The cinema's yellow bulbs flashed in a chasing pattern around its giant sign, the marquee announcing the opening of *Professional Sweetheart*, starring Ginger Rogers. Sam slowed the truck in front of a charming restaurant with a chef statue in the window holding a red, white, and green flag.

"I hope you like Italian," he said as he thrust the shifter into park and silenced the engine. "It's either this or the corner deli."

"I love it." Elsie held out her hand for him to help her down, her enchanted gaze roving the flourished letters painted on the restaurant's front glass.

Inside Marzetti's Italian Bistro, the strung lights and red checkered tablecloths produced the romantic ambience Sam had hoped for. A friendly hostess led them to a table sitting beside a painted wall mural depicting an old stone Tuscan winery and a bountiful vineyard. Only a scattering of patrons sprinkled the restaurant's dining area, sipping the new low-alcohol wine that Roosevelt had approved for sale in March.

Elsie opted for water and ordered spaghetti and meatballs from a short menu of choices. Sam selected the fish, which the maître d' assured them in a pronounced accent consisted of the finest quality fillets. A candle stood between them on the table, the flickering flame kindling a beautiful warmth over Elsie's face, its shadows contouring her gentle features.

"I like your dress," Sam remarked as he unfurled his linen napkin and settled it over his lap.

Elsie self-consciously pressed her hand to the ruffled neckline. "It's Shirley's, actually. Most everything I wear for special occasions is Shirley's. I only have three outfits to my name."

"Why is that?" He reached for his wine glass, filled to the brim like Elsie's with ice water.

"Momma lets us choose something special every year for Christmas from money she's saved all year." Elsie shrugged. "I always ask for drawing pencils or paper. She always asks for fabric. I worked in a seamstress's shop last year, and I always found bits to bring home to her. It's amazing what she can make without even a machine to help her."

A smile pinched one side of Sam's mouth. "The same is true of you and your drawing pencils, I'm sure."

"I don't know about that." Elsie gripped her fork, eyes pinned to her empty plate. "Momma says it's a waste of time, anyway." With a quick sigh, she looked back at him. "I'm sorry about the way she treated you when you came to pick me up. Sometimes she forgets her manners when it comes to the three of us girls."

"She loves you. That much is clear." Sam took a gulp of his water and set the glass back near the candlestick. "It's not every mother who puts so much care into her children."

Her head angled slightly. "And your mother? What is she like?"

Sam inhaled the mouth-watering scent of chicken alfredo and pepperoni pizza arriving at a table near theirs, thinking on the woman who'd raised him. "She's a gem. She works harder than any other person I know. My father has not had the greatest of health, and she's doubled her efforts these past few years to ensure his comfort."

A thoughtful look crossed Elsie's face. "So your parents are still together. I've never met a family like that. Mother has been divorced twice. Maybe more, but she'd never admit it." She tried to cover the hurt with a sunny smile, but Sam saw the pain echoing out through her hazel eyes.

"Elsie, I'm sorry." Her hand tried to dart under the table, but he caught it in his own, his thumb pressing her soft palm. "I don't know what happened to your father, but I'm sorry he's not here anymore."

Elsie gazed down at their hands, her fingers turning to brush his. "Maybe someday I'll tell you the story." Despite the sorrow in her tone, Sam heard hope in her words. *Someday.*

Dinner arrived with fanciful parsley garnishes and a basket of garlic bread to accompany the meal. Elsie immediately reached for her fork, but Sam clasped her hand and bent his head to say grace over their food. She shot him a perplexed frown, but closed her eyes and followed suit as Sam murmured words of thanks to his creator.

After months of canned beans and sandwiches, the flavors of dinner delighted his tongue as if he'd discovered an oasis within miles of desert. The herby taste of sea bass swimming in olive oil, pesto, and garlic erupted in his mouth, parading across his palate in a succulent array. He glanced across the table at Elsie, who daintily tried to twirl her spaghetti and deliver it neatly into her mouth, only to wind up with red sauce seething from the corners. She laughed and covered her lips with her napkin, her bright eyes twinkling over the top of it.

For the first time ever, Sam enjoyed actual conversation with the woman. Over Italian food and a trembling candle flame, she gradually lowered her guard and told him about her life. She had five siblings—not three as he had believed. She had excelled in writing in school, but dropped out to help her mother stay afloat. She loved hot tea, hated mathematics, and always put fresh flowers on the table that she'd grown herself. Above all, she beguiled and fascinated him.

In return, Sam shared the experience of growing up among nine children. "When I was about eleven, we moved from the Tillam-ook area out to Huntington in the eastern part of Oregon," he told her, fingers splayed theatrically. "We rode in a boxcar with our cows on the train, and it was the middle of summer. Us kids weren't supposed to ride with the livestock, so every time the train stopped, Dad would get the four of us into a box to hide before the conductor saw us." He paused, the memory still vivid in his mind. "Finally, the conductor came to our car and said, 'Mr. Tully, you better let those kids out of that box, as it must be sweltering in there.'"

Elsie joined in Sam's chortling, her mouth dimpling prettily. "He knew the whole time?" Her hand covered her lipstick-rimmed mouth, laughter still escaping it. "Your father mustn't have been too skilled at deception."

"Are you kidding?" Sam sat up, his thick eyebrows high. "He's the worst at it. That conductor saw straight through him."

"I'd love to meet a man like that," she said off-handedly, almost as if she hadn't meant to say it.

The chuckling died in Sam's throat, his eyes gazing on her with purpose. "You can if you'd like." He reached out to lace his fingers with hers. A moment passed where the two of them simply looked at one another, their eyes saying so much more than their mouths had yet dared.

A knock on the window beside them jolted Sam from his trance. He turned his gaze to the street, where Walt stood next to a petite girl with dark red hair. "Well, lookie here!" his brother said, jabbing a finger at their entwined hands. In seconds, he had ushered his companion into the restaurant and stood over them.

"How did you get into town without the truck?" Sam asked, unleashing a perturbed frown.

"I have friends other than you," Walt said with a silly grin. "Vi-olet here owns a Cad-ee-lac, don't ya, darlin'?"

Sam extended his hand to the poor girl. "I'm Sam." He gestured toward his date. "This is Elsie." Violet politely bowed her head and shook both their hands before Walt clamped a hand around her waist and congealed her to himself.

"Hey, we're goin' over to the malt shop if you two want to join." His eyebrows wagged mischievously. "They have a mighty fine strawberry shake, if you know what I mean."

Everybody knew what he meant. Davisson's Malt Shop did little to mask the fact that beneath their innocent establishment, an underground club raked in most of their *real* revenue. Sam had accompanied his brother there a couple of times, ashamed to admit he actually liked the atmosphere and the taste of the liquor their government withheld. No way could he take Elsie there after the assurances he'd sworn to her mother.

"Not this time, champ."

"Oh, come on." Walt bent closer and lowered his voice. "The president has practically repealed prohibition anyway. There's no harm in it." He flicked his head toward Elsie. "Looks like your girl wants to go. Why don't you show her a little fun?"

No harm in it. Over the past few years, Sam had put a stumbling Walt to bed an increasing number of nights, right after watching him vomit his dinner. Yet as he glanced at Elsie, excitement shone beneath her soft lashes. In a safe world, he might protect her. From the wiles of a perverse generation, he doubted he could.

"Come on, Sam," she said, innocence lacing her sweet voice. "I want to see it."

And so, Sam convinced himself one visit couldn't hurt.

S am's arm protectively wound around Elsie's shoulder as they walked down the lamplit street toward Davisson's Malt Shop. Elsie glanced at him, worry lines crinkling his forehead and his mouth drawn into a frown. Perhaps she shouldn't have suggested they pop into the dance hall for a few moments, but curiosity had seduced her. The friends who'd spoken to her of the underground business depicted a glittering extravaganza of music and light where everyone was happy and life carefree.

The malt shop sat in empty silence when Walt swung the double doors open across a pink checkered floor. A teenage boy in a paper hat stood behind the counter. Walt made a knowing gesture with his head toward the doors in the back, and the counter attendant nodded approval. Elsie decided the establishment must know Walt Tully quite well.

A short flight of stairs landed them in a small space with only a restroom sign and a door to a bathroom stall beyond. Confused, Elsie spun to Walt, who now faced a blank wall, his fingers running along the corner until they locked on some sort of handle and yanked it back. She watched with amazement as a panel receded into the rest of the wall, leaving another thin panel beneath it.

With an impish grin, Walt hammered three slow knocks on the panel before an opening slid back with a pair of scrutinizing eyes behind it. "What did you come for?" a voice behind the panel demanded.

"I came for a Sunday treat," Walt answered, already rubbing his hands together. This time the wall piece retreated with the other, revealing a room beyond.

Elsie followed the others inside, amazed at the secret world waiting beyond the sliding door. A bar with two attendants fringed the back wall, with mirror paneling behind it and a row of occupied stools perched in front. Beneath a haze of smoke and glowing chandeliers, round tables littered the small space between. To the left, a band consisting of drums, piano, saxophone and a bass fiddle charmed patrons with a sultry jazz medley, a singer crooning beneath a spotlight. Mesmerized, Elsie watched her slinky sequined gown sparkle under the lights as the gorgeous singer swayed to and fro, her voice like silk slipping over skin.

A hand to the small of her back propelled Elsie forward, past the crowd of patrons sipping champagne, guzzling beer, or simply enjoying the company of friends. Sam led her to a space at the bar, where he flagged the bartender down with a wave of his hand. "Whiskey sour for me, please." He shot her an inquisitive, if not altogether regretful, look.

"Nothing for me, thank you," she said.

While the bartender turned to retrieve the order, Sam leaned his elbow against the wooden bar. "You drag me all the way into this ungodly place and then you don't even want a drink?" He shook his head. "You do realize the coppers could raid this place any minute and then your mother would never let me see you again."

Elsie scanned the festive throng, taking in the music melding with laughter and clinking glass. "I just wanted to see it once for myself. I've read about speakeasies in magazine stories. I've had friends regale me with their fantastic tales." Her eyes flickered up to his. "I just wanted to stand here, to be part of it if only for a moment."

A smile edged his thin lips. "Sounds like a writer if I ever heard one." The bartender slid Sam a shot glass, and he lifted the orange liquid toward the ceiling. "Well, Elsie Dawson, was it everything you hoped it would be?"

"It's more." Elsie watched him throw back the whiskey in one swig, his eyes squinting shut at the flavor, she guessed. "You know, I never really understood drinking. It's so harmful that the government had to ban it, and yet so fun that people started clandestine clubs just to keep it flowing."

The alcohol's acidic scent burned her nostrils, carrying so many memories. "I can't remember a time when drinking it wasn't illegal. My stepfather drank, and I thought it must be grand indeed if a good man like him would break the law just to have it. I tried it once when he wasn't looking. I just had a sip, but I thought it was the worst thing I ever tried."

Sam chuckled. "It is an acquired taste. And you're right; it isn't the best of habits to make. It probably causes more harm than good."

The bitter memories stung Elsie's throat. If not for alcohol, maybe her mother and Harry might never have divorced. Maybe she'd still have a father. "Then why do you do it?" she asked, fear creeping into her voice.

Sam stared into his empty glass a long moment, twirling it in his fingers. When his gaze settled back on her, Elsie saw restless tension behind it. "It's never been a problem for me, Elsie." He looked down the bar at his brother, already swigging his third beer. "Walt drinks the stuff like a fish until he can't even stand. I tried to keep up with him once and it never touched me, never affected me the way it did him." He shrugged. "So I don't do it often, and I never seem to want more. Some people need it, but not me."

Comforted, Elsie gripped the shot glass in his hand and set it back on the bar. "Come on, they're doing the Lindy Hop." She gestured toward a group convened in front of the bandstand, whirling and skipping to the band's up-tempo beat. Taking Sam's hand, she towed him up to the gamboling cluster. Thankfully, many nights without a radio to entertain them and a sister up-to-date on all things vogue had taught Elsie a thing or two about dancing.

Sam seemed less sure of himself as he stepped to one side and then the other, letting Elsie perform most of the moves. She swung around him, laughing gaily as Sam strove to keep up, the speed of his feet mounting to match hers. When the last of the song's catchy notes blasted from the saxophone, they both had sweat seeping from their pores, the spotlight's heat simmering into their skin.

Elsie steadied herself against him, his laughter tickling her ear. His strong hand clutched her waist, holding her secure. Elsie pulled back and looked at him, his stalwart chest heaving and upturned mouth gasping for breath. "That was fun." She panted, swiping her sticky curls back from her face.

The hand pinned to her waist constricted, prompting her gaze to entwine with his. His blue eyes glittered beneath the crystal chandeliers, pregnant with adoration. His body shifted closer, his arm hooking her in. Elsie drank in a quick breath as he lowered his head toward hers, the swirl of dancers and the tinkling crystal forgotten. Butterflies danced in her middle as his handsome features fused into the dazzling blur about her, so close his breath showered her skin.

Suddenly another pair of hands jarred her from the beautiful instant. Cold fingers compressed her arms, pinning her against something solid. She looked not into Sam's affectionate face, but wicked eyes glaring back at her, cackling ringing in her ears. *Ralf.* He haunted her, plagued her, and even in this man's gentle arms, she couldn't escape him.

Fighting against him, Elsie broke free and darted backward, colliding with a chair and toppling it. She bent to right it again, ashamed by the probing stares directed from half a dozen people seated near. Sam hesitantly stepped forward, his hand outstretched. "Elsie, what's wrong?" His fingers met her fiery cheekbone. "I'm sorry if I assumed—"

"Nothing's wrong, Sam. It isn't your fault." She recoiled under his touch. His wounded eyes impaled her. "I just need a breath of fresh air is all." Whirling toward the furtive paneled door, Elsie wound between the tables of jovial drinkers, feeling as if running naked before a stadium of spectators. *We're all the same and we all live for similar ends,* Ralf growled in her mind. *If it isn't me, some other man will find you and gladly finish the job.* As she burst through the exit and scampered up the steps, Elsie couldn't help but wonder if Sam would be that man.

Thirteen

"It isn't fair!" Shirley screeched, her voice reverberating through the kitchen and shattering the quiet reading time Elsie had promised Dorothy. "You can't do this to me, Momma. You can't!"

Curled beside her on the bed, Dorothy turned up frightened eyes. "What's happening, Elsie?" she asked, her voice a mere breath in the tiny bedroom.

"I don't know, little one. I'll go and check." Elsie slid their worn copy of *Treasure Island* off her knees into Dorothy's lap and pushed up from the wall they had their backs against. Her feet hit the floor with a quiet thud, her footsteps on the wooden floorboards hardly audible over the ruckus beyond their door.

"Just because *you* never made anything of yourself doesn't mean I shouldn't!" Shirley was shouting as Elsie grasped the door handle and slowly revolved it open. When she poked her head out, she found Momma scrubbing away at the breakfast dishes and Shirley storming around the kitchen on a frantic rampage.

Before she could utter a word, Shirley spotted her and flung both hands into the air. "You won't believe this, Elsie!" She glared at their mother as if she'd just murdered the family dog. "Momma says I can't go back to school in the fall. I'm supposed to throw away my *whole life* just because she wants me around here to keep an eye on."

Calmly, their mother rinsed the sudsy plate in her hand and lined it up with the others in the dish drainer. "Now, you know that's not what I said. We don't have the resources for you to go to school anymore. Elsie had to quit just like you when money was tight."

"Elsie at least got *two years* of high school!" Shirley said, grunting like a rabid wildebeest. "How am I ever supposed to get anywhere in life with nothing more than a ninth-grade education? I'll go for an interview and have to tell them I spent my secondary years doing nothing but *pulling weeds* from the flower beds!"

"I expect you to do a lot more than that," Mother said as she continued brushing the dishes in her basin. "With your good looks, you could marry the richest boy in town if you wanted to. And here you're sitting around worrying about interviews."

"Women are becoming doctors and lawyers and all sorts of things they couldn't before." Shirley paced to the window, setting her fists on her thin hips. With a stomp of her foot, she spun abruptly around. "You tell her, Elsie. Talk some sense into her, please."

Elsie opened her mouth just as Lillian shot her a harsh look of warning. "It won't be so bad, Shirley. You can take some correspondence courses as I've done. There are still plenty of opportunities left if you don't finish high school." Her unwanted response only produced an irritated huff from her sister, whom Elsie knew was more angered by the thought of leaving behind her schoolmates than the piles of homework her teachers assigned.

Sinking into a chair, a defeated Shirley planted her elbows on the table, cradling her face in outstretched fingers. "Momma, I thought you were going to get a job."

"It's not as easy as it sounds, Shirley." Their mother finished her last dish and dried her hands on the floral towel hanging beneath the counter. "Elsie has been trying for months, and she's only found an opening here or there, usually for a day or two. It turns out it's even harder for a woman my age, especially since I have no experience in the workforce."

Shirley's lovely features softened, though her fists still dropped to the kitchen table with a thump. "If you can't find a job, how do you expect us to find one? You've said yourself it's next to impossible."

Lillian's nimble fingers untied her apron at the back and lifted it over her head. "You sew better than most of the design shops, Shirley." Shaking out her apron, she folded it and stowed it in a drawer. "You're going to work from home doing commissions. I cut out the ad in the paper." She pinned her stare on Elsie, a keen promise that neither daughter would escape her duty. "Elsie, you're going to grow most of our food and breed our chickens until we have more eggs and meat than we know how to handle. The market will buy quality produce and poultry from us; I've already spoken to them."

"So you'll have your own little sweatshop." Shirley glared arrows of fire at their mother. "Next we know, you'll have Dorothy selling firewood from her red wagon."

"Shirley, dear, dispense with the drama, if you please." Momma paused at the mirror suspended between the bedrooms and fluffed her hair, replacing two of the pins. "Dorothy still has much to learn from school at her age. Consider it a compliment that I deem you studied enough to be done with it."

Though she kept her mouth pinned tight, Shirley didn't attempt to conceal the eye roll she sent Elsie's way. In truth, her sudden shade of rebellious behavior worried Elsie. Had the newly acquired beau their brother fretted over day and night already influenced Shirley so strongly? Elsie couldn't recall an occasion she'd given Momma so much lip over something she simply didn't want to happen.

"I'm going into town to inquire after an opening at the salon I spied in the paper," Lillian said, crossing the room to retrieve her purse. "Shirley, I want you to help your sister with the chores today." She pulled on her gloves and secured them tight around each finger. "Elsie, no running off to see that boy. You have the weekends to visit with him all you like."

With their disastrous date in mind, Elsie gloomily shook her head. "You don't have to worry about him anymore, Momma." She suppressed the stinging tears behind her eyes. After she'd humiliated him by running out of the club, Elsie had kept on sprinting up the street, even when she heard his voice calling her back. Any man in his right mind would forget about her after such an insulting performance.

If a glint of compassion sparked Lillian's eye, she rapidly crushed it. "I'm not sure whether I should feel sorry for you or glad for your safety." She slung her purse over her shoulder and reached for the door handle. "At any rate, at least you'll be home more to mind your duties."

Elsie gulped back her reaction to Momma's callous words, watching her pull the door open and flood the kitchen in streaming light. A yearning low within her had thought perhaps he'd change her world, had hoped he'd be that special man to walk beside her forever, but her own foolishness had demolished the prospect before it had even taken shape. The men of her past would haunt her, she feared, into eternal isolation.

"What's this?" Momma's question ripped Elsie from her musings, directing her attention to a parcel on the front porch. After bending to lift it, Lillian straightened and skimmed the label. "Elsie, this is for you."

Heart thumping, Elsie accepted the large package from Momma's outstretched arm and set it on the kitchen table. She didn't recognize the bold writing atop the butcher paper. With two pairs of curious eyes examining her every move, Elsie tore into the package and found an envelope inside with her name on it. Beneath the flap rested a card with yellow canaries and violets adorning the front, the note within blasting a thrill straight through her: "Elsie, to bring your dreams into focus. Sam." From inside the cardboard box, she pulled a basic set of paints and a clean white canvas.

"Jeepers," Mother breathed from beyond the open front door.

"Isn't that just my luck," Shirley said. "I will be stuck here making dresses for the rest of my life and Elsie will go running off with a man who buys her everything she wants."

"She will *not*." Lillian marched back through the doorway and jabbed a finger at the woven canvas in Elsie's hands. "Elsie, what did you do with this man for him to give you such an expensive present? I thought I taught you to have a little respect for yourself."

Dumbstruck, Elsie shook her head as her gaze rambled over the oil paints from the deep blues and reds to sunny yellows. "I danced with him, Momma. We had dinner." Her fingertips brushed the rough knit canvas. "Not every man is the scoundrel you'd imagine." For the first time, she imagined perhaps the idea might be true.

"I don't believe it." Momma's head shook vehemently, her fingers tightening on her purse straps. "That man has an agenda—mark my words. You'll stay away from him if you know what's good for you."

Her mother's statement echoed across Elsie's consciousness long after Lillian had stormed off for her interview, a visible tangle of nerves. Deep down, Elsie subscribed to her every word and always had. As she lovingly carried her new items to the bedroom and tucked them in her dresser beside the brushes Sam had won at the carnival, a glimmer of hope lit inside her. What if Momma was wrong all this time? What if life had only dealt her wicked cards with good ones left to distribute? She shut the drawer and went about her day, sure Sam was one of those good cards.

S am's raggedy truck thumped over the countryside beneath the fading colors of dusk, a backdrop of rough-hewn mountains shielding the sinking rays of sunlight. Beside him in the cab, Elsie propped one elbow on her door and stared out over the blackening expanse of fields bowing to the swirl of pink and yellow sky.

The occasional giggle lifted from the truck bed behind her, prompting Elsie to check on the sister she'd allowed to cuddle into the back with her sweetheart. Shirley now roosted in the crook of his arm, throwing back her head in riotous laughter any time Johnny opened his lips to say something impossibly clever. Elsie felt the skin between her eyebrows crease, wary of the silly girl who'd supplanted her demure, composed sister.

Glancing up at Sam, Elsie couldn't miss the pleasant twitch of his mouth as he steered his truck through the vacant fields along the railroad track. "You worry just as much as your mother, you know." His eyes flickered in good humor before he shifted them back to the rutted pasture beyond.

Elsie turned back around, settling her nervous hands in her lap. "Bus told me I'd better not let a single hair on her head come to harm or he'd wallop me." She resisted the urge to look again when she heard Shirley yelp in excitement.

"Ah, he's a lot of talk." Sam waved off the notion with a flap of his arm. "Plus, if he ever did, he'd have me to answer to."

A sense of belonging sprouted at his words. Elsie attempted to hide the shy smile bubbling on her lips, but still it surfaced against her will. Angling her blushing face away from his line of sight, she stared into the blurry horizon and let the cleansing wind rush over her short curls. Momma had warned her to curb her feelings for him, but still they assaulted her like waves thrashing against a seashore.

A black shroud had descended over the countryside by the time Sam shifted the pickup into park and twisted the key to silence its motor. Johnny leaped from the truck bed and lifted Shirley out as easily as plucking a leaf from a tree branch. Elsie's fingers tingled as

Sam opened her door and helped her down into a cloud of diesel fumes.

"We're going to go for a walk," Johnny promptly announced, claiming Shirley with a snatch of her hand.

"Now, hold on a minute." Elsie trod forward after them. "I told Bus I wouldn't let you out of my sight. He'll kill me if I just let the two of you wander off."

Shirley let out a flippant laugh, her blonde hair shimmering in the newly risen moon. "Honestly, Elsie, we aren't babies. We're just going for a short walk to stretch our legs. Bus never has to know."

Elsie's mouth opened to protest, but the pair had already jogged into the darkness, just a bobbing silhouette among the shadows. She spun to Sam, tossing up her hands. "I don't know how I'm supposed to chaperone them if they refuse to stay put."

Sam moseyed to the bumper and unlatched the tailgate, clanking it into down position. "There's no use trying to keep a couple of wild ponies penned in a chicken coop. If they wander off too far, we'll drive the truck out there and take them home."

A queasy sensation stirred in her middle as her squinted eyes tracked them through the underbrush. "I should never have agreed to this. Shirley promised she'd behave herself, and already she's gone back on her vow." Her head shook woefully. "I see why Bus doesn't trust that Johnny a lick."

"Johnny's young and impetuous." Sam crunched through the dry grass to retrieve a woolen blanket from the cab. "He has a few hard knocks left to take in life before he learns he's not in charge of it."

Despite the thin streams of moonlight showering from above, Elsie had lost sight of her insubordinate sister in the cavernous dark. With a hefty sigh, she turned and pressed her body to the cool surface of the truck, watching as Sam unfurled his blanket and spread it over the truck bed. "Now, you're not planning something indecent, are you Sam?" she asked with a sarcastic half-smile. Anything to detract her mind from the worries coursing through it.

Sam lobbed a grin over his shoulder as he smoothed out the plaid-patterned blanket. "Just a bit of stargazing." He flicked his head toward the onyx sky overhead. "I thought maybe you could teach me more about the constellations." After climbing into the bed, he extended a hand to Elsie and pulled her up beside him.

"If I remember right, it was you doing the teaching." Elsie dusted off her dress as she plopped down beside him and hugged her arms around her bent knees. She vainly attempted one last gander at the shadowed field along the tracks, but still her sister's form eluded her among the silver grass bending in the breeze.

When she twisted back to Sam, she caught him studying her. The skin around his eyes crinkled. "I suspect there's a lot left to learn from each other." He looped his arm around her waist and anchored her to him.

Even as she fought it, the overwhelming sensation of warmth and safety rushed over her like moving waters. She could say anything to him, *do* anything, and still he chose not to judge or belittle her. Life with Momma had trained her long ago to censor the imaginative spirit forever cloaked in her placid shell. But with Sam, the real girl beneath pleaded for her freedom.

The couple looked over the vacant fields in silence, as if suspended within the vast chasm of space with nothing but darkness for miles in every direction. Soon the melody of crickets lit the dewy air, swelling in symphonic harmony. A chorus of coyotes yapped at one another, their child-like barks echoing against the mountains. Elsie basked in the sweep of wind rustling the greasewood and scattering the curls around her face.

She sucked in a breath as Sam drew in his arm and stretched out beside her on the flatbed. *Most men are after one thing,* her mother's ominous voice echoed in her memory. The feel of Ralf's hunting hands through her dress still clutched her in fear. Elsie's body shook as she forced herself to recline on the blanket beside him, her eyes welling with hot tears.

She expected him to reach for her, perhaps try to kiss her again, but instead he sandwiched his arm behind his head and stared up at the stars overhead. "It kind of takes your breath away, doesn't it?" He sighed contentedly.

Her chilly limbs began to thaw as Elsie rolled her gaze to the sparkling sky and took in its radiance. She followed the path of glimmering stars as they painted the night in clusters and brilliant bursts of light. She could see Libra to her right, and beyond that Virgo, and the tail of Leo the lion peeping out from beyond the quivering treetops. "It makes me feel so small."

"Me too." A moment swept by the pair, the breeze mingling the scents of earth and bay leaves. "Sometimes I like to imagine the moment of creation—God hanging each star in place, just where it was supposed to go." He looked at her through the dark, studying the outline of her face under the pale moonlight. "Do you believe in God, Elsie?"

Something tightened in her middle. Maybe he wouldn't like her any longer if he knew the truth. "I had a teacher once who taught us a lot of Bible stories," she said carefully, gaze still pinned to the speckled sky. "Momma says if there is a God, he certainly doesn't care much about us." She choked on the last bitter word. Why should he? According to one woman they'd lived next to in Montana, her family was a group of perfect heathens.

Sam was quiet an uncomfortable strand of seconds, then the back of his hand brushed hers. "What do *you* think, Elsie? What have *you* decided to believe about God?"

What do I think? Elsie blinked back her salty tears, the words resonating through her brain. *You don't want to know what I think, Sam.* The world believed in a savior, a rescuer, a protector from times of trouble. Yet still she looked around and saw only poverty and suffering, Hoovervilles crammed with dirty-faced children hunting for a scrap of bread. Momma was right; if God existed, he certainly didn't see her among his worries. The image in her mind appeared less like the fairytale knight so often described and more like the father who'd vanished on a Tuesday morning and never bothered to step back into her life.

Inhaling the potent air, Elsie let her head flop to the side and stared back at the gentle face beside her. Sam's light eyes, like crystal under the moon, glinted expectantly beneath his abundant lifted brows. His lips pursed into a thoughtful smile as his fingertips grazed the soft skin of her hand. She couldn't disappoint him, not a man reared on the gospel of hope, a man who'd probably never had to consider such hardships.

"I don't know, Sam. I just don't know." Elsie swallowed back the burning sensation rooted in her throat, surprised to find his fingers still tracing the veins of her hand.

"It's okay not to know." Sam's chest lifted in a prolonged breath, his eyes scanning the rustling trees. "I've had times when I didn't know either." He swung his gaze back and grasped her hand, his thumb brushing her knuckles. "Would you be willing to go with me to church one day? I won't push you into it, I just"—the admiration in his gaze deepened—"I'd just like to share it with you, that's all."

She nodded, her cheek stroking the woven blanket. "Of course." For him, she would do anything. Her body would attend, even as her heart waited at home. "I'll go if it's that important to you."

Her breath quickened as those work-roughened fingertips caressed her cheekbone. "You're important to me, Elsie." His shadowed eyes searched hers. In the distance a train whistle blasted, harkening its impending arrival. "I don't ever want you to feel as if you have to run from me. I'll always listen, no matter what's on your mind."

Ashamed, her gaze dropped to the red and blue plaid beneath them. "I wish I could talk about it. I wish I could tell you, but I—" She tried to quell her tears, but they rammed to the surface just to think of reliving those moments of Ralf's angry breath on her skin, of his laugh as he shoved her against the wall.

"You don't have to tell me anything." Sam tucked her wayward hair behind her ear. "But I hope one day you'll trust me enough to stay with me. I'm not going to hurt you, Elsie."

The train advanced now, the shriek of its horn bounding across the canyons. Elsie lifted tearful eyes to the blurred man still stroking away the streams of water tunneling over her skin. "I know you're not. I ran because of me, Sam. Not because of you. Sometimes it's easier to run than to face your fears."

Sam didn't say anything, just let his fingers move across her chilled skin, over her eyelids and turned-up nose. Elsie nestled closer, her trepidation giving way to streams of warmth. If she could only trust him, perhaps all the dreams she'd harbored since her little mind had first sparked to life would find fulfillment. She pictured it now—perfect assurance that someone loved her, needed her, that a good man really could devote his whole being to her happiness. Savoring the incandescent vision, Elsie listened to the chugging gears of the approaching locomotive and pretended for a moment that she already possessed such a gift.

Suddenly a scream tore through her musings. *Shirley.* Elsie shot up behind Sam, scrambling and clawing her way to the tailgate. She hardly felt Sam lift her to the ground as she peered through the darkness at two spotlights charging headlong through the wilderness. Her stomach soured. There, within the locomotive's dazzling light, wrestled two figures—one the lithe form of her sister, fighting to free herself from Johnny's grip.

Aching breath tightening in her chest, Elsie sprinted through the ankle-high dead grass. Sam surged past her, his long limbs jetting him toward the tumult. The sides beneath her ribcage yowled in pain, but still she kept on after him, terror growing as her sister's pleading swelled in her ears. The closer she came, the more details emerged—Shirley standing on the tracks within the steam engine's white glow, bright eyes wet with petrified tears. From behind her, Johnny had his thick arms wrapped around her torso, capturing her there, his laughter flitting through the air.

"Johnny, please!" Shirley begged him. "Johnny, please let me go!" He ignored her, his body charged with excited energy as the locomotive hurtled toward them.

With the train only yards away now, its high-pitched whistle screeched again, ringing in Elsie's head. Her pounding legs throbbed with each stride that would never get her to Shirley in time. She watched with relief as Sam reached the pair and tugged Shirley out of Johnny's grasp and into safety. The locomotive rushed past them, blowing back her tangle of curls and scattering her tears to the wind.

Shirley sobbed as she threw herself into Elsie's arms. Her panic only beginning to thaw, Elsie enfolded her quaking sister in a stiff embrace, stroking back her loose strands of hair. Over Shirley's head, she saw Sam jerk Johnny up by the collar and rattle him with a mighty shake.

"What were you thinking?" His livened face loomed over the teenager's imperturbable expression.

"Relax, would ya?" Johnny ripped free of Sam's hold and dusted off his wrinkled shirt. "I was just having a little fun. I was going to let her go." He began to turn away, but Sam caught him by the shoulder.

"You *will not* pull a stunt like that again, Johnny." His teeth gritted. "You could have killed the poor girl. Look at her!" He stabbed a finger toward Shirley, whose face was still buried in Elsie's sweater.

Johnny swung narrowed eyes to the hand gripping his shoulder. "I wouldn't have *killed* her; we were just playing chicken. And I'll do whatever I please." His challenging stare pierced Sam's, his lips puckering into a smug little simper.

Sam wagged his head, his chest surging. "Not on my watch, you won't." Without warning, he veered his fist back and smashed it into Johnny's left eye. With a wail of surprise, Johnny tumbled backward and crashed to the hard ground below. Stunned, Shirley began weeping anew.

Not bothering to look back, Sam sauntered toward them and put a hand to Elsie's elbow. "Come on, let's get going." With a gentle prod, he turned the girls toward the truck and ushered them onward.

"Wait!" Johnny's holler mounted behind them. "You can't just leave me here. How am I supposed to get home?"

"You walk." Sam shoved the tailgate back into place and helped Elsie and Shirley into the cab before climbing into the driver's seat beside them. Johnny's charging footsteps chased after the truck, but already Sam had slammed the gear into drive and punched his foot to the gas pedal.

Shirley spun around with a sharp intake of breath, pressing her palm to the back window. "But it's dangerous out there. What if he—" She halted at Elsie's firm fingers compressed along her arm.

"No, Shirley, no," she whispered, the fury on Sam's face silencing them both. *Forget him,* she wanted to scream. *Forget him and find someone worthy.* Yet as her sister stared longingly at the fading form nursing his injured eye in the muddled moonlight, something inside told her she never would.

Fourteen

E lsie worked away in her garden until she thought her fingers would bleed. With the summer sun seeping into her tanned skin, she pitched her hoe into the malleable earth, crafting perfect rows in which to drop potato seedlings. She plucked yellow ears of corn from the tall stalks until she had a basketful. Her knees ached as she knelt in the dirt and yanked weeds from among her pepper and squash plants.

Weeks ago, Momma had mandated she expand her efforts in the garden while Shirley put her skills to work sewing dresses. Since then, Elsie's little patch beyond the back door had grown from a few rows of vegetables to a miniature farm stretching to the grassy boundary behind them and wrapping around the sides of the house. Though the work proved difficult and her back often protested at the end of the day, Elsie took pride in her accomplishments. Nothing satisfied more than plunking the extra coins into Momma's hand at the end of the week and knowing she'd made a difference in her family's lives.

Today a grand symphony she'd heard once on a friend's phonograph waltzed through her head, the notes twirling on the breeze and sweetening the summer air. Elsie imagined the vast lands of

Camelot as her hands dug and uprooted, fields of endless green with knights charging over them and queens in brocaded silk watching from high windows in stone walls. A body could still work with a mind at play.

Grunting, she pushed off the ground and dusted the caked dirt from her wrinkled skirts. About an hour back, she'd spied an old Buick sitting in the spot Ralf's car used to inhabit, but it surprised her when she twisted back and found the ragged vehicle still there. Perhaps Momma had company. The neighborhood ladies did stop by to share baked goods or help with the chores from time to time, but Elsie couldn't recall one owning her own Buick.

The sky, so clear and bright all day, had relented to yellow and purpling hues. Dorothy would be home from her weekly trip to Daddy Harry's soon, and Shirley had certainly started home already. A woman about a half-mile down the road had a Singer sewing machine she'd offered use of to Shirley as long as she needed it. Her sister had gladly welcomed the idea of escaping their mother's thumb.

Elsie hoisted her crammed basket of corn onto her hip and collected her spade from the soil. Her rumbling stomach announced the late hour. Momma would already be hard at work over the stove, creatively trying to enhance their slim diet of egg and vegetable-based casseroles. Surely, she could use a hand after Elsie deposited her harvest in the kitchen and rinsed her sullied hands at the water pump.

The back door groaned as she shoved it open with her hip and let the outer screen slam into place behind her. "I think you'll be happy with what I pulled in today, Momma. I—" Elsie froze at the sight of her mother seated at the kitchen table, a man she didn't recognize sipping black coffee across from her. "I picked nearly double the amount as last week," she said quietly, tip-toeing toward the counter as if she'd interrupted a prayer service.

"That's very good, dear." Lillian smiled, though her eyes remained flat as she tracked Elsie across the kitchen. "This is my friend Mr. Phillips." Her hand gestured toward the guest at her table. "He's a builder working on the new courthouse in town." A nervous quality twitched at the corner of her full mouth.

Only affording herself a glance at him, Elsie felt her cheeks redden as she nodded toward the stranger and set her bounty on the kitchen counter with her back to them. *Why* did Mother have a man here so soon after Ralf? Why couldn't she go an entire month without the company of a male? Swiping the back of her hand over her perspiring brow, she worked up the courage to face them, if for no other reason than to count his inferior qualities.

Mr. Phillips had on a clean shirt and tweed vest, though from their looks, they were his only set. His sleeves had obvious patchwork done, and the pocket of his waistcoat appeared nearly threadbare. He was younger than Momma, but not handsome. A prominent hooked nose jutted from between two bird-like eyes, the thin mustache over his lips profuse in some portions and lacking in others. Mother certainly hadn't chosen him for his aesthetic virtues, but judging by his clothes and the car he'd arrived in, money didn't weigh heavily in the decision either.

"How do you do, Mr. Phillips?" Elsie forced.

The man dipped his head. "I do just fine, ma'am," he said with a slight twang. "Your momma and I was just enjoying ourselves a chat over coffee." His beady eyes shifted anxiously, his legs beneath the table audibly wiggling.

Elsie's eyes expanded, volleying an incredulous look at her mother. The man couldn't even manage proper grammar. Whatever an attractive, capable woman like Lillian Potter could see in a man like this outstretched the bounds of even Elsie's wild imagination. Momma's dark eyes narrowed, the clear warning in them to bite her tongue.

"Good to meet you, Mr. Phillips." Elsie set her gaze on Lillian. "Momma, I gather Dorothy and Shirley will be home any time now. Did you want me to put something in the oven, or did you begin something for dinner already?"

"Goodness me, I thought I'd told you." Mother laid one hand over Mr. Phillip's while showering him with a sugary smile. "Dorothy is eating supper with her father, and I sent a basket with Shirley when she left this morning. I left some boiled eggs and cold cuts in the icebox for you. Mr. Phillips and I had hoped for a little alone time this evening."

A cold, hard lump suffocated Elsie from low in her throat. A man they hardly knew came to call and already Momma had written them off like a frivolous concern she couldn't be bothered to entertain? Would the rest of their lives together morph into a parade of Ralfs, of Mr. Phillipses, of men she feared yet learned to tolerate? She looked back at this gentleman "friend" and saw her father, a different man consisting of the same material. Her mother attracted no other kind.

"That's alright, Momma." Elsie shoved off the counter and lifted her chin as she strode toward the bedroom. "I'll just grab a sweater and go for a walk. I've been too cooped up in the garden today anyhow."

Against a cloud-dusted sky melding from purple to gray-blue, Elsie hugged her arms around her torso and trekked down the dirt road winding through barren fields of pampas grass. Her limbs throbbed from the day's labor, but worse raged the tumult inside. Physical pain she would gladly bear. Tending her mother's broken heart, hearing her cry into her pillow night after night yet never breathe a word of it in the day, she couldn't endure again.

Elsie's fingers dove into her pocket and squeezed the paper she'd put there moments before. Withdrawing it, she unfurled the folded advertisement and stared at the bold lettering yet again. The faint glowing light of dusk barely allowed her to distinguish the name she'd fixated on since she'd found it—Andrew Dawson. The father she'd always longed to know, the man whose blood coursed through her pulsating veins. Elsie made up her mind to find him, to discover the reality behind the meager story her mother provided, no matter how much it might hurt.

Daddy Harry lived two miles away in a modest house overlooking the Snake River. Though her first thought had flown to Sam at the railroad camp, Elsie knew he'd ask her questions she didn't feel at ease enough to answer. Bus would no doubt hover close by, demanding to know the truth already written on her face. Perhaps her only true safe haven lay at the door of the one person she knew beyond a doubt wanted to be her parent.

She couldn't miss the alarm in his bright blue eyes when Elsie knocked on his door and found his kind face behind it. "Is everything alright, Elsie? Has something happened?" Harry ushered her in without thought, the gentle glow of his porchlight accentuating the worry lines in his forehead.

His family room invited her in with comforting warmth, even with its plain walls and scant furnishings. "Nothing has happened," she said as he snapped the door back in place. "I just—I just needed someplace to go, if you don't mind my coming here."

"Of course, Elsie." Harry hid his concern with a wave of his hand as he moved past her. "I hope you're hungry. Dorothy and I just sat down to supper. Your mother requested I bring her back later—" He paused at the doorway to the kitchen, his eyebrows working. "I guess she must have company."

Choosing not to answer, Elsie trailed him into the little kitchen and found her sister perched at the table with a napkin tucked into her dress collar. "Elsie, you came!" Dorothy beamed up from her spot by the sink, her smile contagious. "Papa made rabbit stew. It's nice and hot." Grinning, she rubbed her stomach in a circular motion.

"I regret that it isn't much." Harry plunked down in his chair and gestured to the seat beside Dorothy. "I'm not quite the cook your mother is."

Elsie sank into the indicated metal chair. Even Daddy Harry's mysterious rabbit stew smelled like heaven to her empty stomach. "I'm sure it will be wonderful." The fact that he even tried impressed her. Momma often asserted that a man without a woman or a maid ate like a pauper, no matter his standing in life.

The company of her stepfather and little sister so enlivened Elsie that she nearly forgot the problems ever looming. Between gulps of warm stew, Dorothy regaled them with tales of hijinks in school, like getting her lollipop stuck in her hair and having the teacher cut it out, or accidentally giving a boy a black eye when they played foursquare at recess. Elsie giggled until her sides ached, in love with the miniature version of her mother, fueled by pure spunk. The sentiment echoed back in the proud sparkle in Harry's eyes when he looked at her—the only child of his body, the personification of his love for Lillian Potter.

"Do I *have* to go home tonight?" Dorothy whimpered, mischief playing in her dimpled cheeks. "Elsie, why don't you spend the night with me here, and we can go camping in the backyard?" Her back bolted upright with the idea, her hands clenching the table's edge.

"Sorry, little one," Harry answered for her, tugging on Dorothy's ebony braid. "Your mother will be cross with me if I don't bring you two back on time. Besides, don't you want to see Shirley?"

"I guess." The girl sighed, her nose scrunching. "All she ever talks about is that boy at Bus's camp. Shirley and Elsie are both too busy with their beaus to play anymore."

Harry's brows lifted, but he only sent a smirk Elsie's way. "Dorothy, why don't you go on and collect your things?" He flicked his head toward her room. Once the girl had obeyed and happily dashed off, Harry aimed his attention on Elsie. "You have a beau?"

Elsie's cheeks heated. "It isn't anything serious." She studied the remnants of her rabbit stew. "You needn't worry."

"I always worry about my girls." Harry ducked his head until their eyes met. "You tell me if he isn't good to you. I won't stand for it." His clean-shaven mouth boosted in a smile, but the gravity of his words still shone through.

"I will." Courage leaped in Elsie's heart. For once, she wanted to speak of the man who steadily captured her heart, inch by icy inch. "He's a lot like you, actually." Someone had told her once that women chose men like their fathers. Imagining another Andrew Dawson in her life, the concept had terrified Elsie.

Harry drummed his fingers over the steel table, his broad chest heaving in a hefty sigh. "I hope that's a good thing. I'm far from the perfect man." His head cocked, pensive reflection shifting the brows set high on his creased forehead. "What about your mother? How is she dealing with all of this?"

Her mouth opened to answer, but the words jammed in her throat. Elsie looked over the humble kitchen—the stove with a missing burner, the stained sink and mismatched plates piled next to it with nowhere else to go. Mother hadn't dealt with it; she'd run into the arms of man after man until she couldn't feel anymore. Harry had chosen alcohol to drown his senses. Momma had chosen relationship.

"She's fine." Her throat closed, dry and irritated. A smothered sensation overtaking her, Elsie pushed off her chair and shook out her trembling hands. "Dorothy should be ready any minute. I'll just—I'll just wait in the car." With that, she spun on her heel and sprinted toward the front door, hardly hearing Harry's repeated pleas to come back.

Outside, the sultry air clamped around her skin and soaked deep. Leaning against the house's clapboard wall, Elsie breathed in the spicy odor of eucalyptus trees and let her eyes adjust to the pitch-like black. Her feet shifted on the porch floor, the boards creaking in dissent. Somewhere along the river, voices and laughter echoed off the canyon walls. A holler of delight pierced the air before a rocket squealed and fireworks exploded across the night sky in blues and whites. Remnant traces of another July Fourth gone by.

She had barely caught her breath before Harry's footsteps pounded through the house, his form appearing outside the door moments later. His head swung in all directions before he saw her standing there by the open door, salty tears peppering her cheeks and rolling to her tongue. Harry let the screen door slip through his fingers, sauntering forward as it knocked against the doorframe.

"What is it you aren't telling me?" The quiet words buzzed in the hot air. He moved into a patch of moonlight that shadowed one side of his face and illumined the other. "Elsie, I want to be here for you. I want to take care of you girls."

She sniffed, trying but failing to quell her tears. "Then why don't you, Harry?" Without meaning to, her voice sounded accusing. "Why are you here, living alone, barely able to care for your own home when the mother of your child is two miles away, having dinner with another man?"

Immediate regret followed her words. Harry stepped back, the pain in his gleaming eyes manifest. "Is it Ralf? Did she take him back?" His chest surged, the fact that he didn't really want to know etched across his weary face.

"No, it isn't Ralf." Elsie swept away her tears with her wrist. "It's someone else—Mr. Phillips this time. And after him it will be someone else, and someone else after him." She shook her head. "There will always be someone waiting in line to take her hand, to *use* her until they've had their fill."

Harry's lips clenched tight, his gaze darting up to the lit window where Dorothy gathered her belongings. "What do you want me to do about it? Your mother is free to see whom she pleases. I lost my say in the matter long ago." His face hardened, but his eyes mourned.

"You are free as well, and yet I see no woman here to cook your meals or clean your untidy kitchen, to hang pictures on your wall." Elsie lifted her quivering chin. "You're waiting for her. You've been waiting since she walked out that door, and you'll continue to wait until she rips your heart to shreds."

Moonlight moved through Harry's slicked hair. He swallowed, his hands digging into his trouser pockets. "I'll not try to deny the fact that I love her. I loved her the first moment I saw her. I'll love her long after they've put me in the ground, I reckon."

Elsie's neck went limp, her head hitting the wall. "Then why don't you fight for her?" She groaned in agony. "Why can't we be a family again? Why can't you be my father?" Her eyes drifted shut, the world whirling around her as if she could disappear and no one would even notice.

"Elsie." Her name rang in her ears and echoed through a mind intent on hiding. "Elsie, look at me." When she raised her head and focused back through the murky light, her stepfather came closer and leaned against the porch column with his arms crossed over his chest. "I will always be your father, as long as you want me to be," he said, a haunted quality to his deep baritone. "But your mother chose to leave me because I hurt her. I hurt her over and over again until she couldn't take it anymore." His head wagged under the moon's rays. "I never want to hurt her like that again."

Sympathy swelled in Elsie's chest. "I haven't seen you pick up a bottle in a long time." Her face brightened as she pushed off the wall. "You could show Momma that you've changed, that you're clean again. I know she would take you back."

His solemn gaze told her she only had pieces of a grand puzzle far larger than herself. "You see me on a weekly basis, Elsie. You don't know what goes on inside these walls when I'm missing her, or when I have a rough day at work." Sorrow swelled in his lonesome eyes. "Liquor has been a problem for me since I was a little boy delivering papers to the local saloon. The patrons thought it would be funny to get me tipsy. It will follow me wherever I go, no matter how hard I run. Your mother knows this."

Elsie choked back her tears, reality slamming into her like a crane crushing the side of a building. Momma chose to live within the pain of broken liaisons because the one she truly desired had wounded her far beyond the others. As she stepped into Daddy

Harry's Model T behind her chatty sister, Elsie reminded herself that Momma had their best interests at heart, even as the thought of her with that grimy Mr. Phillips made her skin crawl.

When she kissed Daddy Harry goodnight and piloted Dorothy up their front steps, Elsie's stomach churned. That old beat-up Buick still snoozed in their driveway, the kitchen and living space empty when they walked into it. Elsie prodded Dorothy toward their bedroom, talking over the low tones emanating from Mother's closed door. She would read Dorothy a bedtime story and hope it distracted her from wondering why Momma had gone to bed without tucking her in, or whose automobile sat in front of their house.

After one last fretful glance out the window, Elsie readied her sister for bed, combing through her long, thick hair and cleaning her face at the washbowl. Once Dorothy had wriggled into her nightdress and brushed her teeth, Elsie snuggled in beside her and opened their copy of *Little House in the Big Woods*. The wholesome tale of the close-knit family living in the Wisconsin forest had often calmed her. Perhaps it would have a similar effect on Dorothy.

The pages turned, one after the other, adventure unfolding in the waning lamplight. Finally, Dorothy's eyes began to flutter, her mouth stretching into a yawn. Elsie kissed her forehead as she leaned over to flick off the lamp, swathing the room in darkness. She hugged Dorothy against her chest, as if to shield her from the chaos spinning about her little world.

"Elsie?" Dorothy asked, her innocence rending Elsie's heart. "Elsie, where is Shirley?"

"I don't know, little bee." Elsie stroked her cheek. "Don't you worry about that. Just go to sleep and all will be as it should in the morning."

Yet as the hours extended on and Shirley didn't return, Elsie doubted her own promise. She didn't dare close her eyes to sleep until the scuffling sounds in the adjoining bedroom ceased and

Mr. Phillips's Buick roared to life, its headlights beaming through their curtains. With one problem gone and the other wandering around somewhere in the night, Elsie clung to the one member of her family she still felt she had a chance of protecting.

Fifteen

Sam sat on the bluffs of the Snake River with his knees bent and his arms lying flat over them. Across the river, a smattering of brown grass curved in the gentle breeze of twilight. His gaze swooped down the jagged canyon walls to the green water winding beneath a dying sun. Watching the foaming ripples, he thought of the path it carved from its trickling beginnings in Wyoming to the treacherous rapids of Hells Canyon until it emptied into the Columbia Gorge. What a journey, and yet the ever-flowing currents still managed to pacify whomever might listen to their music.

Squinting, he glanced up at Elsie brushing away at her canvas, a curious smile pinching her lips as if she had a secret she wouldn't tell him. "Quit turning around or I'll never finish," she said playfully.

With a soft chuckle, he revolved back and threw a dry strand of grass into the chasm below. "How much has the back of my head managed to change over the last hour?" The blood in his veins urged him to jump up and talk to her, no matter what she said.

From behind her easel, Elsie produced a feigned moan of exasperation. "I'm not very practiced yet. I'm just trying to get it *right.*" Her paintbrush thumped into her oil can again, scraping the edge before the bristles dipped into fresh paint and swept over the canvas.

"I'm sure it will be just beautiful, darlin'." When she said nothing, Sam imagined her rosy cheeks and knew his words affected her. They always did, her twinkling hazel eyes and shy smile setting his heart aflutter beneath his breastbone. She didn't have to utter a sound; her reactions always stirred a happy warmth through him.

"So you've been practicing?" he asked, careful to keep his gaze on the meandering river, now catering to several swimmers on the south shore.

"A little, when I have the time and Momma's not around to catch me." The orange bands of sunset deepened as her paintbrush whirled. "I've tried out a few objects on paper since I only have one canvas. One day I tried a tree. Another I painted an apple, but it looked more like a plum. Dorothy thought it was a cow's rear end with the stem for a tail." She let out an airy laugh.

Sam chuckled with her, visualizing Elsie's little sister angling her head sideways with dark eyebrows tapered in confusion. Sort of the way she did when he'd tried to teach her how to launch a marble in a game of jacks. The three daughters of Lillian Potter each had a unique and captivating personality, and yet he deduced she'd happily lock them away to hide them from whatever pain had plagued her own life.

"What about your writing?" he asked. She'd let him read a poem or two, but mostly she'd kept her thoughts locked away in that notebook. "You haven't stopped writing, have you?"

"Oh no." Elsie's shoes crunched the grass as she moved from one color to the next. "But I only seem to have the right fuel to write when I'm sad, and I can only do my art when I'm happy."

Sam couldn't resist spinning back with a clever smirk at her comment. "Does that mean I make you happy, Elsie Dawson?" The light in her eyes answered for her, though her lips simply pursed. "That's all right, you admit it when you're ready." He forced his shoulders to twist back toward the river. He wanted to shout his affection from the rooftops, but whatever unseen force kept her distant had taught him long ago that patience shaped his wisest course.

"It means I'm terribly fond of the back of your head." A gust of wind whooshed over the canyon and flapped Sam's pants against his calves. He watched the dirt lift and spin away with the draft, his mind pondering her jest. Elsie liked him more than she let on; he knew that much. Maybe someday she'd find more of him to compliment.

The minutes ticked on until Sam had endured his share of waiting. His mother had always praised his patient nature, especially compared to the hasty antics of his brother Walt. Yet amongst day after laborious day of sweating under the summer sun to earn a dollar or two, Sam had craved time with the girl whose face occupied his every working hour. Staring into a canyon for hours on end just wouldn't do.

"All right, that's all the time my head was paid for." He hopped up from the ground and shook the dirt from his trousers.

"Ah Sam, now you've ruined it!" Her willowy shoulders collapsed in disenchantment. "I really had almost finished, and you threw off the entire thing."

Sam shrunk the distance between them with a few easy strides. "Even Michelangelo didn't take this long with the Sistine Chapel. Now let's see this mighty work of art before I throw myself off this cliff from sheer boredom." He tried to peer around the edge of her painting to see the results, but Elsie snatched it out of view before he had a chance.

"Sam, no. It isn't finished yet." Elsie held the picture with care at its edges. "If you let me complete it, then I promise I'll let you see." She held out a finger when he only moved closer. "It's no good now. You'll only laugh at me."

He cocked his head. "Darlin', I would never laugh at you." A squirrelly smile engulfed his lips. "You better show me that picture or I won't have any choice." His outstretched fingers wriggled in midair like spider legs in frantic motion.

Elsie shielded herself with the canvas. "Oh, Sam, you wouldn't." Her eyebrows drew down in a scowl, even as a giggle bubbled from her throat.

Sam had discovered weeks ago that even the thought of being tickled drove her to fits of laughter. He advanced on her, reaching around the wooden frame to poke at her vulnerable side. Elsie let out a piercing yelp, throwing the canvas to one side and leaving her other side defenseless for Sam to swoop in and launch an attack up her ribcage. With another scream, Elsie leaped into the air and tried to squirm free once she'd landed.

"Sam, stop it. Stop it!" She dodged the hand aimed at her middle. "Sam, you're going to get paint all over me." She spurted her words between gasps for breath, a delighted pink hue emanating from her skin.

"Not until I see that picture." He lunged around her. Swinging one arm around her waist, he seized the painting with the other, holding tight as she happily struggled within his grasp. Her hands vainly swiped at the air, her creation out of reach. Sam's eyes hurried over the oil landscape, across the thick brown brushstrokes depicting the high cliffs and rich soil, along the river tinted in greens and rippling white, to the sunset splashed across the sky in colors even more brilliant than reality.

"Elsie," he breathed, letting her go. Elsie dabbed paint from her cheek as he continued to drink it in, content to behold himself painted there with one hand hanging over his knee as he gazed out on an unearthly display of God's creation. "Elsie, this is wonderful." He glanced up at her. "This is really the first painting you've ever done?"

She sighed and extended an open palm. "It will be if you let me finish it." Her brows lifted. When Sam surrendered it to her, Elsie whirled it around and hid it, like the very sight of it ashamed her.

"I know I can do better. I wish you hadn't insisted on seeing it the way it is."

Awestruck, Sam stepped toward her, hooking a finger under her chin and propelling it up until her sad eyes looked into his. "Elsie, you really don't know how amazing you are, do you?" The idea both unsettled and astonished him. Had nobody told her? Had nobody bothered to voice the obvious truth to so tender a heart?

Elsie's cheeks bloomed with color as her gaze plunged to the painting in her hands. "You're a kind man, Sam Tully. We should get going. Mother will hang me out to dry if I'm not at home for dinner on time."

With the orange sun descending behind them into the mist, the couple meandered through the fields of high grass until only a warm glow remained of the day's light. Elsie clutched her painting in front, letting her knees bash against the back as she walked. Beside her, Sam toted her folded easel beneath his arm and her small box of paint supplies in his other hand.

"Do you think your mother will want me to stay for supper?" He chuckled, recalling with lucidity the last time he'd knocked on her door and received a lecture about not spending his hard-earned cash on Elsie's frivolous pursuits.

Elsie shot him a sarcastic simper. "Don't press your luck. She's already gone to the work crew supervisor and grilled him with questions about you. It's lucky you're on good terms."

"It isn't luck. It's good sense." Sam disturbed a cluster of dirt in his path and watched the crumbles scatter in every direction. "Now, it's lucky that my boss doesn't pay any attention to our personal lives, or he would have spilled the beans on Shirley and Johnny's little love story."

Elsie lent him a weary expression, concern flashing over her brow. "She didn't come home until one o'clock the other night, and I fell asleep before she showed up last week." Her words tumbled beneath the munching of rocks beneath their boots as they reached a gravel road. "Momma's too distracted to notice and I can't stop her." She sighed deeply.

Understanding, Sam shifted her paint box to his free hand and anchored the other at the small of her back. "Sometimes you just have to let people make their own mistakes. I know you want to protect her, but Shirley is determined to go her own way."

"She's fifteen." Elsie leaned into his embrace, the anxiety evident in her tense frame. "She shouldn't *want* to have her own way; she should want to stay home with me and be a little girl forever."

Silence drifted over them as they ambled down the rocky road, Sam squeezing her tight against him and Elsie roosting her head on his ample shoulder. Dusk had yielded to evening's trance, folding into the yawning darkness until only the occasional passing vehicle illuminated their course in yellow beams of light. "I know you miss your sister," Sam said into her hair, longing to kiss her crumpled forehead and promise away her pain.

"Momma will be furious if she sees this." Elsie held up the painting as they neared the scruffy farmhouse she called home. "There's no good place to hide it that she won't find when she cleans the house."

"Here, give it to me." Sam eased it from her hands, admiring her artistic skill once more in the feeble light. "I have just the place for it. I'll keep it in my truck for the next few days, then I'll take it to Sally's house when Walt and I visit on Sunday."

"Thank you, Sam." She took the easel and paint set from him and glanced once over her shoulder, as if cautious of a snooping mother lurking nearby.

"Elsie, that reminds me." Clutching her hand, Sam regained her attention with a gentle squeeze of her fingers. "We're having a big family dinner at my sister's house this weekend, and I—" He stumbled on the word, unforeseen nerves choking him. "I was wondering if you'd come meet my parents." Fear of rejection stung his surging chest. She'd run away the night they met. She'd dodged the first kiss he attempted to give her. Why shouldn't the prospect of facing the most important people in his life launch her screaming toward the hills?

Yet under the pale moonlight, a dimple emerged in her cheek. "I'd love to, Sam." Her thumb pressed his pulsating palm. Her mouth opened to say more, but instead a gentle smile turned up its corners. "Thank you for a lovely evening." With eyes averted, she lifted onto her tiptoes and planted a swift peck on his cheek.

Sam watched her jog through the misty night air, one hand covering the tingling warmth on his face, heartbeat battering his eardrums. "Elsie, wait!" he hollered, prompting her to spin back with a quizzical expression. The beauty of her slender form, silhouetted in white moonlight, stunned the very breath from his chest. "Thank you for a beautiful life. That's what you've given me, Elsie Dawson."

She waved him off with a laugh, her face radiant. "Oh Sam, you're such a clown!"

But long after she'd raced off through the shadows and climbed the steps to her house, Sam stood like a bronze cast in the stillness, simply amazed. "Thank you, God," he whispered to the star-speckled horizon. He loved her, and still he hadn't found the proper words or time to say it. Sam paced the short distance to his truck and climbed inside, sure no matter what the future held, he could face it as long as the girl with the charcoal pencils never left his side.

The sweet aroma of baked beans greeted Elsie as she scampered up her front steps and twisted the door knob. Inside, the chatter of voices lit the air before she saw three female faces in varying moods scattered around the kitchen. Dorothy sat at the table, blissfully reading from her speller with legs kicking. Above her, Shirley chopped cucumber at the countertop, her beautiful mouth drawn into a scowl and blade hacking away like an angry ax.

Momma had her back turned, and Elsie thought for a moment she could perhaps slip in unnoticed, but as soon as her shoe scuffed the kitchen floor, all eyes revolved on her.

"I was wondering when you'd grace us with your presence," her mother's sardonic tone scathed. She glowered up from her bent position over the table, where she'd just lain a fork and knife beside Shirley's plate. "I had expected your help with dinner tonight."

Elsie tucked her easel beneath the folds of her dress and concealed her paint box behind her back. "I'm sorry Mother, I just—"

"Yes, I know what you were doing, and I know who you were with." Lillian pivoted her back to Elsie, moving around the table until all the place settings sat in perfect array. "You have dirt and paint all over your face. Go wash up. We're just about ready to eat."

Obeying her mother's command, Elsie slunk into her bedroom and stashed her art supplies in the oak dresser before dousing her hands and face in cold water at the washbowl. No matter the ecstasy in her heart over a pleasant afternoon with Sam, Momma always had a way of cheapening it, of transforming the most valuable moments into nothing but wasted time.

When Elsie emerged from the bedroom with skin clean and hair freshly pinned, she saw Dorothy had stowed her reader on the bookshelf and now waited patiently beside Shirley for supper. An empty chair nested by Momma, who had her hands folded as if she intended for once to pray and one impatient eyebrow raised. "Well, hurry up before it gets cold. I want you girls in bed early so we can start fresh in the morning."

Elsie's chair squeaked as she settled into it and accepted the bowl of raw vegetables Shirley tendered. Dorothy stared languidly into the pot of baked beans, her nose wiggling like a blood hound's. "I'm so tired of beans." She plopped her face dramatically into one hand. "Isn't there just one slice of pot roast left from the last time you made it, Momma?"

"No, we finished that days ago." Seizing Dorothy's plate, Lillian ladled two scoops of pungent beans onto the middle and plunked it back in front of her youngest daughter. "Now, you eat what I give you, young lady, or you'll not eat at all."

With a theatrical huff, Dorothy snatched her fork and speared it into a bean. Holding it up in the flickering light, she studied the juice dripping off for several seconds before driving it into her mouth and scrunching up her little nose. "All the other girls eat pot roast once a week. Abigail says they even have pork and sometimes lamb chops—"

Momma slammed her flattened hand on the table, jangling the utensils she'd arranged so precisely at each place setting. "I don't care what Abigail has. I don't care about the other girls!" Her nostrils billowed, the veins around her eyes swelling beneath her flushed skin. "We have beans, and you will eat beans every night until I say otherwise." She whipped out her napkin and dabbed it over her perspiring brow, mumbling about how they were lucky to have any food at all.

Dorothy looked like a turtle retreating into its shell. The normally boisterous girl returned to her meal in silence, stomaching the cuisine their mother had prepared without another objection. Whenever Elsie risked a glance at her mother, she couldn't help but notice her inflamed eyes and jittery hands. Lillian hardly touched her food, instead gazing nervously out the window, her foot tapping an unsteady rhythm in the quiet kitchen.

Once the uncomfortable supper had concluded and Shirley helped Elsie with the dishes, Momma instructed them to all get to bed and not come out until morning. "We have a long day ahead of us tomorrow with the produce market to sell for," she said as she tidied their living space and fluffed the sofa pillows. "I want you all rested for the work we have in store."

Elsie suspected her true reasoning for wanting them tucked away long before she heard a car pull up and a male voice greeting Mother at the door. *Mr. Phillips.* The very thought of the greasy man in his unkempt clothes fired tremors up her spine. Why Momma would ever harbor the least bit of interest in him baffled her, but far worse raged the fear that he'd move in like Ralf and slowly infiltrate their lives until nothing of the mother she loved remained.

"Good night, precious girl." Elsie placed a loving kiss on Dorothy's forehead before pulling the covers snug around her chin. Never mind the fact that her sister would be thirteen in six months' time. Safeguarding her bed as Dorothy's eyes drifted shut and her lips puckered in sleep, Elsie wished she could remain a little girl forever.

Such hope for Shirley diminished each time she defied Mother to see Johnny, until only a distant glimmer still peeped over the horizon. Elsie slipped into her nightdress and crawled in beside Shirley, surprised to find her already snoozing within a ribbon of moonlight. Her head throbbed as Momma's bedroom furniture groaned. She and Mr. Phillips had hardly exchanged pleasantries before retreating there to do whatever men did with women under the cloak of darkness. Despite Ralf's efforts to steal her innocence, Elsie still didn't fully comprehend what he'd intended that day.

Sleep had long robed her in its warmth when something stirred beside her. Elsie bolted up in bed, flashes of Ralf's attack ricocheting through her mind. Her breath slowed as she discerned her sister's outline in the muddled moonlight streaming through the window.

Shirley straightened a finger over her lips as she leaned forward to slip on her low-heeled shoes. "Shhh, you're going to get me caught." As her eyes adjusted, Elsie recognized the red dress she'd borrowed for the carnival snug around her sister's accentuated curves.

"You're not going out at this time of night!" Elsie exclaimed in a whisper, the words both a command and a question.

"Johnny's time with the railroad will be up in another month or so." Shirley ran a comb through her brassy curls and positioned them in a flattering display around her face. "I want all the time with him I can get, and Mother's working me so hard, I never have a chance in the daytime."

Elsie reached for her wrist and clamped her fingers around it. "You can't go, Shirley. It's the middle of the night. Do you know what can happen to you out there alone?"

"I won't be alone. Johnny's waiting for me outside right now." Shirley yanked her hand free and turned to grab the purse she'd left sitting atop the dresser.

Elsie scrambled to the edge of the bed and threw back their shared quilt. "Shirley, if you go I'll tell Momma."

Only steps from the window, Shirley twisted back on her heel and regarded Elsie with pity. "Oh Elsie, not you too." Her perfect blonde tresses shook. "You won't, Elsie. I know you won't. Bus would tell on me, but you would never." With that, she moved to the window, pried it soundlessly open, and crawled through as if she'd performed the stunt a hundred times before.

Elsie's pulse thrashed as she sat in dazed silence. She glanced across the room at Dorothy, who still slumbered with both hands gathered beneath her cheek. Shirley was fifteen. *Fifteen.* She couldn't possibly understand the consequences that her decisions could make on her future life and happiness. The idea of her little sister winding up in their mother's shoes propelled Elsie off the bed and into the main room. If telling Momma saved Shirley's life, then tell Momma she would.

The kitchen light still sputtered as Elsie crept through the living area and held a fist to Momma's door, poised to knock. The masculine voice inside reminded her Lillian Potter had company—not the type she wanted to acquaint herself with in the dead of night. Lowering her hand, she edged backward, endeavoring to soundlessly tiptoe back to her bedroom. She grimaced as Momma's door swung open. Perhaps the doorway's shadows would conceal her.

A cold lump slid down Elsie's throat and exploded in her chest as a man she didn't recognize sauntered forward, buttoning his shirt and tucking it into his waistband. He looked older than Mr. Phillips, cleaner-shaven and more put-together. As he wandered into the kitchen light, memories of seeing that wizened face flooded her. He was a cowboy, a rancher. Bus had worked for him two summers back, hauling hay and herding cattle. Now he stood beside the family icebox, one hand clutching his billfold and the other wrenching out a few crumpled bills. She observed with horror as he tossed them on the table and tucked his billfold back in his pocket.

Just as he reached for a cigar in his vest pocket, he noticed her standing there with a start. Unashamedly, his penetrating stare hunted her from the bottom of her nightdress sitting mid-calf to the open neckline at her collarbone. "How old are you, girl?" he asked, retrieving a matchbox from his trousers.

"Seven—seventeen." Elsie failed miserably to keep the frightened tremor from her voice.

"Hmm," the rancher grunted, thrusting the cigar between his teeth beneath a trim handlebar mustache and touching the hissing flame to its end. "You let me know when you have a birthday." He dropped the match and snuffed it under the toe of his boot. With one last gander at her figure, he tugged the door open and vanished into the night, leaving only the stench of cigar smoke and a bitter taste on Elsie's tongue.

Propping herself against the closed bedroom door, she drank in a lingering breath and tried to shut off a mind already reeling with the terrible truth of reality. She'd long known they were poor, low in the world's eyes, even destitute during hard times. But immoral, indecent—she'd never thought to place her family, herself, in such a category. Elsie went back to bed that night seeing her mother's true identity for the first time, and hating her for it.

Sixteen

"**Y**ou have nothing to worry about. Everyone will love you."
Yet still Elsie couldn't dismiss the nervous jitters budding in her stomach as she clasped Sam's hand and stepped onto the gravel driveway. She recalled with glaring clarity the reception her beau had received upon meeting her mother and braced herself for repayment.

The stony walkway crunched beneath Elsie's heeled Mary Janes as Sam swung her door shut and led her toward the charming Victorian farmhouse with fresh yellow paint and white bracket framing along its gabled roofs. Ahead of them, Walt had his girl Violet by the hand, pointing out objects of note around the neat, grassy front yard. A chicken coop housed a raucous bunch of hens beyond a flower garden of day lilies and purple amaranth. A rope swing dangled from a sprawling oak, where several pairs of eyes peeped from among the leaves.

Elsie's arms warmed and tingled as Sam's gentle hand propelled the small of her back up a set of steps so much more stable than her own. Walt shoved the front door in, holding back the screen for Violet to pass through. Inhaling what felt like a dose of bravery,

Elsie wove among the vibrant potted plants hanging from the eaves and trailed Violet onto an oak planked floor.

The door groaned shut behind them, closing her in. A quick glance around the modest room and Elsie spied a plush brown sofa with two complimentary chairs directed toward an empty fireplace. Besides a set of green pillows and a worn-looking footrest near the hearth, the only other adornment was a braided rug of oranges and yellows spiraling from the center of the floor to the couch. Her gaze snapped back in surprise to a painted depiction of a man clothed in white linens hanging on the wall, one hand over his heart and the other extended toward the onlooker.

"Be careful," Walt hissed in her ear. "Jesus is watching you."

Elsie tossed a grin back at his smirking face, but inside a strange sensation gnawed at her. A neighbor lady had chided her with a similar reprimand once when she caught Elsie sneaking an extra cookie at a picnic. She recalled the critical stare of her elementary school principal as his whiskered lips informed her that Jesus saw everything—down to the most secret of sins she buried in her heart. Elsie lifted her chin and met the painted eyes pinned back on her. If he wanted to look, then let him look.

"Pop." Elsie had not noticed the aging man hunched over in his rocking chair before the corner windows until Sam's reverent tone breached her thoughts. He brushed her arm as he moved past her, strutting toward his father like a man approaching a holy relic. The gnarled fingers clenching the rocker's handrails tried to push his worn body upward, but Sam halted him with a gentle thrust to his shoulder. "No, Pop. It's only Walt and I. No need to get up." The obvious bond between father and sons stirred Elsie's heart as she watched them embrace him one after the other, the tender bend of their arms around his neck ensuring his crooked legs stayed positioned beneath his rocker.

"I see you brought company," their father said, peering beyond their heads to the women waiting at the braided carpet's edge.

"Pop, this is Violet." Walt took a few steps sideways and claimed the girl with a touch to her elbow. His other hand swept toward Elsie. "And this one over here is Elsie." Dipping her head, she felt her face heat as Herman Tully's sagging eyes twinkled slyly.

"Forgive me, ladies"—five shaking fingers lifted their way—"I would rise to greet you, but my sons believe me broken." Despite the cheerless words, mirth still played in his rumpled smile.

Sam clapped him gently on the back. "Not broken, just too important to bother with getting up every time one of your pack comes in the doorway." His gaze swung to Elsie in a proud sort of way. "Besides, Elsie and Violet aren't the pretentious type to expect a big fuss."

"Your mother will make a fuss either way." Herman set his chair to rocking. "She gets awful tired of having nothing but a bunch of men to keep her company. It's a nice change to add another girl or two to the mix."

The group found Sam's mother bent over a countertop in the kitchen, fleshy arms coated to the elbows in white flour as she kneaded and pounded out a sheet of dough. Elsie retreated to the space beyond the linoleum table, amazed at Mrs. Tully's sheer size and apparent strength. Her mother consisted of bones and gentle curves, a bird-like appetite able to sustain her trim figure. This woman had ample hips and bulges beneath her apron strings, her rotund body jiving to the rhythm of her work.

"Looks like some mighty fine eatin', Momma." Walt let out a low whistle before sneaking in to kiss his mother's cheek.

Olive Tully jumped, dusting the floor around her in flour. "Why Walt!" she said, cheeks aglow. "And Sam. I was so busy making my biscuits that I didn't hear you boys come in." She swiped her arms and doughy fingers with an embroidered towel before giving each son a tight embrace.

On sight of their companions, she tugged on her floral-patterned frock and clicked her tongue. "And here you've brought such lovely girls home with me looking like a dusty vagabond."

She tucked in a nomadic chunk of her graying hair before extending her arm. "I'm Olive, Walt and Sam's momma. I would have fixed myself up, but I just got so darned busy with the cooking." Steel-colored sparkling eyes and a dent in her rounded cheek accompanied her throaty chuckle.

The hardened skin of a woman who doubtlessly worked from sunup to sundown met with Elsie's more supple hand. She endeavored to speak, but heard only the whisper of her name before a bashful sensation silenced her. With shame, she laced her fingers in front of her as Violet politely asked if she could help the jovial woman prepare her meal. *I should have known to ask right away. Momma taught me better than that.*

"Oh no, dear, that's all right." Olive Tully waved off her suggestion with a casual hand. "You enjoy your time here." Returning to the counter, she snatched up her biscuit cutter and went to work slicing out perfect rings of dough. "I really only have these to pop in the oven. The gravy is cooking already." Her elbow jabbed toward a gas stove with a giant pot atop it, a thick yellow sauce bubbling within. "I hope you don't mind biscuits and gravy. It's not a fancy meal, but it feeds the whole lot in times like these."

Maybe they'd endured the meal a hundred times without variation, but Elsie wouldn't have known. As soon as Sally's husband and all the older boys wandered in from work, the old oak table filling the Tully dining room crammed with eager faces and hands, all ready for their mother's home cooking. Elsie scrunched her arms in tight, Violet close on her left side and Sam on her right. Silently she counted fifteen bodies all squirming in mismatched chairs as Herman directed them to join hands.

"Dear Lord"—his steady, serene voice quieted the boys' whispering jests—"thank you for bringing my children together again. Thank you for the provisions of food and a home during these trying times. And thank you for your love, Father. For it is in your sacrifice that we find meaning, and in your care that we find strength. Amen." His voice faltered, prompting Elsie to open her eyes to an aged man with tears brimming his lashes.

A hand jetted out toward the food. "*Bert Tully,*" Olive gently scolded, just as the boy's fingers clamped on a fresh-made biscuit. "You know better than that. Guests go first in this household." Olive's eyebrows perked toward the girls seated across from him, coloring Bert's cheeks a rosy hue.

"Sorry, Momma. Would you like a biscuit, Elsie?" Seizing the porcelain tray, he offered one first to Elsie and then to Violet.

"Thanks, Bert." Elsie shot him a shy smile as her palm captured the soft doughy creation still letting off streams of heat. In her home, Ralf had always enjoyed first claim to dinner, followed by Momma. Once Dorothy and Shirley had portioned out their meals, Elsie took whatever they left behind. Here, she felt like a royal as they transferred the gravy boat to her hands first, followed by a heaping plate of cooked green beans.

"Bill, did you pick up the mail on the way home from your delivery route?" Herman asked above the din of clinking silverware. "I'm expecting a letter from Mr. Hargrove any day now."

Bill smacked his forehead with an open palm. "I'm sorry, Pop. I thought of it this morning on my way to the dairy, and then it slipped my mind this afternoon. I'll pick it up first thing tomorrow."

A roguish grin skittered across Bert's thin lips. "He was too busy dreaming about Miss Melinda Travers." He rolled his bright eyes and twirled his fork in midair.

Jim joined in the fun, chuckling despite a mouthful of food. "I saw her outside the hardware store yesterday looking all fancy," he said amid his chewing. "Had on her best Sunday dress and ribbons in her hair."

"*That's* why you had to make a special trip over there after our route," Bert said, one finger speared on his older brother. "Mr. Travers didn't ask you for a favor. You just wanted to see *her.*"

"Shut up, Bert! It's none of your business." Gaze plummeting to his half-eaten dinner, Bill puffed out his reddened cheeks and started pushing his green beans around with the tines of his fork.

"That's no way to speak to your brother," Olive gently chided, leaving her reprimand at that. Elsie suspected from the look on her plump face that she took greater offense at Bert's teasing and would deal with him later.

Several moments meandered over the group with nothing but the scrape of butter knives on Olive Tully's simple white plates and the occasional slurp from a water glass. From the corner of her eye, Elsie saw Sam's lopsided smile and turned her head enough to catch a wink from him. His giant foot nudged hers, yet she playfully pretended not to notice.

His chair groaning over the awkward silence, Jim plopped his elbows on the table. "I stopped by the Bakers on the way home from school yesterday. They had a whole bunch of tools and equipment sitting out by the barn, so I asked Mr. Baker and he said they were selling it all. Moving to Washington to take up logging."

Olive sighed, her gray eyes roaming the red checkered wallpaper. "It was only a matter of time, what with the slim profits for produce these days." She clucked her tongue, her fork sinking into her biscuit. "Sure is hard seeing folks uprooting their families, though. Sally, you and I should take a trip out there and see if we can help Mrs. Baker with the packing."

"A man does what he must to see his family through," Herman said solemnly, taking in each and every face ringing his table. He exhaled, as if attempting to thrust off the weight of his worries. "What about you girls?" His eyes pinned his two guests. "We've done nothing but talk about ourselves this evening. What is it your fathers do? Would I know of them?"

Elsie shoved a bite of gravy-soaked biscuit into her mouth, thankful when Violet spoke first. "My father works down at the sawmill, as do two of my brothers," she said proudly. She had a father to speak of. She had *family* to speak of. Letting the warm, eggy concoction slide down her tongue, Elsie felt crushed beneath the enormous weight of their stares.

"Elsie's father—" Sam started, endeavoring to rescue her.

"My father is a firefighter," she said with a soft hand to Sam's wrist. "He works in the quarries during the slow times to make ends meet." No need to mention the father of her blood, the truly prosperous one whose business sense apparently far outweighed his familial loyalty.

"Well, I think that's lovely," Olive said, her face full of sunshine. "You must be very proud of him."

"You know, our family has history in the mines as well." Sam's father wiped his napkin over his wrinkled mouth before setting it back in his lap. "We spent two summers in the mines of Delano a few years back. There's plenty of opportunity for a man willing to work. Won't be too long before we're packing up the family and heading back down, soon as I hear from our old friend Mr. Hargrove."

Panic tightened in Elsie's gut. Her hand froze halfway to her water glass, her gaze reeling up to meet Sam's. Regret dwelt there, contrition. He'd known his father planned to move the family a state away and still he hadn't warned her. A solid lump squeezed the breath from her throat as she considered the hole Sam's absence would cut into her life now that she felt as she did for him. His fingers moved over hers beneath the tablecloth's edge to comfort, yet still the sting of that unseen fist pummeling her stomach remained.

A dessert of berry cobbler and fresh cream stitched the family together until the children scattered to play beneath the moonlight and Olive took up a mound of dirty dishes. With a wave of her practiced hand, she shooed off Elsie and Violet, allowing only Sally to scrub beside her at the wash basin. Guests should be just that, she said. And so, Walt took Violet by the hand and walked off into the darkness, and Sam told her with a whisper and a squeeze of her arm that he wished to speak with his father alone for just a few minutes.

Body still jarred from Herman's unpredicted news, Elsie moseyed down the porch steps and through the grass, her skin tingling in the balmy evening air. Around the side of the old farmhouse and past a pen of cackling chickens, she spotted a wooden swing suspended from an oak with branches stretching toward a starless periwinkle sky. Her fingers clamped around the bristly braided ropes, holding them still a moment before she plunked onto the seat board and pumped her legs until the wind whistled past her ears and blew away her curly strands of hair.

Far down a jagged hill, Sam's younger brothers and sister Lizzy frolicked in a tiny pond shimmering below white rays of moonlight. Lizzy splashed and giggled, trailing her brothers' lead as they stooped low in the water, snatching up bullfrogs whenever they dared leap beneath the water's murky surface. The breeze carried traces of their laughter up the incline, mingled with earth and reedy pampas grass. Elsie's slippers skidded along the ground, slowing her swaying motion until she could twirl and spin in place around the point of her shoe.

This is madness, she reminded herself. And yet she couldn't unsettle the hope building in her chest whenever she considered her growing bond with Sam. He'd leave her like Papa had. He'd inject life and love into her lonely existence and then drop her as all distant memories are discarded. Yet still she couldn't stop her heart from yearning.

The gentle patter of his shoes in the dewy grass reached her ears before Sam stole up behind her and seized the swing's ropes. "They're a bunch of hooligans." He followed her stare over the rocky soil to the cherished siblings launching chunks of muddy slime at one another.

A bit of her icy exterior melted at the hand crushing her shoulder blade. "They're wonderful." Hot tears ballooned beneath her eyelids. "They're all so wonderful."

A good-natured snort sounded above her head. "You might not think so if you spent much more time around them. It wouldn't be long before those mud bombs would be aimed right at your pretty dress."

"Let them come," Elsie said with a smile. Blinking, her gaze slid the length of the swing to his hand before diverting to his face. "I'm serious, Sam. I've never in my life seen such a family, a *real* family that loves one another and would welcome me like one of their own—" Her voice broke, the emotion behind it teaming over. What would they think of her if they knew her father had abandoned her, if they knew what her mother did for a living? Perhaps it was all just a beautiful, fleeting dream she had yet to wake from.

Warm fingers hooked beneath her chin, propelling her sullen gaze to his. "You deserve this, Elsie." His glittering eyes hunted hers, pulled her into them. "Whatever your father did, I don't care. However you've been hurt, it wasn't your fault." The chest beneath his buttoned cotton shirt pumped in fervency. "That's all over now. You're here with me, and I want this for you. I want you to feel this every day." His fingertips drove into the hair twisted around her forehead.

"Sam, I—" The promise of it all seemed too thick, like a haze she could barely squint through until reality cleared away the fog.

"I know what my father said upset you." His work-worn thumb brushed her temple. "I didn't mean for you to find out that way. The truth is we're still discussing it. I'm still deciding what to do." His thumb descended her face until his palm cupped her cheek. "I don't want you to worry about losing me. It isn't going to happen, Elsie. I won't let it."

Elsie shook her head, her hand anchoring on his. "I'm not worried, Sam. Not about us." A strand of moonlight illumined his furrowed brow, casting shadows over his shifting jaw. In the hours since his father's declaration, realization had dawned on her fretful spirit. Whether it lasted a moment or the lifetime ahead, the gift of his presence had changed her; it had altered how she would see and treat herself forever.

His fingers curled at her cheekbone. "Elsie, what is it?"

"The truth is I've never understood the way you look at me until I saw the affection in your father's eyes when he looks at you," she said, her timidity plummeting like dead weight from her shoulders. "The truth is you're just as kind and devoted as the man who raised you, and I—" Her voice broke, emotion choking her. "I love you, Sam. Whether you choose to stay or go, I love you still."

The fingers pressed to her skin pulsed. Elsie could hardly hear the children's gleeful play against the smash of her own heart in her ears. For several moments, Sam did nothing but stare into her tear-flecked eyes, amazed joy spreading from the corner of his lopsided smile to the wrinkled edges of his eyes. Something inside told Elsie her heart had discovered belonging, long before his body neared and his lips captured hers in tender meeting. In a sweet Oregonian boy she'd found her home, and Elsie doubted she'd ever care to wander anywhere else again.

Seventeen

E lsie's back ached and her head swam in confusion. Adjusting
her shoulders against the unrelenting wooden pew behind
her, she winced when the entire bench groaned in complaint and
several stares flew to her. Despite her interruption, the reverend
persisted with his homily on the honor of hard work. As if many of
his parishioners could avoid it. When Elsie dared to glance around
her, she saw factory workers rubbing their stinging backs and men
from the steel mill with tar under their fingernails. They no more
needed a sermon than a cut in their wages.

Gaze wandering up the walls' intricate cedar paneling to the
stained-glass windows with bursts of sunlight spilling color on the
floors, Elsie wondered if such extravagance wouldn't make better
use torn down and sold off for the community's poor population.
A marble altar adorned the stage, where steps of the same material
rose to meet it in a swirl of cream and black. The octagonal pulpit
from which the minister droned was carved and laced with gilded
trimmings. Even the cleric's robes looked expensive, a pavilion of
velvet drapery from his shoulders to the floor, crimson in color and
pinned at the neck above two golden crosses.

Catching a glimpse of Sam watching out one corner of her eye, Elsie straightened her back and primly folded her hands in her lap. Hadn't she promised him she would at least *try* to sit through one of these antiquated parades? Sam had so much good in him, so much love and compassion for the people in his world. How could any of it come from this place, this den of luxurious boredom, where hard-working people sat for an hour to appease whomever it was who judged and condemned their every action?

The minister's voice soared over the crowd, ringing in Elsie's ears. "We exalt God in our service, dear Christians." He aimed a finger at his audience. "We declare the name of the Lord whenever we take up our daily burdens, when we leave our families behind for the day's toils." Gripping the sides of his pulpit, the pastor lifted up his toes and emphasized his last words with a passion beyond his diminutive body. "Let us then *go forth*, good Christian men and women of God, and be living examples of diligence and obedience to the society in which we live. Let us be the hands and feet of the almighty God we serve!"

With a flourish, the minister landed back on his heels and bent his head. Elsie lifted her hands to clap for his stirring performance, but when all the other attendees remained still, she dropped them back on her legs with a bashful grin. What must Sam think of her, so unwise to the ways of religion, so unpracticed? Surely his mother, seated only a pew behind them, would prefer he spend time with the more respectable ladies perched on the front row clinging to the reverend's every appeal.

When the congregation rose for the final song, Elsie's legs wiggled in strange fatigue. Sam held out the hymnal for her to follow, but she struggled enough with the unfamiliar tune that each word seemed to lift from her tongue an instant too late. "To the work, to the work, let the hungry be fed," she latched on more confidently with the second verse, spellbound by the vivid poetry. "To the fountain of life may the weary be led." The minister's fervent words had landed on hard soil, but the hymnal's rousing message sunk low and planted roots in her. Perhaps she could identify with this church or God himself if he felt this way, instructing his followers to provide sustenance to the poor and fatigued.

Elsie opened her lips to join in the third verse just as something hard bashed into her spine. Whirling, she glimpsed two of Sam's youngest brothers slipping something behind their backs, impish grins on their ruddy faces. "Ollie, what did you do?" she asked the closest one, unable to squelch the smile lifting her own mouth.

With one hand sheltering his laugh, the boy used his other to reveal the model airplane tucked behind him. Unamused, Olive Tully already had one palm out to collect their creative weapons. "Settle down, boys. The service is almost over." But still their legs could not conceal wiggles and kicks, bodies ready to catapult through the summer air.

Elsie began to pivot back with a chuckle just as her eye caught sight of someone she hadn't expected. Over the children's heads, Elsie's gaze latched with his, her breath an unrelenting wall inside, refusing to move. He had on a nicer shirt than last she'd seem him, neatly pressed and buttoned at the wrists. His weathered hands bore a snow-white rancher's hat with a feather, void of the dirt peppering the one she'd watched him screw on his head as he ambled out her front door. But he was still the same rancher—the same man who'd thrown down three dollars for her mother's services and propositioned her before stepping into the night. He tilted his head to her now, a wink creasing one eye.

Flustered, Elsie unhooked her disbelieving stare, intending to direct it back on the book in Sam's hands. Instead, she noticed another familiar face across the aisle—Mr. Phillips, hair washed and slicked this time, a woman and three children lined up beside him on the bench. Elsie's stomach churned, a sour sensation milling inside and leaching into her stifled chest. She tried to focus on the notes adorning the hymnal's page, but somehow, they whirled and swam in senseless order, her thrashing heart pounding a louder rhythm than the song.

Good Christian men and women of God, the preacher had called them. Soldiers armed for the fight, servants of a loving creator designed to lend a helping hand to those in need. *Lies, all of them.* She'd *seen* just how good and faithful those men were. She'd witnessed them abandon wives and families to take advantage of a single mother who desperately needed money to feed her children. At least Momma knew who she was. At least she had the decency to stay away from places like this. Suddenly the lavish room closed in on her, the exquisite cedar walls trapping her in a sea of hypocrites, of puppets on display for a cheering crowd, never caring what they did in the dark of the closet they crawled back into at night.

After the reverend's benediction, Elsie barely found the power to lift her throbbing feet along the hardwood floor ahead of Sam. Head bent to deflect any looks from either of her mother's customers, she watched the shuffling feet until the cement steps outside brought freedom. Squinting through the brash sunlight, she wondered with a quaking fear just how many more of the cathedral's parishioners Lillian Potter had already entertained.

"Ready to go?" Sam bounced down the steps gaily, just having shaken the minister's hand. He turned Elsie toward the old Chevy truck waiting several car lengths down the sidewalk. "Mother cooked up some fine cuts of turkey for our picnic today, and my stomach wouldn't stop grumbling for anything all through the service." He buffed the flat torso beneath his dress shirt with his palm, already two leaps ahead before he noticed Elsie stood frozen in place.

"Elsie, what is it?" One eyebrow lifted over the grin tickling his thin lips. "Not already getting cold feet about our date today, are you? I warned you those boys would have tricks up their sleeves." His gaze darted to his two still very childish brothers whooping as they bounded down the church steps.

Behind them, that self-assured rancher moseyed through the double doors, pausing to offer the minister a friendly word. Icicles pricked her exposed arms. Elsie managed two steps back and shook her head. "No, Sam." How strongly she wanted to run, to find solace in the comfort of escape. Yet looking at the man she'd declared her love for, she knew her instincts would only rupture the divide he'd worked so hard to mend. "I just need a few moments, is all. The service was long. I need to—stretch my legs."

With that, Elsie spun on her heel and marched down the tree-lined street toward a quieter neighborhood—one free of the judgmental stares and whispered rumors of God's supposed elect.

"Would you like company?" Sam hollered after her, a grasping attempt to rescue her yet again.

Without glancing back, Elsie waved him off and quickened her metrical pace. Fields of barren grass lay not far beyond the churchyard. A field to envelop her tears and her screams, to take the beating she wanted to deliver those greedy men—and indeed *every* good Christian who paraded alongside of them.

S am stood on the sidewalk in front of the old church building with his hands in his trouser pockets, staring after the girl who both baffled and enthralled him. She said she simply needed a walk after a lengthy sermon, yet her legs whisked her off quicker than a jackrabbit bounding through a field. She needed *escape.* From him, from God, he really didn't know. Perhaps she'd never expose that part of herself.

Revolving back to the flood of people spilling out the church's wide doors, he spotted Mother, in her wide-brimmed straw hat decked in yellow daisies, greeting their petite minister. Pop had affixed himself to her with one arm looped in hers, the other navigating his cane. Several of his brothers had already flocked to the grassy churchyard to test out their model planes, with Lizzy hurdling behind to keep up, while Bill shyly sidled up to a group of girls huddled around the illustrious Melinda Travers.

With a sigh, Sam watched Elsie disappear into a grove of trees beyond the picket fence bordering the churchyard. His blood pulsed, urging him to follow. But Elsie needed space; he knew this. Attempting to fix her problems would only distance her from him, and he'd already crumpled too many of her walls to go back to that place. *Elsie will admit me when she's ready*, he had to remind himself yet again.

Mother called for her frolicking children to load into the truck bed before she helped Pop into the cab of their rusted Chevy. With a wave, Sam told her he'd join them at the park in a few minutes. The old family vehicle looked like a circus show as it pulled away from the curb, burdened nearly to the pavement with a herd of shrieking children and spitting diesel-scented clouds of smoke from its tailpipe.

The trees over Sam's head blustered in the waning wind, tossing leaves into the summer air to dance and swirl until they drifted to the concrete below. Sam watched the knee-high field grasses bend and twist, their long stalks silver in the sun's garish rays. His mind's eye conjured pictures of Elsie again, the way he'd seen her that first night, all rosy and bashful between flickers of firelight. He'd taken her home, afraid she'd run scared when faced with the daunting size of his family. And yet, she'd kissed him, told him she loved him, surprised him in every way.

Reliving the moment, a shy smile lifted his lips before Sam stuck his hands in his pockets and looked at the ground. He couldn't deny he loved her too, loved the independent spirit that fueled her, even loved the visible scars that made her real. If only she understood why his faith mattered so much to him. She listened politely whenever he approached the subject. She had sat through an entire service and not complained. But still he couldn't miss the hollow disinterest behind her eyes, the animosity she tried to gloss over with that sweet smile of hers. Something about Jesus revolted her, and Sam had no idea how to introduce her to the person in whom he'd found peace, this person she'd convinced herself would only reproach her.

"Afternoon, son." A husky voice and the sweet smell of pipe tobacco startled Sam from his daydreams. He turned to see a lanky cowboy in his mid-fifties with a white rancher's hat and a profuse mustache sauntering up the sidewalk.

"Afternoon, sir." Sam tipped his head, expecting the man to keep ambling past him toward town.

Instead, he hung his thumbs in the loops on either side of his bronze belt buckle and wedged one booted foot in the grass. "I seen you sittin' in church with that Dawson girl," he said, his Western drawl thick and encumbered with a meaning Sam couldn't quite appreciate.

"Yes, sir." He looked into the cattleman's wizened, searing gaze and tried to translate whatever he meant to say. "She's my—" Would Elsie want him calling her his girl? "She's a good friend."

A low grunt issued from the man's chest as he squinted through the sunshine at the Tully's truck just puttering out of sight. Then, his steel-gray eyes raked over Sam, sizing him up. "You look like a nice boy from a respectable family." He swiveled his head away to launch a wad of spit into the grass. "That ain't the type of girl you want to be associatin' with—mark my words."

A chilly streak of fear stabbed Sam's gut. "What do you mean?" Had his affection for her blinded him to some obvious depravity? The impulse to defend Elsie surged over his muscled arms and tensing fists before he even knew her supposed crime.

"Her momma—" The rancher snorted, an ironic laugh accompanying the slow wag of his head. "Well, every man in town knows her momma, and it ain't for her cookin'." Clicking his tongue, he reached for his waistband and yanked it upward. "In my experience, good apples don't fall from no rottin' tree."

Before Sam could even conjure the words to reply, his short-lived companion had touched the felt brim of his hat and meandered down the sidewalk, leaving Sam at a loss. He'd known Lillian

Potter had a live-in fiancé when he'd first met Elsie, but he'd never expected the accusations laid at her doorstep this day.

Far down the street, Elsie emerged from her cover of trees and into the glowing light. Though she'd donned a sad smile, her form had loosened since she'd fled. The simple blue floral gown she'd worn to the dance hugged her slim body, her skirt ruffling and beating against her legs as she walked. Sam held in a long breath, unsure how to release it. What a picture of innocence she made against the tawdry backdrop just painted for him. How he'd silence his heart long enough to discover the truth, he couldn't begin to conceive.

Eighteen

Night crept over the land in a cascade of moving lights, swirling across the heavens like a mother bird stretching her wings over her beloved children. Roosted atop a fencepost with twisted wires uniting it with another, and then another to the distant horizon, Sam watched the spectacle with one elbow propped on his knee and a blade of grass between his teeth. Perhaps he'd never really appreciated the sky until starting his job at the railroad camp. At home, a surplus of roguish voices distracted him, a flood of concerns always washing these moments away. Here, the moon bursting behind the clouds and fiery stars flickering over the cracked earth had voices of their own.

Sam glanced back at the hazy vision of his coworkers carousing around the fire as their nightly routine demanded. A familiar shout fixed his eyes on the reeling form of a man, whiskey bottle in hand, dancing amid the shadows of the sputtering flames. At least enough sober friends stood close by to assure Walt didn't stumble into the fire. His drinking had not only grown habitual, but snowballed into a dependency that he couldn't shake if he tried. Tomorrow he'd quit it, he'd always announce with a rascally grin. Then the next night saw him lurching about incoherently until fatigue sent him awkwardly sprawled out on his bedroll, only to wake again with the sun and a splitting headache that prompted another vow of self-denial.

With a weary sigh, Sam dug his hand into his jacket pocket and fished around until his fingers closed on a circular object. Pulling it out, he pinched it between his index finger and thumb, watching the way the moon struck the small diamond in a glittering display, multiplying its size in pointed rays. Momma had taken him into Papa's study after dinner and slipped it into his hand, enfolding his knuckles in her work-worn palms. "I know my boy," she'd whispered, pride emanating from her storm-gray eyes. "I know you'll give it to her when you're ready."

Now, with frustration draining his lungs of oxygen, Sam scrunched the treasure in his fist until its prongs bit his skin. Grandmother's ring, the holy vestige that had trickled from one woman to the next since before the Civil War, would grace the hand of the one he loved. Or would it? The silent question drifted from him and soared over the vacant fields until he could hardly make sense of it. Would she ever give herself to him that way? Would she ever trust him to love her the way he wanted? Was she even capable after the unexpected accusations divulged to him about her family?

Pop had made his intentions clear that very same night as his rocker croaked through the family room's stillness. "We're picking up and moving, Sam. The decision is clear. We have nothing left for us here, and Mr. Hargrove has promised us a good place to live with plenty of jobs to sustain us." He'd stopped his rocking, his crooked back inclining forward in urgency. "I'll have money left over from the sale of this house. I can buy you some land, help you start the business you've always wanted."

The haunting words echoed in Sam's ears, drowning out the drone of crickets around him. Of course he wanted to go into business for himself. Every muscle in his body *yearned* for it. And he couldn't abandon his family in a time of need—not the very people who'd loved and sustained him all these years. With sad resignation, he thrust his fist into his pocket and limply let the ring tumble back in place. Neither would she. If he'd learned anything about Elsie these past few months, he knew she'd travel enormous lengths to protect her sisters. She'd never leave them, and he couldn't ask her to.

Sam ignored the crunch of running feet as they pummeled the dry grass behind him. Probably Walt again, racing to ask him to join his drunken camaraderie, only to fall on his face in the process. He'd performed the charade too many times. Yanking the earthy-flavored stalk of wheat from his mouth, Sam tossed it into the yawning darkness and couldn't even see where it landed. He'd planned to hop down and take a walk into the wilderness to clear his head, but a sudden commotion near the fire spiked the hair on his neck.

"Walt. Walt!" A familiar voice demanded. "Is Sam here? Where is he?" Sam twisted around to see Elsie's hazy form in the dying embers, frantically attempting to shake his brother from his stupor. Giving up, she dropped her arms and let her head turn this way and that. "Sam? Sam! Are you here, Sam?" The panic in her voice shot fearful spasms through his body.

"I'm here, Elsie! What is it?" He swung his legs over the barbed fence wires and pushed himself to the ground with a thud of his boots on the hard soil.

She reached him in a matter of seconds, her glowing hair disheveled and her shawl halfway off her back, dragging behind her in the weeds. "Oh, Sam, thank God I found you." Elsie seized his forearms in trembling fingers and endeavored to slow her rapid breath in desperate gasps for air. "Shirley, she—she's still not home yet, and this time Momma found her out. We've been everywhere—the school, Mrs. Pearson's where she sews. Momma even has the neighbors scouring the town for her. I know she's with Johnny, but she told me they were going to the picture house. His car isn't there, Sam. I don't—I don't know where else to—" Her gaze flew around the camp as if it might miraculously clamp onto the missing couple.

"Breathe, Elsie." Sam anchored a strong hand on her silken hair and smoothed it from her forehead. "Just try and relax. We'll find them, I promise." Kissing the soft skin above her eyebrow, he drew her quivering body against his.

Elsie pressed her face into his shoulder, wetting his shirt with her tears. "If Momma finds out who she's with, she'll never let Shirley out of the house again. Bus went to Hagerman for the weekend, but once he gets back he'll kill Johnny, I know it."

Sam's firm hand flattened on her back. "We won't let that happen," he said with the confidence of a man who could read the future, even in the face of his towering uncertainty. "We *will* find them, Elsie."

The headlights of Sam's 1926 Chevy pickup cast two streams of yellow light across the fields as they jostled over rocks and craters, eyes wildly hunting the expansive terrain. Sam went everywhere he could think of—the spot they'd stargazed the night of their double date, the grove of trees where he and Bus had once caught Johnny wooing Elsie's little sister. At every turn, the edge of his gaze caught Elsie's shoulders climb in expectation, then plunge back into despair. She would worry herself ragged.

By the time his headlights touched the rickety farmhouse the Dawsons called home, Elsie was propped against the pickup door with one hand cushioning her face against the glass and eyelids drooping. Sam threw the car into park and hopped down before she had time to fully wake and comprehend it.

"Sam, what are you—" She weakly protested as his arm hooked around her and gently dragged her from the cab. Her eyes sleepily opened to the little house with yellow light pouring from every window. "No, I can't go home until we find her. I promised Momma."

"It does no good to keep on looking for her half asleep." Sam placed a hand beneath her arm and guided her toward the porch steps. "I'll keep searching, Elsie. You just try and get some rest." Fixing both of her hands on the porch railing, he deposited her there and scurried off to his truck before Lillian Potter had the chance to detain him. Watching from the driver's seat, he made sure Elsie had climbed the steps and disappeared inside before he shoved the gear in reverse and rammed the truck toward the main road.

The lonely ride into town flung anxious shivers through Sam's extremities. He gripped the wheel, gaze still flying about as if one second with his guard down would mean his failure to locate the wayward girl. The incandescent glow of street lamps and window displays shone like a beacon as his rumbling pickup neared Main Street and rounded the corner. Despite the late hour, patrons still dotted the sidewalks here and there, rushing to catch the midnight movie showing or staggering to their automobiles after a riotous night on the town. Sam took a quick gander at each and blazed past them, parking his truck in an empty slot in front of the closed market.

The chasing bulbs of the picture house framed a marquee advertising James Cagney in *Footlight Parade*. The freckled teen in the ticket booth advised Sam that he'd seen Shirley come and go with her date hours ago, just as he'd told the handful of other concerned citizens who'd questioned him. Discouraged, Sam walked the street until his feet ached, popping into the few businesses still open and checking the alleyways behind them.

At the edge of town, he spotted a group of young men carousing in an abandoned parking lot, three worn pickup trucks backed together with their tailgates positioned down and big band music streaming from a radio. As Sam approached, he noticed several girls perched under their arms. Unless she'd dyed her hair or utterly disguised herself, Shirley wasn't among them.

"Hey Sam, what's steamin'?" one of them shouted, proudly exhibiting an amber bottle of beer—and not the legal kind, Sam guessed.

Sam casually sidled up to the party, leaning his elbow on the truck bed and surveying the group again. Tommy, the one who'd hailed him, had joined the railroad crew straight out of high school only months ago. A couple others he'd seen around town. All, no doubt, knew the infamous Johnny Mills.

"Hey, Tommy." Sam dropped his gaze to the graveled lot and then back at Tommy, trying to force ease into his demeanor. "You seen Johnny around these parts tonight?"

Tommy's mouth popped open, though he stole a glance at his comrades before answering. "Johnny? No, not since we all met at the cinema." He swung an apprehensive look back on Sam. "Seems like an awful lot of people are out looking for him, though. He's not in trouble, is he?"

Sam made a clicking sound out the side of his mouth. "Not unless the police find him before I do."

"The *police?*" Tommy's eyes exploded. "I didn't know the police was on his trail. What did he do that was so bad? He wasn't jaywalking again, was he?" The teenager slapped his knee with an awkward chuckle, though no one in his party felt the urge to join him.

An easy smile lifted Sam's lips. "Now, Tommy, I think you know the law when it comes to grown men entertaining fifteen-year-old girls." His gaze drifted across the gathering, over the girls of questionable age themselves, their stares now sheepishly pinned to their laps. "We wouldn't want anybody to spend the night in the slammer over a simple misunderstanding."

Tommy visibly swallowed. "Listen, Sam, we don't want no trouble." His worried glance flitted down the darkened street to the malt shop still lit up on the corner. "I heard Johnny say something about going to Davisson's after the show. Maybe he's still there. I don't know nothin' beyond that."

Sam reached up and ruffled Tommy's dark hair. "Good man." He pounded the truck's aluminum side with his palm. "Now, you take these nice ladies home before their mothers start to worry."

Davisson's Malt Shop. The clue couldn't mean anything less than the den of depravity lurking beneath its innocent shell. Sam punched open the establishment's double doors and marched past the sleepy attendant behind the counter without affording him a simple hello. After taking the stairs two at a time, Sam located the secret panel on the wall and knocked three times as he'd watched Walt do.

Contrary to the dozing street corner outside, the blind pig tucked below it thumped to the rhythm of buoyant jazz. Sam ventured into a haze of smoke and drunken hollers, realizing the underground club probably grew wilder as the night evolved. The lone sultry singer who'd last time occupied the spotlight had been replaced by a troop of showgirls in short costumes, swinging their voluptuous legs about for the pleasure of their patrons. Mostly men filled the tables between the stage and the bar, gambling rather than dancing, plastering themselves with liquor rather than bothering with civilized conversation.

Trailing the smoky, vanilla scent of bourbon, Sam wound through the crowded room to the gaslit bar flanking its rear wall. "What can I get ya?" a barkeep yelled above the ruckus while slopping vodka into several shot glasses and sliding them toward waiting customers.

"You know a kid by the name of Johnny Mills?" Sam asked, slipping into a stool left vacant by a man stumbling off toward restroom.

The barman reached a lower shelf to retrieve a tall bottle of gin and another of rum from under the counter. "Sure, everybody knows that creep. Wasn't in here but more than an hour ago."

Alarm seized Sam's tautened muscles. "An hour ago? So he already left?"

"Yeah." The bartender's slick hair glimmered in the chandelier's beams as he bobbed his head. "Saw him running out of here like his tail was on fire. Never seen that kid so worked up before."

Sam's brow furrowed as another patron ordered a rum and coke. He leaned in, watching the barman skillfully mix the desired creation. "What about the girl?" he asked, quieter this time. No need to bring any more shame on Elsie's family.

The bartender shot him a perplexed look as he set the order down and swept the customer's money into his waistcoat. "I didn't see a girl. He ran out of here alone. Didn't even bring any of those baby-faced friends of his with him."

Sam scrunched a fist at his mouth. "Well, if she didn't come here with him, where did she end up?" He envisioned Lillian Potter with fangs exposed, tearing him from limb to limb if he didn't find her.

"Listen mister, I didn't say he doesn't come in here with girls." Sam looked up to find the bartender cleaning glasses with the rag once strewn over his shoulder. "The guy gets around plenty." His head flicked toward a door along the deserted side wall that Sam hadn't noticed before. "We have some back rooms people rent by the hour. Kids like to come here and, you know..." His lips twisted dryly. "Your friend ain't a stranger around here."

Sam's throat dried, his stomach roiling. Just the idea of that weasel wanting to steal that beautiful girl's innocence discharged rage through his pulsing veins. Pushing off the bar, he aimed himself straight at the indicated door before a voice halted him.

"So, you were just going to sit here and let me give you all this prime information and then not even order a drink?" The bartender scoffed. "Some friend you are, pal."

Sam peered back, considering the man's words against his better judgment. "Give me a scotch on the rocks." Not that he needed more encouragement to hunt down and pummel Johnny Mills.

"That's more like it." The barkeep dipped a metal scoop into his ice bin and poured the tawny liquid into the glass. The ice crackled and clinked as the drink landed in Sam's hand, and he sloshed it back without even taking a breath. Slamming it back on the bar, he left his informant with payment plus a hefty tip for his help. If his report didn't lead to Shirley, at least it had properly fueled him for the challenge ahead.

Inside the door the barman had indicated, Sam found a dark hallway with several doors lined up on either side. He tried a handle to find it locked, a perturbed voice behind it shouting, "You mind?" Half the doors were ajar, the rooms beyond them empty. Another open door revealed a group of young people sitting in a circle on a made bed and talking quietly amongst themselves. One door at the far end remained, seemingly closed except for the shaft of muted light escaping it.

Oh Lord, be with me. Unsure what to expect, Sam pressed his palm to the grainy wood and released a slow breath before quietly propelling the door inward. Inside, a lamp flung eerie shadows over the vacant walls and chilled his already restless limbs. Then, just a silhouette in the lamplight, he finally saw her—the crumpled form of Elsie's sister, scrunched in a ball atop a disheveled bedspread.

"Shirley." Sam pushed past the bothersome door. The shadows gave way to details—the rip in her dress sliced to the skin above her knee, her mangled blonde hair sticking to a clotted cut on her mouth, the purple skin dotting her regal cheekbones. Recovering from his shock, Sam eased two hands beneath her and scooped her wilted body from the bloody sheets beneath.

Though hardly awake, the girl recoiled.

"It's only me, Shirley," Sam spoke to the petrified blue eyes straining to appear beneath her drooping lids. "It's only Sam. You're safe now."

Shirley tried to speak, but it only resulted in a throaty cough, her head rolling into his shoulder blade. "Don't—" she finally wheezed. "Don't tell Momma." The whisper was all she could manage before her eyelids slumped again and her body sagged against his.

Heartbroken, Sam carefully led her down the hallway and into the riotous club, his arms barely feeling the weight of her. The laughter and roaring died wherever he ventured to step, the heated games of poker and gin suddenly not so important as revelers beheld the broken and bleeding girl asleep in his embrace. The music quieted; the showgirls adjourned their seductive dance. Sam spotted the barkeep frozen with glass in hand and gave him a nod of thanks, then trekked through the glowing light, the drip of her bloodied face spattering a trail behind him.

He hadn't a care for the leather upholstery of his truck cab—only for Shirley's comfort—as he eased her into it and took off toward her home. Heart battering out of his chest, Sam forced his foot to drive slowly over the rutted road so she wouldn't wake, wouldn't feel it, wouldn't have to face the trauma of whatever had happened after she'd let Johnny Mills coax her into that sleazy backroom. Caught somewhere between rage and mourning, Sam squeezed his fingers around the steering wheel and tried to pray—mainly for Shirley, but also for strength not to murder the man who'd attacked her.

Elsie ran from the house as Sam's pickup approached, now alert and panicked as ever. She gripped the edge of the passenger window before the truck had rolled to a stop, her round eyes fixed on the girl inside. "Oh Sam, what happened?" Her hand flattened over her gaping mouth, her eyes glistening with tears. "Oh God, Shirley!"

Sam focused on the task at hand, tenderly hauling the injured girl from the cab. "I found her at that club in town." He hoisted her into his arms. "Someone said they saw Johnny, but he wasn't there when I arrived." Sam left the truck door ajar, conveying the limp woman to the front porch as Elsie frantically examined her cuts and bruises.

"She looks terrible!" Her fingers brushed Shirley's cheek. "Bus is never going to allow Johnny to live after tonight."

"If he knows what's good for him, the little coward has already skipped town." Sam ascended the porch steps just as the house's screen door swung open and Lillian's stark face rushed out from behind it.

"Jeepers." A crisper fear than he'd ever seen darkened her normally stoic features. "Bring her inside." She motioned, holding back the door. "Bring her into my bed."

Sam obeyed, lugging Shirley through the kitchen and into the tiny living space. On the way, Dorothy popped out of their shared bedroom, rubbing her sleepy eyes with the back of her hand. "Momma, what's wrong?" She caught a glimpse of her battered sister and swiftly awoke, her bare feet walloping the living room floor. "Is that Shirley? Is she dead?"

"Get back into your room," their mother ordered with a jab of her index finger and her iciest of looks. "Dorothy, I mean it. Get back in there and close the door, and *don't* come out until morning."

With Shirley safely tucked into her bed and an ice pack cooling her injured brow, Lillian turned her questions on the only man in sight. "Where did you find her?" she demanded.

Sam glanced at Elsie, who sat at the kitchen table. "At the—at the malt shop, Ma'am."

"At the malt shop." The words dripped off her tongue like rotten sludge. "Perhaps if I were a better woman I wouldn't know what you meant. And I suppose she was with this Johnny fellow nobody has felt the need to inform me of?"

Swallowing, Sam achieved the slightest of nods. "I believe so, yes. An employee saw him run out—"

"And next you'll tell me you had nothing to do with it?" The ebony pools of her eyes lit with fire.

"He didn't!" Elsie said from behind her mother. "I found Sam at the railroad camp and asked for his help. He wouldn't hurt Shirley, Momma."

"He lied, and that is enough for me!" Lillian propped her fists on her reedy hips.

"He never lied to you," Elsie said with head cocked, imploring her. No wonder the girls felt such a need for secrecy. Sam sensed he was doomed no matter what he told her.

"An omission is a lie!" Lillian marched toward Elsie, teeth gritted. "He lied, you lied, Buster lied. You even had my youngest child lying to me about where her sister had gone. And all this could have been avoided if someone had mustered the courage to tell me the truth instead of leaving me in the dark!" Her foot slammed on the linoleum floor, unsettling the chairs positioned around the table.

Fury seethed under Elsie's beautiful skin, but she quelled it beneath her pumping chest. Sam knew her well enough now to read the unspoken words teeming from beneath her abundant lashes. *An omission, Mother? As if you don't have any of those yourself? As if you don't have a revolving door of dangerous men coming in and out of this house? Shirley is only imitating your example.* Yet as her breathing slowed and her jaw relaxed, he witnessed with amazement the restraint she must have practiced with her mother a thousand times by now.

Maybe he could help her, in however small a way. "Ma'am? I know this isn't my place, but I—"

"It most certainly isn't your place, and you're no longer welcome in this house." Lillian's feet hammered to the door until she was posted beside it, pulling it open and showing him his exit route.

"Momma!" Elsie charged to her feet. "Momma, I'm ashamed of you."

Lillian lifted a cool eyebrow. "Believe me, the feeling is mutual."

With one last glance of regret in Elsie's direction, Sam honored her mother's wishes, lifting his feet out the door and into the starry night. Blood still dotted his cotton work shirt. He could still smell the sticky sweat and salty tears caking Shirley's skin. Yet somehow it all evaporated from his memory when Lillian's final words reached his ears.

"I never want to catch you around any of my daughters again. You hear that, Sam Tully? You are *never* to see Elsie again."

The door smashed behind him, jerking his every muscle. Elsie's sobs wrenched at him. But Lillian Potter was right; he had failed her. Shirley could die and he had no one to blame but himself. He'd ignored the wrongdoings transpiring beneath his nose, choosing to believe they'd work themselves out despite his inaction. And so, he sauntered into the black, his conscience weighing as heavily as his shattered heart.

Nineteen

Dreams had often tortured her during difficult times, but never like this. Elsie saw herself on a dusty oak floor, a little girl of only two years. A dry breeze from the open window lifted the lace trim of her best dress, tickling the skin beneath. Her chubby fingers clamped on her only toy, a ragdoll with yellow yarn for hair and eyes made of two black buttons. "Betty," she said with adoration, clutching the cherished doll to her chest. Her dolly's companionship showered her in peace, even amid the shouts and screams emanating off the walls.

Somewhere down the hallway, a door slammed and angry footsteps thrashed the uneven floorboards. Elsie recoiled, her dolly's head smashed safely in the curve of her neck. Moments later, her father's reddened face materialized in the doorway, two cold eyes raking over her miniscule form. With a huff and a sneer of his curled lips, he whirled toward the front door with a large suitcase in one hand and a box of treasured possessions in the other.

"Papa, wait!" she called after him. "Where are you going?"

As if propelled by a waterwheel, he turned mechanically back. "I'm getting as far away from this place as possible," he said, voice like steel. "I'm getting as far away from this house, from your mother, from *you* as I possibly can, and I'm never coming back."

The words stung Elsie's vulnerable little heart. She climbed to her feet, her doll dangling from one hand and dragging on the floor as she approached his colossal form. "But Papa, don't you love us?" Seizing one giant finger in her supple grip, she pressed it until she thought her heart would burst. "Don't you love *me?*"

Andrew Dawson stared down at her with the eyes of a merciless hawk about to devour its prey. "No." The single word cut through her like the sharp point of a spear. "You don't deserve my love and you never will. You don't deserve any man's love. You're nothing but a worthless, spoiled little girl who will grow up and amount to nothing in this world. You'll never matter to anyone."

Elsie woke with a jolt. Through her blurry vision, she found an indentation on her wrist where she'd lain her cheek and fresh tears rolling to her elbow. Sitting up, she flung her gaze over a snoozing Shirley and then at the window, where birds tweeted in the almond tree against a bright blue sky and full sun. She must have fallen asleep while tending to Shirley's wounds.

The muscles in her back protested as Elsie unfolded herself from her chair and meandered toward the washbowl. Lifting Momma's rosebud-painted pitcher, she poured cold water into the bowl and doused her face with it. Of all her recurring dreams, she hated that one the most. She could barely even remember Papa's face, let alone the moment he had stepped out of her life for good. She hoped instead of the harsh words her mind chose to conjure that he'd stooped low and kissed her, told her he'd miss her, left her with a feeling of belonging to someone.

"I hope you're planning on bringing me some of that water," a voice croaked behind her. She spun around to see Shirley groggily opening her eyes, a slight smile edging her lips. "I'm completely parched." She winced as she swept a hand over her bruised brow.

"Shirley." So excited she forgot her sister's request, Elsie hastily dried her hands on her dress and dashed back to her chair. "Oh

Shirley, thank God." Snatching Shirley's flaccid hand, she pressed it to her cheek and basked in the warmth coursing through it.

Chuckling hoarsely, Shirley lifted a perfectly arched brow. "That bad, is it?" She lightly pressed her knuckles to her discolored cheekbone and cringed in pain. "At least he didn't get the good side of my face."

Elsie set Shirley's hand back on the bed, unable to laugh. "So you remember what happened?" She'd hoped perhaps Shirley's unpleasant memories would wash away.

"All too well." Shirley swallowed, the action appearing burdensome. "A whole group of us went to the movies, and then—" She paused, a cautious shame pricking her eyes. "And then we went to this underground club. I'm ashamed to say I've been there lots of times with Johnny. His friends like to pick a backroom and just sit around talking and smoking. They say it's the only quiet place you can find where the coppers won't be on your tail for breaking curfew."

"Then his friends left you behind," Elsie said, almost frightened to discover the answer. The beautiful little girl she saw staring back through Shirley's eyes deserved only love, care, undying protection.

Shirley barely nodded, her skin reddening beneath the stains of purple. "They all decided to leave and I wanted to go too, but Johnny said just a few more minutes. He said all sorts of romantic things to make me stay—how I was the only girl for him, how he'd longed for just a moment alone with me all week." Her gaze plummeted to the pink lace-trimmed bedspread covering her broken frame. "Something didn't feel right to me, but I had this strange urge to please him."

Elsie's heart picked up speed. "Shirley, he didn't—" The vile words died on her tongue, a fresh vision of Ralf's wicked face assaulting her memories.

"No." Shirley couldn't look back, her eyes instead revolving to the window. "We started kissing, and I could tell from the way he moved that he wanted more. I thought for a moment that maybe I wanted it too, but then his hands were everywhere, and I just—" Her voice broke, a lone sob escaping as tears swelled beneath her lashes. "I told him I wasn't ready. I'm only fifteen, and I don't want to be that type of girl, even for him."

Shirley's wet gaze climbed to meet hers as Elsie ironed a reassuring hand over her flaxen hair. "He ignored my words and just kept at it. I tried to move away, but he pinned me to the bed. I screamed at him to stop, but he hit me—over and over again." The tears fell faster, her shoulders jolting with each cry. "He said it was too late. He said I *owed* him after all this time. He tried to rip my dress open, but I fought him with everything I had. He hit me so hard I nearly blacked out. I knew I couldn't fend him off much longer, so I just laid there. I stopped breathing. I pretended he'd killed me."

Heart rending, Elsie's arms instinctively enveloped Shirley's quivering shoulders. "Oh Shirley, I'm so sorry." She pulled her tear-stained face against her chest. The shifting strands of light from the window flickered over Shirley's hair like drops of honey. "I am *so* proud of you for finding a way out. That took great courage."

Sniffing, Shirley swiped her nose with the back of her wrist. "It took me long enough to try," she said between hasty breaths. "I'm so ashamed of the way I acted, the way I treated everyone. You tried to warn me, and I was too distracted by Johnny's good looks and charm to even care." Her head shook. "I should have stuck with Joseph Hatley and at least made Momma happy. He wouldn't have ever tried a thing with me."

Elsie squeezed her, a sardonic chuckle escaping her lips. "Ah, we all have to make mistakes at some point, Shirley. It's part of growing up." With a reassuring smile, she cupped her sister's velvety cheek. "Someday, maybe when you have a few more years behind you, you'll meet a man far beyond Johnny Mills or even Joseph Hatley. You'll meet a man who makes *you* happy, not anyone else."

Shirley's twinkling eyes creased. "A man like Sam Tully? He loves you, Elsie. I can see it. And now that he saved me, Momma can't possibly have any objections to him."

Elsie toyed with the frilly edge of Momma's bedspread and chose not to respond. Better to save that conversation for another day, when Shirley hadn't already riddled herself with guilt. To conceal the hot tears budding beneath her eyelids, Elsie turned toward the laundry basket she'd left beside the bed and returned to the task of folding towels and clothes. At least there she found distraction. At least there she didn't constantly think of *him*.

"I saw him, you know." Shirley leaned her head against the floral-carved headboard. "When Sam came through that door, I thought it was Papa." Her simple statement prompted Elsie's attention quickly back to the sad smile etched on her sister's face. "I see him everywhere, Elsie—in the workers who scythe the wheat fields along the highway, in my teachers at school, even in the butter and egg man. I don't even know what he looks like, and still I see him." Her gaze collided with Elsie's. "For a moment I thought he'd finally come to rescue me."

A sudden ache enveloped Elsie's chest. How could Andrew Dawson have left them behind as easily as the week's refuse? How could he have chosen not to know this beautiful creature, fashioned from his own body? Elsie doubled the washcloth in her hand and held it briefly to her chest. "I'm sorry you had to grow up without a father."

Shirley's head shook. "I grew up with a picture in my head of him, at least. As a little girl, I imagined who he was and pretended to know him. It was probably all too romantic and overblown, but it was mine." She slid one hand up her willowy arm, as if hit by a gust of cold air. "What I wouldn't give to know if there's any truth to my musings, to at least know if he's dead or alive and what took him away from us."

For an instant, Elsie pondered the advertisement she'd tucked beneath her unmentionables in the bureau. She'd thought about telling Shirley a hundred times that she'd found their father, yet somehow the possibility of hurting her always squelched the idea. "Why do you care, Shirley?" She set a neat stack of towels in the wicker basket. "He didn't care to know us."

"No, he didn't." Shirley crossed her arms and sighed. "But we both know Momma had something to do with that, I think." Her gaze darted to the closed door. "At least then I might know a little bit more about myself. Or maybe why in the backroom of that club, I thought I deserved what Johnny did to me."

Sam paused his hammering long enough to straighten his back and wipe his clammy brow with the back of his arm. Pain volleyed from his shoulders to his tailbone. The clash of the anvil meeting railroad spikes still clanged in his pulsating eardrums. He glanced over his shoulder at the sun, just melting into the horizon in a parade of orange and yellow bands. Most of the workers had already begun to gather their tools and mosey their way back to camp. With a hefty sigh, Sam lifted the anvil over his head once again and drove it into the solid spike below.

October. The normally pleasant month, just days from fruition, loomed over his head like a storm cloud threatening to rain over his perfect summer. The nearly finished railroad track stretched beyond his toiling hands, winding among the valleys and through barren fields until it disappeared behind a mountain range that would soon be capped in snow. Soon, no reason would exist to keep him here in the wilderness of Idaho. No reason the world cared about, anyhow.

"The boss only pays you until sundown, you know," came a soft, feminine voice behind him. Sam hid his pleasure behind a furrowed brow and angled back to find Elsie only feet away, garbed in her blue cotton smock with white flowers, a picnic basket suspended from the crook of her arm. "I brought you a hot meal. It was the least I could do to say thank you for saving my sister."

Tearing his gaze from her to the hard earth, Sam trudged over it and dropped his anvil atop his small pile of tools. "I didn't save her. Someone would have been by to help sooner or later." He pulled a rag from his pocket and wiped his hands on it. "She would have survived either way."

Elsie's feet trampled the dry weeds between them. "Yes, but the right type of person? Sam, Shirley could easily have been assaulted in other ways if you hadn't pulled her out of there when you did." She let the horror of the idea swarm the sultry air between them as the crickets sang in place of real conversation.

Sam shut his eyes, attempting to block out the image of Shirley's battered body, just a heap of helpless bones in the muddled lamplight. If someone had harmed her in such a way, he'd never forgive himself. The guilt of knowing he'd played a part, however small, in her attack already seared into his gut until he could barely breathe. And here this beautiful girl wanted to bring him dinner in her gratitude.

"Any word on Johnny?" Elsie asked when Sam said nothing.

With eyes squinting at the fading sunset, Sam rubbed harsh knuckles against his scalp. "Skipped town, just as I thought he would. The coward didn't even pack up his things, just drove right on out."

"He thought he'd killed her. Shirley told me she played dead to make him leave her alone."

Sam exhaled with a wheeze and shook his head. "It figures. Seems Bus had him pegged all along. Here we were, trying to give the boy the benefit of the doubt and Bus could see right through him." His gaze wandered across the retreating bunch of men to Elsie's brother, his withered form barely lifting the tools slung from his shoulder. "Poor man blames himself for not intervening sooner."

"And you don't?"

"It's different, Elsie."

"Is it?"

Sam twisted back and dared to latch eyes with the hazel ones staring back. Elsie cocked her head, the faintest of smiles dimpling the corner of her mouth. "I know you blame yourself, Sam Tully, and I blame myself too. But if anyone deserves the blame, it's Shirley. She knows it. She understands now that she should never have gotten mixed up with the likes of Johnny Mills, and maybe next time she should pay more attention to her family's advice." She wagged her head. "It isn't a burden for you or Bus or anyone else to take on their shoulders."

Sam shoved the rag back in his pocket. "I'm sure your mother feels differently. She practically threw me out of her kitchen, remember?" *And for good reason,* his inner voice reminded him. Hadn't he failed Elsie just as he'd promised Lillian he never would?

"My mother can worry about herself for a change," Elsie said. She stood taller, hands on her narrow hips and chin thrust into the air. "She only behaved in such a *despicable* manner because she blames *herself.* It seems everyone around here wants to take credit for Shirley's mistake."

Smoke from the freshly lit campfires wafted past them, nipping at Sam's nose. "She'll never trust me, Elsie. Every time she looks at me, she'll feel betrayed." The shoulders beneath his work shirt drooped. "How do I have the relationship I want with you when your mother thinks I'm a liar?"

Despite his gloomy words, a sparkle ignited her eyes. "I'm nearly eighteen, Sam." Shifting her picnic basket from one slender arm to the other, she stood regally, appearing more like a grown woman than she ever had. "My mother would disapprove of Clark Gable. She'd say he was too old for me and far too worldly. A man like Nelson Rockefeller? Too materialistic. What about the kind young man who delivers the groceries? Much too poor. He'd never amount to anything." She chuckled, a lilting, angelic sound. "You see, Sam? It's up to me to choose who I want to be with.

My mother will come around eventually—when she sees who you really are."

Sam glanced at his dusty boots, the edges of his mouth lifting as if tugged by strings in spite of his resistance. "I don't suppose you'd want to be with a tall awkward fellow who couldn't string together a proper hello for the girl who brought him dinner?" His thin, apologetic smile beseeched her.

Elsie thought for a moment, her fingertip tapping her chin. "I have just the way you can make it up to me, Sam Tully." Traipsing through the tall grass, she located a clear spot and spread out a thin blanket from inside her basket. "Come on, I'll tell you all about it over some food."

So, Sam Tully sat down to a nocturnal picnic with the *woman* who'd captured his heart, at last making up his worried mind. The family he loved so dearly would have to wait. Lillian Potter would have to placate herself. He would get Bus's permission tonight.

Twenty

"**A**re you sure you want to do this?"

Sam's question hardly brushed Elsie's ears as they pulled up in front of the Larkspur Inn, the Chevy's engine sputtering until he turned the key and it cranked its farewell. One glance out the crusted back window afforded her a view of the road behind them, a swirl of dust against the mountainous landscape. *There's no going back now.* She snatched up her weathered handbag, a castoff of Momma's from years ago. "I have no other choice," she said, eyes transfixed on the structure ahead.

The Larkspur Inn bore no resemblance to the grandiose picture her imagination had fashioned. Where she had expected an imposing establishment with tall pillars and marble steps, a clapboard building with the siding falling off stood in its place. She had envisioned lanterns in the windows and claret drapes, diamond chandeliers casting rainbows into the street, and instead found a peeling signboard and a spittoon by the rusted door. An old dog, filthy and flea-bitten by the looks of him, kept watch on the rickety front porch, his glassy eyes lazily scanning the road.

A painful bulge strangled Elsie's taut throat, but she swallowed it with effort as she stepped out of the truck and tidied her wrinkled dress. All day she and Sam had traveled the seemingly endless roads to get here. All day to think about her father, to wonder what he'd say and to stretch her memories as far as they could, trying to remember one detail of his face. All day to imagine her mother, bitter with rage, disowning her over such a loathsome betrayal.

Elsie's legs felt as if made of rubber as she strode up the dirty path and took the stairs one at a time. At her request, Sam hung back at the truck, body rested on the grill and feet crossed at the ankle. He'd save her from this if he could, but Elsie knew she had to face her father alone. She had a thousand questions, none of which she could voice with an audience nearby.

The inn smelled of cheap rum and pipe tobacco as Elsie stepped through the front door, heartbeat thumping in her eardrums. Clearly, the law was flouted in this place. Elsie glanced around the room and spied several men sipping coffee—or rather, a stronger substance masquerading in coffee cups. They appeared not to notice her as they conversed amongst themselves, some enjoying a game of cards, others listening to the Primo Carnera fight on a radio fixed to the far wall.

Rather than the check-in desk she'd expected, a lengthy bar with a row of stools flanked one side of the room. Above it, a chalkboard advertising an assortment of coffee flavors and simple foods like sandwiches and French fries adorned the wall. The remainder of the room, with planked floorboards and circular tables scattered throughout, had the quality of a 19th century saloon. Elsie guessed it once must have served such purposes, and from the dust motes floating in the air that it hadn't been properly cleaned since.

Timidly, she sidled up to the counter, behind which a man stood staring at the blasting radio, one hand set to wipe down the bar with a rag but never actually accomplishing it. With each bellow of the announcer's imposing voice, the man either cheered or yelped, his free hand mimicking a boxer's jabs. No more than thirty, the barkeep surely wasn't Andrew Dawson, Elsie decided.

"Eh—excuse me," she asked, angling her head toward the man's line of sight. He hollered, stomping his foot in response to the ruckus from Madison Square Garden. Elsie frowned, thwacking her palm on the counter. "Excuse me," she tried again, louder this time.

The barman shoved her a singular glance, one that started at her face and darted quickly downward. "Renée's in the office." His eyes already focused back on the speaker, from which the announcer was singing another blow by Carnera. The man flicked his head toward a closed door at the end of the bar with the word "office" elegantly scrolled in frosted glass.

"I'm looking for Andrew Dawson," she said over the radio's din and the increasingly excited pack of patrons.

Shaking his head, he didn't bother to rip his gaze from the wireless. "He'll pay you, but Renée hires all the girls. You need to see her first."

The girls? Elsie's brow wrinkled, her gaze sprinting around the musty room. The inn contained not a single woman that she could see, its sole employee now jumping around like a chimpanzee as the broadcast declared a knockout and victory for his boxing hero. "Do you think I'm a waitress?" They certainly appeared to need one.

With the match concluded, the barman begrudgingly threw her his attention. "Look, lady. Call yourself whatever you'd like—a waitress, a wench, a *lady of the night.*" He rolled his eyes. "I don't care. Just quit botherin' me, would ya? If you want a job, I already told ya. Renée is in the back."

The words echoed in her ears, the bitter taste of bile collecting on her tongue. "Lady of the night," she barely whispered, reality sinking low in her gut. "You think I'm a prostitute." A raging heat erupted at the base of her throat, steaming up her jaws and into her cheeks.

"If you want to get right down to it." He tossed her a mocking grin before turning back to his work behind the counter.

Nausea spun in Elsie's stomach until she thought she would vomit right there for everyone to see. For the first time, she noticed another doorway beyond the radio, the trace of feminine laughter trickling through its beaded curtain. No wonder no other women graced the establishment. Her father was a hustler, a panderer of women. Her fingers trembled atop the counter's glossy wood. Her instincts shrieked at her to run, as hard and as fast as her legs would carry her away.

"Jerry, did you log the newest shipment in the books?" a second man's voice breached the fog of her thoughts, slowly pulling her out of them. "I want to be sure the ledger adds up this month. No more surprises." Elsie looked up to watch an older man saunter past the barkeep, his blond and gray hair slicked back, a tweed vest and knotted necktie concealing a dense torso.

Elsie's mouth dried as Jerry stood at quick attention and satisfied his boss's every demand. The elder gentleman, so familiar and yet unknown to her, bent low to retrieve a crate of clinking bottles from beneath the counter. When his piercing blue eyes flickered upward, Elsie saw Shirley staring back at her.

A crinkle creased the man's eyebrows, the same look Buster gave her whenever he disapproved of her actions. Amazingly, she saw kindness in those puckered eyes. He had a strong face to match his form and a nose that dragged downward toward a thin yet jovial mouth. "May I help you, miss?"

"I—" The proper response died on her tongue. What could she say to the man who'd created her and then left her behind as if she'd never mattered?

He exhaled thickly, plunking his knuckles on the counter and glancing over his right shoulder. "Jerry, go tend to the kitchen. I'll man the counter for a while." Turning back, he stared at her an excruciating thread of seconds before shame crept across his weathered face. "Are you Elsie or Shirley?"

"Elsie," she said, attempting to mask her pain. "I'm Elsie, sir."

Andrew Dawson wagged his head, wonder sparking his gape. "I never thought I'd see your mother again." His eyes roamed every plane of her face. "Yet here she is, looking out through you." Uncomfortably, he scratched the back of his neck and shook his head. "I'll be darned if you don't look just like her."

Elsie's gaze tumbled downward beneath her lashes, her cheeks glowing. Momma was so beautiful. "Shirley looks just like *you*."

"Poor girl." Andrew chuckled, his face mirthless. "How did you find me, anyway? Did your mother get wind that I'd moved up here?"

"No, I—" She reached into her jacket pocket and produced the folded flier she'd found tacked to the bulletin board in Twin Falls. "I saw the advertisement for kitchen staff when I was looking for jobs."

Concern deepened the lines of his aging face. "Do you need money? I don't have a great deal, but maybe I could scrounge up a dime or two—" His leather-skinned hand reached for the cash drawer, prompting Elsie to stand tall.

"I didn't come here for money." Her voice sounded more grown than she'd expected.

Her father's hand froze on the drawer handle. "Then what did you come here for?"

His question, though gentle, sparked a pinwheel of emotion inside her. Why *had* she come? To satisfy a curiosity that had been burning inside her since childhood? To seek revenge on a mother who wished to deny her happiness? Sinking onto a barstool, Elsie met his hunting gaze with vulnerability. "I don't know." She shrugged. "I guess I thought I'd find out who you are, find out—" Her voice faltered. "Find out why you left."

With a sigh, he lowered himself to his elbows and squared his gaze on her. "Do you think that's why I went away? Because of you?"

"Well, I don't imagine so." She couldn't help studying every inch of him this close—the way his brows tapered downward, the flecks of green in his bright eyes. He must have been so handsome in his day to have caught Momma's fancy. "But I can't help wondering why you never came back."

"Your mother and I—" Andrew shook his head, a slight dimple emerging above his mouth. "We were a whirlwind, honey. We started so young, when everything felt possible. The more we spun, the more out of control we got, until one day we'd destroyed everything in our wake." He looked back on her with regret. "Well, almost everything."

He reached beneath the counter and produced a bottle of liquor. "By the time you came along, all we ever did was fight." After overturning a coffee cup, he emptied a stream of alcohol into it, replaced the cork, and shoved the bottle out of sight again. "Your mother thought I was cruel, which I do hate to admit I can be. And I couldn't stand her need for control."

Elsie leaned in. "So you thought it was better to split the family up? You thought it was better for us never to know our father?"

A moment lingered with only the carousing of the inn's patrons to fill her ears as Andrew stared into his forbidden drink. "I'm loath to concede that I did," he said, a new rasp in his voice. "We tried life apart for a while, but Emma and John were old enough to be confused by it all. They would cry whenever they left your mother's and cry again when I brought them back. They couldn't handle being dragged from house to house, so eventually we decided that no further contact between us would suit everyone best."

"But Momma begged to see them again." Elsie's brows cinched, her fingers splayed on the bar. "I saw her letters. You never answered a one of them."

Sadness pierced his eyes. "She told me before I moved to stand firm, no matter how much she pleaded. She knew she'd miss them more than she could bear. But we made that decision together, and I couldn't go back on it." He reached for her hand. "Not even when it killed me."

Elsie stared down at the veined hand covering hers. Why should she trust a word he said—a cad, a deserter, an immoral opportunist? "Did it really mean all that much to you?" He'd spent a lifetime flouncing along the edges of her life, and now he feigned to care when convenience dictated it?

"Do you think I *wanted* to leave you?" Andrew's eyes widened, challenging her to crumple or dismiss him, she couldn't be certain. "Do you think I wanted to receive news of my baby girl in a letter, of all means?" His head shook vehemently, disturbing the perfect order of his oiled hair. "I questioned our plan more times than I can put a number to. Truth be told, I still do." His elbows plunked on the counter, one palm grinding his furrowed brow.

Despite her resolve to remain icy, a bit of warmth seeped through and began to melt the façade Elsie had spent a lifetime erecting. She felt for the man, had sympathy for a person who'd trampled on her existence since it had begun. Disgusted with herself, she thrust up her chin and glared down her nose at him. "Shirley *still* thinks you're coming to rescue her. You know that? She's the most beautiful girl you've ever seen and she's only attracted to boys who will hurt her."

Eyes still sheltered in his open hands, he gave a slow, mournful shake of his head. "I had hoped with a mother like yours that another man had stepped up to fill that void long ago. A better man than I ever was." Andrew thumped his knuckle against the glossy wood, regret deepening every line of his face.

"The truth is—" Her father's red-rimmed gaze flitted to the curtained window, where tractors and beat-down cars alike clogged the air with clouds of dust. "The truth is Shirley deserves so much better than me. You both do." His stare darted to his feet before making its purposeful climb to hers. "It's no excuse for what I did. It's no—justification. But you can't go through life punishing yourselves for what a foolish young man chose to do those many years ago."

A bizarre sense of liberation sprouted low within her. Elsie felt an enormous burden freed from her shoulders and something like reprieve crawling into its place. Punishing herself. Is that what she'd done? A glimmer of sunlight caught her eye, aiming her attention at the reflection of a girl with soft brown curls and cherry cheeks staring back from the mirrored wall beneath the signboards. For the first time, Elsie saw her innocence, the blameless role she'd played in the faded scheme of her beginnings. Her tiny presence at the age of three hadn't an ounce of power to sway her parents' actions, yet how many stones had she hurled at the woman that child had grown into, convinced the fault of every heartache lay at her feet?

Despite her turmoil, a grin touched the very crook of her mouth. "Momma said you were a pig-headed scoundrel. She said if a man were on his last dime, you'd somehow cheat him out of two."

Andrew flashed her a quick smirk and threw back his drink, finishing it with a wipe of his wrist over his clean-shaven lips. "Your mother always did have a way with words, especially when they involved her assessment of my depravity." A shimmer of fondness danced in his eyes as his glass clanked back on the counter. "I've never met another woman like her." He sighed, dragging himself from a sea of old memories. "How is she after all this time? Beautiful and ruthless as ever, I would guess?"

"More than you know." Elsie thought of her mother, bent over her steaming kitchen stove crafting whatever she could from garden vegetables and the butcher's humblest cut of meat from last week's leftovers. "She's fairing fine enough. Making due with what she has, doing what she can to survive." *Doing what she never thought she would,* her heart concluded the shameful thought.

With a laden glance at the beaded curtain, her father sank into a sigh. "Aren't we all?" He blinked, as if noticing her there anew, a guiltless creature to guard against his immorality. "Don't go making a mess of yourself the way we have, you hear?"

"No." Elsie flicked her head once. "No, sir."

From the back office, a woman emerged, older yet slim and sophisticated. She wore a frilly white blouse, charcoal pencil skirt, and matching fitted jacket. Her dark head, styled into a high bun, darted left and right before centering on Mr. Dawson. "Andrew, darling," called her tight French lilt. "Are you nearly ready? I have to close up at the market today before we go home."

"Yes, dear," he called behind him, his eyes never leaving Elsie. "Do you want to come over for supper? Renée wouldn't mind."

As if a spring had released beneath her, Elsie instinctively popped from her seat. "No, I have to get back to my—" Her open hand gestured toward the window, where Sam had his muscled arms rested against the truck cab, his fingers drumming the chrome. "I have to go."

"John and Emma sure would have liked to see you." Andrew clicked his tongue ruefully. "They live in town, you know. They both have children of their own."

Elsie clutched her handbag in front of her. "Maybe I could write to them. If you send me their addresses."

"I'll send it in response to a picture of you—and Shirley. Don't forget Shirley." His cheeks creased, the eyes beneath his graying brows almost misty in the gaslight.

With a barely perceptible nod, Elsie turned on her heel. She had wanted so badly to hate him, especially seeing what earned him a living. Yet as her heeled Mary Janes tapped their way to the door, she couldn't help noticing their buoyancy. His wicked deeds stacked high against him, a public chronicle of his sin. Their shared genetic inheritance, or perhaps merely his humanity, endeared him to her. Maybe she could embrace him in his broken state and hope he'd someday mend.

"Elsie." Her hand had just met the grainy door when she heard him call her name. She spun back to find her father mere inches away, his chest pumping. Tossed like a wave toward her, he trapped her in a hug that volleyed warmth to the soles of her feet. "Thank you for this," he said against her hair. "Thank you."

Twenty One

The little town rested in quiet serenity as Sam drew back the bed covers and set a glass of water on the nightstand. At home, darkness attracted a fresh crowd of revelers, girls set on dancing the night away, families streaming in droves to the movies. Even his work camp, isolated beneath the twinkle of stars, had the occasional train whisking past, its horn echoing from mountain to mountain. But here in the stillness, in the midst of a seemingly deserted town, one could almost hear his breath melding into the blackness.

Curious, Sam stole a glance at the door to their motel room, where Elsie stood on the little balcony overlooking an empty street. The moon had crested a mass of clouds, a silvery river of light cascading over her hair. How her soul must ache from the day's affairs, unexpected joy mingling with the renewed pain of picking at an old wound. His forearms stung with the urge to get up and wrap them around her. To bring her some type of comfort. But the girl he had come to know, had come to cherish as his own blood, could only receive his help in her own time.

Lord, show me how to bring her solace, his heart pleaded as she turned from her meditations and swept a hand over her arm. The weather had begun to change, wafting a chilled breeze into the room and tossing her hair about her shoulders. Elsie shut the door and paused there a moment, her head cocking to the side as she observed him with a sad smile.

Without a word, Sam dropped to the foot of the bed and patted the blanket next to him, glad when she assented. Silence swallowed them, their hands intertwined, the rhythm of their chests falling into restful synchrony. Elsie's head angled sideways until it met his shoulder, the sweet citrus perfume of her hair swarming his senses. *Peace.* The single word tolled through his busy mind. *Here is my peace.*

"We probably could have gotten a free room at the Larkspur Inn," she finally ruptured the quiet. "I have it on good authority that every guest thoroughly enjoys themselves." She reddened at her own joke.

"Oh, Elsie." Sam broke free from her, his fingers tucking her wayward hair behind an ear before anchoring at her chin. "You don't have to be so strong all the time. You can tell me about it, you know."

She shrugged, a dismal complacency crossing her weary face. "I can't really say how I'm feeling. It's all just a jumble in there. Relief that he seemed to care about me. Sadness that he didn't care enough to come find me." She stared down at the strong hand gripping hers, her fingers contracting. "They made a terrible plan together, but at least Momma fought it. She didn't let go of John and Emma without sacrificing her own sanity."

"Maybe that's why she tries to protect you so fiercely. Maybe she's afraid of losing you the way she did them. She let go for just a moment and they slipped through her fingers forever."

Elsie searched his gaze, raw unease plaguing the amber flecks of her eyes. "It's different, Sam. She—" Fighting the tears budding between her lashes, Elsie swallowed and tried again. "They both thought that permanently dividing our family would save us the heartache of continuously ripping us apart and putting us back together. But what she does now—the constant need for control, the manipulation—that's purely to elevate herself."

Sam let his gaze wander the room, from the peeling paper on the wall to the antique chest of drawers in the corner. He would rather die than hurt her more. "Did you get the feeling that their marriage could have been salvaged if not for that attitude?"

"Of course it could have. My father was a self-admitted rascal, but we've all experienced how my mother behaves when she thinks the world isn't going her way. My father wasn't good enough for her. Harry was no better. She could have tried to help him with his drinking, but instead she chose to blame him for her every problem and push him away."

The hurt in her had rammed to the surface, as if Lillian Potter sat between them and prodded Elsie with an unseen finger. Sam decided not to venture on when Elsie defensively knotted her arms over her chest and flared the nostrils set high over her pursed lips. Her father had stamped out the crooked road that had brought them here and yet her mother took the liability for it. Could he really blame her all that much? Even the men at the railroad camp whispered about their mother behind Bus's back.

"How am I going to go back there now?" Elsie asked, absently chewing on her thumbnail. "Mother will skin me like a cat. She won't understand."

Sam slid one hand down his pant leg, sweat licking the fabric. "What if you didn't have to?" His gaze darted to the embroidered bedspread and back up again, daring to meet hers. "Go back there, I mean."

Her curls shook. "Do you have a better plan?" Frustration furrowed lines between her brows. "I can't exactly stay here with the Father of the Year."

Ignoring his rapid pulse, Sam swallowed the burning sensation stifling his throat and plunged ahead. "I might. If you're willing to accept me."

The seconds crawled over them, feeling so much longer than the gentle ticks of the clock on the wall. Elsie's head angled, a rosy hue leaking over her cheeks. "What do you mean, Sam?"

"Listen, Elsie, I want to rescue you. This mess with your parents—I wish I could take you away from it all." Seizing her hand, Sam paused for a breath of courage. "But so much more than that, I want to spend my life with you. Not to rescue you, but to fight alongside you."

His free hand dove into his pocket, swallowing the cherished heirloom he'd carried around since the night she'd declared her love for him. Could he really do this here, now? The trust echoing back in her shimmering eyes silenced any question still lingering in his heart.

"This ring belonged to my great-grandmother." His fingers unfurled to reveal it, inciting a gasp. "My mother gave it to me the night she met you." Sam's grip tightened around hers, one side of his mouth lifting in simple joy. "She must have known one day I'd be sitting in a crummy little hotel room, holding your hand, asking you to marry me." The final word barely squeezed from a throat choked with emotion.

Elsie smothered a laugh with one hand, then quickly swatted him with it. "Did she tell you what my answer would be, Sam Tully?"

Scratching his chin, Sam shot her a rascally smirk. "Come to think of it, she didn't quite get that far." His head cocked inquisitively, his eyebrows lifting. "I guess I hoped you'd say yes?"

"Yes." Catching her breath, she bobbed her head enthusiastically. "Of course my answer's yes." In a flash of movement, she was in his arms, enfolding his body in hers. Elsie's warmth, the soft cushion of her lips as they linked with his, launched a wave of surety through him. Sam found her slender finger and slipped the ring over it, not quite a perfect fit, but dazzling as if it had found its own way to her.

Leaning against him, Elsie examined the diamond in awe. "How long did you plan this?" Her knuckles twisted in the dim lamp rays, oranges and yellows flickering from within. "Here I was, complaining about my mother, and you had this hidden away."

Sam laughed, pulling her head against his shoulder and combing his fingertips through her hair. "I didn't plan to do it here, that's for sure. I thought I'd ask you under the stars or maybe down by the river." Wincing, he thumped his brow. "I was in such a rush, I forgot to get down on one knee. It was supposed to be so much more romantic than this."

"No, Sam. Stop." Her hand reached up to cup his face. "It was perfect. The most romantic thing that's ever happened to me."

He sighed, savoring the feel of her rising and falling against him. "My mother would have told me to fancy up."

"We're not fancy, the two of us. And that's okay."

Several moments coasted over them, pregnant with optimism and glorious splashes of future triumphs. In this instant Sam could be anyone, do anything, reach for the dreams he'd thought impossible to attain. Yet still he felt a nudging, a reminder of all that could crumble beneath him if he didn't address reality.

"You know what this means, don't you? You know where I have to go."

Her chest ballooned and deflated again slowly. "Nevada." The word sounded distasteful, like a task she'd put off all week and only begrudgingly picked up again.

Sam squeezed the soft fabric of her shoulder. "What about Dorothy and Shirley? Can you bring yourself to leave them?"

She looked up through a veil of curved lashes. "Shirley proved herself the night you found her in that club. She used her brain. She got out when it mattered. I know she's learned her lesson and she won't let Dorothy go down that same path."

"And what about you?" Sam slipped his hand from her elbow to her wrist, hooking her closer. "I know the desert isn't exactly your idea of paradise. Do you think you'll survive it?"

Her gaze matched his—unblinking, resolute. "With you I could go anywhere." Her fingers entwined with his, an unspoken oath passing between their fitted hands. Elsie laughed lightly. "I'll dream us up a home in Connecticut with dormer windows and a backyard of forests and endless sea."

Sam's lips curled. "That's right, I forgot you could do that. Why don't you dream for us a fishing boat while you're at it, if we're to live right on the water."

"Of course. And a lovely wraparound porch where I can paint great works of art and sell them in artist colonies."

"How about a couple of kids?" He could already see himself skipping rocks with them in the picture she painted.

"No, Sam." Her hair brushed his smooth-shaven cheek. "I won't have to dream those up."

Sam took a long look at her endearing face in the muddled lamplight before bending low to kiss her again, his love full and brimming over. Whatever he'd done in life to deserve such a gift from God, he'd never know. Yet in this moment he committed to spend the rest of his days treating her as the priceless treasure he saw in her now.

When the last street light had flickered into darkness and the moon slid behind a mask of clouds, Sam realized the mere minutes it felt like he'd held her had transformed into hours. Elsie slumped in the crook of his arm, her prolonged breaths tickling his skin. At his stirring she woke, a yawn stretching her lips before a sleepy smile captured them.

"It's time for bed," he whispered through her hair, easing her backward and settling her against the pillows. Elsie lazily dropped her shoes at the side of the bed before driving her legs beneath the covers and tugging the blankets up to her chin. With a kiss to her forehead, Sam drank in her scent before flicking out the light. In the obscure black, he unbuttoned his shirt and removed his belt, finding his way to the bed he'd laid out for himself on the floor by feel.

"Goodnight, Sam," she mumbled just as his head met the pillow he'd crumpled beside a dubious radiator.

Sam sighed happily and extended his lanky body beneath two layers of knit blankets. "Good night, my future wife."

❦❦❦❦❦ ❦❦❦❦❦

T he wild grass bordering the road home didn't crunch beneath Elsie's shoes the way it had only weeks before. With the rise of autumn came scattered rainfall, winds that howled off the mountain canyons, and a smell like fresh laundry after Momma pulled it down from the clothesline. Elsie could barely make out her footsteps as she journeyed beneath the muted moonlight, but she'd planned it this way, asking Sam to drop her off a half-mile from home. She couldn't risk another confrontation. After all she'd faced within the last two days, she simply lacked the strength.

Elsie realized the time when at last their farmhouse emerged into view, a black monster etched into the gray landscape beyond. Momma usually kept her bedside lamp on until late into the evening. Somehow it brought her comfort. Yet tonight, not a single shred of light seeped from the muntin-barred windows. If she didn't know otherwise, she would have believed the house abandoned to its humble surroundings as so many before it.

With a plan to sneak in her bedroom window, Elsie sidled up to the house and tiptoed around the daisy beds. Shirley had done it enough times and not been caught. She could manage once. She had just reached the side of the house, her fingers brushing the flaking boards, when her mother's voice lifted from the porch.

"It isn't like her, Harry. I know something is wrong."

A thick breath lodged in her throat. Elsie peaked around the corner to find a hazy form pushed up against the front door. "Elsie's never gone anywhere on her own," Lillian's haunted voice whispered into the darkness. "It's been two days. She could be anywhere." Elsie squinted, her mother's outline materializing in the dim starlight.

The woman, so regal by day, sat crumpled on the front porch, her fingers bent against the boards as if to claw through them. Behind her, Harry leaned against the door, one leg tucked near him and the other beside her. "You know Elsie," he said gently. "She's a good girl. You know she won't do anything foolish."

"Do I?" Lillian's voice scathed, loaded with sarcastic animosity. "She's done many foolish things lately, things I thought she'd never do. That girl has shown me nothing but contempt and rebelliousness since she took up with that *boy*." The final word was spat, like it disgusted her to let it reside even a second on her tongue.

"The boy who took her to the carnival?"

"The boy who brought my daughter home half-beaten to death." Lillian's nose flared above her uncompromising mouth. "I used to have three smart, obedient daughters. Everything changed when that boy walked into her life."

Elsie made a fist, her knuckles jamming into the house's splintered siding. Of course she would blame Sam. Sweet, uncomplicated Sam. The man embodied everything she'd never be. Well, she couldn't stop them from marrying—not now that Elsie had turned eighteen. Blood pumping, she determined to march forward and tell her mother just what she'd been doing these past two days, to watch the shock and horror flood her face at the mention of her long-estranged husband. Then something in her mother's demeanor froze her.

Despite her callous speech, Lillian's lithe form had wilted like the stem of a dying flower. Her hair, usually pinned neatly at the nape of her neck, cascaded over one pronounced cheekbone. One thin hand rose to shelter her forehead, her eyebrows scrunching like she had a headache.

Harry covered her shoulders with soothing fingers, working softly at her rigid muscles. "You know better than that, Lillian."

Her mother's body heaved with primal sobs, convulsing in heartbreak. Her cries howled into the night for several minutes before Harry eased her against him, cradling her head to his chest. Her tears fell unchecked, etching paths down her skin and staining his shirt.

"She still loves you, you know. They all do. Your girls will always love you."

Lillian sniffed, shaking her head. "I don't deserve it." Her voice quivered. "Shirley was sneaking out to see that boy for months and I never suspected a thing, Harry. I should have noticed. I should have *done* something. She—she could have been killed." Her thoughts drowned into weeping again, and Harry wrapped her tighter into his hold.

"But she wasn't. She's home and she's safe, and tomorrow is a new day to make however you want it to be." Yanking a handkerchief from his shirt pocket, he unfurled it and handed it to her.

Lillian stared at the embroidered cloth a long moment before wiping her nose. "I don't know if it is. I used to think my divorce was the worst thing I would ever do. Andrew left, and I imagined I'd already sinned so badly, only a lifetime of good deeds could make up for it." She closed her eyes, visibly shunning the pain. "And now I can barely see that day, the woman I was. She seems like a saint compared to the reflection that stares back at me in the mirror now. Her sin was only a shadow of the depravity that was buried inside of me."

Harry's fingers entwined with her hair as he stared into the misty fields of solid black. "No sin is too much to come back from." His chin nested lightly on her head. "No transgression can destroy the bond between two people if that bond was strong enough in the first place."

She sank into him, deflated, devoid of all hope. "You wouldn't say that if you knew what I'd done. If you really saw me for who I am."

Harry's strong hand dove into the darkness and hooked her chin, tilting it upward. Lillian lifted grieving, ashamed eyes to his, her soul exposed and bleeding in her vulnerable expression. "I see you. I will always love you, Lillian Potter. No matter what you do, no matter how far you run. I'll never stop."

Elsie sagged against the farmhouse wall and gazed up at the white moon just emerging from a bushel of clouds. It radiated so much beautiful light, transforming the gloomy sea in which it swam. She wanted to believe her stepfather's sentiments more than anyone, to believe in the clemency of God, the goodness of humanity. How long had she floundered in that fathomless abyss, terrified the light she saw vaguely in the distance was only her mind's own composition?

"I'm so worried," her mother's voice shuddered across the distance between them. "I haven't been able to sleep since she left. Food only turns my stomach sour." The cadent chirp of crickets swelled along with Elsie's guilt. "I wouldn't blame her if she never comes back to me."

One last glance over the porch railing gave Elsie a view of her mother and Harry in a crystal ribbon of moonlight, fear engraving their faces as they gazed at the road in expectation. She meant to turn aside, to steal the secret glimpse of her mother's heart and tuck it away as she always did. Yet this time, a quiet voice propelled her forward, emboldened her to confront the barrier forming between them before she could no longer see over it.

Stepping to the porch rail, Elsie swallowed the knot in her throat and gripped the posts. "I'm here. Momma, I've come back to you."

Twenty Two

These walls before had caged her. The eyes around her had screamed her imperfections. The last time she'd passed through these doors, Elsie had been running away. Now she approached her future, an exciting synthesis of trepidation and hope bubbling within her. Forcing her head high, she gazed beyond the small smattering of people dotting his family church, past the claret drapes and stained glass that had once unsettled her, and up at the one aspect of her life which truly mattered—Sam.

Breathing in, Elsie stepped onto the velvet aisle runner. The organ medley swelled in her ears, the perfume of lilies from the altar luring her forward. She fought a dizzy sensation as she sauntered on, her world veiled by a short piece of netting from her hat. Elsie clutched the simple bouquet of peonies bundled in her hands, terribly aware of her simplicity. Shirley had made her the finest dress she could for the occasion from white cotton and scraps of lace, but still it wasn't a real wedding gown. Inwardly, she imagined a satin dress that flared at her feet and a Juliet cap with embroidered rosebuds. Her knee-length frock had little decoration, but at least it had been fashioned with love.

Across from Sam and his brother Walt stood Shirley and Dorothy, each with their own tiny bouquet, their dresses miss-matched but lovely. The weeks had healed most of Shirley's bruises, reflection giving way to penance and growth. She had decided she'd double her work at sewing commissions, tucking away the extra money until she could afford secretary school—someplace exciting and far—away from their rural life, away from Momma.

Thinking on the night she'd returned from Shelby, Elsie's lips trembled beneath the dewy lipstick her sister had applied. "I've come back to you, Momma." She'd been so sure *this* moment would mend the expanding cavern between them. Lillian had sprung up, dumbfounded, her gaze darting through the dimness. After her words of affection, Elsie half expected an embrace or perhaps an expression of relief. Instead, her mother's eyes hardened like two black stones glittering under the moon. One jabbed finger directed her inside the house, *now*.

Elsie held tight to Harry's hand as he guided her into the kitchen. Storming past them, Momma quickly found a lantern and lit it, unwilling to brighten the whole house and wake the slumbering girls. The kerosene flame spat trundling orange light over Momma's arms and accusing face as she sat across from Elsie at the kitchen table and silently demanded answers.

With an insecure glance at Harry, Elsie opened her mouth to make an excuse, yet only the truth emerged, so vivid and beautiful she couldn't hide it. "I was with Sam. You know that, Momma. We went to Shelby for the weekend. I should have told you but I didn't."

"Shelby?" Lillian's dignified brow wrinkled. "What in the world would you be doing in Shelby?"

Elsie swallowed back the dry lump in her throat. "Meeting my father." Her gaze flicked to Harry. "My biological father, I mean."

Lillian's lower lip descended slowly, shock and pain doing a tug-of-war over the high planes of her face. "Are you trying to hurt me, Elsie?" Both hands coiled into fists on the table. "That man is a miscreant and he never cared a whit for this family."

"Yes, but I had to know that for myself." She watched her mother's face soften in the lamplight. "Momma, you were right. I saw who he is and how he lives, and we're probably better off not knowing him." Her voice choked. "But he's *my* father and I had to meet him face to face—to leave the past behind me, if nothing else."

"And you had to go traipsing across the countryside with that boy to do it. You had to bring disgrace on this family—"

"Momma, *I* did not bring disgrace on this family." Shame leaked from every pore of her mother's fair skin, birthing regret. "We did nothing the least bit dishonorable. I'm going to marry that man, Momma. He asked me and I agreed." For the first time, she exposed the hand ornamented with the simple diamond once worn by Sam's ancestors.

Lillian's fist thumped on the table. "Over my dead body, you will." Her teeth gritted. "Elsie Dawson, I forbid it. You give that ring back first thing in the morning, do you hear me?"

"No." Elsie knotted her arms over her chest and pointed her chin out. "I'm eighteen, and I *am* going to marry Sam Tully on the first weekend the local church is available. There's nothing you can do to stop me short of killing me."

The soft hollows beneath Lillian's cheekbones pinkened, her eyes snapping as if staring down her greatest enemy rather than her own daughter. "Don't expect me to be in attendance, then."

"Lillian, think about what you're saying," Harry said calmly from behind tented fingers.

"Don't expect to sleep in this house and eat from my kitchen while you disobey me in such a fashion." Her mother's lips trembled and her fingers quivered even as she forced back her chair with a skid and directed Elsie out with one perfectly aimed nail.

Harry rose, his palms pushed out in petition like a reluctant referee. "Have you already forgotten what you told me right outside that door?" His eyes pleaded with her to show reason. "I know this isn't what you want. I know it isn't."

"I decide what I do and do not want." Lillian's face stiffened, visibly trying to halt the tears welling in her dark eyes. "I want you to leave."

And with that, their lifelong bond ended, never to be grabbed up and patched the way it had so many times before. Against the cold rush of panic and grief coursing through her unwilling limbs, Elsie marched into the night and walked down the country road until her feet begged her to stop, then sank into a thicket of tall grass on the roadside and cried into her hands. She'd meant to travel until she reached Sam's camp, but the lights on Harry's Model T weren't far behind her. The father she'd loved from childhood scooped her from the ditch and brought her to his home, tucking her into bed like his own little girl. Afraid of losing her, he'd called Momma in regard to her upcoming nuptials. Yet as the days wore on and she planned a wedding absent of her mother, Elsie mourned her as if death rather than pride had stolen her.

Now, advancing to an altar decked in white flowers symbolizing hope and new beginnings, Elsie held out her hand to Sam and savored his warmth. Here rested her future—in the palms of the man who'd stolen her heart, the man who'd never let it be crushed. Squelching her heartache, she promised herself that if she ever had a daughter, the world would burn before she let her feel alone.

The couple came to stand before the pastor, who waited in wide robes with Bible in hand. Sam squeezed her hand, and she thought at first she'd find a wink or a lopsided grin when her eyes climbed to meet his, but instead he flicked his head toward the scant crowd. Following his gesture, Elsie sucked in a quick breath. There beside Harry sat her mother, looking everywhere else, but present all the same.

Elsie took her vows to Sam before his Christian parents, under the filtered lights of colored glass depicting Jesus and a host of devoted disciples. His deep voice imparted such fervency, sounded so sure, as he promised to love and protect her, to unite with her in the sight of his beloved God. Maybe she'd never understand it. Maybe she'd always find in this strange deity an abstract concept to divide them. But as he slipped the thin circle of gold over her finger and cemented their oaths with a kiss, Elsie hoped somewhere deep within that he did exist, and even more that he cared the way Sam thought he did. With her new husband's fingers laced in hers, Elsie felt for the first time that nothing in the world could shatter her happiness.

❧❧❧❧❧❧ ❧❧❧❧❧❧

"It was lovely, son. A dream." Olive leaned in to kiss Sam's cheek, her skin emanating a lilac perfume she only wore on special occasions. "And you!" She reached out to embrace her new daughter-in-law. "Aren't you the prettiest bride I ever saw?" She stood back to admire Elsie's lace gown, her fingers grazing the cap sleeves.

Sam's cheeks dimpled as he watched his wife self-consciously fluff her hair under such praise. "I'm so happy you and Sam will be joining us in Nevada," his mother said, the dahlias on her straw-hat bobbing. "Goodness knows we'll need a feminine presence out there in the middle of the desert. It was nothing but an endless pile of dusty laundry and hunting stories the last time we lived there."

One by one, all of their guests passed by in the fellowship hall of his family church, offering their well wishes or a piece of wisdom to launch their marriage into tranquil waters. A group of his youngest brothers sidled up in a clump, their grins both timid and mischievous, each with arms concealed behind their backs. At once, they all yanked out model airplanes like the ones they'd assaulted her with in church and presented them to Elsie, inciting a shower of her beautiful laughter.

Most of their attendees had broken off to enjoy the humble array of finger sandwiches and punch his mother had prepared when two familiar faces approached their receiving line. Harry O'Donnell propelled Lillian toward them with a gentle nudge. Her dark eyes never left the floor as Harry took Sam's hand in a firm shake, then moved on to sweep Elsie into a loving embrace.

Sam's throat felt like sandpaper as Lillian's gaze pointed at his shoes, then his knees, until their tormentingly slow climb arrived at his face. The two pools of ink beneath her feathery lashes pierced through him. She placed one gloved hand over the cinched waist of her fur-lined dress jacket and one on her reedy hip. "I love my daughter very much," she said, tone hard as granite.

"Of—of course you do," he stammered back, unable to produce better words. "I love her, too. Mrs. Potter, I would never—"

The pristine white of her upheld glove shut him up. "I will tell you when I'm finished." One brow arched disapprovingly on her ivory forehead. "I did not approve of this marriage. You went behind my back to court my daughter even after I told you not to. You whisked her off to Montana and proposed to her when you knew it was my express wish that you leave her be." Her full lips pressed into a rigid line despite the emotion flaring her nostrils. "And now you're taking her away for good—into a place as wicked as hell itself, into the devil's playground."

Lillian stared for a distressing period of seconds into the pink flower on his lapel, her eyes misting with tears. "The fact is she's a woman now, and nothing I say really matters all that much to her." Her gaze caught his like a hooked fish. "She's yours now. She's your responsibility, your person to protect. I've done my best these eighteen years, and now you must pick up the reins where I am not allowed." Her hand jetted out to pump his in one solid shake. "She's precious, Sam Tully. I expect you to treat her that way."

Her free hand gestured his turn to speak, but Sam could only manage an astounded nod. "Yes, ma'am." Inwardly scrambling, he had almost gathered the courage to produce another sentence when he noticed she'd moved on to his new bride.

Lillian Potter stood with both hands on Elsie's arms for several seconds, either admiring or critiquing Elsie's appearance, Sam couldn't tell. Then she folded her into a possessive hug, her lips whispering muffled words into her ear. When they finally disconnected, Elsie's skin glowed and tears brimmed in her wheat-colored eyes. "I'll miss you too, Momma," Sam heard her murmur over the piano chords just striking up from the old Baldwin near the refreshment table.

Elsie's mother swung her gaze back to him. "It's a wedding." She simpered. "Don't look so serious, my boy."

It took little time for Walt to entice a group of guests to join him on the marred oak floor of the fellowship hall, their numbers growing as the music livened. To the sprightly tune of "Oh! Susanna", Sam whirled Elsie around and laughed with her when they forgot the steps. Song rolled into song until Walt started showing off his skills and tried to teach everyone the Charleston, a dance he'd learned at one of the many marathons hosted in the town's high school gym. The couple stumbled out of the ruckus with skin flushed and hearts pumping.

"I'm going to the powder room," Elsie said between breaths, brushing back a mass of curls that had fallen in her face. "I must look like I got married in a barn today."

"Do you want something to drink, my darling?" Sam asked.

"Water," she tossed over her shoulder as she strode to the restroom. "Or lemonade. Or—" She swiped a hand through the air. "You'll figure it out. Anything cold sounds wonderful."

As Sam approached the refreshment table, the beautiful display his mother had laid for them tempted his growling stomach. He popped a cucumber sandwich into his mouth, followed by a pig in a blanket and a cookie dotted in melting chocolate chips. Sam reached for the punchbowl's glass ladle just as someone clapped him on the back.

"Brother!" Walt exclaimed, excitement still teeming from his every pore. "This is one mighty fine party, if I do say so myself." Sweat trickled from beneath his ashy hair, collecting beneath his arms and soaking through his dress shirt.

"It wouldn't be the same without you," Sam said with a wry grin before he put his cup to his lips and began to drink.

Walt's hand shot out to halt him. "Don't drink that, it's swill." He bent over and reached for the jacket he'd left draping over a chair and righted himself with flask in hand. "Here. Pink lemonade is a woman's drink." He exchanged Sam's paper cup for his sloshing tin.

The cold metal pressed into Sam's palm. "I don't want this." He pushed it back. "Not today."

"Come on, it's a celebration." When Sam waved him off, Walt cocked his head slyly. "If you won't do it in honor of your own wedding, do it for mine." His large hand flew up, revealing a thin circle of gold around his ring finger.

"You fool, when did you do this?" Sam chuckled, embracing his brother with a congratulatory whack to his shoulder blade. "How mad is Mother going to be when she finds out her eldest son got married without her there?"

"I already told her. And she was." Walt spun the ring around absently with his thumb. "We just decided on a whim-like. Ran off to the courthouse last weekend. Didn't want to make a big fuss."

"You're not going to be a daddy, now are you?"

Walt scowled. "Now, you would go off and suggest a thing like that. There are other reasons to marry, you know. *Love* comes to mind." His gaze meandered to the pretty girl with auburn hair crooning by the piano. "The truth is I ain't never met a girl who got me all worked up like that one, and I wasn't about to run off to Nevada and leave her be just so some chump could run up and snatch her out from under me."

A genuine smile lifted Sam's mouth. He knew love when he saw it. "Well, I'm glad, brother. I'm really glad."

"Ah, enough of this." Walt speared a finger at the flask still lodged in Sam's hand. "I poured my heart out. You go and drink for me or I'll be insulted."

"Now, I can't have that." Unscrewing the lid, Sam threw Walt a playful wink before he tossed back the flask and drained its contents down his gullet. It took several swallows, his brother's hoots and applause smashing in his ears as the sweet whiskey forged a burning path down his throat and into his stomach. When at last he came up for air, his senses felt fuller, stronger. He felt like he could conquer the world.

Sam hardly noticed that Elsie had returned from the ladies' room, her gentle eyes watching him cautiously as he slammed the flask back in his brother's open palm and shook his hand. Like Walt had said, it was a celebration. A rare splurge he would only allow himself to enjoy on the best of occasions. Yet as he swept up her hand and kissed it, Sam found himself surprised at how much he *did* enjoy it, and how much he wanted to do it again.

Twenty Three

*D*iligence is the mother of good luck. Elsie couldn't remember if she'd first heard the words of Benjamin Franklin in school, or from her mother's persistent repetition. Either way, she retold it to herself often as she went about her work in their desert home, attempting to create a future for her family rather than merely dream of one.

Elsie was so good at dreaming. On the hard days, she imagined herself as Cinderella, busily scrubbing the floors in wait for the day she'd blossom into a princess. Or perhaps a young maiden locked in a tower, cursed into performing menial duties until the rescue of a handsome prince. A smile edged her lips as she thought on it now, bent over a queen-size mattress and tugging at the cotton sheets. She had her prince and still the work remained. The only truth to her childhood fairytales lay in the encompassing love she felt just looking at him.

After wadding the old sheets into a bundle and stuffing them in her laundry basket, Elsie took a folded set from a rocking chair and neatly spread them over the bare mattress. Her back ached and sweat seeped into her hairline as she wrenched the corners into place, but she refused to stop until a perfectly made bed allowed her to deposit a crisp quilt over it. Elsie stood back with a hand on her hip, inspecting her toil with pride. Her last bed of the day.

Exiting the simple yet tidy room, she locked it with her ring of keys and walked her pile of dirty sheets to the washroom. Months in this foreign place still hadn't gotten her used to it, but every day she learned a new strategy to ensure her survival. With the money he'd saved, along with a generous leg up from his father, Sam had purchased Oasis, a little motel and service station that served as a watering hole to travelers along Route 40. While Sam ran the bar and café downstairs, Elsie and Sally kept busy in the guest rooms. If anything, all the hard work only distracted her.

Elsie plunked her heaping basket on the floor of the laundry and gazed out the window. Beyond the string of dusty cars and trucks parked along the front, nothing but a long stretch of asphalt and endless miles of sand swelled to a murky horizon. Even the winter, dry and listless, had brought colder temperatures but no greenery, no life with the turn to spring. Inwardly she wondered if this would be the only view the years would ever bring. Sam loved this place. He loved it with an intensity that frightened her.

Reminding herself of her many blessings, Elsie shoved the sheets and pillowcases into the machine and poured in a liberal scoop of soap. She'd never had a washing machine before, never even dreamed of one. From Roosevelt's work programs under the New Deal to monetary reform, so many aspects of life had improved. The collective breath of America, held for so long, could finally release.

An envelope with Momma's handwriting scrawled across the front waited for Elsie in her personal mail slot behind the front desk. She tore it open, her eyes feverishly scanning the pages of news from home. Momma had written twice a week until her letters began to mention Harry more and the woes of her miserable life less. Now they arrived sporadically, the hope etched within her inky lines of flourished cursive leaving Elsie with no doubt that she'd allowed herself to love him again.

"How is your mother?" Sally hailed from inside the back office. "Anything new at home?"

"Only raving reviews of Dorothy's performance in school." Elsie rounded the bend to find Sally seated at the oak desk, reading glasses perched on her sizable nose and a stack of receipts in front of her. "Now that Shirley's gone off to study in New York, all of Momma's attention is fixed on the poor girl."

"It's not so bad to have your parents all to yourself." Sally's brows rose, an obvious allusion to the eight children who'd come after her. "It will certainly keep her out of trouble."

Elsie folded the letter back in its envelope and tucked it safely in a rose-patterned box with the others. "Ah, Dorothy's no trouble. She'll go further than all of us, I'm sure, and she'll make it look like the simplest thing in the world."

Above the sound of Sally's chuckle, the front desk chime announced a new visitor. Elsie glanced at the mirror beside the desk to find a tall man in a smart hat and tailored suit standing at the logbook with briefcase in hand. Eyebrows cinching, Elsie cautiously bent over her sister-in-law. "Sally, look at that man out there. Do you think he looks like John Dillinger?"

Despite a roll of her eyes, Sally leaned far enough back to catch a glimpse of his reflection. "Oh Elsie, that man is far too handsome to be John Dillinger." She let out a breathy laugh.

Elsie's eyes widened. "Pretty Boy Floyd?" With every report of mobsters and bank robbers terrorizing rural America, Elsie was more certain one would waltz through their doors and demand their every last cent. Each day, it seemed like a new one sprang up—Ma Barker, Clyde Barrow and Bonnie Parker, Baby Face Nelson. Her imagination ran wild with visions of machine guns and shoot outs.

"Much too tall." Removing her glasses, Sally leaned back again and chewed the end of an earpiece. "You know, he does look an awful lot like John Paul Chase."

Elsie sucked in a breath. "He does? Who's that? Is he danger-ous?"

"He's one of them. The Dillinger Gang." Sally wiggled her thin fingers like spider legs. "He is supposed to be hiding out from J. Edgar in Reno." When Elsie only gaped at her in horror, Sally swiped a hand through the air dismissively. "I'm only joking, Elsie. He isn't *John Paul Chase*. You're far too easy to frighten." Pushing her glasses back up her nose, Sally returned to her work. "Help the poor man, would you?"

Heartbeat hammering in her throat, Elsie held one hand over her pulsing ribcage. "Land sakes, how am I supposed to go out there now?"

Somehow, the courage came to her. As Elsie rounded the bend into the lobby area, the fragrance of fresh-plucked lupines floated over her. Nevada's landscape didn't paint with quite as lovely a brush as Idaho or Montana, but still she devoted time every sunrise to scouting fresh flowers and using them to adorn the motel. Today, the tall purple flowers sat proudly in a glass vase with a lacy ribbon atop the front desk, accented by yellow arnica and tiny white verbena.

The man's dark eyes aimed over the top of them at Elsie as she took her place at the counter. With the slightest of smiles, he removed his hat and dipped his slicked shock of raven hair. "Ma'am," resounded a low, Western-tinged voice.

"Checking in?" Elsie's gaze darted to the sign-in log. Sally was right—the man looked like something out of a Harper's Bazaar advertisement. No criminal could look that sophisticated.

"Yes, ma'am." He deposited his hat on the counter and took the pen from its stand. "That's if you have room. I'm sorry, I should have phoned ahead. The truth is I'm traveling quite a great distance and I haven't seen a place to stop in some fifty miles."

"Oh, we have the room." Elsie snatched a key from one of the vacant cubbies and plunked it on the desk. "We get a lot of such travelers here, but they always seem to enjoy their stay enough to return."

He glanced up from signing his name with a congenial smile. "I'm sure I will." He held her gaze a moment before scribbling out the rest of his information. "You make quite the first impression."

Unsure if he meant the hotel itself or her in particular, Elsie hid her blush with a quick tuck of her hair behind her ears. "Are you here on business or pleasure, Mr.—" She tilted her head to decipher his broad handwriting. "Mr. Winston?"

"George Winston, of San Francisco." The man's large hand spurted out to offer hers a shake. "And I like to think of it as both. My company has me overseeing a new project in Salt Lake over the next few months, but I don't mind appreciating the sights along the way."

Elsie's skin tingled as she allowed his hand to cover hers. "It's nice to meet you, George. I'm Elsie. If there's anything you need, don't hesitate to let us know."

"Well now, I might just take you up on that." Stooping to collect his bags, he tipped his head again before stalking off to the stairwell. With a half-turn back, he lifted an eyebrow. "By the way, what do people do for fun around here?"

"Well, there's the bar and café right there. There's a restaurant down the way." Elsie scrunched her nose, her hands clasped demurely behind her back. "I'm afraid there isn't much else until you reach Salt Lake."

George shrugged, his eyes raking the service station visible through the front windows. "I figured as much. Looks like a fine night for some reading." His gaze pinned back on her. "Good to meet you, Elsie."

Though she couldn't pinpoint why, Elsie watched their new guest lumber up the stairs and disappear from sight, the trail of his musky cologne still lingering in the lobby air. She shook her head, her feet pivoting back to the office where mountains of work remained. Perhaps she'd never seen a man that striking in real life;

perhaps one had never treated her so kindly. Either way, he'd be gone before the next night anyway.

Pen still scribbling across her receipts, Sally didn't bother to look up. "Now that wasn't so bad, was it?" Wadding up a piece of scratch paper, she tossed it toward Elsie. "He's awfully charming for a crazed felon."

꧁ ꧂

Glasses pinged and jangled. Laughter roared. Whiskey poured like waterfalls into the empty tumblers of bar patrons and over the cherry wood they thumped each time they demanded more. Revelry lived on into the night, every night, unhindered and lawful despite the disapproval of women's groups and religious societies. Sam wiped up the bar and tossed the towel over his shoulder, standing back to admire his kingdom. Whatever he had been or wanted to be, he'd wound up here, a proud business owner, a man who provided for his family.

A *den of sin*, Lillian Potter had called Nevada while bemoaning her daughter's decision to marry. So far, he'd beheld only a wasteland filled with the hardest of workers, who dragged themselves into the only watering hole for miles at night to relax over a respectable pint of ale. With Roosevelt's merciful end to prohibition in December, Sam had sprung for free drinks that first night and inaugurated a tradition among the locals to include his bar in their nightly rituals. The more they imbibed, the comfier the Tully house became.

Sam reached for a crystal glass in the row he'd left to dry and stacked it carefully with the others along the bar's mirrored back wall. Out of the corner of his eye, he caught Walt shuffling in through the back door, body sagging and face like a sleepwalker's. His brother offered him a tip of the hat as he rummaged through Sam's liquor supply and helped himself to a double portion of rum. Walt stretched with a moan, his back cracking in protest, the liquor spilling over his lips and staining his whiskered chin. Who could blame him, really? At the conclusion of a twelve-hour work day, not much else calmed a man's nerves quite like it.

"Sam!" A faintly slurred voice rose behind him. "Sam, I'll take another."

Sam turned back to one of his most lucrative customers, a pudgy old drunk named Rufus who sold shoe shining kits by the highway. "I'd hate to send you back to Bessy drunker than a walleyed skunk," Sam said as he retrieved his bottle of Rufus's favorite brandy and pinged the neck over the empty glass's rim.

"Ah, she's used to it." Rufus's eyes widened with anticipation as the liquid glugged into his glass. "Woman wouldn't want to deal with me without my spirits, anyway." His laugh revealed a set of discolored teeth before he tossed back his order in several large gulps and contentedly wiped his face with the back of a wrist.

"You drinkin' tonight, Sam?" one of the patrons farther down the bar asked, lifting his glass in salute. "The Cubs are settin' up for a win tonight."

A roar sprang up from the corner, where a group of men huddled near the wireless, alternately playing cards and slamming them down when the game heated up. From the exuberant shout of the sports announcer, it sounded as if old Kiki Cuyler had landed yet another homerun for the team from Chicago. Sam flipped a glass from his collection and sloshed in some whiskey, holding it high in celebration. "Long live the Cubs!" he declared to the revelers through the haze of cigar smoke, basking in the onslaught of hoots and stomps.

The time trickled by in work amalgamated with merriment. One by one, Sam's patrons grabbed their coats and stumbled out the door, eager to catch a few hours of shuteye before the sun beckoned them to yet another day of cruel labor. Sam collected their dishes and scrubbed them, forming tall stacks for the café's use in the morning. After he swept, he straightened the chairs and wiped the bar down until it sparkled. Only one last task to accomplish before going home to Elsie. Reaching beneath the counter, Sam slid a drawer open and pulled out a mint from a canister within. His wife always worried when the lingering scent of alcohol reached her nose. Better to put her mind at ease.

The spring air already carried a hint of summer as Sam ambled down the dusty path between the motel and the cabin he shared with Elsie. In Oregon or even Idaho, winter's frosty chill would cling to the evenings like dew quietly dripping from a leaf. Here, in the vast space between mountains and rivers, in the vacant wilderness, not a whisper of wind blew over the sand and scrub brush. Sam could feel summer already soaking into his skin as his shoes pressed imprints into the dirt over the ones he'd made in the morning.

To his surprise, he found their little home vacant. The bedroom where he removed his hat and shoes displayed a beautifully made bed topped with a patchwork quilt and embroidered pillows that smelled of sprinkled verbena. Steam clouded the kitchen, where the robust odor of tomato and sage lifted from a bubbling pot of stew on the stove. Sam spied a loaf of bread baking in the oven, and a sitting room with a cup of tea and open-faced book resting on the end table.

Then, a shapely silhouette on the back porch pinned a smile on his face. With ginger footsteps, Sam eased the screen door open and crept toward her. Elsie had her hair fastened at the base of her neck, but still a rebellious piece hung toward the notebook she had perched on the railing. She furiously scribbled something, only to erase half of it and brush off the eraser bits before jotting down whatever superior idea lived in her head.

"Writing up a storm, I see." Sam enclosed her from behind, his arms diving beneath hers.

"Oh, Sam." She jumped, covering her racing heart in one hand but filling his ears with a delightful laugh. "You startled me. Yes, I was trying to write a poem but it isn't much. Just a little bit of nonsense, really." After flipping her notebook shut, she tucked it into the pocket of her apron.

"It isn't nonsense if you wrote it." If only she understood how proud she made him to have a wife of talent and imagination. "An ode to the beauty of a greener place, maybe? Canada? New England? Ireland?"

"It was actually about my life right here." A gentle smile pursed her lips as her shimmering eyes met his. "About love."

Heart moved, Sam pressed his lips to hers in a tender kiss that deepened as they stood together. When he pulled back, his thumb traced the shadow cast by the silver moon over her cheekbone. "I'm sorry I'm so late. I meant to be home as soon as you finished dinner, but you know how they like to linger when the game is on."

Elsie rested her cheek against the side of his face, her fingertips descending his arms until they laced with his fingers. "I forgive you this time." She sighed—a breathy, contented sound. "I can't say I didn't sneak a few crackers in the pantry, though. There's only so long we can wait."

His satisfaction swelled at the mention of his child. Sam's palms journeyed to her midsection, his fingers spreading over the small mound already forming beneath her floral print dress. "Then I'm sorry to the both of you," he whispered into her sweet-smelling hair.

The echo of a coyote yowled in the distance, answered by another and another until a chorus bawled a medley of discordant shrieks. Beyond them, Oasis appeared desolate except for a lit room on the second floor, casting a yellow glow against a black sea of sky. Sam held tight to his bride, listening to the rhythm of her breath, savoring his life. *Thank you, God. I couldn't have pictured it better. I couldn't have dreamed all this up.*

The fingers he'd pressed to the precious life blooming inside her softly scrunched her dress. "Do you think dinner can wait a little longer?" he asked, relishing the beautiful blush that spread over her cheeks.

Elsie nodded, and without a word, Sam took her hand and led her into the house.

Twenty Four

The waking sun had just breached a distant, milky horizon when Elsie set about her day's work at the motel. Normally she paused to watch it spill gradually over the jagged landscape in a glittering cascade of flaming orange and to pluck a few wildflowers for the front desk. Today, she felt like scrubbing away at her worries, far from any creation that might force her into self-reflection.

After sorting the morning mail, Elsie snatched up her feather duster and headed for the stairs. Halting a moment before the mirror on the landing, she critiqued herself as always. She could still wear her white collared blouse without exposing her delicate state, but the wide-legged brown trousers beneath had strained to their utmost without ripping. The cheeks beneath her wide, lash-framed eyes flushed near the color of the red bandana tied around her head. Soon, none of her clothes would fit, and she'd have to don one of those shapeless frocks that alerted everyone to the pregnant lady waddling through the door.

Sighing, Elsie tried to resign herself to fate as she ascended the second set of stairs and plunked her cleaning supplies on a round table between a set of cushioned lounge chairs. The rays of sun filtering through the window revealed the layer of dust already forming on the furniture after several days of neglect. With the growing weight within her, Elsie tried to avoid climbing those stairs whenever she could manage it.

She set to freshening the room—wiping down the woodwork and shaking out the chair cushions. She took a push vacuum from the closet and ran it over the Persian rug they used to cover the gnarled floorboards. From the framed photos on the walls of nature's wonders to the frilly curtains she'd sewn herself, Elsie had tried to dress up the white stucco and lonely hallways they'd met when first purchasing the desert inn.

Humming to herself, she moved to a low bookshelf housing her most cherished possessions and began to straighten them. A couple of books lay scattered throughout the room—one on the windowsill, another open on the settee. At least they'd caught someone's fancy, she thought as she returned them to their cozy home along the wall.

"So you're the person who stocks the library," a baritone voice swam into her thoughts.

Elsie allowed herself a moment's recess before turning, her lips fighting the smile that instantly sprang to them. "I wouldn't really call it a library." Her gaze flitted up to the man whose frame practically filled the sitting room entrance. "It's just a few scraps I pick up here and there. Books people leave behind when they visit, donation pile hand-me-downs, that sort of thing."

George took two sizable steps into the room, his sturdy form towering above her. He looked just as smart as he had at check-in, with dark hair slicked back neatly and pleated trousers void of a single wrinkle. Today, however, a sweater vest had replaced the tie and stiff suit coat he'd arrived wearing. Elsie noticed the book in his hand before he extended it to her.

"Well, I certainly couldn't put this one down. It had me up practically half the night."

Flipping the book over, Elsie smoothed her fingertips across the familiar blue jacket. "It's one of my favorites." She reverently stroked the yellow lettering. "Gatsby's reckless love for Daisy despite everything she does to him, it's heartbreaking, but it's—" Her mind lurched for the right word as dazzling images of F. Scott Fitzgerald's work spun through her imagination.

"Illuminating," he helped her, directing her gaze back to the deep-set eyes staring back.

"Illuminating, yes. Inevitable." Elsie shook her head. "He worked all those years, and for what? A woman who turned out only to be a dream, a projection he'd fashioned from a lifetime of greed and striving for more *possessions.*"

George's eyebrow hooked. "I take it you don't put much stock in worldly assets, then." Elsie couldn't miss the flick of his gold-plated wristwatch as he combed a hand through his hair.

"I'm certainly a child of my time." She chuckled. "When you have nothing, you come to realize how frivolous it all really is. A hearty meal and warm place to sleep—that's most of the needs one really has for happiness. What good was Gatsby's wealth to him in the end? It destroyed him."

A dimple grooved his smooth-shaven cheek. "I couldn't agree more. I'd like to read more of this Scott Fitzgerald's work."

"Oh, I do have one more, but I left it at home." Elsie shoved *The Great Gatsby* into line with *The Canterbury Tales.* "It's brand new, and I've only read the first few chapters, but it's beautiful so far. *Better* than this one, I think."

"Well, I'll have to read it when I come back through." George thrust a hand into his pocket, an air of timidity touching him as the toe of his shoe dug into the rug. "Listen, Elsie, I was thinking of going down to the café for breakfast and I thought maybe you'd like to join me?" He shot her a smile of supplication, handsome enough to make any girl swoon. "Maybe you could share some more book ideas with me. I don't meet many sophisticated women on the road."

The fact that a man like George Winston had called her sophisticated while she had a handkerchief knotted on her forehead and a feather duster in one hand nearly made Elsie burst out laughing. Instead, her hand instinctively rose to shelter her middle, where the diamond and gold band on her ring finger revealed as much as the fingers pressing her clothes tight over her swollen abdomen. "I—" Words refused to form in her parched throat.

George practically jumped in shock. "I'm sorry, I didn't realize—" His hand washed over his open mouth before one pointed finger jutted toward her. "You didn't have that on yesterday. I looked."

Self-consciously, Elsie twisted the ring around her finger with her other hand. "I take it off when I do laundry. I don't want to risk it falling in the machine and getting destroyed. I'm sorry, I never meant to—"

"Please don't apologize." George stopped her with an upraised palm. "The fault is mine. Truly." Fiddling with his rolled-up sleeves, he sidestepped awkwardly and jabbed a thumb toward his hotel room. "I should be going anyway. Salt Lake is still a few hours down the road."

Watching his tree-like form slink down the hall, compassion flattened her. "George, I am truly sorry."

He paused for a moment at his door, hand clenched on the knob. "I wish you the best, Elsie." His gaze alighted on her only an instant before he vanished into the room.

Elsie covered two burning cheeks with her palms, unable to suppress the disbelieving smile that had crept across her lips. At home in Idaho, the thought of such a handsome and cultured man ever taking notice of her had evaporated with her mother's every assurance of Elsie's shortcomings. If their station in life hadn't dissuaded him, Shirley certainly would have. Now a bizarre excitement stirred within her, blood channeling through her veins like unhindered river water.

Snatching up her cleaning supplies, she could only laugh and wag her head at the reflection she passed in the stairwell. Momma would never believe it.

❦❦❦❦ ❦❦❦❦

"**P**ass the bread!" someone insisted down the table from Elsie, prompting a line of hands to convey a napkin-covered basket down one side until it landed before the ravenous requester. He and two others shoveled into the basket like it contained the very last biscuit on earth.

"Bert, I do wish you would use better manners," Olive scolded with a click of her tongue. "A simple please and thank you won't hurt you, you know."

Her offending son halted mid-bite, a piece of biscuit in each hand. "Sorry, Mother," he blurted, unable to annunciate with the half-chewed mush clogging his mouth.

Mrs. Tully sighed, her thick lips crinkling. "We're not farm animals." Her gray head shook as she demurely placed a bite of dumpling in her mouth.

Elsie shared a smirk with Sam before diving into her own food. Just the savory scent of Olive Tully's famous chicken and dumplings billowing through the house had tortured Elsie's middle during the pain-staking process of making them. A long day's work in the motel coupled with the developing child within her had set loose a ferocious appetite. The first bite of chicken exploded in her mouth, a perfect blend of flavors—onion, carrots, celery, and bay leaves, swimming in a creamy sauce. Though she'd made the dish alongside Sam's mother many a Sunday, she doubted she'd ever possess the skill to create the looks of satisfaction she saw bursting on faces around her.

"This is some fine cookin', Ma," Walt said the words suppressed in Elsie's crammed mouth. He tipped his head toward a bottle on the counter. "Would you pour me a little wine, sugar?" he asked Violet with a flirtatious grin.

His wife obliged, sloshing the claret liquor into Walt's water glass until it was practically overflowing. Elsie watched in horror as he consumed more in alcohol throughout the night than actual food, and finished his meal by uncorking a second bottle.

"I'll take some," Jim announced proudly, holding out an empty glass to Walt.

"You will not." Olive snatched it from his hand. "Drinking is legal now, not underage drinking."

Jim lifted up on his palms. "But the Millers do it. Every last one of them, down to that little kid who's always lighting firecrackers down by the mines."

"Maybe that's why he's daft enough to be lighting firecrackers near a mineshaft," Herman said with a twinkle in his eye. His hand tremored as he speared his fork into his chicken.

"Ah shucks, Pop, it ain't so bad." Jim plopped his elbows onto the table, cradling his face in his hands. "One drink couldn't hurt."

"If I believed you'd never tried the stuff, I think I'd be pretty apt to believe in Mother Goose herself," Walt said with a wink, clinking the bottle neck over Sam's glass. "You'll be a man someday, Jim. Then you'll be able to drink and smoke and go see them long-legged gals in the casino shows."

Olive's fork pinged on her plate. "Now, don't you go putting such unchristian ideas into my boys' heads." Beyond her, a trio of young sons grinned from behind sauce-smeared cheeks and hands.

Unable to keep her gaze on her plate, Elsie watched as Sam lifted his glass to his lips, emptying half down his gullet before setting it on the table. Every Sunday, when the Tullys herded their pack together for family dinner, it seemed like he drank more. Walt had already poured him two before this, and the way he mindlessly swigged them burned an uneasy ache in her stomach. Visions of Daddy Harry stumbling home drunk taunted her. "I never seem to want more," she remembered Sam telling her on their very first date. If only she could trust that.

After the evening meal and a dessert of home-churned strawberry ice cream, Elsie found herself as every Sunday with the other women on the Tully's wraparound porch. The younger children seized the hiatus from work to run around the dusty earth, playing tag and hopscotch with fingertip-drawn squares. Walt, Sam, and the older boys played poker in the kitchen, their shouts occasionally surging through the windows. Their father sat in his old rocker by the railing, silently watching the oranges and pinks of dusk melt into dark as the stars emerged.

Elsie pulled her gaze from him and back to the crochet project in her hands. As much as watching the Tully patriarch brought her peace, she would have a baby by autumn and no warm clothes in which to dress it.

From the next rocker, Sam's mother fanned herself with a book discarded on the table beside her. "I, for one, certainly won't miss this heat wave." She pushed the sticky strands of hair off her neck. "If there ever was a time to miss Oregon, summer is it. What I wouldn't give for one of those pleasant Julys under the evergreens."

Violet glanced up from the task of brushing rouge polish over her nails. "At least we don't have the burden of sweating for two." Her cherry lips pursed in sympathy. "You poor little dear, I can't imagine how you must feel in this heat."

With a contented smile, Elsie placed a palm over her engorged middle. "It isn't so bad. Summer won't last forever."

"And your *condition* won't last forever." Olive reached out to cover Elsie's hand in hers, weathered fingers caressing her belly. "Then I'll have a beautiful new grandchild to dote on. God made mothers to become grandmothers." Her eyes smiled.

"It's been far too long since I've had one is what she means," Sally said sarcastically.

"And I'm too busy looking after Walt to think about babies." Violet laughed, displaying her freshly-painted nails and blowing on them. "Besides, I'm not quite ready to sacrifice my freedom.

Give me a few more years of youth before I'm strapped down to a tableful of screaming children." Her thin eyebrows tapered. "Sorry, Olive."

The mother of nine simply laughed, her bosom quaking. "I'm not offended. I like my tableful of screaming children."

Sally peered dubiously over her own knitting at Violet. "What could possibly be so thrilling around here that you just have to hold onto it for a few more years? Surely you can't mean the fun of hanging out at Sam's bar. Or hunting with the boys. There's literally nothing else to do around here."

"Well, Elko's not all that far. And they have casinos and night-clubs and all sorts of shops." Violet sat up, her palm thwacking the arm of her rocking chair. "I almost forgot. We went to the picture house last week and saw the most divine movie. *It Happened One Night.* Elsie, you'd love it. Clark Gable is so handsome, it's impossible not to swoon."

Elsie sent her a smirk while Olive chuckled gaily again. "At my age, I might want to skip it," she quipped, fastening a hand over her heart. "Swooning could be hazardous to my health."

Above all four women's laughter, Violet rose and pecked her mother-in-law on the cheek. "Oh, Olive, you'd love it too, I promise."

The project in Elsie's hands came back into focus, the strands of green yarn weaving over one another, a miniature armhole beginning to take shape. She hardly heard Sally lean over and whisper, "*That's* who that man looked like."

Elsie's forehead scrunched, her gaze still pinned on her knitting. "Hmmm?"

"That man who checked into the hotel a while back. You remember him. Tall. Handsome. Dressed like he owned a retail chain. He didn't look like John Paul Chase; he looked like Clark Gable."

Elsie's fingers clamped on the downy threads of yarn, her needles working faster. "Did he?" She hoped her warming cheeks didn't show too much color. "I can't say that I noticed." Her ticking needles were hardly audible over the heartbeat in her ears.

Sally guffawed. "How could you not have noticed? The man looked like a model from the cover of Life magazine."

With a shrug, Elsie hooked one sarcastic eyebrow. "I'm a married woman," she said with a pursed grin.

Sally leaned in, her arm brushing Elsie's as she shielded her mouth with the back of her hand. "Well, so am I, but even married women have *eyes*."

An uneasy sensation bit at Elsie's middle. Under her ribs, her child kicked, her guilt deepening at the reminder of her baby's presence. The fact that she, a newly married woman and mother of a growing infant, had allowed herself the slightest attraction to a stranger, drove pangs of self-reproach into her throbbing chest. She could just see Momma now, her dark eyes flashing in disapproval, standing over her and repeating the oft-spoken mantra of her childhood: "You never appreciate anything, Elsie. You've never been one to realize what you have. Soon enough it will be snatched from you, and then you'll wish you had it back."

Fear jolted Elsie from her chair, the arches of her feet aching under the sudden weight. "I'm awfully tired. I think it's time I turned in." She crushed a hand over the expanding bump beneath her dress, an easy excuse to combat any questions.

"Of course, dear. You need your rest." Olive reached up to embrace Elsie, her fleshy arms compressing lovingly, as if hugging her own child.

"Good night, Elsie," Violet chirped alongside Sally's wave.

A quick glance inside the house gave Elsie a view of an abandoned kitchen, empty beer bottles and cards strewn everywhere, the stench of cigar smoke still lingering. Sam must have left already without telling her. Gripping the porch rail in curled fingers, Elsie carefully descended the steps and ventured into the night. The cabin she shared with Sam sat at the end of a short string of homes occupied by Tullys, not long enough a walk to quiet her rampant thoughts. If only she could squelch her own vanity, let go of the pride that swelled in her each time she imagined that handsome stranger asking her to breakfast. What good were his advances, anyway?

Elsie crossed her arms over her chest and shut out the world. The vast space of blackened desert stretching in every direction brought too much silence, too much room for reflection. She tried with all her might to focus on the strident call of a cactus wren, the sand stirring beneath a blast of warm summer air. Anything but the face of that man, the idea inside of her that she must have invited his attraction. Ralph's callous words the day he'd attacked her slithered through the recesses of her mind. *"You wanted this, my little älskling."*

Shivering, Elsie turned the corner of the dusty path and nearly collided with the silhouette of two men, barely visible in a sliver of moonlight. Hopping backward, she balled her fists at her chest, ready to defend herself the way Sam had shown her.

"Woah there, pretty lady. Watch those fists," a familiar voice halted her, one darkened hand outstretched to deter her.

Elsie squinted through the muddled dark, her eyes adjusting. "Walt? Sam?" Their jubilant faces emerged one detail at a time. "What on earth are you two doing out here?"

Sam pivoted back, burdened under the weight of Walt's arm strung over his shoulders. "I'm just helping Walt home. He's had a few too many." The brother in question giggled and hiccupped, attempting fruitlessly to tuck in his belt protruding from its buckle.

"A few too many? Why, he's three sheets to the wind!"

"Hey!" Walt speared one finger up and stood tall. "I'll have you know I only have *one* sheet, and it ain't anywhere but on my bed." He tried to walk toward her on his own, but one boot tripped the other and he took Sam down in a ball of drunken swears and laughter. In horror, Elsie watched her husband flailing in the dirt with him, his skin flushed with delight as his body rippled with mirth.

Her head cocked in disappointment. "Oh no, Sam. You too?" The idea planted an ache in her chest.

Getting his feet under him, Sam unsteadily hoisted himself before leaning down to help Walt, still sprawled out like an overturned tortoise. "I'm fine, honey." The words slurred into one another. "Go on home and get some rest."

Elsie stomped forward, one hand on her hip. "You're not fine. You think you're helping him, but you can barely walk yourself."

Stopping in mid-action, Sam left Walt sitting in the dust and swiveled back to her. A sternness had infused into his gray-blue eyes, a cruelty Elsie had never seen before. "I'm fine," he said, firm as the final ruling of a judge. "Go home."

"Yeah," came Walt's garbled voice from behind him. "Calm down, would ya? It's just a few beers. It's not like he's running out on ya."

Tears pricked her eyes as Elsie stared back at the man she'd pledged her life to, almost as if looking into the eyes of a stranger. The kind smile, the warmth she'd found in that face on the night he'd danced with her in the glow of lanterns had been usurped by a cold glower demanding she leave. Spinning on her heel, she marched with her head high back to their little home, vowing to keep her emotions in check until solitude embraced her.

The heavy air inside their cabin stifled her. Elsie rushed to a window and then another, frantically shoving back the curtains and throwing them open. Her throbbing feet begged for release. Elsie dropped to the bed and unbuckled her shoes, throwing them across the room rather than stowing them neatly in the closet as usual. The shoes bashed against the wall, clattering as they tumbled to the floor. Walt's words tolled through her mind. *Just a few beers.* And wine before that, and bourbon at lunch time. Sam hadn't thought she'd notice, but she did. She always did.

Swinging her feet over the bed, Elsie lay back and stretched herself over the homemade quilt Momma had gifted them. She'd spent a lifetime trying to outrun her mother and now she would do anything for just a word of her advice, for a moment of comfort in her arms. One tear plumped and fell, tunneling a warm path down her arm. Then another, and another, until Elsie lost herself in sobs. Rolling to her side and cradling the life inside her, she cried into the night and pleaded with a God she wasn't sure existed.

Twenty Five

T he copper pot atop the stove rumbled as the heated water inside roiled and spat, throwing up puffs of steam. Sam took a handful of thin spaghetti from the containers Elsie had smartly lined up beneath the cabinets and snapped it in half. The dry pasta slipped from his fingers into the scalding bath. On the next burner, a pan bubbling with aromatic tomato sauce, oregano, and sage infused the kitchen in the scents of an Italian eatery. *Not too shabby,* Sam thought to himself, proud that he could take up the reins when the demands of pregnancy burdened his wife.

He glanced at the closed bedroom door, then at his wristwatch. Elsie had slept horribly the night before, back pain assaulting her at every turn, preventing the precious hours of sleep she needed. No wonder she'd slumbered the better half of the afternoon away, a windy desert storm outside not even enough to wake her. Sam had come home early from the bar, surprised to find a quiet house rather than Elsie slaving away as she always did.

As if roused by his thoughts, footsteps thumped in the bedroom beyond, and the doorknob revolved with a click. Elsie appeared beneath the doorjamb, hair disheveled and perplexity knitting her brow. "What time is it?" Her gaze darted to the Bavarian cuckoo clock on the wall. She gasped. "Oh Sam, I'm so sorry. I should have started dinner hours ago."

Sam tossed her a carefree chuckle. "You were sleeping like an angel. I would have hated myself for waking you."

"But now I hate myself for making you cook dinner after a long day at work." She waddled through the living room, her enormous belly forcing her to masquerade as a penguin. "Here, let me finish. You go relax." She reached for the wooden spoon in his hand, but he angled a playful elbow her way.

"I'm perfectly capable." His hand stirred the sauce cooking over a hissing blue flame. "It's you who should be doing the relaxing. You're resting for two now." He winked.

"You dear man." Elsie reached an arm as best she could around either side of his torso and snuggled her head against his back. "Whatever I did to deserve you, I'll never know."

"I'm glad to impress." Sam clicked off the burner and dumped a metal colander into the sink. "Just wait until you try my famous spaghetti and meat sauce." Kissing the tips of his fingers, he spread them out like a starfish. *"Delizioso!"*

Elsie simpered at him as she wandered to the easel propped up near the window, a half-finished painting adorning the canvas. "Don't get too cocky or you'll be cooking dinner from now on." Plopping onto her stool, she tilted her head and studied her artwork with a sigh. "It isn't quite right, is it?"

"It's the framework." Sam turned to the sink, emptying the hot water into the strainer. "You don't have enough load-bearing beams. That barn would crumble right to the ground." Upon turning back, he couldn't miss the disapproval puckering her lips. "But that isn't what you meant, is it?"

Elsie's head shook emphatically. "No, it wasn't, thank you very much." She gestured back at the oil depiction of an old barn sitting amid a field of pampas grass. "I was going to say that there needs to be a tree or some type of vegetation to pretty it up. Here you go with *beams.*" Her eyes rolled.

"Sorry, honey. I don't know much about art, but *building*, I know." He drenched the naked pasta in the pot with the fragrant sauce and swirled it around. "This is just about ready if you don't mind setting the table."

"Ah, something to do!" Elsie eased herself off the stool and made for the cupboard, selecting two stoneware plates before bending to the silverware drawer. "I should mention before I forget that I received another letter from my mother today." She shuffled to the table they'd nestled into the corner of their tiny kitchen.

Just the mention of Lillian Potter set his heart to thumping. "Good news, I hope." Remarkably, she had sent them positive accounts all year long, from Dorothy's induction into the honors program to her remarriage to Harry.

Elsie shrugged as she neatly flanked their plates with a silver knife and fork each. "If you consider her coming down here for a few weeks good news. She wants to help with the baby."

Groaning, Sam dramatically threw his head back as he carted the pot from the stove and set it on the trivet Elsie had laid on the table. "*Weeks?* Do you know how long it's going to take her to make us want to move again? Certainly not weeks."

Absently smoothing a hand over her stomach, Elsie hung her head. "I know, but she is my mother and she will help us." Her bed-flattened curls shook. "Honestly Sam, we don't know anything about taking care of a baby."

"I know." Sam pulled her close, his lips brushing her forehead. A voice tempted him to remind her of *his* mother, the woman who'd raised up nine of her own and had already mentored Elsie so much. Sometimes only one's own mother would do, he decided.

Sam swept a strand of hair off her forehead and tucked it behind her ear. "I have Bill cleaning up the bar tonight. He's old enough to help run things now, and he can see to the customers while I spend more time here with you." His eyes wrinkled into a grin. "I imagine this baby will be quite enough for both of us together."

"Oh Sam, you have no idea how much relief that brings me." Elsie melted into his hold, her head burrowed beneath his chin. "I'd imagined being alone here all day with the baby, feeding him and keeping him clean. The idea was simply terrifying."

The downy tendrils of her hair slid beneath his open palm. "Well, I can't be here *all* day. Mother and Sally can help out when I'm gone."

Elsie straightened, a look of concern flooding her childlike features. "But I thought you said Bill could run things." Her pink lower lip protruded, her look so vulnerable Sam wished he could promise her everything.

"He can help, but I have a business to run, Elsie. Not only is there the bar and café, but the service station and the motel. It's a lot to handle, even when I leave my brothers and sisters in charge." His chest pumped. If only he could convey how difficult it all really was, how much stress he felt pressing on him to succeed.

"Well, I guess that's true." Elsie studied his rising chest, her fingers absently playing with a button. "What if Bill took over the bar, though? You could run the rest of it, just leave the work there to him."

Sam caught the bashful glint in her eye and felt gut-punched by it. "Elsie, you know I can't do that." The strong arms enfolding her fell lax. "This business is my dream, everything I've ever hoped to accomplish. I can't leave parts of it to be mismanaged by somebody else."

Withdrawing, Elsie took a prolonged breath before replying. He knew the reason behind her hesitance. He saw it every time he touched a bottle to his lips, any occasion he allowed himself a glass of wine with dinner. She'd reduced him in her mind to a common drunk, a lush. He, the man who'd lifted her out of poverty and provided a roof over their heads, sustenance to nourish her. Her judgment haunted him every day, beaming in silent glee through every disappointed twist of her face.

"Is the bar your dream, or is simply owning a business what you want?" The honey-brown depths of her eyes searched his. "When we first met, you did everything in your power to dissuade me from places like that."

He blinked, a hard lump climbing his throat. "Those were different times." He released a raspy breath. "*This* is what I want now."

Her eyebrows scrunched, almost in pity. Her head cocked, her misty gaze imploring, like she was hunting for something unattainable inside. Then, as if giving up, Elsie lumbered to the front door and slipped on the shoes she'd left in the entryway. "Well, I'm off to the restroom before we eat." She yanked the door open. "This child must think I'm a jungle gym."

Breath hard in his chest, Sam stared after the closed door for several moments before surveying the meal growing cold on the table. A pot of spaghetti, bread and butter from the icebox, a colorful salad with vegetables he had painstakingly sliced in order not to rouse her. No matter what he did to show his tremendous love for her, it never seemed enough. It never surmounted the faults she so easily unearthed in him.

With a grunt of frustration, he stomped over to the loveseat and jammed his hand behind one of the cushions. His fingers rifled futilely before closing around a bottleneck and tugging it into the light. Elsie's opinions be darned. He only had this one life, and he would enjoy himself. Tossing back the bottle, he emptied half its contents down his gullet in several glugs, the sweet burn of whiskey calming his thundering nerves. Recorking it, he shoved the bottle back into its hiding place before Elsie returned, rearranging the pillows and swiping a hand over his whiskered mouth. It was just a vice, he reminded himself as he plunked down at the kitchen table. It was just a means of survival until life eased up on him.

E lsie heard her mother's voice in the front room long before her boots clomped outside the bedroom door. "I'll be darned if I stand around here and chitchat while my daughter lays up in bed," she said, Harry's gentler voice muffled in the background. "You men folk can exchange all the pleasantries you'd like."

The door squealed open, Lillian Potter's beautiful face peeking around the edge before she burst through it. "Oh good, you're awake." She tramped forward, stopping just short of the bed and perusing Elsie's swollen body with hands on her thin hips. "Well, aren't you two just a sight for sore eyes?" A twinkle glinted below her perfectly arched brows.

Elsie's heart fluttered, strange relief washing over her. "You came." *And just in time,* she thought as her hands reached out to cradle the massive lump beneath her nightdress.

"Yes, dear, I'm here." Her mother tossed her corduroy jacket on the chair beside the bed, along with her purse and hat. "And so is Harry and your sister Dorothy. Shirley *would* be here if she hadn't insisted on becoming a modern woman and running halfway across the country."

Elsie's eyebrows cinched. "Momma—"

Lillian brushed away the one curl that had managed to escape her hair clip and crossed her arms defensively over her chest. "I don't know what the magazines call it, but I call it selfish."

"Momma, please."

As if snapped from her daydreams, Lillian gazed at Elsie a long moment before dropping to the bed beside her. "Yes dear, of course." Her voice softened, her work-worn hand meeting Elsie's over the mound between them. "This is not about your sister, or her rebellion. This is about you and this perfect little being you're about to bring into the world. My first grandchild." She stared reverently at Elsie's torso, rising and falling under a cascade of morning sun from the window.

With a twinge of guilt, Elsie glanced at the small table beside her bed. In its drawer, she had pictures of all of them—her lost brother and sister, the four grandchildren Lillian didn't know she already had. *Someday*, John and Emma had decided. Someday they would meet her again, but they needed time.

Elsie smiled, taking in her mother from the powdered glow of her ever-so-slightly aging skin to the frilly collar of her mint-green day dress. "You look happy, Momma." Happier than she'd seen her in a long time—maybe ever.

"Most days I am." Lillian's full lips turned up poignantly as she traced the thread of Elsie's nightgown with her fingertip. "Dorothy is certainly pulling her weight in school. She's at the top of her class."

"And Harry?" Elsie could hear the Scots-Irishman's warm voice exchanging dialogue with Sam in the kitchen.

Her mother's eyebrows climbed. "He's talking about moving to California." She chortled. "Yes, me in California. Can you believe it? Apparently, it's wildfire country and there's no shortage of work for a fireman."

Time ambled by, the seconds ticking audibly from the cuckoo clock outside the bedroom door. The urge to unload her worries, to tell her mother every secret problem in her marriage tugged at Elsie mercilessly. She scrunched a fist around the patchwork quilt Lillian had sewn by hand and broached the subject with caution. "And you *are* happy?" Her voice quivered like a frightened pupil in school. "You haven't had an issue with Harry's—*vices?*"

Lillian eyed her sideways while she plumped Elsie's pillows and ironed out her sheet's creases under her palms. "If you're asking if he's been drinking, the answer is no." Rising, she found all manner of work to do around the already tidy room—raking out the fringes of the rug, pushing the curtains along the rod so they hung symmetrically over the sill. "As far as I know, Harry hasn't had a drop since we've been married." She turned to the porcelain chamber set by the window.

Hope quickened Elsie's pulse. "What's different this time? What changed about him?"

Wagging her head, Lillian lifted the flower-adorned pitcher and splashed water into the washbowl. "I don't know that he really changed, just accepted. He knows that he has a problem, and he's willing to face it this time." She reached for a small towel folded in the corner and pressed it into the basin. "He goes to meetings at the local church now. We keep liquor out of the house. He doesn't try to hide it or pretend it doesn't exist like before."

Elsie watched her mother ring the washcloth out and let the rush of water ping the sides of the bowl. "What—" How could she even say it? "Well, what do you do, as his wife? What do you do to help him?"

Towel in hand, Lillian shrugged as she sank back on the edge of Elsie's bed. "Whatever I can do, I suppose. Encourage him, support him." She flipped the sopping cloth over in her palm, gazing at it thoughtfully. "You know, it's funny. I used to blame myself for Harry's problem. I thought he drank because of my moods." Her mouth lifted into a simper. "I guess what I didn't understand at the time was that ignoring it only fed our troubles. He needed me to stand up, be strong, face the monster right along with him."

The inky pools of her eyes speared through Elsie, diving to her heart. "You are all right, aren't you, Elsie?" Her mother pressed the cool cloth to her forehead, dabbing along her temples to her cheekbones. Her hand paused to swipe a tear away with her thumb, the fragrance of her skin like a field of poppies after a rainstorm. "You and Sam, you're all right?"

Breath high and tight in her throat, Elsie thought for a brief moment she might burst into a mess of tears and admit everything—her sadness, her loneliness and feelings of inadequacy whenever Sam chose a bottle over her. For months she'd masqueraded as a happy, dutiful wife, the heart beneath her smile crumbling each day he stumbled in late, his breath reeking of brandy. But what could she do, really? Ask him to stop? Sam respected her mother's opinion about as much as a dog respected privacy.

So she painted on the face again, a little wearier this time, a little more broken. "Yes, Momma. We're fine." She'd recited the lie enough times, she could almost believe it.

A sudden tautness seized Elsie's middle, not so much painful as surprising. Elsie spread her fingers wide over the bump, the sensation gripping her tight before releasing and rippling over her body. "Momma, I think—" Elsie gasped in delight, the thought suspended in the air. "I think I felt something."

Already in motion, Lillian pulled back Elsie's blankets and fetched a bag she'd left at the door. "Dorothy, come," she ordered over her shoulder, loud enough to reach the living room. She plopped her valise on the chair and opened it, revealing a collection of rags and ointments within. "This is the beginning." She leaned over the bed and kissed Elsie's brow. "Just remember, no matter what you feel, this is nothing millions of women haven't lived through before you."

Twenty Six

"Dad-blame it, would someone let me in there?"

Sam paced the creaking porch with thunder in his heels. The wooden boards beneath his boots groaned in angry protest as he stomped over them, teeth gritted and fingers interwoven with his hair. Again he heard her howl in pain, again her toe-curling screams and the barked orders from her mother. Each new sound from inside their little bedroom tortured him, like fresh cuts to an old wound.

A hand meant for comfort clutched his shoulder blade. Sam looked down into the storm-gray eyes of his mother, sympathy teaming from her round face. "This is normal, Sam—I can assure you. Every woman goes through this before she welcomes a child into the world."

Unconvinced, Sam bit his thumbnail and threw his gaze back to the window, where he could vaguely see the outline of his wife, bent over and writhing in agony. "Why is it taking so long? Why does she only seem to be getting worse?"

Olive's plump fingers drove gently into his muscles. "It gets worse before it gets better. Once it's over, she'll feel nothing. No pain. It goes away in an instant, and then you two will have a beautiful baby to adore."

Despite the consolation, Sam heard nothing but his wife's shrieking. He clenched his eyes shut, but still it charged at him like a furious bull. Elsie was begging her mother for relief, anything she had to pacify her pain. He knew he should have chanced the hour's drive to the nearest hospital. They could have helped her, sedated her, done *something* to end her torturous misery.

"Help! Help me!" she pleaded, echoes of her wailing ringing in his ears. Sam steadied himself against the porch post, his fingernails digging into the wood and peeling the paint. Every furious pump of his blood compelled him forward, roared at him to spring to action. To stand here helplessly made him feel weak and useless.

Elsie screeched again, her panicked petitions plunging into his skin and tunneling through his body. "That's it." He pushed off the rail, tramping toward the front door. "I'm going in there. I don't care."

Violet hopped into his path. "Sam, stop it. You can't." Her hand rose up to block him. "I was just in there, and believe me, you don't want to see all that's going on. You can't help her."

"Honey, she's right." Olive clasped his wrist in both hands. "You won't be able to end her pain any more than they can. Lillian is a skilled midwife. She knows what she's doing."

Rage rammed through Sam's veins, at once rousing and suffocating him. "I can at least hold her." Frustration percolated from every pore of his heated face. "I can at least tell her I'm here, show her I'm with her instead of out here doing nothing!" His hands flew out on either side, imploring her gatekeepers to lower the walls set impossibly high between them.

His mother's fingers loosened, her head falling to the side. "It isn't a man's place. It just isn't done."

Defeated, Sam slumped against the aged siding and drank in a breath to his boots. *Lord, bring me peace. And God—give her strength.* The discordant melody of his wife's cries reverberated from ear to ear until he thought he'd go mad. Digging in his pocket, Sam dragged out his flask and unscrewed the top. A little whiskey would calm his nerves. Just a few sips would get him through this. But before he could think, he found himself with an empty canister, trudging through the dust to Oasis for more.

E lsie slumped into the pillow her mother had propped against the headboard, feeling like a weed assaulted by rain. For hours, pain had racked her body, rumbling over her in waves until she thought she'd die. In her worst moments, Elsie had almost wanted it. Now, a giggle burst in her throat and bubbled into uncontrollable joy across her face. The new voice that speared the thick air silenced all the others.

Through sagging eyelids, Elsie peered across the room at her mother, who held a tiny, wiggling package in one hand and wiped the child's skin with the other. The baby wailed, pink fingers grabbing at nothing, little knees kicking reflexively. Lillian whispered into the child's ear as she bundled it tight and pivoted back to Elsie.

A sense of awe took hold as Lillian presented Elsie with her child. "It's a girl," she said, tears ripe in her dark eyes. "You have a perfect little girl." Lillian stooped to lay the newborn child in Elsie's arms, pausing a second to cup her cheek before standing back in admiration.

Elsie's finger dragged the blanket away from the baby's face, her disbelieving stare taking in every inch of her. Coffee-brown irises peered out from thick, downy lashes, her eyelids blinking at the intrusive light from the window. She had a delicate feminine nose and perfectly plump cheeks that dimpled when she pursed her fleshy pink lips. Heaving a contented sigh, Elsie wove her fingertips into the child's hair, thick and sable like her mother's. She had known love, but never a love like this. Never the all-consuming adoration that encompassed her as she stared into her child's newly opened eyes and stroked her cherry skin.

When at last she managed to tear her gaze from the precious gift in her arms, Elsie looked inquisitively up at her mother. "Where is Sam?" She couldn't wait to introduce them.

Lillian stopped her frantic cleaning long enough to swipe her wrist across her perspiring forehead. "He had to step away for a moment, Olive told me." Concern flickered in her eyes, but she expertly disguised it with an easy smile. "Not to worry, dear. I'm sure he'll be back any—"

Just then, the door surged open. Sam stood behind it holding the knob, his chest pumping in fury. "I'm here." Awestruck, he tiptoed around the bed. His gaze pinned on the little creature now wiggling and fussing in Elsie's arms. Silently, Sam slid into the empty spot beside her on the bed, his quivering hands extending toward his newborn daughter.

Proudly, Elsie transferred their child into his strong hands, leaning back to observe the pair. Sam's lips parted and his jaw slackened in wonder as he gazed on the baby. She reached her arms to his face, her little fingers brushing the light stubble of his cheeks. Tears burgeoned in Sam's eyes as they swung back to Elsie. "She's the most beautiful creature I've ever seen." The words barely escaped his choked throat. "Thank you, Elsie. Thank you."

Her mother's footsteps tapped out the door, barely reaching Elsie's ears. She'd left them alone to bask in the pleasure and amazement of their new role as parents.

"What should we call her?" Elsie asked.

"Well, I know we talked about naming a girl for one of your sisters." Sam ran his thumb down the baby's cheek.

"Shirley." There could be no one to name her for but the blue-eyed companion of her youth.

"Yes, Shirley." Sam's gaze lifted, the devotion on his face not only reserved for their daughter, but for his wife. "I'd like to name her after you, too, if that's all right. Shirley May, her middle name after yours."

Elsie found his hand beneath the child's blanket and squeezed his fingers. She'd never have conceived the notion herself. "Okay."

Sam moved little May back into her arms, relaxing against the headrest. "She looks like your mother." He chuckled. "How did she manage that?" His head snuggled Elsie's shoulder as he offered a finger for the child's hand to curl around.

Cradling the baby warm against her breast, Elsie savored the sight through eyelids drooping and lifting until sleep threatened and soft breaths escaped her lips. Sam leaned close and kissed her forehead, his free arm encircling them both. Elsie didn't even care about the trace of bourbon she detected on Sam's breath. He had to have been nervous, after all. No, here in the perfect space of warmth and comfort, of newly formed familial bonds, she found peace. As long as the three of them stuck together, the evils of the world couldn't stand against them.

"I love you, Sam. We are going to be okay." She repeated it to herself before the world vanished and sleep took hold.

Twenty Seven

The desert wind howled and rattled the shutters as Elsie pulled on her daughter's mittens and hand-knit coat. The three-month-old giggled and tugged at the yarn, her bright, curious eyes like two drops of chocolate in cream against her velvety skin. Elsie smiled and lifted her from her bassinet, pausing a moment to brush noses with her. Scrunching up her tiny face, May recoiled with another melodious laugh.

Pulling her jacket tighter around the both of them, Elsie opened the front door and stepped into the icy morning. Immediately the cold captured them in its ruthless grips, compelling May to burrow herself deeper into the cavern of Elsie's jacket. Elsie clasped the child to her bosom and trekked across the frozen path, careful not to slip on the frost coating everything in sight.

Sam's gas station lay only a couple dozen yards from their home, yet the journey felt so much farther with a child in hand and stiff legs attempting to keep them steady. The desert floor looked more naked and desolate than ever, the sage and brittlebush frozen over and flowers shriveled beneath the frost. Capped with white, the distant mountains thrust back the whistling wind, bits of snow swirling about and driving into Elsie's eyes.

As she approached the service station, she saw a vacant Cabriolet parked next to the pump, its black paint and gold trimmings glinting in the morning sun. Sam stood at the door to the building, probably tallying up a customer's bill.

"We missed you this morning at breakfast," she said to his back. They'd missed him too many mornings to count lately.

Flinching, he spun around. "Well, hello, darling." He wore a smile despite the exhausted lines around his eyes. "How are my girls this morning?" Leaning in, he left a quick kiss, first on Elsie's lips, then the rotund cheek of their baby girl. May chortled and stretched her stubby fingers toward him.

"We're very busy, aren't we, sweetie?" Elsie held her tight despite her attempts to reach her father. He wouldn't have time to play with her anyhow. "We're low on everything. I have to run to the market for lunch food, and then I'll go see to the hotel for the rest of the day. I assume you'll be home by afternoon?"

Sam scratched the forehead below his fedora, his eyebrows scrunching. "I have to attend the bar tonight. You know that, Elsie."

Elsie's head cocked, her entire body sagging. "Sam, don't tell me you forgot about tonight. I've been telling you about it for weeks." At his look of confusion, Elsie sighed. "Remember? You're supposed to watch May tonight so I can go with Violet to the winter—"

"The winter rodeo. I remember now." Sam chuckled, though no humor lit his face. "Whoever heard of such a thing?" He shook his head. "Well, I hate to say that I forgot to make arrangements, but perhaps Bill can handle the bar tonight on his own. Mother's already busy with the café or I would ask her to take May."

"Please, Sam. It's very important to me. It's the first time I've been out since the baby, and I was really looking forward to spending some time with Violet."

"I know, I know." Sam held up both hands as if instating a wall between them. "It's not like I'm running around having fun myself, you know. I haven't had a night out since May was born either."

Despite the chilly air, Elsie's cheeks burned hot. Her incredulous eyes bore into Sam's, but they met only blank apathy. "Are you kidding me, Sam?" Her voice rose. "You're at that bar almost every single night of the week."

He blinked hard. "Working, Elsie. I'm putting a roof over our heads."

"Drinking and playing cards—it's not exactly what I consider working." Elsie huffed, the passion in his eyes annoying her. Why should he feel any justification in putting his carousing on the same level with her work at home? "I bust my back from sunup to sundown running that motel, and I do it with an infant on my hip to boot. Forgive me for wanting one break. I forgot you had so much *work* to do at the bar. My regards to Walt and the town drunk."

Elsie knew her words had stabbed into Sam's soul when the fire in his eyes turned woeful, his nostrils ballooning as he held his emotions in check. "I think you'd better go now," he growled, his gaze flitting to the girl squashed against Elsie's chest. "I'd rather you not rub off on our daughter. I'd hate to see her turn out like her ma."

His boots crunched the gravel as he marched out to collect money from an unseen customer beyond the pumps. Her eyes stinging, Elsie swiped at a stray tear and supported herself against the doorjamb. Little May angled her dark curly head, concern flashing on her innocent face. Forcing a smile, Elsie cupped her cheek and kissed her lightly on the nose.

"Hey, Else, I'm headed back to the motel," Sally's cheerful voice sang in her ears. Elsie turned to find her sister-in-law a few feet back, one arm full of legal pads. "Need me to take the baby?"

"Yes, Sally. Thank you." Elsie forced her quaking voice to steady as she transferred her kicking child into Sally's grasp. "That's very helpful. I need to run to the market, but I shouldn't be more than a half hour."

"Oh, that's all right. Take as long as you need." Sally tickled May below her ribs, inciting a fit of giggles from the baby, who gnawed on drool-soaked fingers. "You know I can't get enough." May in arm, she sauntered off toward the hotel. Last month, Sam had fixed up a play area in the office that occupied May many hours of the day while the women worked.

Grateful for Sally's intervention, Elsie collapsed against the freshly painted siding of the service station and inhaled a long drag of frozen air. Sam had disappeared, as had the Cabriolet, leaving her alone to ponder the words exchanged between them. She hated to speak to Sam that way, loathed even more the self-hatred that grew inside to recall his hurtful words. Whether alcohol or just the work of their own hands, the last few months had broadened rather than rebuilt the chasm between them.

Steeling herself, Elsie lifted her worn body off the wall and headed for the market. She was just about to round the bend of the service station when a large figure nearly collided with her. "Oh, I'm sorry." Elsie jumped back, her hand over her stomach.

"The fault is mine, miss," answered a smooth baritone.

Startled, her gaze climbed the smart sport coat and scarf to the square jaw and thick eyebrows of George Winston. "Why, it's you, George. What are you doing here?" It was all she could think to ask, her distress over Sam fading to embarrassment.

"Just coming back through on my way to San Francisco." George adjusted the feathered hat over his gelled hair. "My work is finished in Salt Lake City—at least for now."

Elsie squirmed under his unyielding gaze. "That must be your fancy car I saw at the pump a few minutes ago."

"Yes, I parked it at the café just now." George gestured around the corner with his thumb, his stare unmoving. Elsie felt exposed beneath it, his dark eyes taking her in like a painting on display at the Louvre. "Listen, Elsie. I don't want to interfere, but I saw what happened just now—with your husband. I was standing right over there."

Elsie plastered one hand to her heated face. "I'm so sorry. I'm mortified."

"Don't be." His hand shot out, gently crushing her fingers. His warmth and the icy flakes on his gloves met her skin. "*I'm* the one who is sorry. I didn't mean to spy, but now I can't help wondering if there's something I can do to help."

Tears pressed into her eyes. Elsie dropped her gaze to her boots, silhouetted by a puddle of melted snow. "No, George. Thank you, but there isn't anything you can do." She tried to pull her hand away, but he held it until their stares intertwined again.

"I mean it, Elsie." His solid chest inflated and fell back again. "Any man lucky enough to be married to you should have the good sense to treat you right. If he's out drinking every night and then comes home talking like that, he doesn't deserve you."

A mirthless laugh escaped her lips, a visible cloud of vapor in the winter air. Elsie's shoulders shrugged, defeated. "And yet he has me." How many times had she told herself she didn't deserve him, or any love at all, for that matter? How often did she convince herself that her existence alone warranted such treatment?

George's head shook. "It doesn't have to be this way. You don't have to resign yourself to a death sentence just because there's a ring on your finger. This is the 1930's, not the Dark Ages. If you're unhappy, you should get out."

"Oh, yes?" One eyebrow hooked as she scanned the ashen canvas of desert. "And where would I go?" Live in a tent like her family had as children? Prostitute herself as her mother had? She couldn't do that to May.

"San Francisco, for starters." Elsie's gaze slung back to his at the bold statement. "I think I could make you happy, Elsie. You *and* your daughter." George shifted closer, his spiced cologne permeating her senses. "I can't stand to see you hurting this way when I know I could give you everything you could ever need or want."

Overwhelmed by him, Elsie took a quivering step back. Her gaze slid from the fine wool of his trench coat to the shimmering black Cabriolet he had stashed by the motel. She was fairly certain he *could* give her any material possession she desired, along with the intellectual companionship she craved on nights alone in their tiny house, counting the minutes until Sam came home. For a brief moment, she entertained the notion, picturing herself wrapped in mink and attending the opera, hand in hand with the one who held hers now.

Her throat dried. Shame flooded her at the gleam of silver winking back from her ring finger. "George, I can't—"

"Just think about it, Elsie. Give it a day." His gaze darted over the empty service station and beyond, checking for Sam's return. "That little diner you told me about down the road—I'll be there. Tonight. Come find me."

She wagged her head. "I'm going to the rodeo tonight."

"Come after, then. I'll wait for you." George's thumb brushed her knuckles, plunging the guilt deeper. "I'll wait all night if I have to. Just please come, Elsie. I want to take care of you."

At last yanking herself free of him, Elsie twisted around and propelled her feet over the slippery terrain. Her worry fused with an aching hunger growing inside her. She wanted more, needed more. Grunting, she pushed her crocheted scarf over her numbing lips and forced herself not to look back at the pair of eyes staring back. George Winston was a dangerous man, and if she didn't watch herself, his charms might just sweep her into the fantasy she'd always coveted.

The headlights of Violet's 1929 Cadillac Fleetwood speared into the night like a pair of eyes gazing into the abyss of black. The highway, all but abandoned by this time of night, spread to the distant mountains like a narrow ribbon twisting among the sagebrush. Elsie stared into the flecks of snow whirling past her window, her mind ablaze with terrible musings. Even the bright lights and roaring crowd of the rodeo hadn't dispelled her doubts and fears, nor the gnawing guilt she'd felt just listening to George's proposal.

"What you're so darned fixed on thinking about, I'll never guess." From the driver's seat, Violet tossed her a roguish grin. "It's that cowboy, isn't it? The big one. Your cheeks lit up hotter than a red iron when he came charging out on that stallion."

Elsie's hands instinctively flew to her face. "They did not!" Heat reignited the skin beneath her palms.

Her sister-in-law's chortle filled the small space. "Don't worry, I won't tell Sam. A girl would have to be dead not to notice that man's backside."

"Violet, really!" Elsie attempted a scowl, yet the urge to giggle bubbled up anyhow until they both succumbed to irrepressible laughter. The scattered lights of home already gleamed under the cloudy December sky when the women at last regained self-control.

Violet gripped the steering wheel in one hand and reached for her cigarette box with the other. "Do you mind lighting me up, darling?" She extended the tip of one toward Elsie in her elegant hand.

Obliging, Elsie flicked on Violet's jeweled lighter and watched the orange and blue flame hiss to life before touching it to the woman's cigarette. Violet immediately relaxed against the leather seat, dragging in long drafts of smoke and puffing them out again like a glittering steamship sailing over the Atlantic. That's what Elsie imagined, anyway. Violet, so fashionable with her red-tinged hair falling in soft waves, her gloved arms and faux-fur wrap. She almost looked like a magazine cover.

"You want one?" she asked, eyebrow hooking. "They're not the best, but they're the best I can afford."

Elsie glanced down at the shimmering cigarette box on the seat beside her and smiled. "My mother would tar me. I tried to sneak one out of Harry's jacket one time as a child and she hit me with a willow switch so many times, I swore I'd never touch the things again. She told me they dry out your skin and turn your gums black."

"Well, it's a good thing your mother's not here," Violet said with a sardonic chuckle.

The smoke from her cigarette alone had already smothered Elsie in a cloud of soot. Her nostrils felt plugged with the stench of tobacco. Her eyes stung and watered. "I think I'd better not." She waved her hand. "It can't be good for you—inhaling all that smoke."

Violet's radiant eyes rolled up in her head. "Come on, Elsie. Live a little. Besides, you're wrong on this one. All the actresses in Hollywood smoke, and I don't see any *charred gums.* My doctor smokes. If it were really all that bad, they wouldn't recommend it, now would they?"

Elsie merely simpered in return as the Cadillac turned off the highway and charged up the asphalt drive to Oasis. The string of houses the Tullys occupied sat in quiet tranquility, so unlike the bar still lined with patrons' cars and streaming wild tunes from the jukebox. Apparently, drinking was a late-night sport. Disheartened with the prospect of seeing Sam after their spat that morning, Elsie inwardly vowed to make peace as the hum of the Cadillac's engine sputtered to a stop in front of their little house.

"Until next time, then." Violet leaned in to embrace Elsie, her lilac perfume briefly subduing the ashy aroma. "I had a lot of fun tonight. You're a good girl, Else."

Lingering a moment, Elsie savored her warmth. "Thank you, Violet," she whispered into her hair. "Thank you for tonight." How many nights her sister-in-law had cried over her own husband's vices, she couldn't imagine. A painful lump materialized in her gullet as Elsie realized she'd only been thinking about herself.

Elsie's boots crunched the gravel as she trekked the short path she'd lined in daisies. The house seemed almost abandoned, save for the single lamp glowing in the family room window. With a sharp breath, she eased the screen door open and stepped inside. Her problems wouldn't go away by simply ignoring them.

Odd. Violet's cigarette smoke must have followed her in. The brash taste of it still loitered on her tongue. So strange that it could still singe the edges of her nostrils. Elsie tiptoed a few feet into the house before she caught sight of orange flames dancing in the kitchen.

Springing to action, she sprinted through the family room, hardly noticing her husband sprawled on the couch. *Could he be injured?* Before she could reason it out, her hands were hunting through the kitchen drawers, retrieving the towels she'd neatly stacked there this morning.

Smoke rushed at her like a tidal wave. Elsie choked and coughed into the crook of her elbow, her eyes smarting. Somehow, she fanned out a dish towel and aimed it at the billowing monster, beating it into oblivion until she thought her arms would break. A pot crashed from the stovetop, blanketing the floor in a cascade of scorching water. Elsie kept on until the flames died beneath her dish towel, swirls of suffocating smoke sweeping through the kitchen.

"Elsie?" She could barely make out Sam through the haze, rising and squinting her way. Behind the closed door at his back, little May's piercing screams rose.

"Sam, are you all right? What happened?" Elsie dashed to open several windows before meeting him by the loveseat.

As if in a stupor, Sam's brows wrinkled, his bemused gaze darting from the blackened stove to the flooded kitchen floor. "I—I don't know." He pushed his fingers through his unruly hair. "I was just making a bite to eat on the stove and I must have fallen asleep."

Elsie moved closer, her fear converting to rage at the glazed look in his eye, the fresh stains on his white cotton shirt. "Could *this* have had anything to do with it?" She stooped to snatch up the empty whiskey bottle he'd haphazardly let slip under the coffee table. She hurled it at his chest, her own pumping in violent fury.

Catching the glass bottle in his large palms, he gaped at it for a long moment, as if his mind languidly sauntered to grasp her racing accusations. "Elsie, I don't know—"

"Yes, you do, Sam. You know exactly how this happened." Her heartbeat hammered. The arms beneath her wool overcoat shook. "You chose to lay around drinking, *again*. You could have burned down our house. You could have *killed* our daughter." Tears pricked her eyes as Elsie spun around to answer May's frightened wails.

"I'm sorry, Elsie," she heard from behind her as she crashed through the nursery door and scooped up her frantic child. "I didn't mean to do it."

"I don't care if you meant to do it," she hissed through gritted teeth, her clenched hands shoving the hysterical child into her winter jacket and boots. May's pouty lips trembled, her dark eyes bright with tears as she peered from one parent to the next.

Sam tried to halt her with a hand to her elbow. "You don't know what would have happened. I probably would have woken up any minute and put it out myself."

Disbelieving, Elsie allowed her gaze to search his. "And if you hadn't, Sam?" Tears burned so close beneath the surface, she could scarcely keep her voice steady. "If you hadn't, I'd be a childless widow. All because you can't control yourself." With a force she didn't know she possessed, Elsie ripped free of him and hoisted the screaming child on her hip.

"Where are you going, Elsie?" Panic tautened Sam's vocal chords.

"I don't know. Away from you." His footsteps pounded the wooden floor behind her, his protests dead in her ears. Elsie refused to look back. Holding May tight against her, she strode down the porch steps and out beneath the canopy of winking stars.

All down the row of houses, lights flicked on and commotion stirred. Olive, a blue terrycloth robe hugging her rotund figure, hurried out of her house and across the gravel drive. "Is everything okay, dear?" Her soft hand smoothed back May's chestnut curls. "We heard yelling and smelled smoke coming from your home."

"Everything is fine," Elsie said flatly, her flaming glare flying to Sam, who stood clutching their porch post.

His mother's gaze followed, flickering over the fear-stricken man drenched in a puddle of moonlight. Understanding deepened the lines of her blue eyes. "Why don't you let me take your little girl? You need rest, child."

Elsie's arms closed around her baby like a vise. "I can't let her go. What if something else happens?"

Olive's gentle hand clutched her shoulder. "You're very shaken up, understandably so. Now, you know I love this child more than anything in this world. I'll take care of her, darling. I'll make sure she is safe. We both know you need to calm down before you can mother her the way you want to."

Elsie's anger fizzled every second she stood staring into her mother-in-law's reassuring moonlit eyes. She felt like a melting snowman being sucked to the ground, about to disappear into an insignificant pool of sludge at any moment. Her fingers slackened until the child was free from her, until she stood alone in the quiet drive, her gaze locked with the man who would never be all he had promised her.

When resolve at last warmed her icy body, Elsie marched toward the house and thrust past Sam in the doorway. Pausing at her antique vanity mirror, she combed through her disheveled hair and reapplied rouge to her dried-out lips. She replaced the stockings that had ripped when she chased after the fire and strapped on her Mary Janes. Five clicks of her heels and she stood at the bowl Sam threw his car keys in and seized them without a word to the form still slumped against the doorjamb.

This time, her husband didn't question her intended destination. Elsie hopped into the cab of Sam's truck and twisted the key, awakening the whirring engine. Red light painted the front porch as she rammed the truck into reverse and stopped it mere feet from where Sam stood beneath the eaves. For an instant, Elsie took in the image shining back in the rearview mirror—the broken man sagging against the house, his strong jaw still set determinedly, but eyes pleading with her to stay. She swallowed the cold lump in her throat, her fingertips drumming the steering wheel. Then she threw the gearshift into drive and pressed her foot to the gas pedal, compelling Sam's old truck over the rocky drive and toward the diner, where another man waited.

Twenty Eight

Like the desolate landscape around it, Rosie's Diner sat only a quarter-mile down the highway from Oasis—a grim, squat building with little decoration and clumsy signage. One could easily miss it if barreling down the road, it blended so well with its wilderness setting. Flecks of dry paint clung to Elsie's fingertips as she pushed open the whiny front door and passed beneath the bold black letters simply spelling out "diner".

Despite its lackluster outward appearance, Rosie's offered a tranquil retreat from the raging cold and snow outside, a cozy haven for the locals not pursuing the carousing spirit of Sam's bar. Half a dozen square wooden tables nearly filled the small space, beyond which sat a row of inviting, if not a little threadbare, booths that Rosie had refurbished herself from scraps left behind during the Depression's upheaval.

The woman herself, clad in a polka dot dress with a shawl collar, turned from pouring a cup of coffee upon Elsie's arrival. "Oh hey, Else. Go on and pick a seat. Is Sam on his way too?"

Stiff from the cold or her own nerves, Elsie couldn't be sure, she hardly felt herself nod. "Uh yes, we're meeting a friend here." Heat must have poured from every inch of her face. Seven or eight pairs of eyes had already pinned on her from around the restaurant—all aware of her deception, she guessed.

Oblivious, the restaurant's matron bounced back toward the kitchen. "Oh, good. Well, I'll be along in a minute to take your drink order."

I can't do this. Elsie's heart pumped furiously, the blood in her ears a torrent. How silly of her to believe she could meet a man not her husband, let alone in a room full of his friends. Beneath her woolen jacket and button-up twill dress, her stomach flipped over and again. The fingers clutching her purse trembled. Spending her courage, Elsie did an about-turn and started for the door.

"Elsie!" his voice halted her midstep. She revolved to find George at the corner booth, one hand raised in salutation.

Elsie tried to ignore the curious stares of Rosie's customers as she slinked between their tables toward him. From the corner of her eye, she glimpsed Ben, a local miner and one of Sam's best friends. The Andersons, their neighbors from down the road, gawked at her quizzically as she brushed by their table without a word of greeting. Elsie pursed her lips doggedly. If she chose to leave Sam, they'd all know soon enough anyway.

"I didn't think you'd come." George looked her over excitedly before catching her in an awkward hug.

"Neither did I." Elsie shyly lowered her gaze as George stepped around her to remove her jacket. Her arms tingled despite the tepid temperature inside the establishment.

Trailing her companion's outstretched hand, Elsie slid into the booth just as Rosie marched up to the table. "What can I get you to drink, Elsie?"

"Hot tea, please." Hopefully it might settle her fitful stomach.

Rosie bobbed her head. "And for Sam?"

Elsie couldn't miss the twitch of George's dark brows. "I'll let him decide when he gets here."

"One tea coming up." Satisfied, the restaurant's jovial owner disappeared again, leaving Elsie to gaze inelegantly at her hands.

How could she answer the perplexity on George's striking face? They both knew her coming here was a sin.

"I had to say that Sam was coming. Everybody here knows me. They would know—" Elsie choked on the very words. They would know what she was doing there.

With a nod of recognition, George perused the small crowd of patrons, all taking turns glancing their way. "Ah, I see." He reached for his water and took a sizable gulp. "Well, are you hungry?" His fingers flicked toward the half-eaten dinner on his plate. "I still have half my sandwich, or we could order you something."

Her stomach churned at the thought of food. "No, but thank you, George. Violet and I ate at the rodeo."

A lengthy silence stretched between them. Elsie's tea arrived, a welcome tonic for her parched lips and throat. The porcelain cup warmed her icy hands as she savored the heady blend of black tea leaves and chamomile, studying George over the rim of her cup. He had such bold, chiseled features. His deep-set brown eyes stared pensively into his coffee cup over a straight nose and slightly dimpled mouth. Not a hair stood out of place atop his creaseless forehead. How a poor country girl like her had wound up here, considering the advances of such a refined suitor, she could hardly imagine.

At last, he sighed. "Listen, Elsie. I'm just going to say it." He swallowed, his hopeful gaze hooking with hers. "I'm so glad you came tonight. My whole trip to Salt Lake, I couldn't stop wondering what might have been between us if you hadn't had that ring on your finger."

Shoving down the pangs of remorse biting at her, Elsie forced a feeble smile. "I wondered too. I mean, I don't meet many men who dress in suits and adore literature out here in the middle of the desert."

George joined in her quiet chuckle, his face filling with joy. "So we both felt something special." He bit his lip as his stare dropped to her hand on the seat beside him. Covertly, he inched his fingers toward hers under the table until their skin met.

Skitters raced up Elsie's spine as he turned her palm over and swept her fingers with the tips of his, then laced them in his balmy grip. For a moment, the thrill of it captured her in its claws, heat rushing up her arms, pulse hastening. Then, the memory of a similar day jolted her back to reality—the moment Sam had seized her hand under the lights of the midway. Gasping, she slipped her fingers from his. "George, I—I'm not ready. I'm still married. I haven't even decided—"

"Of course." He straightened abruptly, slicking an uneasy hand over his hair. "I understand. I'm sorry, Elsie."

Tears sprang to her eyes. No matter how hard she pushed, Sam wouldn't quit nagging at her. "Tell me something about yourself," she said, craving a distraction. "Anything."

George considered her question, his brow working. "Well, I live in the Embarcadero. I have an apartment that overlooks the bay." The smile crept back onto his lips. "I enjoy Chinese takeout and going to the theater. Alone, mostly."

Her head cocked incredulously. "You can't tell me you don't have a string of girls just waiting for you to take them out."

George's broad hands splayed before him. "I do date occasionally. But there really aren't a lot of women interested in the things I like." His brows rose, his robust chin settling on his fist. "They're more concerned about their hairstyles, or—Ginger Rogers's latest wedding."

"Both very important issues. If we don't know about Ginger Rogers's latest wedding, how are we supposed to know how to do our hair?"

White light from the restaurant's hanging bulbs glinted in his eyes with his laugh. "See? That's why I like you, Elsie. You're witty."

The compliment soaked into Elsie, probably too deep for her good. Lifting her teacup, she swigged a little more of the dark liquid and let its warmth relax her. "You know, I never thought a man like you would be the least bit interested in a girl like me." Would that have changed her decision to marry Sam?

George volleyed her a dubious look. "How can you say that? You're charming. You're beautiful. Any guy would have to be half-dead not to see that." His gaze, weighted with longing, plummeted to the lips she tried to keep from quaking.

The heavy air of Rosie's Diner enveloped her. The couple at the next table had just been delivered grilled sandwiches and fries, the aroma of grease and hot cheese snatching her back to earth. Perhaps she'd imagined them dining in a Parisian café, or relaxing after a show at George's favorite theater. Yet glancing around at the eatery's shabby diners, the men's hands tinted with clay, the women in their homespun versions of New York fashions, Elsie remembered the way of things. She recalled with beautiful nostalgia the young man in his tilted fedora and rusty old truck who'd picked her up for the carnival, who'd danced with her in the soft glow of lantern light and awakened a love inside her she hadn't known she could feel.

Her misty eyes lifted to the movie star-like man staring back. "This is a mistake."

George frowned, evident disappointment tugging at his mouth. "How do you mean?"

"I came here tonight because I was mad at my husband." Her arms crossed over her chest, her fingertips digging into her skin. "I wanted to feel desired again. I wanted to feel good about myself."

He leaned forward, his gaze leveling with hers. "Elsie, you *should* get to feel good about yourself."

"Yes, but now I feel ten times worse." Elsie shook her head, the enormity of her poor judgment crashing in on her. "I have a husband at home who loves me. I have no business even entertaining the thought of you, let alone meeting you here."

Drinking in a prolonged breath through his flared nostrils, he slumped back against the booth. "Elsie, I really think we could be something. I really do."

Elsie's head angled, her curled locks tickling her arm. "Based on what? Four short conversations with me?" The silverware jangled against the tabletop as Rosie stomped by, Elsie's tea rippling in circles. "You don't know me, George. Not really. You're a kind man. You're handsome and smart and sophisticated. You're everything I've always convinced myself I wanted."

Yet now, with her lifelong vision of happiness sitting before her, Elsie desired only the security of the arms she knew. "Sam, he knows me," she said shakily, pausing to swipe a hot tear from her cheek. "He knows the good and the bad in me. We chose each other. We promised to stand by each other no matter the trial." How foolish she felt now, running from him in his hour of need, picking anger in the face of his shortcomings. "That's what I need to do, George. I'm sorry."

George's fist thumped the table softly as he released a cathartic breath. "Then that's what you need to do." He shrugged.

Elsie gave him a gentle nudge. "You should go find a nice girl. Preferably one who doesn't come with a husband and child."

His full lips curved upward. "You got a sister?"

"I do, but she's far out of your league."

Slipping out of the booth, George jerked his head toward the door. "Come on, I'll walk you out. I think the town gossips have had their fill." He assisted Elsie in pushing on her overcoat before dropping a few bills on the table for Rosie. Elsie ambled with him through the dwindling gathering of spectators, eager to return home and speak with Sam. They had a long road ahead, but now she knew she only wanted to walk it with him.

S am plodded through the snow-flecked night to his bar like a man defeated. The roar of the lively jukebox inside danced in the wintry air, neon lights illuminating the otherwise black panorama in festive reds and greens. Still intoxicated, Sam nearly tripped on the icy threshold. One hand flew out to steady himself against the doorjamb, his world a befuddling jumble of lights and sounds.

Inside, the cheerful banter of his patrons plugged the small space. His eyes swept over the little fir tree they'd driven into the forest to find. Elsie had decked it in tinsel, glass balls, and golden bells. *Some Christmas,* he thought somberly as he put the embellished tree behind him and pointed himself toward the bar. Pretty soon he wouldn't have a wife to come home to, let alone to pick out Christmas trees with.

Sliding into an empty stool, Sam thumped his knuckles on the shiny wooden bar. Bill, who'd had his back turned, revolved around with glass in hand. "Get me a Jack and Coke," Sam ordered, rubbing his eyes with his palms. "Make it double."

Bill paused, a clean towel buried in his glass. "You don't look so good, Sam. Maybe I should pour you a seltzer instead—"

"Just get me what I asked for," Sam growled. His little brother wouldn't have a job if it weren't for Sam's bar, and now he presumed to defy him? The requested drink slid into his hands, Sam's fingers clenching around the glass like a vulture snatching its prey.

"Rough night, eh?" Bill plunked the second glass in front of him, eager to meet Sam's approval.

"Something like that." Sam sloshed down the first offering with little effort, the icy ping flooding his ears, the carbonated potion fizzling in his throat. "I don't want to talk about it."

The little world he'd fashioned provided a welcome escape from reality. Sam faded into it, a backdrop of imbibing drunks and triumphant sports fans. Only two years ago, his own business had seemed an impossible dream, the elusive key to his perpetual happiness. How empty it all felt now—the liquor slopped across tables, cards, and hands. The jabbering and the stumbling, the obnoxious roar of inebriated clientele. Some vision he'd chosen to bring to life.

Sam could hardly taste the whiskey mingled in the second glass. Unsure if Bill had tricked him or he was simply losing his senses with each swallow, he set the glass back down half-empty. His eyes stung. His unkempt lips trembled. He saw only her face—the soft golden-hued eyes, the pink lips and turned-up nose. Those eyes had once looked on him with such hope, such trust. Now the disillusion in them shattered him, drove him into the very dust. How he had failed her in so many ways.

The front door creaked open, blowing in a burst of chilling air. For a moment, he imagined Elsie whisking through it, the howling wind tossing her short curls, a placid warmth enshrouding her. He would go to her and apologize. He would give it all up; he would flip his entire world over for her. But when he turned and saw only the dismal face of his friend Ben, Sam sank even further into his overcoat.

Ben's boots walloped the uneven floorboards as he sauntered in, dusting the snow off his jacket and calling out greetings to his fellow clientele. Two steps behind Sam, he clapped both hands on his shoulders. "Crying in our whiskey, are we? You're a sad-looking spectacle if I ever saw one."

"Just doing my part to welcome in the holiday season." Sam lifted his glass in an apathetic salute.

Ben moved around him, dropping onto the next barstool. "Well, I can't say as I blame you." He summoned Bill with a flick of his head. "I'd probably be knee-deep in the stuff already if my wife was running around with a guy like that."

Frowning, Sam watched him order a scotch through his bleary swirl of vision. "A guy like what?"

"That guy she's cozying up to down at Rosie's." Ben wagged his head, a low whistle blasting through his teeth. "What is he, a politician or somethin'? Fancy guy like that ain't nobody from around here, that's for sure."

Sam's fist crashed on the bar, inciting a row of glasses to topple and shatter across the floor. Swearing under his breath, he shoved out of his chair and stomped toward the door, leaving behind a group of gawking patrons. The walk to Rosie's, which normally took a good ten minutes in the snow, felt like a flash in time. Head awhirl and soaked to the knees in glacial water, Sam stumbled up to the diner in time to find Elsie and this mystery man coming out the door, talking and laughing with one another.

Steam surged from Sam's hands to his arms, leaking into his flushed face. The man led Elsie out with a hand to the small of her back. She chuckled at something he said, her cheeks pinkening and eyes bright. Sam charged into the moonlit parking lot, his feet barely keeping him steady over the icy ground. "So it's true," he said before they could even process his presence.

Elsie looked at him like a stranger. "So *what's* true, Sam?"

"You and this guy." Sam stabbed a finger toward the tall man he now recognized as a guest at the motel. "I didn't quite believe it when Ben told me he saw you two together, but now—" He gulped back the emotion inching up his throat. "I didn't take you for a cheater, Elsie."

Her sad eyes flashed in the light from the restaurant window. "That's because I'm *not* a cheater. George here is only a friend, and—"

Her words faded into the black night as Sam clomped over the crunchy snow, his sights aimed on her companion. "Did you think you could steal my wife, huh?" he barked, his volume rising with his blood pressure. "Did you think she was part of the room accommodations—like some free drink, like some mint on your pillow?"

George stepped backward, his gloved hands extended before him. "Listen, friend. I don't wish to quarrel."

"Friend?" Fury rammed into every cell of Sam's quaking body. "You bring my wife here and you call me a friend?" Against any judgment left in him, he came toe-to-toe with the broad-shouldered man and stuck a pointed finger in his face. "You have twenty minutes to get your stuff in your bag and hit the road, pal. I'm not going to tell you twice."

"Sam, really," Elsie said from somewhere behind him. "None of this is George's fault, and if you would just let me explain a minute—"

"Stay out of this, Elsie." A headache knifed through Sam's skull. His stare drilled into George, now only inches away. "If I ever see your face around here again, I'll turn it into putty."

George unfurled proudly. "I'm not afraid of you." His gaze held steady.

"Oh yeah?" Sam threw off his overcoat and began rolling up his sleeves. "You're not afraid?" He shoved a challenging hand against George's chest. "Why don't we have it out right here, then? Me and you?"

"Sam, please," Elsie said. "You're drunk."

Let her call me drunk. Let her undermine me one more time. She'll see. Sam spat into the snow, hardly feeling its chill as the other man tossed his jacket into the heap and presented his fists. Sam's focus narrowed, away from the crowd gathering outside Rosie's Diner, away from his wife's shrieking pleas, from her restraining hand on his arm. He'd fought many a contest with Walt and his other brothers. He'd endured hours of bare-fisted pummeling—bleeding, bruising, testing. He could handle one cowardly city slicker.

Despite his inebriated state, Sam managed to dodge the first fist that flew at him. Then another. To the roar of Rosie's patrons, he returned the offense with a jab to George's stomach. Undeterred, the stranger lunged at Sam full-force, nearly toppling him. Wedged between two brawny arms, his cheek stung in a sudden blow. Wrestling free, Sam regained his senses and reeled his arm back, ready to release it into George's vexatious face. But instead, his fist contacted something solid behind him.

A feminine yelp of pain made Sam spin around. "Elsie," he said, stunned to find her pressing fingers to a bleeding mouth. He reached for her arm. "Elsie, I'm so sorry. I didn't mean to—"

"No." She ripped free of his grasp. Her eyes spoke a million regrets over him—years she'd never have back, decisions she couldn't change. "No," she repeated, a sense of mourning capturing her amber-streaked eyes. "I've had enough of fighting. I'm going home. Do not follow me."

Sam watched his wife trudge through the snow, climb into their old Chevy, and slam the door. He watched until the vapor from the exhaust pipe cleared and only a distant blur of the taillights still glowed in the abyss of night. The crowd outside of Rosie's dissipated. George bent for his overcoat and threw an awkward grimace Sam's way before rumbling away in his Cabriolet. Alone in darkness, the bitter cold seeping into his exposed skin, Sam hung his head and prayed for an answer he believed would never come.

Twenty Nine

Elsie frowned as she bent over her vanity and splashed cold water on her face. For a few moments, she allowed it to roll off her skin and plink to the washbowl below. Eyes shut, she searched with one hand until it closed around a towel, then slowly swept it from her forehead to the chin below her trembling lips.

Sighing, she pivoted away and reluctantly reached for her gray woolen jacket. Her Mary Janes clicked through the house as she made her way to the door. The barren Nevada tundra, frosted in a shell of frigid ice, warned her to turn back. But Elsie had no choice. She could only avoid facing the inevitable for so long.

The cold bit her nose and mouth as she approached the Tully household. Sam had retreated here, she guessed, since the horrid display he'd made outside of Rosie's the night before. Olive had brought her fresh pancakes that morning with warm maple syrup. Sally had insisted on watching May between her feedings. Sam's family provided a network of support that would never forsake him, even in his darkest hour. With sad resignation, Elsie realized if she parted with Sam, they would vanish along with him.

Three taps on the front door incited not even a stir from inside the little house. Elsie bit her lip, trying again. How unusual not to hear the whoop of a child or the scamper of feet from within the household. Thwarted, she turned to go just as the door screeched open on its rusty hinges. Herman's friendly face stilled the anxious heart throbbing in her chest.

"Well, hello there, Elsie." He teetered onto the porch, clutching his cane. "I was just coming out to have a sit in my rocker." He gestured toward the wooden chair lounging by the steps.

Elsie frowned. "But it's so cold out here. You'll catch your death."

"Oh, psshaw." Herman waved her off with a crooked hand. "Can't be any worse for me out here than in that stuffy house. It's too quiet for me to even think in there."

A half-smile caught her lips at the ironic statement. "Sam isn't here?"

"Not a soul but me." Herman plopped into his rocking chair and gazed out over the frozen landscape. "Don't know as I've been so alone in some twenty years. Everybody must be out doing something more *important.*" He looked at her sideways, a glint in his sagging eyes. "Don't suppose you could spare a few minutes to chat with an old man?"

After the emotional week she'd endured, a moment's reprieve from life was enticing. "I can't think of anything I'd rather do," she said, easing herself onto the porch swing beside him.

Minutes passed, both Tullys musing in separate worlds, a swirling dust of snow littering their view beyond the porch rails. Now and then a car passed on the highway behind them, the motor's hum and whoosh of tires through the snow zooming away. Finally, Sam's father shifted his gaze to the hand Elsie had rested beside her, the diamond and gold band encircling her finger.

"Heard there was an awful lot of commotion over at your house last night." His brows knit as his light eyes climbed to hers. "You're all right, aren't you, darling?"

Elsie's breath trapped inside her chest. The compassion in his tender gaze buckled her. "Yes, Herman, I am." She tried desperately to suppress the tears ramming to the surface. "It's nothing you need to worry about."

Before she could speak again, his crinkled hand had found hers, squeezing lightly. "You can call me Pop after all this time," he said with a thin smile. "If you want to."

Nodding, Elsie swiped at a warm tear rolling past her nose and squeezed his hand with a sad smile. Her father-in-law noisily settled deeper into his chair, his hand lifting to scratch behind his ear. Straight salt-and-pepper hair flanked the sides of his head, a gleaming dome of freckled skin. Elsie caught a whiff of his aftershave and sank deeper inside herself. He must have used the same bay rum that Sam dabbed on his cheeks after lathering them up with his brush and shaving away the prickly hair.

"Sam is an awfully stubborn person," Herman said, slicing into her thoughts. Elsie looked up to find him bobbing his chair with one foot. "He's just like his mother. You could never tell that woman what to do a day in her life. You'd have more luck telling her to do the opposite."

Elsie angled her head in curiosity. "Olive? Why, she's nothing but a beam of sunshine on a rainy day."

Herman released a hearty chuckle. "Well, that she is, my dear. That she is." He held up one weathered finger, a smirk tugging his lips. "But she's a pill, too. Don't let her fool you. During the years we mined in Delano, she refused to stay at home. *Refused.* I told her the mines were no place for a woman, especially *my* woman, and she hit me over the head with her chopping board."

Elsie's mouth hinged open. "She did not."

"Well, practically." Herman shook his head, his eyes alive in the memory. "I had no choice but to let her, and here I was—the only man with a wife working beside him every day and still coming home at night to cook all the food and bathe the children." His thick brows rose. "Poor woman worked herself so hard that her hands and feet were bleeding with callouses. Wouldn't tell me either, until I caught her one day, rubbing ointment into her skin. I told her, 'Sweetie, you can't do *everything*.'"

"Did she listen?"

"Of course not." Herman snorted. "She slowed down for maybe a day or two and then *bam*, she was right back at it." He clapped his hands together. "Wore herself so thin she had to take up vices to cope. Eating too much was one. Even took up drinking for a time."

Elsie folded her legs beneath her and leaned nearer. "Wow, I would never have guessed." She stared a moment into the hands working in her lap. "That does sound like Sam."

Herman regarded her solemnly a long moment before he drew in a raspy breath. "I think you, more than anyone, must understand how I felt in those moments. It sure ain't easy being married to a mule sometimes."

Her mouth pinched into a grin. "And yet here we are."

"Here we are." Herman nodded, his rocker squeaking with every movement. "Elsie, I—" He paused, picking his words delicately. "I can't tell you what's right for you, what will work in your own marriage. But in my experience, if you really love someone, the way I see you clearly care for Sam, you fight. You don't let anything get in the way of what you could be together."

Elsie blinked back her stinging tears. "He's making it very difficult, Pop. I'm not even sure how much fight I have left in me." Body quaking, Elsie pulled her arms tight around herself.

"I know. I know." His hand reached out to cover the forearm of her jacket sleeve. "I've watched my son this past year—where his priorities have shifted, how he treats you." His head drooped wearily. "I can't say I've always been proud of what I've seen. But Elsie, he loves you. No matter what false front he's chosen to show you, he loves you more than anything in his life. When he looks at you, I can't miss it. It's the same look he had the first time I took him to an auto race. He was mesmerized."

Her loose curls shook. "Mesmerized? By *me*?"

Herman's hand tightened on her arm. "By *you.*" His eyes locked with hers. "The woman he chose to marry, the queen of his heart." He shook her gently. "Elsie, Sam loves you. Now you need to love *yourself.* Stand up. Tell him how you feel. From the moment I first met you, I could tell you didn't give yourself half the credit you deserve."

Elsie covered her flaming cheek in one hand. "You could really tell all that?" She sighed. "It's true, I've never had confidence in myself or my own abilities. You see, my father—he left when I was a little girl. My mother was so harsh with us, I guess I just began blaming myself for everything. I'd imagine a world I hadn't come into—one where my mother and father had stayed together and been happy—without me." The tears came unchecked now, dripping down her skin and plunging to her overcoat.

"You blamed yourself for what you couldn't have prevented." Herman gingerly reached across to the table by the front door and produced a black leather book embossed with gold letters. "Elsie, I know your earthly father forsook you. He left scars on your heart that he could never mend." He held out the book to her, his hand trembling slightly. "But I hope you'll find solace in these pages—that you'll let your heavenly father restore all that's been taken from you."

Accepting the worn Bible, Elsie traced her fingers along the gold leaf words adorning the cover. From time to time, she'd picked Sam's up and read it. Within the fading leather, she'd found stories greater than life, bemusing passages she couldn't quite decipher, poetry as moving as any of the greats she'd read before it. But hope? Restoration? Could she really find such treasures in a centuries old book—in the imperceptible God Sam threw his faith into?

Somehow, a memory formed in Elsie's mind. Her mouth curved, the vision of it dancing before her eyes as if the day she'd lived it. "When I was a little girl, my stepfather left to do business in the city. He was gone a long time, and when he returned, he brought us girls back the most beautiful gift we'd ever imagined—a little ballerina made from blown glass that twirled on her foot when you spun her."

She looked through the snowy air at Herman, whose eyes glowed in rapt attention. "She was such a lovely thing. We cared for her as if she were a live pet. I think Shirley might have even tucked her into her own private bed at night." Elsie shared a laugh with the older man.

"But I remember being so scared. I thought certainly one of my little sisters would break her, so I'd never let them stop her if she was spinning. I'd reach in and quickly grab her before she could fall." Elsie mimicked the action, her fingers clamping on nothing.

Exhaling, she watched the breath from her nose curl in visible wisps. "Sometimes I feel like that little glass dancer. If I spin, and I spin, and I spin, and I spin, then nothing can hurt me. I won't have to crash, as long as I keep moving. But if I stop—" Elsie gripped the porch swing's chain, the thin steel pressing into her skin. "If I stop, then I'm sure to fall. I'll shatter into a million pieces and I won't ever be put back together."

"Unless..." Herman's rocker halted in mid-squeak, a playful expression lighting his features. "You let someone stop you. Expert hands. Hands that won't let you fall." One finger jabbed at the book in her lap. "You'll find them here, Elsie." He shot her a look, both kind and wise. "You'll find those hands have already been reaching out, waiting for you to let him hold you."

Touched, Elsie clutched the Bible in one hand. "Perhaps you're right." She'd have to find out for herself.

"You can't keep spinning forever." Herman shivered despite his promise that the cold wouldn't affect him. "Whatever happened to your glass dancer, anyway? Do you still have her?"

"No, Dorothy left her on the floor and Momma stepped on her." She giggled at the absurd memory. "So, I guess it isn't a perfect analogy." Elsie stilled, her gaze pinning on Herman. "Thank you, Pop. Thank you so much for this." Before she could even process it, Elsie found herself standing over the man, her arm draped lovingly around his neck, embracing him in gratitude.

"Now let's get you inside! I don't care what you say, it *is* freezing."

Love yourself. Stand up. Fight. Herman Tully's words echoed through her mind as Elsie marched her way to Sam's bar that night. All day, she'd pondered what she would say to help her husband understand, what she could do to mend their broken relationship. Now, with the colored lights of his bar emerging from the shadowed buildings, her heart thumped wildly. This moment would either fuse them or fracture their marriage forever.

Inside the establishment, only a handful of customers remained, most of them ringing a table with cards and poker chips scattered across it. The two seated against the long, polished bar looked about ready to keel over in exhaustion or intoxication—she couldn't tell. With the scent of cheap vodka singeing her nostrils, Elsie glanced at the gold and red garland she'd hung in the window. Beneath it, the tree they'd chosen together had already dried out, as if giving in before the holiday had even passed.

With a breath of courage that only absorbed the stale odor of the place, she set her sights on the tall, lanky man behind the counter. His shoulders sagged and his steps came slowly, like a man already half-pummeled to death in a boxing ring. Yet still—still he had to listen. She couldn't stand another day of this distance between them.

"Sam," she called, her fingertips anxiously drumming the wooden counter.

Her husband turned, his brows lifting. "Elsie," he said almost reverently.

She gulped back her fear. "We need to talk. I've been thinking about this all day, and I just—I just can't wait any longer." Elsie tried to ignore the inquisitive stare one of Sam's patron's volleyed from down the bar.

Sam sighed. "I want to talk too, Elsie. I really do. But right now, I have customers. I can't just get up and leave." He moved to replenish the prying man's drink, filling his glass with a deep red liquor.

Her hand tightened on the bar, her knuckles blanching. "Can't Bill do it? He's right around the corner at the service station. Besides"—she motioned to the pitiful showing around her—"this isn't exactly a party. If we could just go to the backroom for a few moments. There's some things I need to get off my chest."

Setting his jaw, Sam rolled up his sleeves and put his fists on the counter. "No, Elsie." His tone hardened. "We'll talk later. I'm not leaving my bar." The fire in his eyes told her he wouldn't back down, the muscles of his forearms tensing.

"Fine." Elsie made quick work of the buttons on her jacket, shedding it and tossing it over a barstool. "If you won't leave the bar, then we'll just have it out right here. Get me a drink." Pulse thundering, Elsie stepped up and slid atop a barstool, attracting the attention of the poker players in the corner.

"Elsie, what are you doing?" Sam shook his head. "You've hardly drank a drop in your life."

"Well, it looks like we're changing that tonight." Elsie perused the bottles lining Sam's bar, colors ranging from dark to clear. "Give me something strong. What do you always drink? Whiskey? Give me a whiskey."

Sam leaned in, his forehead scrunching and eyes glaring. "Are you trying to cause a scene or what? I'm not giving you a drink."

Compelled by her building rage, Elsie reached into her coat pocket and produced several bills. "You'd deny a paying customer?" She threw the money across his gleaming bar. "Get me a whiskey *now*."

Sam took a few seconds to glance around and see that all eyes in the room had fastened on him. "All right, fine." He flipped over a tumbler and reached for his scoop.

"No ice. No ice, no water, just whiskey."

Grunting, Sam tossed his scoop back in the bin of ice with force and snatched the whiskey bottle from among his collection. The amber liquid splashed into Elsie's glass, nearly filling it as he shoved it in front of her. Sam slammed the bottle down again, inciting the others to jingle.

"Thank you." As Elsie's fingers curled around the dripping glass, she realized with a sense of panic that every eye had shifted from Sam to her, eagerly awaiting her next move. Sam was right. She didn't even know what whiskey tasted like. She stood a very good chance of vomiting the moment it touched her throat, but she had to get his attention *somehow*.

Steeling herself, she bored one last look of determination into Sam before throwing her head back and glugging the entire glass of whiskey in one breath. Cheers and laughter rose up around her, unable to drown out the ringing in her ears. Her throat stung. Her nose and eyes felt like they were going to explode with pressure. Yet still Elsie managed to set her glass down demurely and twist her gaze back to her husband.

She saw torment there, the agony of a man already defeated. Elsie's lips burned and trembled. "It's all for *this?*" Tears blurred her vision. "Our marriage, our family—you would give it all up for *this?*" He slumped at her words, his whiskered mouth opening to say something but never accomplishing it.

"I've had enough." Bolting from the barstool, Elsie didn't bother to retrieve her fallen jacket on her jog out the door. The winter wind whipped her hair from her bobby pins, flapping her dress against her legs and chilling her exposed arms. Elsie's boots staggered through the crunchy snow, reeling her toward the service station. Outside lay a lone brick dusted in frost. In utter frustration and pain, she picked it up and flung it at the station's window, gasping as the pane of glass splintered and shattered in pieces across the snow.

Bill emerged from inside the service station, eyes round and mouth agape. "Elsie, what on earth just happened?" He scanned the landscape behind her for a madman that didn't exist.

"Elsie." Her name rushed through the howling wind like a resounding gong. She froze, hardly feeling the cold against her skin as she turned. Sam's eyes pierced through her before landing on the station, a saddened astonishment filling them.

Sam lifted a fist to his mouth, lurching two steps before fixing in place again. His bewildered gaze washed over her. "Elsie, why would you do that? That window's going to cost a fortune to fix."

Shaking, more from her own nerves than the frigid temperatures, she forced her voice not to falter. "I'm leaving you, Sam." Elsie could scarcely believe her own words. Her heart ached as she watched his mouth drop open, the air escaping his lungs as if she'd punched him hard in the gut. She swallowed back the enormous lump in her throat. "If this is what you want—to run this bar and come home drunk every night, then I have no choice. I have to protect May. I have to protect *myself.*"

Elsie thought she'd crumple at the hurt leaking over her husband's handsome face. "I wanted to stay here and fight," she said, her disheveled head falling to the side. "I wanted to walk with you through this, but I can't help someone who insists on going alone." Her voice cracked, her soul mourning the very thought of unlinking her life from his. Head spinning, she pointed herself toward their house.

"Elsie, wait." Sam covered the distance between them in seconds, his large hand spurting out to catch her wrist. When she lifted her tear-filled gaze to his, a plethora of emotions swam across his face—confusion, rage, panic, grief. Sam blinked into the falling snow, then pulled her against him.

Before she could speak, Elsie found herself in Sam's arms, her head on his shoulder, his hands grasping her like she'd disappear at any moment. His solid chest rose in waves, his lungs panting for breath. His fingers knit with her hair, his hot breath on her neck. "Please don't go," he whispered urgently. The scent of bourbon and aftershave mingled beneath her nose as he held her tighter.

Tears sprang to her eyes. Elsie pushed against him. "I'm so sorry, Sam." She didn't dare meet his injured gaze as she broke free of his embrace. "I have to."

"Elsie," he tried again, weaker this time.

Willing herself not to look back, she forced her way through the snow and told herself it was all for the best, even as her heart ached in brokenness.

Thirty

S am awoke amid the chairs scattered about his bar, his arms
wrapped around a table leg. He blinked, half expecting to be
holding Elsie, until dismal reality set in. Groaning, he rolled onto
his side and rubbed at a throbbing spot on his lower back. A hard
wooden floor would never make a suitable bed, and yet he hadn't
found the strength last night to lay his weary body anywhere else.

Sitting up, Sam took in the feel of the empty bar, so lonely in
the morning light streaming from the far windows. Tiny motes of
dust floated about the space, trapped in sunlight. Dirty glasses and
peanut shells still littered the designated poker table, their musty
scent assaulting his nose. Even in this deserted place, the tinkle of
wind chimes Elsie had hung at the service station drifted in.

With a miserable sense of accomplishment, Sam rose from the
floor free of the dizzy or groggy sensations that had plagued his
mornings these many months. He hadn't swallowed a drop last
night after Elsie's revelation. The assembly of alcohol behind his
bar had called to him, enticing him to drown his sorrows in
their comforting embrace. He passed by them now with the same
queasy feeling stirring in the pit of his stomach. No matter how

much they tempted him, he hated their crippling effect on his life, the havoc he'd let them inflict on his marriage.

The backroom of his establishment housed personal items Sam needed on such occasions—a toothbrush, a razor and lather brush, a comb to style his hair. Sam took an agonizing look at himself in the small mirror tacked to the wall before running the comb over his head. He'd have to grab a shower over at Mother and Pop's, but in the meantime, he needed some sense of normalcy. Maybe a cup of coffee at the café.

With a labored sigh, he snatched his jacket from the hook on the wall and thrust his arms into it. He caught sight of himself in the mirror again—the sprinkle of whiskers over his strong jaw, the lines furrowing the skin around his eyes. He looked so much older than he had only a year ago, a fresh new business owner with limitless ambitions. Would he have recognized then the man staring back at him now, disillusion teeming from his tormented eyes?

Sam leaned his head on the mirror, his arms bracing his exhausted body on the wall. How clearly he saw her now, standing at his bar and pleading to speak with him privately. *What a fool I was.* He'd only wanted to avoid the conversation, to put it off as long as he possibly could. The truth was, when he'd first seen her face in the lighted mirror behind the bar last night, he couldn't help but see the innocent girl he'd first spotted at a porch rail, brush in her hand and hair floating on a breeze. How far he'd led her from that naïve young woman. How much he'd failed her in every way. Sam had assumed with a twisted gut that she'd come there to tell him she'd fallen for another man. He simply hadn't mustered the courage to face it.

But oh, how her words had cut into him like a jagged shard of glass—"I'm leaving you, Sam. I have to protect myself." Not because of this George Winston fellow, not because she'd grown tired of their marriage, but because he'd pushed her away. For months, she had pleaded with him to let her in, to let her help him.

And Sam had convinced himself he could fix it on his own, that he wouldn't put the burden on his beloved.

Last night, he'd watched the only woman he'd ever loved walk away from him, knowing she'd made a decision he could no longer change. Overcome, Sam had dropped to his knees and stretched out his arms, begging God for another way out. He'd knelt there for what felt like hours, the wet ground seeping into his trousers, ice and snow cascading over his face. When all that met him above was a sea of eternal black, a cold resolution sprouted deep within him. He'd lost her forever.

Pulling himself together, he pushed off the wall and reached for his keys just as the bells on the front door jingled to announce a visitor. He must have forgotten to lock up the night before. "We're closed," Sam called out as he rounded the corner, eager to shoo away whomever had breached his secret orb of depression.

"Even for an old friend?" Leonard Hargrove's jovial face peeped in through the open door.

"Mr. Hargrove." Sam strode forward to pump the man's hand. "For you we're always open." Anything for the person who'd single-handedly provided jobs for half his family during their most trying times. Sam gestured toward the bar. "Can I get you anything?"

"Oh, no. Thank you." His visitor plastered a hand on his rounded paunch of a stomach, his head shaking above a thick scarf and double-breasted coat. "I'm too old to be drinking this time of day. I just thought I'd drop in and see how business is going for you these days."

The mention of his livelihood produced an involuntary flinch from Sam. He hadn't wanted to give it thought quite this early. "Oasis is thriving." He shoved back the memory of what it had cost him. "The bar, especially, gets a lot of regular customers."

Mr. Hargrove pinched his hat off and held it in both hands. "Yes, I've noticed that driving by here. Seems like there are more cars every time I do." He pointed a thumb toward the service station, where Bill had already swapped the broken glass with a crude piece of drywall. "What happened there?" He laughed. "Drunken fight turned ugly?"

Bobbing his head, Sam nervously clutched the back of the chair in front of him. "Something like that." No need to divulge the embarrassing fact that his marriage was in ruins.

"Sam, I don't want to take up a lot of your time," Mr. Hargrove said, seeming to miss the woe Sam tried to conceal. "I'm a businessman, as you know, and I haven't ignored the work you've done around here. You've turned a ramshackle bunch of buildings into a prosperous enterprise— no small feat in this economy."

"Thank you, sir." Sam rubbed the back of his neck. If only he could really enjoy the success.

"I have a proposition for you, my boy." Mr. Hargrove reached into his overcoat and produced a rectangular piece of paper. "I'd like to buy Oasis if you're willing to sell it. I'm not one to haggle over prices, so I'm offering a figure that should more than compensate you in your future endeavors." With a dramatic flourish, he extended the check in front of him.

Breath stuck in his chest, Sam plucked it from Mr. Hargrove's grasp. His eyes scanned the check swiftly, his heartbeat picking up speed. "This is far more than I bought it for." One hand raked his hair. "I don't know what to say."

Mr. Hargrove chuckled. "Well, you could accept. I know this place probably has a lot of sentimental value for you, your first business and all, but Sam, I really think this could be—"

His steady flow of words ceased as Sam lunged at him, throwing his arms around his thick shoulders. "Mr. Hargrove, I accept! I could kiss you right now." He laughed, taking in the rounded sum on the paper again.

Mr. Hargrove held out two flat gloved hands. "That's quite all right. The hotel and bar will do just fine."

Sam's hand jetted out in promise. "It's a deal," he said, sealing the pledge with a firm shake. "When do you want us out by?

Tomorrow? How about tomorrow?" His excitement bubbled, his knees springing him from one foot to the other.

"I can't say I expected so much enthusiasm." The entrepreneur gripped the lapels of his jacket in two fists. "A month should be sufficient. I don't want to rush you with the holidays and all."

"Oh, that's fine. That's fine." Sam could hardly hear him over the rush of his own thoughts. "Listen, Mr. Hargrove, I don't mean to be rude, but there's somewhere I have to be." He trotted toward the door, then spun back around and dropped the check into Mr. Hargrove's hands. "Here, you hold onto that until the deal's done and we're all set to hand the keys over."

With one mission in mind, Sam tossed the door open and dashed across the snow. In the midst of suffering, he'd called to the one who'd made him and pleaded for a way out of the mess he'd constructed. Now, in the sunny light of day, the answer dared his heart to hope in a way he hadn't thought he could in a very long time.

❧❧❧❧❧ ❧❧❧❧❧

Nevada's glorious mountains had never spoken to Elsie the way they did that December morning. Clutching Herman's Bible close to her chest, she stared into the pointed crags, peeping out among blankets of untouched snow. The sun sparkled off their white surface, glistening across the flatland scattered with aromatic sagebrush. Whatever became of her, she wouldn't forget this place.

Elsie peered down at the frosted ground, the flowers she picked in summer now wilted and hiding beneath the desert floor. She imagined herself among them, a once beautiful creation pummeled and forced into the dark by a seemingly endless winter. *I will rise from this,* she promised herself. *Even though I walk alone, I will not falter.*

Opening the worn book in her hand to where she had marked it, Elsie found the scripture she'd discovered that morning. "The Lord is my shepherd; I shall not want. He maketh me to lie down in green pastures: he leadeth me beside the still waters. He restoreth my soul." She breathed, the whistling wind tossing back her unpinned hair. An incredible calm descended over her despite the turmoil raging within. Somehow, she already knew the truth of those words, already felt an unseen hand at her back, guiding her forward.

Elsie swiped at her cheek as two tears dropped and puddled atop the black ink. In recent months, she'd corresponded often with her brother and knew she'd have a home with him where he'd settled in Oregon. But oh, how her heart shattered to imagine really leaving Sam for good, to even think of taking his daughter that far away. She knew he'd always have a piece of, if not all her heart. Hadn't she pledged it to him forever?

"Sally said you'd gone for a walk." At first, Elsie thought his voice merely a figment of her overactive imagination. How she'd yearned to hear it these last few hours, going about her daily routine with no sense of purpose. When she turned back, her heartbeat rushed to find him standing there, that fedora tipped over one brow, his thumbs working the suspenders beneath his jacket.

"May just went down for her nap," she said, her dry voice hardly audible over the howling wind. "It seemed like a good time to get out of that stuffy little office." To a place she could actually breathe again.

He cocked his head. "You're still working at the motel, even after all that happened between us last night?"

"It won't do any good to be idle." Elsie's hands fidgeted with the buttons on her dress, her gaze plummeting to her small-heeled shoes. "I'm no slouch. You put a roof over my head, and until I figure out my next step, I'll earn my keep."

His head shook slightly, his eyes compassionate. "Oh Elsie, you owe me nothing." Clearing his throat, Sam shifted his weight to the other foot. "Have you decided where you're going yet?" The pain written across his brow said he really didn't want to know.

Elsie bit her lip to keep it from quivering. "I'm not sure yet. Not so far you won't be able to see May when you want to."

Sam's forehead furrowed, the heft of her words appearing to crush him. He nervously rubbed the back of his neck. "Listen, Elsie. I'm aware this won't change your decision. I just need you to know." His steady gaze hooked with hers, his boots carrying him one step closer. "No matter where you go or what you do, I'm never going to stop loving you. *Never.*" He blinked, moisture illuminating the blue of his eyes. "It's my own stupidity that's brought you to this point, and I hate myself for it."

The unquenchable urge to comfort him erupted within her. "Sam, you don't—"

"No, Elsie, please." His large hand extended in front of him, his fingers spread. "I have to say this." He twisted off his hat and stared at it in his palm for a long moment. "I brought you out here with the promise to give you a place to build our family, to give you a life that made you happy. I broke that promise." His eyes climbed to hers again, vulnerability ablaze in them.

Sam heaved a thick sigh. "I should have listened when you wanted to talk. I should have accepted your help when you first saw I had a problem." He swallowed hard, his chest surging. "Last night, I was a fool to turn you away when you reached out to me. I was a fool when I saw you with George Winston. I've been nothing but a fool, Elsie. I see that now."

Elsie knit her arms over her chest. "I had a part in that, you know. I had no intentions with George, but I never should have met him at Rosie's. I was lonely and hurting and afraid." Her cheeks burned in disgrace to admit it, but Sam deserved her honesty.

"I caused that hurt." Sam's shoulders quaked as he gazed deeper into Elsie's eyes than she ever remembered. "If only I had realized it sooner—before I drove you past the point of no return." His head shook. "I'm so sorry, Elsie."

The wind picked up, whirling a bundle of sagebrush into the air and mercifully shielding Elsie's face in hair. She couldn't let him see her tears or the desire she still carried for him. How long she'd ached to hear these words, but they were only that. Words. Another string of broken promises with nothing to back them up.

Flinching, she comprehended within her jumble of thoughts that Sam had drawn close. His hand moved to sweep the loose strands of hair from her face, tucking them behind her ear. With tender care, he did the same on the other side, his fingertips lingering on her neck a brief moment, a smile flicking the edge of his lips.

"I only ever wanted you to put us first," Elsie said, determined not to let her love for him suck her back into this trap. "I wanted you to *show* us we were more important than all these ambitions you'd built up in your head."

Sam's gaze drifted over every inch of her face as if memorizing it. "Oh Elsie," he whispered, his tone heavy with adoration. "If I could have that time back, you'd never question your worth in my eyes again." His hand reached up to cup her cheek, his thumb smoothing her cheekbone. "You are worth more than the world and everything in it. You are worth more than life itself."

Elsie closed her eyes to block him out, tears squeezing into her lashes. *Words. Meaningless words.* Yet somehow, she knew he meant every one. "I don't *want* to love you." She tried to ignore the gentle pulse of his thumb on her skin. If she could only shut off these feelings that held her captive.

"Elsie, look at me." When her head shook once, Sam slipped his knuckles down her jaw, this thumb resting in the cleft of her chin. "*Please look at me,*" he said, voice raw and husky.

With a breath of courage, Elsie lifted her head and dared to let her eyelids drift open. Before her stood a man with his heart open, every wish or longing he'd ever harbored centered on her. She studied him a moment, his chest moving in fervency, his nostrils flared and lips compressed. He had on yesterday's shirt. He smelled like the bar, all liquor and cigar smoke. But something had changed. Something in the depths of his eyes bespoke the truth that he would trek the whole world over if it meant pleasing her.

"If given the chance, would you start over?" His eyes searched hers. "If I could take you away from this place, to somewhere that would make you happy, would you go? Would you take your imperfect husband's hand and trust when he says he'll grow every day until he's everything you'd hoped he'd be?"

"Sam." Elsie's trembling hand found his, her fingers lacing the hollow spaces. "To me you were perfect in your imperfections." Her eyebrows narrowed. "But I can't rip you from your dreams. You've always wanted this. You think you can so easily part with it, but I know you. They'd have to drag you kicking and screaming from that place—"

Elsie halted at the grin erupting on his face. "What is it?"

The fingers entwined with hers tightened. "Elsie, I sold the bar this morning." His laughter converted to joyous tears.

"You what?"

"Oh, darling." Sam ironed his free hand over her wild hair. "I always wanted my own business, yes. But Elsie—*you* are my dream. You and May are the reason I draw breath every morning. I can start another business in Oregon or Washington, or Timbuktu, if that's where you want to go." He lowered his forehead to touch hers. "But I can't *live* if I don't have you."

In spite of the wall she'd carefully erected between them, joy breached its layers until light and love trickled through her every part. All her life, she'd walked the earth believing an insidious lie. She'd never amount to anything, never be worth more than a passing fancy to cast aside. Now, gazing into the eyes of the man she'd sworn her life to, the truth of God's love enveloped her. He had fashioned her for so much more. He had created her to love and to share in the encompassing pleasure of being loved in return.

Her head shook, her face stretching into a smile. "Sam Tully, I love you."

In a flash, his mouth found hers, his lips caressing hers in tender meeting. Sam fastened one arm around her and pressed her to him, his warmth cloaking her in perfect serenity. He hugged her close for a very long time, his strong hands promising to never let go.

When at last they parted, Sam sent her a clever grin, one hand extended to receive hers. "Come on, Elsie Tully," he said with a wink. "Let's go plan our life."

They walked back to Oasis, hand in hand, ready to conquer the world—together.

More About This Book

I have wanted to write this book since I was a little girl, when my grandmother would sit me down in front of a warming fire and read me the stories of her childhood. I loved her more than anyone in the entire world. She threw me tea parties with stuffed animals, helped me build sheet forts around her little house, and was the first person to sit me down with a pencil and encourage me to write. She was pure magic, and so much of who I am I owe to her.

Unfortunately, I never knew my grandfather. A fire took him a few years before I was born, but I feel as if I know him from the many loving stories passed down to me. He was a good man with a true heart. I am honored to descend from them both.

This book is a heavily fictionalized version of their love story with little sprinklings of family stories passed down through the years. It is by no means a family history or meant to depict people as they actually were in my grandparents' lives. The events of this novel and characters' personalities are products of my imagination.

That being said, the ending was very important to their real story (spoilers ahead). As I've heard it told, my grandfather did have problems with alcohol while running several businesses in Nevada. By that time, they had several children. Desperate, my grandmother confronted him at his bar, downing a stiff drink and throwing a brick through the service station window, as in the book. My grandfather fell to his knees that night and begged God for a way out. The next day, he sold the business on a handshake. They had a happy, 46-year marriage that produced five children and many descendants.

I've always been inspired by what the people of this generation went through, and how strong many of them became as a result. I hope you enjoyed the peek into this time and the love story that this author owes her life to.

Thanks

Special thanks to all my readers, both old and new. Your kind words of encouragement have made all the difference in my writing journey.

This book would not be the same without countless hours of research done by historians and genealogists. In particular, I would like to thank my cousin Samuel Tooley for his work organizing so much family history and making it accessible. It was so valuable to me when plotting this novel.

A huge thank you to all the family and friends who continue to read book after book and offer your insights. I am indebted to the incredible people in my life who make each day worth living.

Books by Laurie Sanford

The Winds of Freedom

November Rain

Moon Over Blazing Star Field

Midnight Road to Heaven

The Memory Chase

The Guardians' Plot

The Moon King's Bounty

Traitor Isle

To Capture a Unicorn

Stand-Alones

The Glass Dancer
For exclusive scenes you can't get anywhere else, head to www.la
uriesanford.com/signup.

About the Author

Laurie Sanford is a writer of historical adventure and romance. Her first series, the *Winds of Freedom* trilogy, tells the story of a young woman whose experiences on an antebellum cotton plantation lead her on a journey of self-discovery and ultimate freedom. Her new series, entitled *The Memory Chase,* is an adventure through Napoleonic France and beyond, through the eyes of a woman devoid of memory.

Laurie attended Pacific Union College in Napa Valley, where she earned her Bachelor's Degree. She studied to become a teacher, but wound up as a dispatcher, a job she loves and finds fulfillment doing. Laurie is happily married with two small children.

When she's not at work or wrangling little ones, Laurie enjoys writing (her first love that now comes in fourth in line), reading or watching anything historical, traveling (33 states and counting), exploring nature, playing guitar, and studying genealogy. Having a family is the greatest blessing she has ever been bestowed, and everything she has she owes to Jesus Christ.